Passage

JOHN DAVID MORLEY

Passage

JOHN DAVID MORLEY

Published in 2007 by Max Press,
an imprint of Little Books Ltd,
48 Catherine Place, London SW1E 6HL

10 9 8 7 6 5 4 3 2 1

Text copyright © 2007 by John David Morley

Design and layout copyright © by Max Press

A CIP catalogue record for this book is available from the British Library.

ISBN 978 1 906251 00 0

Typeset by Decent Typesetting, Swindon 0870 350 2930

Printed ar ⸻ m, Kent

I would like to thank the three musketeers:

Chevalier Antoine 'Faites vos Jeux' Amadé
Chevalier Giuseppe 'Bugzy' de Longshanks
Demoiselle Maxmilienne Deslivrets

who have helped further this passage

THE FIRST NIGHT

Tahuantin-Suyu

At Christmas a box was left by an anonymous caller at the Franciscans' shelter on the Upper East Side in New York, containing the mummified but still living remains of a five hundred year-old man. Such, at least, was the claim made in a letter accompanying the box found inside the porch by Father Anselm, who was on duty that evening.

Shutters on the front of the wooden box opened to reveal a metal-framed glass case, two foot high but otherwise similar to an antique carriage-clock case. Inside, it seemed tethered to the ceiling by its ears, hung a bat-like figure measuring about eighteen inches; a ghoulish creature hardly recognisable as a human being. In fact it did not hang by its ears but was supported by a wire brace fitted to the spine and anchored to the rear wall of the case. Though shrunken in proportion to the rest of the body, the head still appeared enormous on the tiny frame beneath it. The mummy did not move at all during the ten minutes Father Anselm studied it, nor was it possible to detect any sign of life in its eyes, hidden behind dark glasses.

The inmate of the case required no care, the covering letter said, no feeding or cleaning or any other sustenance beyond a periodic renewal of the batteries. Its natural bodily functions had long since been terminated, the inner organs gutted and replaced by an artificial circulation system supporting a waste-free metabolism sewn up inside. All it required was someone to hear confession.

Technically, at least, this didn't appear to present any problems. To talk to the inmate it was necessary only to flick the switch marked TALK, to listen to him the switch marked LISTEN. But looking at the wizened doll that showed no sign of life, Father Anselm hesitated to do so. To attempt to engage in conversation with this waxwork figure seemed ludicrous. He suspected someone was playing a practical joke on him. Perhaps because Father Anselm was apprehensive of making a fool of himself timidity got the better of kindness. Depositing the case on his desk and locking up his office, he went out. He was kept very busy for the next few hours attending to the callers who were already showing up at the shelter.

It was not until the shelter closed at midnight that Father Anselm found time for a second inspection of the inmate of the glass case. He noticed that a change had taken place. A green light on a display at the base of the case now illuminated the words PLEASE ACTIVATE LISTEN SWITCH. Pulling up a chair and sitting down at the table facing the case, he proceeded to do so. Soon he began to hear a faint rustle, or not even that, perhaps just a background of silence from inside the case that was different from the silence outside it, surrounding Father Anselm in his own office. It was like the murmur of the sea inside the old man's shell.

Father Anselm flicked the TALK switch and cleared his throat. "I am Father Anselm," he said. "Is there any way I can be of assistance to you?" He sat waiting in the silence that emanated from the interior of the case, hearing nothing but the slight rustle out of the loudspeakers at the corners of the base.

"I am much obliged to you, Father Anselm" a young man's voice eventually answered, although the figure in the case appeared just as lifeless as it had before. "Don't be surprised to hear the voice of someone far younger than I am. It is not mine. I myself am unable to speak except by means of a voice synthesiser, and this is the voice that has been installed. Nor am I able to hear you with my own ears, but only thanks to a device that transforms incoming sounds into digitised impulses and feeds electric stimuli to my brain. In fact, all that is left my own body is the use of the index and middle finger of the right hand to push buttons on the control pad of the life-support system you can see attached to my hand. Give me your honest opinion, Father Anselm. Can these artificial aids be seen as in any way invalidating the integrity of the confession I am anxious to make?"

"Not if it comes from the heart."

"Ah, the heart."

The old man fell silent, and again Father Anselm heard the sea-like murmur inside his case. Looking at the motionless figure, pinioned like a butterfly in its glass case, Father Anselm felt pity for him. He was ashamed that he had at first been reluctant to talk to him for fear of being taken in by a hoax.

He activated the TALK switch. "In the letter accompanying your, er,

4

habitat, the box that was left on my doorstep this evening, some remarkable claims are made as to your antiquity. I hope you will forgive me for wondering just how....after all, five hundred years...."

"Of course," replied the old man. "It is only natural to wonder how such a thing could be. Well, I am the victim of a time warp to which I was subject in Tahuantin-Suyu in the sixteenth century. I was not the only victim of the decelerating time syndrome we fell into there, which was the reverse condition of the accelerating time sickness we brought to a civilisation far more ancient than ours. A fatal sickness, I need hardly add, that very quickly led to its extinction. I cannot rule out that in a remote village, high up somewhere in the Andes, there may be others among my hundred travelling companions during that murderous baptism of the New World who have survived the intervening centuries as I have. But if there are I have not managed to locate them, despite all my efforts to do so..."

The voice trailed off.

"Murderous baptism?" quizzed Father Anselm. "Those are terrible words."

"As terrible as were the deeds they describe."

" Is this the matter you wanted to talk about?"

"Mainly about that. But first I must tell you how I was taken from my home and joined Dom Pedro's ship on a voyage to the so-called New World. There I was adopted by Taiassu Indians and spent my entire youth among All-Creatures-Being-In-The-Forest, until to my misfortune I was caught up in the conquest of the ancient kingdom of Tahuantin-Suyu. We came for gold and in exchange brought the Rushing Wind Sickness of which all the people fell ill and died, while we became heirs to the timelessness of Tahuantin-Suyu and could never die. I am afraid it will be a long night, Father Anselm. And that is only a small part of what is on my mind."

"I am at your disposal until Father Gregory comes on duty at six o'clock," said Father Anselm.

"Then let us begin right away," said the inmate of the box with a sigh of what sounded like infinite weariness.

The Ocean Sea

When his ship's writer died suddenly during the night the fleet lay at anchor on the river, all ready to sail at dawn, the admiral Dom Pedro Felipe sent factors ashore to the Spanish Jew to obtain a replacement for the dead man, but finding only the Jew's ward, Pablito, the factors made do with the boy and carried him off to the New World. Whether the Spanish Jew, or the Spanish merchant, as he was known in Lisbon, where he had fled from the massacre in Cadiz, would have consented to my removal, and whether anyone would have respected his wishes had he refused, were questions that remained unanswered, as Zarate was absent at the time. I was lying half asleep in the merchant's house, day-dreaming on a warm fringe of light from the ovens where women were baking bread, confusing smooth golden loaves with the arms removing them from the ovens, when two strangers picked me up and hustled me outside. They held me under the arms and carried me between them downhill to where the ships lay moored on the Tagus. My kidnappers bundled me aboard with no sound on my part or the least attempt to struggle. For sheer terror I did not make the slightest sound.

There was no wind, but the ship slid mysteriously out into the estuary with furled sails, moving more quickly than the current that bore her. All around stood walls of darkness and fog. I heard the splash of dipping oars beyond, a voice saying we had been taken in tow for a few miles but that the wind could be expected to pick up as we came nearer the sea. So it went on for an hour or two, this sliding forward immersed in darkness, until a breeze began to tug at the white shirts of the men standing rigidly staring ahead, the tow boats cast off, and the ship sprang alight as the sailors swarmed up into the rigging. A brisk wind followed, but the fog stayed. Gradually it grew lighter, surrounding us with a wax-coloured sky, under which the ship hardly seemed to move. At intervals the admiral instructed the sailors to sound the ship's bells. Behind us we heard the answering bells of the fleet, less and less distinctly, until at last they became inaudible.

For days the caravel sailed alone without a visible sea or roof of sky, imprisoned in the fog that swallowed up its wake and shut off whatever might lie ahead. The ship rode wave by wave on each stretch of sea as it was unravelled, its passage only in the present, from one moment to the next, as if it came from nowhere and had no destination. The ocean seemed less to be carrying the vessel forward than moving along with it, creating among the ship's people the impression that they had put no distance behind them at all. Our sea passage narrowed to a river between banks of fog. I seemed to be in a dream. Terror had given way to numbness, numbness to fits of weeping for my frustration, my homesickness, disbelief that such an outrage could have been done to me and my impotence to do anything to change it. Standing on a box to give myself more height at the writing desk in the admiral's cabin, where I listened to our creaking progress through the mist in the pauses between dictation, I sometimes thought that if I rubbed my eyes three times I might wake out of this dream and find myself back home on the Tagus. But the admiral continued to substantiate the dream with his bony presence, a gaunt, dishevelled sort of man with so many corners and such obtuse angles about his rambling person, including cavernous eyes set back on ledges, sharply pointed beard, a forehead creased into a perpetual frown, that there seemed to be no end to him.

Dom Pedro was a gruff old man whose behaviour I often found strange, but he never treated me unkindly. Whenever he started up out of those rigid trances into which he was prone to lapse, forgetting everything around him, he smacked his head with his hand, peered out of the cabin window as if seeking his bearings in the fog, and uttered an exclamation. Between absences he dictated his instructions that were to be copied out and passed round the ship's company. Should they encounter the inhabitants of new lands, they must find out what commodities they had to offer, notably gold, silver and precious stones, in exchange for the mirrors, coloured glass, ivory combs, Venice glasses and shoes of Spanish leather the colonists carried with them for the purpose of trade. Further, they were to pay close attention to the navy of the native inhabitants, how they constructed ships, sails, tackle, with what ordnance, armour and munitions the navy was equipped, how their soldiers were armed, what force of pikes and halberds they had, and the disposition of all such forces by sea and land. But above all it was their duty to teach the inhabitants the true religion. In this connection, he asked me many questions about Zarate and the Jewish faith. Although brought up to believe I was a foundling who had been left at the Jew's door and adopted by him, I had heard rumours that I was his natural son by a serving woman in his household. The schooling I was given, equipping me to debate with the most learned men of Lisbon by the age of twelve, seemed to support these rumours, for why would the Jew have taken such pains with the education of a mere foundling? Naturally I took care not to mention any of these matters to the admiral, for Jewish ancestry might be a dangerous thing, as I had learned from Zarate's own life. From Zarate I had also learned that one must accept one's fate, not fight against it, whatever it was, and gradually I came to accept it was my fate to be a captive on this ship.

Dom Pedro Felipe brooded in silence, exclaimed, sighing as he dusted off the top of his head and asked me if I had taken everything down. I then helped the admiral strap on his breastplate, handing him his sword and helmet, for it was his custom to inspect the ship wearing full armour. As his eye ranged over the hogs-heads of salted beef and lard, sacks of biscuits and skins of wine, the admiral gave the impression of carrying out calculations in his head regarding the number of persons on the voyage, its probable length and what eventualities would have to be met in the undesirable but not unlikely event that it turned out to be longer than planned. In his irreproachably dignified way, Dom Pedro Felipe accepted responsibility for the welfare of his people, even if he showed them little warmth.

One hundred and sixty-four souls aboard the *Sao Cristobal* had been consigned to his safekeeping, the majority of them settlers. Professional tradesmen such as blacksmiths, carters, miners, even a printer, and a considerable ecclesiastical appendage, made up of friars, priests and nuns, had embarked in their wake. The clergy had in their charge six girls, Orphans of the King, raised by royal charity and now subject to royal prerogative, who were being sent out to the New World to breed colonial subjects for the king. They were meek, mouse-faced, pock-marked girls, each equipped with a dress and striped bonnet, a trunk containing her dowry, and a pension from the king to compensate any suitor prepared to overlook the lack of more conspicuous personal charms in a wife. In the hierarchy of the ship's population that descended from Dom Pedro Felipe and Master Joao, the pilot, the Orphans of the King came last, ranking only above the animals, the horses, cows, sheep, goats and hogs brawling in their pens in the hold, which was where the admiral usually ended his

8

inspection of the ship. Dom Pedro was the absolute lord of this ark. During the long, wearisome fog that hung in the sails and shrouded the sea it often seemed to the ship's people as if the vessel contained the last living things on earth.

On the sixth morning of the voyage we awoke to find the fog had suddenly disappeared. A stiff breeze was bowling the caravel across a chipped blue sea that ran steeply down to the horizon. I had never seen such emptiness. I cried and was terribly afraid. We found ourselves on the edge of the fabulous Ocean Sea, where it was said that a vessel would depart from one world and enter the next. The ship was running down to the rim of the horizon like a stick being pulled over a weir. But towards noon the admiral came out onto the half-deck with the pilot, Master Joao, who seemed quite unimpressed by this heaving desert, having negotiated it a number of times already. The pilot squinted up at the sun, visible for the first time since we had left Lisbon, and then down at the run of the sea. Pronouncing the ship to be steady enough, he removed an instrument from the box he was carrying in order to take measurements and determine our position. Master Joao took the height of the sun at midday and found fifty-six degrees, and the shadow was north, by which he calculated the ship's position more or less, since he had to measure with floating instruments, to be seventeen degrees distant from the equinoctial. This course was too far south, he found, and he gave steerage instructions to the helmsman. Looking from the sea to Master Joao's charts, where the ocean had been reduced to lines and numbers, I recognised in these abstractions a power of the human intellect that was no less great than the mass of water all around us. I became less fearful of the vast expanse of the Ocean Sea, of whatever was hidden in it and might emerge from its depths during this voyage into the unknown on which Dom Pedro's fleet had embarked.

Fine weather continued, the temperatures rose, and when one morning the sister ships of the *Sao Cristobal* were sighted behind us on the horizon, two specks that materialised in the great emptiness, many of the ship's company wept for joy. The admiral ordered a Te Deum in thanksgiving for this miracle. The voyage proceeded now by varying shades of blue, from a solid blue-black swell through midnight blue streaked white to transparent green seas with turquoise tints, laid out like a flowing mosaic floor. The ship's company gravitated to the upper deck. There the mariners sewed and sang, played the pipe and the fiddle and fished with hooks hung over the side of the ship. While they were walking on deck with the younger hidalgos the Orphans of the King removed their bonnets and allowed their hair to flow freely in the wind, drawing attention to marriageable attractions that until now had been hidden. The Orphans befriended me. I became very fond of the smallest of them, a squint-eyed girl called Francesca, no taller than myself, although she was already fourteen. Together we sat on the upper deck and watched the pageant of the Ocean Sea, the plunging porpoise schools and the silver arcs of flying fish tensed in mid-air, shimmering fishes all around us as far as the eye could see. The light rebounded from their scales, giving the surface of the water a solid silver sheen, as if they intended to snare the ship and run it aground. Two sister ships, erratic attendants, sometimes hovered on the horizon, swooped in and came so close that we were able to see the people on board. Sometimes our attendants slid off the edge of the sea and left the *Sao Cristobal* alone in the emptiness.

Carrying the trade winds full in its sails, the ship soared under a cloudless sky across the western sea. Listening to the caravel, I could hear it run in tune with the wind dead through the middle of that gusty ocean plain. The sails braced and boomed, giving sound to the wind they had caught with a clap in the canvas and held fast. My spirits soared with that sound. When the *Sao Cristobal* crossed the equinoctial line I looked up at night to see the unknown constellations of the southern hemisphere, densely crowded nebulae glittering in the inky heavens. Sometimes the sea was no less brilliant than this star-strewn sky. The waves came charged with phosphorescent light, which the pilot attributed to a species of luminous creature living in the water. As the waves broke against the side of the ship they opened into chasms of fire, so that she seemed to move in a surface of flame, leaving a long train in the burning wake behind her. I could feel the respiration of the sea, of the tides rising and falling on its shores, of rivers flowing down from mountains into estuaries, and all the earth's breathing through the great watery diaphragm of the ocean and the flowing firmament above, the inhalations and exhalations of a universe in unceasing motion, and I knew I would never resist this motion, never stay in one place, I was built on water, my bones were fluid, this river ran through my veins and I would flow with it. I discovered my design and carefully hoarded this secret inside me.

The *Sao Cristobal* had been at sea for six weeks when the sailors sighted land, but what they had said was shore was not land, but only cloud. Then the sky was covered with so thick a mist that it could have been cut with a knife, and we no longer saw the sun or the stars. For days the ship lay becalmed. Buckling on his full armour, a sign of the gravity with which he viewed the situation, the admiral clanked up and down the deck all day and night. He began to lose the use of his eyes from want of sleep. For many hours he stood motionless beside the pilot, who was unable to use his navigation instruments unless the sun was out, staring at the ocean, trying to see what the pilot could see. Master Joao watched the run and colours of the ocean. He trawled from the stern, pulled fish and seaweed out of his nets, sniffed them and tasted them, and said we must be near land. The sailors caught by hand a bird which was like a tern, with the claws of a gull, but it was a river, not a sea bird. All night we heard birds passing, the motion of their wings, wheeling and beating the darkness overhead. Then there came to the ship, at daybreak, two or three land birds, singing, which raised our spirits, and afterwards, towards evening, they flew away again. At sunset on the following day two pelicans passed the ship, flying south-east and coming from the west-north-west, where we could be certain of making landfall soon, the pilot said, for these birds slept on land. In the morning they flew out to sea to look for food, but never further than twenty miles from the shore. All through the night the ship's company kept watch, straining to see through the dark.

At daybreak, where there had been nothing before, we saw a fixed line marking the horizon. The decks were slippery from the moisture that had collected there during the night. It seemed to be not spray, but dew. Sailing closer, we could make out a dark green shore, covered with large trees growing down to the water's edge., but all this vegetation provided no convenient place to land. We continued sailing along the coast a few miles from the shore, until we sighted the estuary of a broad river, and coming within a few hundred yards of the land we could make out green meadows, criss-crossed by streams and dotted with groves of trees bearing orange-coloured fruit, where we saw people reclining in the shade and walking naked along the shore.

11

The Indies

Master Joao, the pilot, went ashore to measure the height of the sun with the astrolabe, and informed the admiral that the latitude was eleven degrees south. The fleet must therefore have made landfall in the southern region of the Indies, he said. The Indians, so called, since they were the natives of this land, seemed hospitable enough. As their force and their true intentions towards strangers had not yet been established, however, the admiral allowed no one to leave the ship. In that temperate zone, with a balmy off-shore breeze, the ship's company spent the night very comfortably above deck.

In the morning, three large canoes came down the river. Some twenty-five men sat in each of them. Having come well within range of a lombard shot they stopped rowing and shouted a lot of words. As they showed no inclination to venture any further, Dom Pedro ordered a tambourine to be brought to the poop, and told the young men of the ship to dance, thinking it would please the savages. But on the contrary, they regarded it as a signal for war. They abandoned oars and laid hands on their bows and arrows. Seeing this, the admiral ordered the entertainment to cease and told the men to bring crossbows to the deck, but Master Joao said it would be sufficient to show them what power the lombards had, and the effect which their shot produced. For this purpose he ordered one to be loaded and fired at the shore, where by lucky chance it demolished the top of a palm tree. A loud shout went up from the canoes and the Indians rowed away as fast as possible.

For the sake of his ships' safety the admiral ordered them to pull off a greater distance from the land. Some two hundred Indians returned to the shore, forming long lines, swaying back and forth and chanting. When darkness fell they lit fires, and the entwined lines of dancers with burning torches wove flickering patterns in the night. With great excitement I watched from the safety of the ship as the Indians placed lamps in the bows and stern of one of their long canoes and pushed off from the shore, with many others swimming, although the fleet stood off two miles from the land. When they came to the ship, making salutations and signs of their peaceful intentions, ladders were let down over the side to allow the Indians to come aboard.

By the light of torches burning on deck we were now able to make our first inspection of the inhabitants of the New World. They were well-built, not one of them over thirty years of age, with good faces, handsome bodies, and coarse black hair cut short, like the hairs of a horse's tail. The men carried their sex in a pouch attached to a string around the waist, in which it lay curled up like a snail, plain enough to see, while the women went entirely naked, their privy parts so high, so closed, and so free from hair that I felt no shame in scrutinising their nakedness. Some of these girls had red, white and black patterns painted on their bodies, with small grey feathers stuck onto the skin. They moved noiselessly on bare feet among the ship's company, touching our clothes, and making crooning sounds deep in the throat, like doves; then, becoming bolder, fondling our bodies, as if to find out whether we were made of flesh and bone like themselves. With mimes the Indians gave us to understand that the ships with sails were birds with wings, which must have flown down from the sky. They kissed our hands, placing our feet on their heads as a sign of their subjection. How foolish the admiral's instructions to the fleet now sounded in my ears as I watched these naked creatures move among us — that we were to pay close attention to the navy of the inhabitants, their construction of ships, how their soldiers were armed, and the disposition of all such forces by sea and land!

The Indians had brought with them parrots and cotton threads in balls, spears made of wood and other gifts, which they spread out in front of Dom Pedro Felipe. From his grave and motionless demeanour, or because he was the only person seated, they took him to be the cacique in command of the fleet. In return, the admiral gave them red caps and glass beads, which they wore around their necks with expressions of great pleasure. Dom Pedro paid close attention to the ornaments which the people had hanging from a hole in the nose, for they seemed to be pieces of gold. By signs he was given to understand that, going round the island to the south, one might find a cacique who had great vessels of it. A gleam lit up in the admiral's eye. He came creaking forward out of his chair to obtain more information regarding the locality of this hoard, but at this moment all the Indians stretched out on the deck, just as they were, their privy parts exposed to view, and to the surprise of the ship's company fell fast asleep.

I looked down at the sleeping Indians and then around the circle of faces contemplating them in the flickering light of the pitch flares burning on the deck, the hidalgos who desired their women and their gold, the factors who were hungry for their lands, the friars who aspired to claim their souls. Seeing such guilelessness on the one side, such resourceful greed on the other, I had a premonition, a vision of that unconstrained quality of life in which the Indians swam as naturally as porpoise shoals swam in the sea being transformed into a river so thickened with blood that it ceased to run, while the friars I watched stepping forward with blankets to cover their sleeping nakedness seemed to me to be death-bringers, already shrouding the first Indian bodies.

The Requirement

When Dom Pedro Felipe stepped ashore he knelt and put his lips to the ground, kissed the crucifix he was carrying and dedicated the land to God, I was hardly less startled than the people native to the land. The Indians stood watching under the trees, clicking their tongues. The admiral took out a parchment, first placing it on his head, as a sign of submission to its will, before touching it reverently with his lips. Then he read aloud from the parchment for everyone to hear. God created all the world and gave it to St. Peter for his kingdom. Successors to St. Peter, the popes, who were his earthly representatives in Rome, made a donation of the mainland of the Indies and all its islands, to be divided between the kings and queens of Portugal and Spain. The terms of the Requirement, the legal document by which he claimed possession of this new land, laying down the obligations of the Indians to become loyal subjects and converts to Christianity, would have to be waived until later for lack of a common language, when there were interpreters to convey their meaning to the Indians. At this time, therefore, he would do no more than take possession of the land.

The admiral swung up onto his horse and galloped off down the beach. After a while he returned, drew his sword and plunged his horse into the sea. Wheeling and splashing in the shallows, he faced the crowd assembled on the shore and cried out in a tremendous voice: "Long live the high and mighty monarchs, the most gracious kings and queens of Portugal, in whose name I take and seize, real and corporal, actual possession of these seas and lands, and coasts and ports and islands of the south! And if any other man pretends any rights to these possessions, I am ready to defend them in the name of my sovereigns, who are paramount in these Indies with all their seas!" After making this declaration the admiral fell silent and glared all around him, as if expecting submarine challengers to rise bodily out of the empty sea. But there was no answer other than the sound of dried fronds creaking in a palm tree and waves lapping gently on the shore. He spurred the horse back on land, dismounted, took a dagger from his belt, with which he cut a cross in the trunk of the tree, and then carved crosses in other trees, three altogether, in honour of the Holy Trinity. He called on all the people watching him to bear witness to what he had done, and that no one had come forward to dispute his claim. The notary was instructed to draw up a deed to that effect, the ships' writers to copy the document and to convey it to the local cacique.

Not a word of this declaration of the seizure of their land was understood by the Indians. They followed the rituals with close attention, impressed by their solemnity, in particular by the spectacle of a cacique astride a horse, talking to an invisible tribe in the sea. Above all they were fascinated by the exorcism of the cross, whose image they found everywhere, on trees and banners and chains worn around the neck, and which they watched being drawn in the air by the two or three hundred people celebrating mass on the shore. The Indians raised their hands to make the sign of the cross with them, knelt when our people knelt, crooned in their throats at the sound of murmured prayers, all of which the friars noted with satisfaction, for it showed a natural aptitude for the true religion.

To me it seemed that the Indians were the aboriginal possessors of a natural paradise unknown to us who had come to steal it from them. They lived in such ease, surrounded by such plenty, that they disdained effort, and accordingly they had no understanding of value. The soil was so fertile that seeds falling on the ground in the evening rose up overnight as green shoots. The ripe burden of fruit trees hung in clusters on the village roofs, succumbing instantly to the touch. Fish sprang out of the streams into open mouths, crowding the coastal waters in shoals so dense they could hold up a swimmer on the surface of sea. The people went naked yet seemed to have no sense of sin. When a woman took a liking to one of the men from the ships she rubbed herself up against him to show her pleasure. In the evenings the Indians sat down in groups on the meadow under one of the great spreading trees, where men and women were sometimes joined in union that we knew only as an act performed secretly in the dark. When I went to spy on them they found me in my hiding place and drew me into their circle. Love between men and women was carried out in the open, surrounded by laughter, crooning, by playful exhortations and the sound of tiny flutes, placed in the nostril and piped on two or three stops by inhaling through the mouth and breathing out through the nose. But the Portuguese felt shame at what they did with the Indian women and hid with them in the forest. As for the friars — having arrived at paradise, the friars found they were unable to go in. At first they said nothing, biding their time, but it was from this seed of envy that so much of the ruthless zeal to reform the Indians sprang.

Entering the Main

Dom Pedro Felipe made his dispositions, disembarked livestock and grazed the animals in the meadows on the shore, supervised the construction of a primitive fort to shelter the people in case of attack, and sailed away round the island to the south in search of the cacique with the vessels of gold. I joined an expedition up the river as ship's writer to Master Joao on board the brigantine *Salvador*, with instructions to make a careful record of whatever we encountered on our journey into the interior of the country. The picturesque appearance of the river's banks attracted all our attention. The stream was a dark brown flood half a mile wide. Along its shores grew an endless forest, as thick as the bristles on a brush. A flock of white herons escorted the *Salvador* upstream. At every bend we would see half a dozen of these birds perched on some dead tree overlooking the water, but as soon as we came in sight they took flight, until, coming round another bend, we would find them settled in front of us again, and so on up the river.

The sight of the birds, glimpsed against the forest green in ghostly white flight before they disappeared at each bend in the river the moment the brigantine came into view, began to have a disquieting effect on us. The sailors believed the white herons to be birds of ill omen. As the river narrowed its colour darkened beneath the dome of enclosing trees. Late one afternoon the ship caught fast on a snarl beneath the surface. Dom Joao told us to gather brushwood and light a fire on the shore, where we would rest for the night before floating the ship in the morning and returning to the mouth of the river, for there was nothing to keep us in this desolate place. I took the opportunity to go ashore, as at this point on the bank there was a clearing that made it possible to penetrate the dense jungle, and I went off in search of brushwood.

Only when standing under those enormous trees I had hitherto seen from the elevated deck was I able to appreciate the true dimensions of a tropical forest. Projecting from some of these trees were immense buttresses, forming complete wooden walls that suggested a makeshift house in which I imagined a family might comfortably have lived. The roots of the trees rose high above the surface of the ground, as if they stood on many legs, forming archways through which I could easily pass. The floor of the forest was strewn with decaying fruits, lid-shaped leaves, twisted legumes, like peas a yard long. I wandered into the jungle, looking up vast tree trunks, the tops of which were hidden in foliage of similarly extravagant growth. Enchanted at first, I gradually felt oppressed by an uncomfortable feeling of no longer being in proportion with these surroundings. I retraced my steps to the river. I had gone, I thought, no more than fifty yards, but when I had returned at least that distance I still had not reached the river. Here it might have been better to stop and shout, to attract the attention of my companions. Instead, I continued the same distance again before I hollered at the top of my voice. I could almost hear the sound of my shout being absorbed by the mass of forest, muffled and at once buried by that lush green cushion into which it sank. I shouted again, and again, listening with dismay to that dampening effect of the forest, swallowing up my voice as soon as it left my body.

I realised I was lost. For a moment I was seized with terror. Then I prayed to God. He chose for me a direction in the forest and I walked a couple of hundred yards, counting the steps and carefully marking my way. Having hollered several times, and received no answer, I returned to the spot from which I had started and walked the same distance in the opposite direction, when I hollered once again. My plan was to walk a fixed distance from the same spot to the four points of the compass. But as darkness was now falling I looked around for a place to spend the night. I found a large rock by a stream with an overhang near the base. It formed a niche in which to shelter. Curling up inside, with my back against the smooth stone, I lay awake full of anxiety, listening to the strange sounds of the jungle night, wondering about all the things that might happen to me. In fact I had already fallen fast asleep and had begun to dream, and in no time at all it was already daylight.

At once I was wide awake. On the ledge of below me two handsome cocks were parading in the bright morning light. They were tall birds with rusty brown plumage and jet black combs, and they strutted up and down, showing off their plumage, I thought, to intimidate their opponent before commencing the fight. But on the contrary, they inclined their heads, making scooping motions with their necks and wagging their combs more as if they were bowing to each other, like courtiers. The quaint notion came into my head that the cocks had not come here to fight but to dance. The cocks circled one another solemnly, bowing and jigging up and down with a great puffing and rustling of plumage, when one of them suddenly squawked and flapped its wings, and the other bird immediately flew away.

Leaning down over the ledge I saw that the remaining cock had been caught in a snare. A noose appeared to have been formed of some fine and resilient creeper. The cock must eventually have stepped into it and been unable to extricate itself, drawing the noose only tighter around its claw in the struggle to escape. The other end of the creeper had been tied to a root, indicating that the snare must be man-made. Whoever had laid the snare would probably come for the bird before long. Settling down in the thickets by the stream, I decided to wait. I had hardly taken up my position when something or someone fetched me a blow across the head. Everything went black in front of my eyes, and I lost consciousness.

Pig Indian

With this blow on the head I was born again to begin life, and perhaps to end it, as an Indian. Maybe this was my place in the divine arrangement of the world of which Zarate had often spoken. It was my doom to be adopted into the tribe of the Taiassu, or Pig Indians. They lived deep within a forest so dense and entangled that not even other Indian tribes who inhabited the littoral and sometimes came up river in their canoes, chose to venture into it. Three Pig Indians, making their way to the rock where they snared male gallo birds who came there to play, had followed with amazement the tracks and counter-tracks I had left in the jungle in my blundering attempt to find my way back to the river. They established at what point I had stepped into the igaripé they regarded as their house stream, the hiding-place in the bushes where I sat waiting for them, and all of these actions of mine in the course of half a circuit of the sun across the sky were so baffling to them that they had become intensely curious even before they set eyes on me. They had never seen such a pale, so manifestly confused and feeble a creature, and contemplating the partial fur that grew extraordinarily on my body (which was how they made sense of my clothes) they had serious doubts as to whether I could be the same kind of animal as themselves.

The narrative of my capture was told many times and passed into Pig Indian lore. Woodcock and Grasshopper had suggested killing me at once, a proposal they conveyed with a rather casual mime of putting a blow-pipe to their lips, to the great enjoyment on the part of their listeners, although never without a certain discomfort on mine. To Guaratinga-acu, or Great White Bird, I represented a valuable article of barter, worth perhaps a dozen of the best calabashes or two wives from the Mud Indians; a point of view he represented with energy when he returned to the village with my unconscious body dangling from a pole like a flayed capybara, and found a number of tribesmen more in favour of eating me. The tribe parleyed and decided to let the drums speak. So the drummer rang the changes on the hollowed-out blocks of wood known as manguare, and they came from far and wide, the Woodpeckers and the Mouth of the Fish Indians, the Toucans and the Armadillos, the Ashes and the Calabash Indians, painted and feathered for a feast, laden with gourds of manioc liquor. Sliding into consciousness and sliding back out of it again, I took down with me the brief, undesirable impressions of the surface to which I was exposed, of lying naked in a dark flickering place where I was being poked and pried by many fingers, in my ears, my mouth, my ribs, my anus, while my brain throbbed with the drumming of the manguare that seemed to be inside my own head. All of these impressions crowded in on me as a continuous jet of black fluid, pouring me into some vast space where I seemed to dematerialise and become nothing. This was the moment of Pablito's death and my rebirth as a Pig Indian called *pimwe*, or White Water Bird, a name that commemorated the paleness of my skin and the sacred stream on which the Taiassu believed me to have entered the world.

For the Pig Indians, the igaripé on which I had been found was the stream of life, on it I had entered the world. The fiction that I had just been born arose necessarily as a means of accounting for my otherwise inexplicable arrival, and it required my adoption by Taiassu parents so that I could be accepted as a member of the tribe. This responsibility fell to the person who had adopted me, Guaratinga-acu, the tsushaúa, or foremost man of the tribe, and his wife Palm. She clasped my head tightly between her thighs and groaned when Guaratinga-acu pulled me out. This formality completed, I became their child.

Like women and other male children under the age of about five I was not expected to wear a breech cloth. Nakedness was an attribute of infancy. The string tied to my ankle was not a means of keeping me prisoner but of keeping me out of harm's way, perhaps knocking over a cooking pot and scalding myself, for example, during the hours of the day when the malocca was less frequented. The post to which I was tied supported a palm-leaf roof that sloped all the way down to the ground on either side. The house, or malocca as it was called, was over a hundred feet long and as broad as it was high, with flaps at either end through which the inmates ducked in and out.

At night, when the house was full, about a hundred men, women and children lived in the malocca, the hammocks of each family arranged around its own fireplace. A main aisle ran the length of the house, the communal space around which the individual families lived. Here the children played and the small bristly pigs from which the Taiassu took their name wandered up and down at all times, poking their snouts into corners in search of food. In the side aisles stood the cane presses for squeezing manioc to extract the juice for making caxiri, earthenware vessels in which it was fermented, calabashes for drinking and gourds for fetching water from the river.

Gradually my eyes became so accustomed to the gloom inside the malocca that I did not feel it as dark. I lay on the floor, filthy, naked and sore, unaware that I was being ignored by the inmates only because they were still waiting for the women of the tribe to complete the birth that has been initiated by Palm. The prone stage of infancy, during which a child might be expected to sleep eighteen hours a day, had already been summarily dealt with to the satisfaction of the tribe, for while recovering from concussion I had passed my days in a semi-conscious state. As I slowly recovered, I began to take interest in what was going on around me.

At dawn, the women of the great hut were the first to stir, boiling water and making a beverage from an infusion of herbs and lemon grass, which they drank before they went down to the river to bathe. The men were preoccupied with curious exercises, pushing their palms upwards over their heads and grunting, while the women fetched water in gourds and tended the fires before leaving to work in the manioc plantations in the forest. They returned to the malocca before the men, their hair freshly oiled, their skin glistening from the evening bath in the river. When the men came in the women inspected their feet for jiggers that might have worked their way into the skin during hunting forays through the jungle, removing them with the tip of a palm-spine. Smells of cooking, the chatter of wives, the cries of children and the crooning that hushed them into sleep drifted upwards with the smoke from the fires, lingering under the palm thatch as day passed imperceptibly into night.

Within a week of birth I was a giant toddler, not much smaller than the proxy mothers who were breast-feeding me. My foster mother Palm had weaned her own child, but in my capacity as the child of the tribe I could be shared out among the three or four other women in the malocca who were nursing at the time and able to provide me with milk. This was the stream of life on which I would continue to enter the world until I had been weaned by the women of the tribe. The first in a series of communal teats that would be put at my disposal in the following months was originally presented to me by stealth, inserted between my lips when I was still

in a delirious state, suffering from a burning thirst. The comfort and relief
I found at this anonymous breast helped to undermine my resistance on
the first occasion a woman came to suckle me and active collaboration
was required on my part. I saw how children of three or four years interrupted their play to run to their mothers and suckle while the women sat
at their chores, how even house pets, a capybara whelp and a tiny monkey,
sometimes hung at those tap-like nut-brown teats. The breast offered a
universal nourishment, and was subject to a rule of life that made no distinction between human and animal needs. For a time I was permitted
nothing else. In this diluted form I became acquainted with, and by slow
degrees adapted to, the unfamiliar taste of Taiassu food echoed in my
mothers' milk, those ferocious curassow stews, laced with peppers and a
great variety of amphibians, reptiles and nutritious insects, which I might
have found indigestible had I been launched straight into them. From my
wet-nurses I gradually absorbed, by other forms of osmosis, a taste for Pig
Indian life in a much more general sense. What at first seemed rank and
overpowering in its animal nature, a dense tribal existence whose customs
were as barbarous as the mud-packed, blood-soaked floor of the malocca
under which the Pig Indians buried their ancestors, I came to relish for
just these strong, clear instincts and the extravagant vitality that was an
expression of the rain forest in which it flourished.

Great White Bird

Guaratinga-acu hung a thumb-size pot of curare on a string around his
neck, took down his bow and arrows and ducked under the flap of the
malocca. He glanced doubtfully at the sky, pushed upwards and groaned,
as if shelving some invisible heavy matter that threatened to fall on him,
and said that now I had come of breech-cloth age we must go into the
forest to clothe me. I was able to understand what he said. During all the
time I lived in the great hut where I spent my proxy childhood the inmates
spoke to me without ever expecting me to speak back, for small children
were incapable of speech. In silence, like an infant washed over again and
again by the same recurrent sounds, I absorbed the Taiassu language as
naturally as I took into myself the milk of my loan mothers. Recently,

among the loan mothers, there had been much talk of breech-cloths. Laughingly they tweaked my sex when it stood up in the mornings, told me I had come of breech-cloth age and repeated this many times, less for the benefit of my understanding, I could tell, than for their entertainment. So I affirmed what Great White Bird said and he showed not the least surprise that in the interval of stepping outside the malocca I had finally learned to talk like a grown-up Pig Indian.

We walked in silence through the cool morning until we came to a grove of scarred trees, all with their bark stripped from the trunk, but Great White Bird pushed further on into the jungle in search of untouched trees. The grove was like an abandoned gentlemen's outfitters, plundered for so long by Pig Indian ancestors that nothing but ruined trees were left. Only the breech-cloth tree, as it was called in Taiassu, provided the sort of bark considered suitable for the manufacture of loincloths. In order to get the genuine article it had now become necessary to make a half-hour trip into the jungle. When a suitable tree was found, Great White Bird cut a strip of bark six feet long and a foot wide. Peeling off the outer bark and the milky inner skin, he rolled up his purchase and took it back to the river. Here it was soaked in water and beaten with a mallet until it became as supple as a piece of cotton, and I was presented with my first breech-cloth.

To my foster father Great White Bird, tsushaúa of the Pig Indians and maker of my first breech-cloth, I formed a closer attachment than to any other Indian, including my wife Lemon Grass. Guaratinga-acu was not their headman. In that egalitarian society there could have been no such thing. He was the foremost speaker in his own malocca and at the tobacco palavers under the giant rain tree where tribal business was discussed. In the Taiassu language, "to lick tobacco under the rain tree" was indeed how the process of tribal government was referred to. Great White Bird was not a particularly effective speaker. Far from it. When broaching any topic other than practical matters in hand he became extremely diffident. This was a common tribal trait. Taiassu men seldom looked at one another when talking, and unless taking part in tobacco palavers they did not much like to stand still either.

How many conversations I had with my Pig Indian father in the jungle while we walked in opposite directions or stood back to back, looking up at the trees. Sometimes he even chose to remain hidden in the thickets when instructing me in forest lore. His diffidence being what it was, Guaratinga-acu needed many hunting expeditions with me before he felt prepared to bring up the subject of his name. Calling a person by his name, he cautioned me as soon as he was out of sight up a tree in order to dislodge a monkey he had shot, still hanging from a branch by its tail, might bring misfortune on bearer of name and was to be avoided for that reason. To know a man's name meant to have power over him. You could squeeze his name in your mouth and unintentionally grind it between the teeth. For this reason it was necessary to have a second, secret name, known only to oneself, in the event that the first name died. Names associated with one's genitals were recognised as warding off harm most effectively. Pig Indian relatives you called mother, father, son, daughter, brother, sister. Members of other tribes you called man or woman. He scrambled down the tree. Do you understand, son, he said, examining a leaf he was holding in his hand. Understand, father, I replied. It was a potentially emotional moment, which must have been why, turning his back on me and peering intently up at the forest, Great White Bird said he thought that a pair of agouti had been here just before us. He added that in dry weather they could catch a scent at extraordinary distances. More than likely they were now to be found drinking rainwater out of the broken gourd under the calabash tree I had no doubt noticed when we passed it on our way earlier that morning.

Pig Indians and their neighbouring tribes had a sense of the locality born in them. They could tell that when the sun was in a certain place in the sky, perhaps an hour ago, six Indians had passed that way carrying a tapir, which had been killed when the sun was there, indicating another position, meaning two hours earlier. They judged by the sky, the weathered side of trees, the flight of birds, the run of animals, the exudation of sap from a broken twig. From Great White Bird I learned how to read all these signs. My training with bow and arrow, with blow-pipe and poisoned dart, fish nets and cudgels for hand-to-hand fighting was not of primary concern to my father. He left this aspect of my education to his nephews Woodcock and Grasshopper, the sons of a brother who had been tsushaúa before him, a warrior killed in a legendary battle with the White Earth Indians, who lived beyond the swamp. With the bow and arrow I remained a poor marksman, unable to hit anything smaller than a monkey, laughed at by boys who were barely into their breech-cloths, but who could be relied on to impale darting pirati at a glance when they came up river to spawn. I had instead the hand, the lungs and the eye of an expert blow-pipe sleuth. At sixty paces I could bring down a small bird, larger animals at over a hundred. Great White Bird took mechanical skills such as the handling of weapons for granted. They did not interest him. What he wished to impart to me was knowledge, to teach me, as he said, everything that lay between the roof and floor of the Pig Indian world.

One of the first things I learned from him was that the roof of this world was about to fall down. Only the unceasing daily efforts of all the forest children, particularly the Pig Indians, could avert such a disaster. This was manifestly true. On emerging from the malocca in the mornings, sometimes when still inside it, the Taiassu tribe made a great show of staggering, as if shouldering a huge burden that had been placed on their shoulders. Only with some difficulty were they able to straighten up, lifting that burden over their heads and putting it out of harm's way. My father was most reluctant to speak of this collapsing roof and their efforts to prop it up, disappearing behind a bush when he did so, because invisible powers were always watching and listening, and might be offended by what they saw or heard. He did not say so, but clearly he only addressed the subject because of tribal dissatisfaction with my contribution on this score. By making it a matter of my personal responsibility if the roof fell down he was tactfully exhorting me to greater endeavours. Raising the sky when I got up in the mornings would become as natural an action as taking my bath in the river, and in time I felt as uneasy as any other Taiassu if for some reason I had neglected to do so.

From my father I learned with certainty what for a long time I had suspected from the behaviour of Pig Indian boys when we were out together in the jungle. Sometimes they went rigid and rolled their eyes, paralysed with fear. I thought they had got wind of their greatest enemy, the jurupari or jaguar, pig-mauler and snatcher of children out of their hammocks in the night. Often the jurupari was just an unspeakable presence the Indians sensed around them. The Taiassu inhabited an unstable world in which the sky threatened to cave in, floods were poised to submerge the forest floor, the sun might disappear and village fires go out. And when the moon, neglected by its mother, began to wane, drifting in a cockle-shell boat across the sky, children could unaccountably lose the will to live, or be set by demons to eating earth until they died. In the world's mysterious sounds and its unaccountable happenings, the sudden looming of night in the forest, the rushing of the igaripé when the rains fell, the commotion that shook the still air when a storm broke over their heads, my father saw the signs of work performed by the spirits of animals to whom the Taiassu had done violence. From the lizard that slept during the months of the rainy season our tribe had stolen sleep, drawing it with fish hooks through the lizard's eyes, and out of those sleep-trawling lines the Pig Indians had spun hammocks, where they forever bound it fast. From the fox with eyes that glittered in the dark on his nocturnal wanderings through the forest our people had taken fire to light their huts, from the sucuruju the winding rivers in which the great water serpent coiled and uncoiled his body. Our hunter-ancestors had murdered the toucan and the red-tailed macaw, from whose bleeding plumage the sun issued as a ball of fire. During the rainy season, when the days were long, it was carried by a snail, but during the dry season, when the days were short, it flew with a humming bird across the sky.

Mud Indian

When Palm became ill with a fever, Great White Bird sent for the medicine man Green Ibis, whose Taiassu name was Corócoró, to come and cure his wife. Green Ibis had her carried out of the malocca and placed in a hammock under the rain tree. He rolled tobacco leaves, building a cigar as thick as his wrist, as long as his arm. He told the women to boil mimosa seeds and strain the liquid off, into which he cut slices of the skin of a jararaca, a small, dingy snake, prized by the medicine man for its virulent poison. After this brew had simmered for a while in the pot and been allowed to cool, Green Ibis drank it off in one go. Lighting his cigar, he began to puff vigorously, blowing smoke over the unconscious woman in the hammock. The potion he had drunk was gradually taking its effect. He got down on all fours, growling, leaping, working himself into a frenzy. Then he bent over Palm's body and began sucking it, spitting out what he had sucked, and when it

26

failed to emerge to his satisfaction, pulling it out with his hands and throwing it onto the ground. Exhausted, the medicine man sank down and fell into a trance-like sleep. When he awoke, Palm's fever had gone. She opened her eyes and went to bathe in the river.

Pig Indian boys who brought him the snakes he needed for his cures Corócoró rewarded with charms, intoxicating potions and aphrodisiacs, according to their age. Woodcock had begun to show an interest in aphrodisiacs at a time when Grasshopper and I still preferred the thrill of inhaling niopo secretly with Green Ibis in his forest den, a safe distance from the village. The medicine man considered Otter too young for this. He gave him instead bird's-claw talismans to guide his arrows to their mark in the jungle, so far with mixed results.

After receiving from Great White Bird the rat-skin pouch symbolising his elevation to the tobacco palaver, Woodcock now considered himself too old for clandestine narcotic sessions, and he was more interested in pursuing widows into the forest in any case. He became particularly officious in the business of seeking out a certain kind of poisonous toad, required by Green Ibis for his medicines, after it had been disclosed to him how the skin of the toad could also be used for the enlargement of the genitals. A strip of skin taken from the freshly killed toad and wrapped overnight round the penis caused it to swell up spectacularly. For several days it remained in a rampant, semi-erect condition that widows found irresistible. The male provider of this satisfaction, however, underwent considerable discomfort in the process. Grasshopper and I inspected Woodcock's bloated member with interest but not the least desire to follow his example. We went back to drying mimosa seeds, mixing them according to Green Ibis's instructions with quick-lime and baked clay to make niopo snuff, packing it in snail shells and inhaling it through hollow bird bones that were inserted in both nostrils. Floating on this soft blue niopo cloud, we rode dreamily out over the roof of the jungle, were transformed into birds, swam with the fish in the streams and sometimes, just for the sport of it, rent the odd jurupari with our bare hands.

After one of these excursions, flying over the village of the Mud Indians, Grasshopper decided he would play a trick on them that had come to him in his niopo dream. He persuaded Woodcock's favourite widow to go to the place on the river where the Mud Indian women fetched the clay with which they made their pots, and describe to them Green Ibis's marvellous device for enlarging a man's parts, and what pleasure Woodcock had thereby given her. She was provided with a good supply of toad skins, cut up in much broader strips than the usual treatment prescribed, and instructed to tell the women that their men should make a poultice like a sheath, which they must wear from sunrise to sunrise three times in succession. The Mud Indians were known as a sluggish, gullible tribe, whose men preferred pottery to hunting. They had none of that nimble, bristling quality characteristic of a Pig Indian warrior. Their element was clay, which they were rumoured also to eat. Unlike all other tribes of the forest, who oiled and painted their bodies, they applied layers of it to the skin, not only as a protection against the sun but, it seemed, for the sheer pleasure of mud. Accustomed to barter their pottery for Taiassu hogs and medicines, the Mud Indian women were not suspicious of the widow's suggestion. The rest went according to plan, for Tijuco women had an easy way of it with their Mud Indian men, as Grasshopper well knew.

More times than he could count, the sun travelled across the sky, and a delegation of bow-legged Mud Indians came to lick tobacco with the Pig Indians under the rain tree. In their hands they reproachfully held up for display the toad-skin poultices they had worn about their parts, showing between their legs the sorry results of having rashly allowed themselves to be persuaded to do so. Their spears were gross and misshapen, covered with sores, and in some cases beginning to curl up at the ends. They complained that on account of the discomfort which had begun with the poultices they had been unable to make any use of their spears, nor could their wives endure them. They came for redress. Guaratinga-acu ordered calabashes of caxiri to be brought, and sat down for a palaver with the guests that continued all day and night. The Mud Indians went home drunk, having been promised that Taiassu warriors, with their superior hunting skills, would come and free the Tijuco community of the tapir who was devouring the village manioc patch. Upon the departure of the delegation Pig Indian wives were kept busier than ever making fresh supplies of caxiri, as the tobacco palaver continued its deliberations under the rain tree for a second night, after which its members became incapacitated and did not stir out of their hammocks throughout the following day.

As Grasshopper's malocca and niopo brother, eating from the same pot and floating together on the blue cloud, I was bound to help him with the tapir hunt that had been entrusted to him by the tobacco palaver. It was entrusted, not imposed, a commission rather than a punishment, for punishment was unknown among the Pig Indians. Although a heavy, cumbersome animal, the tapir was notorious for still being able to elude even the best hunters. It was as quiet as any animal in the jungle and possessed a very keen scent, but it was not so much the contribution of my blow-pipe that Grasshopper needed on the hunt as my moral support. On account of its feeding habits, only at night could the light-shy tapir be hunted with hope of success. For an Indian this meant enduring all the terrors with which his imagination embodied the dark. Unthinkable that Grasshopper should be left to face them alone. Having determined where the tapir was feeding in the Mud Indians' manioc patch, we built a platform between two trees, high off the ground, and there we waited from dusk on, back to back and as still as death, Grasshopper with his bow and arrows and I with my blow-pipe, our bodies smeared with the resin of the tree in which we had made our lair. The tapir came silently in the darkness to browse in the manioc patch, betrayed only by an unexpected sound of digestion after the animal had already begun to feed. We heard the unmistakable report of a fart, an urgent pellet of compressed air, as palpable as solid dung, deposited beneath the tree. Though we could see nothing, we shot our arrows in the direction of the sound, which was followed by trumpeting squeals and the trampling noises of a stricken animal. We heard him crashing through the bushes. At dawn we climbed down from our hiding place, tracking the tapir to the spot where he lay with limbs already stiffening and partly devoured by ants.

Grasshopper's telling of the hunt of this tapir who had been the victim of a fart convulsed his Pig Indian audience, calling for several calabashes of caxiri while the animal was roasted and eaten under the rain tree by the inmates of our malocca. Pantomimes were volunteered, encores demanded, the affliction of the Mud Indians recalled, their plight conveyed with obscene gestures, doubled and trebled, renewing the tribe's hilarity, until men and women lay back on the earth like upturned insects, legs feebly threshing the air.

Shadows

Every year when the pirati came from the ocean, ascending the sweet water to spawn in such swarms that the tremor of their passage could be felt on the banks of the great river, an expedition of Pig Indians would journey to its confluence with the igaripé on which they lived, and build shelters near the village of a friendly Indian tribe called the Pirairú, or Mouth of the Fish. We stayed in this settlement on the river for the duration of the pirati season. If we had laid in stock what we harvested when the pirati came we would have fared better in the lean season. But forest Indians were not accustomed to set by for the future. We lived in the present and did not possess a future, not even a prospect of death. Our men and women, parents and children died, but still we did not believe in the necessity of death. It was caused by the intervention of something or someone whose magic was more powerful than our own. Left to ourselves, we were immortal. Our fluid present state was like the flight of a butterfly across a sunlit clearing. In this earthly moment there existed nothing beyond the brilliant surrounding haze, the warm pulse felt with each stroke of the butterfly's wings.

In my Pig Indian incarnation, my rain-forest-blossom of youth, I learned that I was immortal because my soul could pass in and out of my body at will. In our tribe, our elders had long known and passed down to us that during sleep the shadow of a man passed out of his mouth, wandering in the places of which it dreamed in much same the way that Grasshopper and I passed out of our bodies when we rode on the blue niopo cloud. While the body lay in the hammock, the shadow felled trees and planted manioc, shot fish and rustled leaves to make the great anteater believe that rain was falling, for then the tamanduá would turn his long bushy tail up over his head to shelter from the rain and stand stock still, making it easy for a hunter, even one who was fast asleep, to dispatch him with a blow on the head. To dream was to be there, muscles tensed for the encounter with the forest beasts, goosepricks bubbling on the skin when a cold wind blew through the gloaming of the hunter's sleep.

Taiassu never woke one another during their dreams, believing that if they were interrupted before the shadow had returned to the body the sleeper would die. On our way to the morning bath in the river

Grasshopper and I told each other our dreamings, where we had been in the shadow world, and all the things we had done there. The dreamings of the tsushaúa foreshadowed the wanderings of his tribe. He hunted, he fished, he travelled up river for news of dead kinsmen in their land beyond the mountains, eluding the juruparí who sought to kill him on his way. From his dreamings Great White Bird foretold the coming of the piratí, the birth of a child, the failure of a crop, the end of the rains. When he dreamed he had seen White Earth Indians crossing the swamp in order to enslave the Pig Indians the tribe dug pits on all paths to the village, lined them with poisoned stakes and hid in the jungle, where they remained until the danger had passed. The tsushaúa told his dreamings at palavers under the rain tree. His dreamings were told and transformed by others who added their own, passing through a hundred mouths until they became Old Stories, grafted onto the memory of the tribe where they took root and became embedded in the grain of Taiassu lore.

Woodcock, Grasshopper, Otter, the elevation of all my youthful peers was dreamed by Great White Bird, and they duly received from him the rat-skin pouch that entitled them to lick tobacco under the rain tree with full-blooded Pig Indian warriors, but for some reason this privilege was still withheld from me. I remained a dependent at my father's hearth in the malocca, prevented by tribal custom from planting my own tobacco or manioc or from cooking my own food. I resented this dependence. I had no wife to remove thorns and jiggers from my feet, receiving me with hot cassava cakes when I returned from my forays in the jungle, no one whose task it was to cultivate my manioc patch, to brew me a calabash of caxiri or to paint me for a tribal dance. The widow who desired my bauble and would sometimes snatch me for her enjoyment into the forest was not the person with whom I wished to share that most delicate gesture of intimacy among the Taiassu, the exchange of lice, or whatever titbit one happened to come across when grooming one's body and presented to one's partner to devour.

Meanwhile, Great White Bird continued to dream me in celibacy, a warrior-in-waiting whose hammock still hung at his fire, and who entertained his malocca with stories of the Elsewhere. The Elsewhere was allegedly drawn from my dreamings, in fact from the far side of the horizon of my dim recollections of life before the Pig Indians. With the point of a stick I

31

scratched a map on the floor showing Lisbon on one side, the Spanish Main on the other and the limitless ocean that lay between. The pointed stick traced in the dust my spoor through the Elsewhere, from the city with its innumerable inhabitants, houses, shops, churches, the ships in which I had been carried across the sea with hidalgos on horses, soldiers and friars, until I had ascended the river with the pirati to be spawned in the igaripé flowing beneath the Taiassu village. In comparison with the expanse of the Elsewhere I represented it to the Pig Indians as a mere pin-prick in the dust. Such were the dreamings I laid out for the inspection of my elders, for I had been there, my soul passing out of my mouth while my body remained in the hammock beside the tsushaúa's fire.

These earth pictures and the stories that accompanied them were a source of inexhaustible entertainment to my fellow Pig Indians. Notions such as that of an ocean in which all the igaripé as far as White Earth ter-ritory beyond the swamp would have been entirely swallowed up, or of canoes for three hundred warriors, which were blown along by the wind in a sail of such dimensions it could only be imagined by supposing that all male inhabitants of the three maloccas contributed their breech-cloths to its making, caused the whole tribe to lie down on the ground and howl with laughter. The great river over which the sun rose to the east and the swamp to the west, into which it fell bleeding when it died during the night, circumscribed the whole world, or what in Taiassu was called All-Creatures-Being-In-The-Forest. Around two hundred and fifty Taiassu lived in three large huts by a river, an entire people. They were similar to the Toucans, the Mouth of the Fish and the Tijuco, or Mud Indians, who were their immediate jungle neighbours, but they remained sufficiently different in their conjugation of verbs, in their body painting, their views of the origin of the world and the flavour of their soups, to constitute a distinct tribe. Less than a dozen tribes constituted mankind in its entirety. Gradually I regressed to this view of the world, accepting the subordinate nature of the Elsewhere, and in the course of time my memories of it became less real to me than the shadow world of dreamings. They sank below the surface of my mind, and it was only in the shadow world that I would sometimes still find myself back in Zarate's house. I became a com-plete Indian.

Between tears of laughter when he listened with the others to these absurd recitals of mine (the faces of the audience always averted from me as mine was from theirs, so that we appeared to be engaged in conversation with different parties, both absent), Guaratinga-acu seems to have been troubled by doubts about my orthodoxy within the order of All-Creatures-Being-In-The-Forest. Against my dreamings from the Elsewhere he pitted his own from the Here. He cocked his head and began to dream me askance from about the time Lemon Grass first sidled up behind me during the village dance.

When a hundred men stamped in a line under the rain tree, beating up the dust around the fire, so that all one saw was a tangle of feathered bodies in snatches of firelight, a young man might not pay too much attention to the girls who slipped into the line behind him and hung onto his shoulders, for girls did so all the time. It was not until Lemon Grass had repeatedly done this, and then withdrawn into the bushes, making quite sure I noticed, that I knew I was being invited to a tryst. When I followed Lemon Grass into the jungle, and she spat at me and scratched my face, it was clear I had found special favour in her eyes. Girls had spat and scratched me before, but playfully, leaving few marks, nothing compared with the trellis of wounds that had been drawn across Woodcock's face by the fingernails of many admirers. It was not only passion but jealously that caused the girls to mark a man with their nails. The more marks he bore the more desirable he became. When I first took off my breech-cloth to impale her snake-like body, winding around me inside the forest bower which Lemon Grass had built from branches and palm leaves and strewn with violet trumpet flowers for trysts with her lovers, she scratched me and hissed and spat like a lynx in an unmistakable declaration of love. I returned to the malocca duly mauled, my desirability much enhanced, displaying my scratches with pride to my peers. Guaratinga-acu's wife Palm made a loud clapping noise with her tongue when she caught sight of me, imitating the puff-throated manakin bird, remarkable for a stupendous love call out of all proportion to his diminutive size. All the women around her, many of them loan mothers who not so long ago had given me the teat, repeated the call gleefully, laughing and flapping their arms as they made clapping noises with their tongues. Only Great White Bird, swaying rhythmically in his hammock as he prepared to pass into guácu, a state of unbeing which was practised by the Taiassu to give greater calm to the body and mind than any sleep, cocked his head a little further on one side amid this flurry of flappings and explosions, and chose to say nothing.

My father's shadow passed out of his mouth, dreaming me into that lopsided view of All-Creatures-In-The-Forest he held from his hammock, dreamings which he made and related at the tobacco palaver, not of his own doings in the shadow world, but of mine. Since the dreamings of the tsushaúa, once they had been disclosed to the palaver, were held to anticipate what would come to pass in the upper world, they imposed an obligation on the person he had dreamed to fulfil his destiny.

Guaratinga-acu's dreamings for his foster son Pimwe routed him along solitary paths as the tribe's pig herder and trader, ferrying swine up the igaripé and then the great river as far as the village of the Tenimbuca, or Ashes, on the rocky border of the mountains where the souls of dead Indians resided. The Tenimbuca were a dwarfish, foul-smelling people who lived in fear of their proximity to the dead. As a prophylactic they smeared ash on their skins and dwelt in caves, on the walls of which thrived a white phosphorescence, much prized by downriver Indians for the salt-like properties otherwise lacking in their rain-forest diet. So I unloaded hogs and took on board my balsa raft a cave-wall crop of saltpetre, trading a part of it on my journey downstream for the nets of the Pisá Indians, for birds from the Tucános and Uacarrás, and for the hides of armadillos from the Tatús. It was a lonely, miserable life as a hog trader among these savages, enduring the pig-taunting jibes of strangers and, even worse, their hospitality, submitted to deluges of cheap caxiri and kawana beer, missing my hunting companions and all our familiar haunts along the igaripé of my native village. Moored somewhere on the great dark river, amid the brawl of sounds that wrangled at night in All-Creatures-in-The-Forest, I opened my mouth in my sleep to let my soul fly out to the bower of Lemon Grass, my face itching to be scratched, my spear eagerly at tilt, only to be met by Guaratinga-acu standing at the entrance with his head on one side, barring my way.

Outdreamed by my father, dreamed out of my own dreamings, deprived of my hunting rights even in the shadow world, I complained bitterly to my foster mother Palm when I returned to the village, and asked her for magic. Lemon Grass had meanwhile left her father's malocca and was housed in her jungle bower, living off roots and berries and eating earth, it was said, because she was pining for her absent lover. Palm took me on one side and said: your father is jealous of Lemon Grass, that is all. He knows that some day Pimwe will hang his hammock above her hammock in her father's hut, and then he will lose his beloved White Water Bird to a wife. But there is a natural way that is stronger even than a tsushaúa's dreamings. There is no need for magic. Go and find Lemon Grass, and when you next come home, speak with her father, give him arrows, an axe, a piece of shingle to prove you have a roof over your head to offer his daughter, and hang up your hammock in his malocca. The rest will take care of itself.

So I went into the jungle to Lemon Grass's bower, where I lived with her until the time came to set off on my travels again, and when I next returned to the village Lemon Grass was working in the manioc patch with a swollen belly, hatching the egg I had laid inside her. I gave her father arrows, an axe and a piece of shingle, as Palm had said, and went into the forest to fell trees and burn scrub and to clear a piece of land where the women would plant manioc. When the bride's family had seen to their satisfaction that I was able and willing to prepare land to provide food for them, I carried my hammock into her malocca, hanging it up above the place where Lemon Grass slept. Thus we became man and wife. The belly of a young girl, growing round and taut for everyone to see, was the stratagem chosen by Palm to outwit Guaratinga-acu, leaving him with no choice but to recognise my new status.

Soon afterwards he related under the rain tree a dreaming that happened to come to him at this time, in which he had seen me brought to bed in expectation of the coming child. As it would have been unfitting for a man to give birth before he had licked tobacco with his peers, I was presented with the rat-skin tobacco pouch that admitted me to the palaver. The tsushaúa bent forward to the tribal tobacco pot, dipped into it a tobacco stick and conveyed a little of the liquid to his mouth. Man after man came forward to do likewise, myself last of all, thus signifying the agreement of the tribe. My father clasped me in his arms. His embrace was brittle, there was no strength in his arms. Thus in the moment of my triumph I was sad, realising that Great White Bird had become an old man, and that the Pig Indian belief in immortality was a dream of the soul, on which my father's body would soon be broken.

Earth Puddle

Lemon Grass went out alone into the forest one morning to an already chosen place where she squatted down and gave birth to the child on a bed of leaves. The mother tied up with a fibre the snake of life that had bound their bodies together, bit through it, ducking the squalling infant in the river before she covered its body with resin and smeared it with clay, according to the custom of the Mud Indians ancestors on her maternal side. Having flattened its nose with the palm of her hand, she passed the child to her mother and went out to work in the manioc field.

My son was brought to me in my hammock where I had already been lying for some time in preparation for the birth. I received him with joy, of which I gave no outward sign, however, as to do so would have brought him bad luck. I avoided all hard labour or the consumption of food that might prove harmful to the child, in particular meat, so that the new-born would not resemble any animal whose flesh I had eaten. Until his navel healed I remained on a diet of yams and cassava, with a calabash of caxiri under my hammock which the women in my hut always kept replenished.

Villagers visited me during my confinement, bringing gifts and good wishes for a speedy recovery. Even the Mud Indians came to inspect their new relative. They seemed pleased with the child's baked terracotta complexion, distinctly lighter than was usual among the Tijuco, and presented him with a handsome set of earthenware utensils. We licked tobacco together and they performed a dance to celebrate the birth. Under the pretext of passing on to her offspring a lighter skin colour, Lemon Grass had secretly continued to eat clay throughout her pregnancy, a superstition she had inherited from Mud Indian womenfolk. Perhaps it was this which accounted for the boy's turbid appearance. Blotches that passed over and as quickly vanished from the surface of his skin, like a patchwork of clouds moving across an uncertain sky, seemed to reflect some process of rumination, deep inside the child, still vacillating in his loyalty, on the rash, obscure and clamorous nature of his conflicting heritage, for here lay the issue of a stupendously casual union of the old with the new world.

By her marriage Lemon Grass became entitled to a corner of her own in the common house, to her own pots, a hearth around which to hang up the new family's hammocks. In a council of relatives and elders that assembled around me in my confinement it was decided to give our son the name Earth Puddle. The boy would be entrusted with his name and sworn to secrecy once he had been weaned. Until his navel had healed, and what was left of the snake sloughed off of its own accord, he lay with me in the hammock where I dreamed him into life. With Earth Puddle I became, in the flesh, kin of the Taiassu, through him I was now bound inseparably to All-Creatures-Being-In-The-Forest.

During all this time the child remained my responsibility to feed and clean. Sticks and leaves served as dishes and towels. Before Lemon Grass left the malocca in the mornings she milked her breasts into a palm leaf. She did her mother's duty but showed no love. Resting the leaf on the flat of my hand, I turned up the edges to give it a cup-like form. From this vessel I gave Earth Puddle to drink as long as his mother was out of the house. He had a sturdy little body and a phlegmatic disposition, vindicating his mother's belief in the good sense of having reinforced the infant with clay. It had closed the pores through which vital spirits might have escaped and done incalculable harm while this little piece of human pottery was still in the making inside her.

A cousin without Mud Indian ancestry, and without the addition of clay to the pregnant mother's diet, which Lemon Grass regarded as providing a protective glaze to the child inside, happened to die at the same time Earth Puddle was born. To Lemon Grass this afforded proof of the superiority of Mud Indian midwifery. Believing the child's death to have been the mother's own fault, she was wholly unmoved by her grief. It was during this time that I recognised the gulf that lay between me and my wife. She remained deaf to the heart-rending scenes that went on outside the malocca where the bereft woman stood milking her breasts into the air, weeping and calling on the little one to return to the places where it used to play. Her mourning only ceased after everything the child had ever touched, everything the parents possessed, had been burned, so that they stood there naked and destitute as the day they were born, and were able to begin life again.

After she had given birth to her first child and established her own fire place in the malocca Lemon Grass seemed to lose interest in scratching me. I tried to lure her back into the bower she had built in the forest when courting me, but she rejected my advances. I did not take this personally. After a birth Pig Indian women withheld themselves from their men at least until the child could walk, sometimes until it had been weaned. Like all other husbands in this situation, I turned to the widows of the tribe for relief. But unlike most other wives, who seemed content with this arrangement condoned by tribal custom, Lemon Grass was always following me into the forest and spying on me. She humiliated me at the tobacco palaver by darting at my breech-cloth and tearing it off, exposing me to the tribe. I was forced to retire into the forest and remain out of sight until I had made myself a new one. My wife pursued me into the jungle and placed large black stinging ants on my private parts, causing them to swell up painfully. I had no choice but to submit to this treatment, prescribed by Pig Indian custom as the revenge that might be taken by wives on husbands who had been unfaithful to them for whatever reason.

Lemon Grass was a complete slave to tribal custom, imprisoned in a mesh of taboo that separated men and women as completely as if they had been different species of animal. Whenever the men played jurupari music with vibrating turtle shells, fifes and deer-skull whistles the women had to turn their backs, for they were not allowed to see the instruments on pain of death, although Guaratinga-acu assured me this threat was not to be understood literally. I tried to reassure my wife. But Lemon Grass became so terrified at the sound of jurupari music that she disappeared into the forest and remained hidden for days.

It was the same with many other tribal taboos. Although men did no cooking as such, they sometimes grilled what they brought back from the forest. At my wife's fire place this was forbidden. She would no more have helped me with a tobacco crop than she would have dreamed of admitting me to enter her manioc patch. These were the respective preserves of men and women, on which the other sex was absolutely not allowed to trespass. What she ate when her blood came or where she trod, how she painted herself or oiled her hair, when she looked at the moon or turned away, crossed water or did not: in the observance of a multitude of rules in her daily life my wife adhered to the vast unwritten compendium of Pig Indian custom with far greater strictness than other Taiassu women. This was in part attributable to an influence of her Mud Indian ancestors, notoriously fixed in their ways, in part to her own stubbornness. For all that she was a good wife. The conscientiousness with which she removed the jiggers from my feet when I returned to the malocca was irreproachable. Her cassava cakes and agouti stews were unsurpassed.

I dreamed our son Earth Puddle into life in a hammock in the malocca's warm half-darkness shared at all times with upwards of a hundred people, interlaced with the smells of cooking, the recital of dreamings, the cries of children and the songs of their mothers. I put the first grasshopper in his mouth and set him astride his first pig. Inside the malocca his only enemies were the blood-sucking bats that dropped from the rafters during the night to feed on exposed flesh. These vampires could leach blood so softly that they never woke the victim, nor did they leave any evidence of a wound. Their nocturnal visits were sometimes not noticed until it was too late, and children died from loss of blood. From the time Earth Puddle shed his navel cord and was laid in his own little hammock his mother put pepper on his forehead and toes to discourage the bats. During the day she took him with her to the manioc patch where she worked, or into the forest where she gathered berries and roots, covering his body with a film of clay to protect him from the sun, according to Mud Indian fashion.

But it was I and the men of the tribe, not Lemon Grass, who brought the boy up. At a very early age, before I gave him his first bow and arrow, I taught him the call of animals and the song of birds and how to imitate them in order to stalk them better. When he was weaned he received from me a net, and before he went down to the river I showed him how to make expert casts under the rain tree in pursuit of imaginary fish, trapping broken pieces of earthenware or a pile of leaves and dragging them behind him into the malocca.

By the time Earth Puddle's ears were pierced with a thorn and he began wearing bird bones to widen the passage, there was nothing that remained a secret to him. The boy had watched male and female copulating, he knew that old people left the village to die in the forest, and that sometimes they were accompanied by an armed tribesman to ensure them a swift dying. He had seen blood and violent death and eaten the human flesh of prisoners, hostile Indians who penetrated the Taiassu forest. No one knew where the strangers came from. A long spell of peace followed the intrusion, untroubled by the feuds that were constantly breaking out between the forest Indians and their enemies who lived in the open lands beyond the swamp. Earth Puddle lived like a rain drop poised in the great balance of All-Creatures-Being-In-The-Forest, not aware, as I was, of any divide separating himself from the animals. He saw that all the inhabitants of the forest behaved not so differently from himself. They used sounds to communicate with one another, courted their mates and multiplied like man, living part of the time in families in dwellings they built, dividing labour between the male and the female, they made enemies, they formed alliances, and like man they lived off the flesh they hunted and the fruit they gathered. Undiscovered by time, it seemed to me that Earth Puddle would remain suspended in this changeless balance for ever.

But a new wind began to blow through the forest, first registered by Great White Bird on the fringes of his sleep. In his dreamings he heard a sibilance like a rushing of wings, borne down river to him from the domain of the dead. As they came closer the tsushaúa related these whisperings under the rain tree and interpreted them for the tribe. He said the wind was caused by the souls of Indian ancestors who had taken flight from the sacred mountains. The ancestors had been dis-turbed — here he licked tobacco and spat — by what appeared to be some kind of giant centipede, an animal made up of many parts, which crawled and ravaged its way through the forest. Guaratinga-acu stared up into the rain tree, as if seeking confirmation there for what he had witnessed in his sleep. The centipede had the face of a man and the torso of an armadillo, he said, which grew out of a juruparí larger than any he had ever seen. On the night he recounted this dreaming the tsushaúa was heard to groan out loud. Wherever Great White Bird's shadow had flown during the night, when morning came his shadow had not returned to his body.

I wrapped my father up in his hammock and buried him in a sitting position under the place where it had hung. I broke his bow, placing it with his tobacco pouch and a quiver of arrows in the grave alongside the body. With his disappearance under the malocca floor the tribe's mourn-ing for its tsushaúa also ceased. His spirit had departed, signalling the end of an earthly existence that would continue in the shadow world. But Palm's face turned to stone. The wife of the tsushaúa did not move, until one day she got up unseen and slipped away into the forest. Grasshopper and I retrieved the old woman's body and buried her under the malocca floor with the pots she had used, smashing them beforehand so that her ghost would not return to ask for them in the spirit world.

The tribe licked tobacco under the rain tree all night long to appoint a new tsushaúa. We consulted with the medicine-man, Corócoró, as to the meaning of these two deaths. We did not doubt that they had been brought about by the malice of the dead persons' enemies, using magic more powerful than their own. Corócoró rolled a cigar as long as his arm, smoking it in Pig Indian fashion with the burning end in his mouth, and blew smoke at the assembled tribe. After Green Ibis had drunk one of his poisonous concoctions and worked himself into a frenzy, throwing himself onto the ground, the voice of the dead tsushaúa issued from his mouth. Great White Bird's voice announced to the awe-struck tribe that his shadow had been killed and eaten by the White Earth Indians while crossing the great swamp in his dreaming. Guaratinga-acu would be free to depart for the sacred mountains only after his death had been avenged. This was an appeal from the father of the tribe to all his sons, natural and adopted, to Páca, Woodcock, Grasshopper and myself, Pimwe, which had to be acted on at once. Each went to his malocca to fetch his weapons, averting his eyes from his wife – for to see or be seen by her at such a time meant great misfortune – and set out before it began to get light. But Woodcock's wife, Palm Shoot, came up from the stream where she had gone to fetch water, and glimpsed her husband as he was stepping into the forest.

Beyond the Swamp

Stricken we fled through the shadows along the paths foreseen in our father's dreaming, like arrows we sped to our doom. We ran past the Mud Indian village in the early light, averting our eyes from the women washing on the opposite bank, along the igaripé to the great river. We followed the river as far as the caves of the Ashes before turning away from it in the direction of the setting sun. We came into a forest where I had never been. I was lost. My life which had been bound up in a tight seed scattered out of me in all directions. For the second time I felt myself being torn out of the foundation of my life. With every step I took forward I was losing what

I loved. Dislodged by the tremors set in motion by my flight, I could hear the rain drop falling which had been poised in the balance of All-Creatures-Being-In-The-Forest. My son was falling out of the green bower that had been his paradise. But such was the persuasiveness of the dead tsushaúa's dreaming, the sound of the rushing wings he had described so clearly audible, that I never hesitated in this impulse towards my destruction.

We reached the great water and burned out of a log a pirogue to carry us across the swamp. On the far side we stepped onto a bleached shore, strewn with the stumps of dead trees from which the territory of the White Earth Indians took its name. No Indians actually lived there. Wandering Carib and Tupi tribes had their encampments here when they travelled up river on their raiding parties from the coast. On this white graveyard of a shore, where the Taiassu's greatest asset, his ability to be as motionless as the plants around him, no longer gave him an advantage, Páca bled out his life in our first skirmish with a marauding tribe. Páca, who had come to avenge his father by eating the enemy who had eaten him, was himself roasted and mainly devoured the same night, while his subsidiary limbs continued to victual the marauders on their journey downstream. The rest of us who had been captured knew what fate awaited us. The Caribs bared their teeth and bit their arms to make plain to us that we too would be eaten.

We were brought to a dirty village in a land of scrub and a few straggling trees, standing in the plain as if to commemorate the jungle that must once have flourished there before it was burned down. On a dozen stakes, driven into the earth outside the malocca, the heads of the victims eaten by the tribe had been impaled. While Woodcock was hustled into the mal-occa I was taken with Grasshopper to a smaller hut and left tied up out-side.

Then shouting began inside the malocca, a horde of men and women came out, Woodcock in their midst, jeering and poking him with pointed sticks, on which pumpkins were impaled and filled with something that made them rattle. The Caribs used these pointed rattle-sticks to goad their prisoner and to make a great noise at the same time. They chased Woodcock round in circles until he was so exhausted he fell to his knees. A warrior came forward with a club and struck Woodcock such a blow that even from where I was sitting I heard the skull crack open. A second blow followed while Woodcock was still on his knees, exploding his head. His brains spurted out as he pitched forward onto the ground. The women at once poured boiling water over the corpse and flayed it. They severed the arms and legs from the trunk, split the trunk back and front and carried these dismembered parts in triumph round the malocca. While the men were roasting his flesh the women boiled the entrails, adding leaves and herbs to make a stew. I watched them barbecue the genitals as a delicacy for the tsushaúa's wife. When I heard Grasshopper's voice from inside the hut, asking how our brother was, I broke down and wept. I said to him that Woodcock was now lying on the fire being roasted, and that I had just seen the first portion of him eaten.

All night long the revellers drank and danced, stumbling in and out of the firelight, until the last one disappeared inside the malocca and the village fell silent. Towards dawn a light wind rose, spraying sparks through the darkness. I heard a faint jingle. I saw columns of mounted riders with lances and pennants, the horse-hooves noiseless, as if shod with cloth, betrayed by no more than a chink or a glint of light on steel. In closed ranks immediately behind them stood foot-soldiers in breast-plates, helmets and bearing halberds, pitched like a shadow across the open plain. As I stared at this ghostly army, waiting for it to dissolve, it began to move, gathering speed and bearing down on the village, not ghostly at all but a real and terrible doom. The first Indians who came rushing out of the malocca were speared by the riders' lances, snatched up in the air like dolls and dashed to the ground. The foot soldiers swarmed around the malocca, impaling with cold steel the naked bodies that tumbled out, the men, children, women with babies just as they came, most of them still half-asleep, and tossed fire brands up into the roofs. In a short time the village was ablaze. The Indians ran out of their burning house into the waiting swords. They were run through, clubbed and cut down, all the inhabitants of the village massacred within a few minutes.

I was sitting tied up outside a hut that still remained whole on this ring of fire when I was noticed by one of the riders. He wheeled his horse and came forward at a trot, lowering his lance. The man brought the horse about in leisurely fashion, so that he could lean and dispatch me with a thrust from the saddle, for he was not going to bother to dismount to kill me. He was already drawing back his arm to make the thrust when my mouth opened of its own accord and I heard myself exclaim "Holy Mary, Mother of God!" The man's arm jerked back and his neck shot out, as if these two movements were part of the same mechanism. He rose half out of the saddle. In this attitude he froze, his lance tilted, the tip resting on the ground, as if to lend him support, peering down at me in disbelief. "Christian?"

I looked up and saw Guaratinga-acu's vision of a man with the torso of an armadillo, appearing to grow out of a jurupari larger than any he had ever seen. The armadillo was the conquistador's ribbed steel breast-plate, the jurupari the horse on which he was mounted. I looked up mutely at the gaunt figure leaning on his lance and inspecting me from what seemed to be a very long time ago. The pointed beard was now rusty grey, the face wasted, the head grizzled, but unmistakable for all that. The admiral Dom Pedro asked me who I was, and sensing the danger I was in I began to lie about my past. I told him that I was the son of an Indian woman by a Portuguese. He asked who had taught me the true religion. I said a priest had come into the territory of the tribe and converted many people.

Dom Pedro asked if the tribe had eaten people. I assured him we most definitely had not. We had been captured and were about to be eaten by cannibals ourselves. He nodded and said it was just as well if our tribe had not been among the Indians whose custom it was to eat people, because to do so was a very great sin. He lifted his lance, pointing at the burning village behind him, the ground strewn with corpses. These Indians, he said, had ambushed one of his men on his way to fetch water, killed and eaten him. This was why they had followed them on a journey up river that had taken them many days, to punish the savages who had been guilty of such a terrible sin. There was a whoosh and crackle of fire behind him as the roof of the blazing malocca caved in. When he turned to look his face reflected the light of the flames, burning with a dark reddish colour like molten iron. The wages of sin are death, Dom Pedro Felipe said, and he put his spurs to his horse.

Jurupari

Thus I became a mestizo in a moment of mortal need, but of cowardice for all that. I had as much sense of kinship with Indians whose blood I did not share as of strangeness towards the Europeans whose blood ran in my veins. My mestizo status was accepted without question by the Spanish and the Portuguese, who did not care, but by the Indians, who did, it was regarded with mistrust. Where did my allegiance lie? Once outside the Taiassu village where I had spent my youth I would never be able to come back inside an Indian community. My forest life was now embodied by Grasshopper, sole survivor of my Pig Indian past. Only with each other would we ever again be able to speak the Taiassu language, share a universe stored in memories that had meaning now for just two people.

With Grasshopper I licked tobacco at night on the deck of the brigantine that had brought the admiral's expedition upstream from the coast. I taught him the rudiments of the Christian religion, knowing that without religion he was doomed. Grasshopper understood the narratives I told him, but for the explanations I tried to draw out of them he expressed contemptuous disbelief. Why had the warrior-hero who submitted to death on the crossed branches not used his magic to escape? I cast around for means of conveying to him Christianity's fundamental ideas, but Pig Indians did not think in abstract terms. There was no way of saying "God is Love", because the Taiassu language had no word for God, or for love.

With the God who was love I had difficulties myself. The jurupari who was violent and cruel and could only be appeased by sacrifice seemed much more real than the God of love. Was there one God for the white men and another for the Indians? Had the God who was love told Dom Pedro Felipe to burn a village and put the inhabitants to the sword because one of his men had been eaten? The massacre of the Indians seemed much rather the sacrifice to a jurupari than to any God who was love. The Spanish expeditionary force had only completed what we ourselves had set out and failed to do. The killing had been carried out with more thoroughness than the usual small raiding party of Indians might have been expected to accomplish with bows and arrows and fire-hardened sticks, but for the strategy of surprising an enemy when he least

expected it, and for the cold-bloodedness with which it had been executed, Grasshopper felt only admiration.

On board the brigantine he closely watched the admiral for some sign of
the manner in which he communicated with the jurupari from whom he
received his instructions and whom he was repeatedly seeking to appease
by making the sign of the cross. Dom Pedro was his own pilot now, using
instruments to determine the ship's course that were also new to me. The
sight of him silently engaged with sextant and charts, on which he made
notations it was his habit to read back aloud to himself, inspired in
Grasshopper a feeling of even greater awe than the unimaginable sea that
now engulfed him. I stretched out my hand and asked: what is this around
you? The great river has flooded, Grasshopper answered. And what of
these ships, I asked, these canoes so large they can float a malocca across
the great river? It is just as you told us under the rain tree, Grasshopper
said with equanimity. The wind blows into the great breech-cloth and
pushes the canoe over the flood. All these things happen in the Elsewhere,
just as you saw them in your sleep. From this answer I understood that
Grasshopper believed he had died and was now in the shadow world.

The crew of the brigantine had been recruited by Dom Pedro in Cadiz.
There the admiral had fitted out ships for the expedition when his petition
was favourably received at the court of Spain. After returning empty-
handed from his earlier voyage and suffering long neglect at the hands of
the Portuguese, the admiral's ambition to lead an expedition into the interior of the New World had ironically been fulfilled by his country's enemy.

Many times during the voyage we were summoned by the admiral to
give an account of Indian life, the food the Taiassu ate, how they built their
houses, how they could find their bearings when travelling in dense
jungle, how they conducted their marriages, their alliances, their wars and
many other things he was interested to learn in detail. He gave me a letter,
with instructions to present it to a factor called Antonio when we disembarked in Santa Maria de la Antigua. The factor would make arrangements for the mestizo and the full-blooded Indian to be accommodated as
dependents attached to the admiral's household there, for a time would
come when he might need us, he said. After two weeks sailing along the
coast we reached a settlement on the west shore of a gulf. Originally the
settlement had been known by its Indian name, Titumate. When it was

captured from the Indians by the Spanish it was christened Santa Maria de la Antigua, in honour of a pledge the commander had given to Our Lady of Antigua, whose shrine was venerated in the cathedral of Seville, to make a pilgrimage to the shrine and adorn it with jewels if she granted him victory. I was told that hundreds of Indians had been killed in the battle, not a single Spaniard, God be praised, and this was apparently the way things usually went in our wars with the Indians.

Titumate

The Spanish flotilla arrived in Titumate at the beginning of the wet season, the very worst time of year. The ships rode on a swell under a low roof of cloud while the food, munitions, horses and men were brought ashore in a torrent of rain, soaking them so thoroughly that they would not dry out for weeks. I asked for the factor Antonio and was directed to the only building on the waterfront. It was surrounded by a stockade in the middle of a wasteland of mud. The factory comprised one vast empty space. There were racks along all the walls, crammed with hogsheads, crates, sacks, and a counter running the length of the room, on which a Negro lay asleep. Grasshopper was more fascinated by the sight of this black man than by anything he had seen so far. But for that profound awe in which Pig Indians held the mystery of sleep he would have rubbed his hand against the Negro's skin to see if the colour came off. So we squatted down on our heels against the wall, waiting for the factor to arrive, until eventually we fell asleep.

We were woken by a bright light. A small, wizened man with a goat-like beard was holding up a flare and scrutinising our faces as he muttered something about his factory becoming a hostel for all kinds of vagrants. I asked the man if he was Antonio, and presented him with the admiral's letter. Antonio read the letter with arched eyebrows that gave him the appearance of being permanently amused, even when, as now, he was not pleased at all. He had just returned from a journey up river, he said; land was being cleared for new plantations; he had to supervise the loading of the timber which Indians would be bringing to the shore during the next days; and besides, in darkness and such weather it would be impossible to

47

reach the governor's house. This explanation for being unwilling or unable to comply with Dom Pedro's request was given in a not unfriendly manner. The factor had a springy, mellifluous speech, indicating that he was not a native Spanish speaker but an Italian; Genoese, as it turned out. He lit an oil lamp, handed it to the Negro with instructions to give us some food, and told us he would come back the next day.

The Negro did not answer or give any sign of having heard what the factor had said, but as soon as he had gone he climbed down from the counter to fetch us bread, cheese and wine before resuming his position on the counter. The Negro's silence had an unsettling effect on Grasshopper. He climbed up the wall racks and curled up on a shelf, saying he would rather sleep there than with the Negro on that wooden hammock, as he called it. All might I walked barefoot up and down the stone floor, slapping the soles of my feet on the ground as I listened to the crash of the rain on the roof, repulsed, like my feet, by the hardness of tiles, not absorbed by the jungle roof and floor. I thought about stone roofs and floors and hammocks that refused to bend with the weight of a body, and how different this antagonism of borders was from the suppleness of the Indian identity within All-Creatures-Being-In-The-Forest. We were so much a part of it that in guácu it would sometimes seem the body supported the hammock on which it lay, and the great forest trees stood upside down, balancing on the fretwork of their upmost leaves, with their trunks growing out of the sky.

When the rain ceased I blew out the lamp and lay down on top of the counter. In the darkness I was aware of the Negro's body, lying rigid at the far end of the counter, as emitting some peculiar force under which the grain of the wood must eventually crack. I could feel the heat exuding from his body, and along this line of straining heat travelled a faint hum, opening up like a wedge of light, growing wider, this hummed dirge that was the Negro's grief. The dismal twang resonated in the wood and penetrated my bones. All night long I lay on his beam of sound as if it were my own ache, unable to sleep, until the Negro got up with the first light. I followed him outside, raising my shoulders to the sky and pushing it up with a groan.

The sheet of rain clouds hung so low over the ocean that a ship could not have passed between without losing sight of the top of her mast. Along the shore a mumbling kind of procession inched its way. The procession was made up of men in harness dragging tree trunks. These were the Indians the factor Antonio had set to work. Having cleared the forest for the plantations inland, they were now bringing the logs to the shore for shipment to Spain. When the Indians reached the harbour front the Negro went out to them with a long rope spooled off a winch. He hitched it around the tree trunks and hauled them in over the mud, all day long without ever seeming to tire. The Indians came and went until darkness fell, the Negro returned to the factory, took his dinner of bread, onions, cheese and wine and lay down again on his counter. His body went rigid while he slept, generating heat lines along the counter, splinters of ache. I could feel it coming through the wood, jarring my bones, that hum of some immeasurable sorrow.

For days we watched Indians in harness drag brasil wood along the beach, until the waterfront was stacked from end to end with timber piles. The factory disappeared behind a forest, dismembered and laid out in piles of corpse-like trees. The Indians wanted to know from me why the white people carried forests across the sea. I said they needed brasil wood for dyestuff, palisander for making furniture and other hardwood for building ships, since they had cut down all the forests in their own lands. The Indians listened to these explanations in silence. Perhaps they were unable to understand me, or perhaps they couldn't comprehend that anyone would do something so foolish.

A messenger arrived from Antonio, a mestizo, who had been sent to fetch us to the governor's house. Grasshopper was persuaded to climb down from his shelf. I was relieved to leave the factory and its strange Negro, who either worked like a horse with no sign of tiring or lay motionless like a stone on the counter as if he were dead. The mestizo was a high-spirited fellow, cheerfully negotiating the bleak prospect of Titumate in the rainy season, the waist-deep holes into which we unexpectedly sank, the sodden makeshift houses on the point of collapse, the torrents of filthy water that swirled the excrements of the town around our legs, as if these discomforts had been invented for our amusement. Even Grasshopper, who was grey and feverish, began to rally under the impact of his exuberance. Something about this effervescent manner, which in a mestizo seemed so displaced, struck me as familiar. Then I saw in him his father,

49

the Genoese factor Antonio, whose eyebrows continued to arch in an expression of amusement even when confronted with something he didn't much like. Antonio's son told us he was called Arapásso.

Arapásso brought us to a house with a door and windows in the European style but otherwise resembling a miniature malocca. I thought this an unlikely residence for a governor of His Hispanic Majesty, even for one as Spartan in his habits as Dom Pedro Felipe, representing the Crown in as precarious a colony as Santa Maria de la Antigua. But when an Indian woman came out of the house I understood that she was Don Antonio's wife, and that this was where the factor lived. The woman had the same stocky figure as Arapásso, the square face of her son and the same broad nose, which she must have flattened at birth with the palm of her hand as vigorously as her mother had flattened her own before Arapásso's father had been able to intervene. She was followed by a clutch of children of diminishing size but with increasingly protuberant noses, and in the elevated contours of this succession of noses, lined up behind one another like a miniature mountain range, I recognised not only the likeness to the husband but the effect of his restraining hand on the nose-flattening instincts of his Tupi wife. There was something very comical about these sleek Indian children displaying the same knob-like apparatus in the middle of the face, like toys wanting to be wound up, which was at the same time very poignant, for they reminded me of my son Earth Puddle, whom I knew I would never see again.

After all the ordeals we had been through since leaving Pig Indian territory, Grasshopper and I settled into the hammocks, and, more generally, into the familiar Indian hospitality provided for us by the factor's Tupi wife. It was a restful stay, including prolonged spells of guácu punctuated by delicious armadillo and iguana stews, in an atmosphere not so different from the malocca to which we were accustomed. The factor himself was absent, Arapásso explained to us with his usual cheerfulness, because he had been detained in the governor's house on charges of embezzlement. Apparently the admiral was unlike any governor Santa Maria de la Antigua had seen before, a fanatical servant of the Spanish Crown, whose interests he saw jeopardised by a morally corrosive combination of Indian climate, Indian duplicity and Indian women. That white people did not generally thrive in this wet heat, became disease-ridden, listless, debauched, losing all sense of morality at the prospect of gold, all control of their passions under the influence of naked women entwining their bodies around them — these were the unavoidable consequences of the colonising ambitions which had brought them here. Many of the colonists embarked on the carracks that left Lisbon and Cadiz as casually as if they were going on a short voyage along the coast, a shirt in one hand and a loaf of bread in the other, with no other provision for the future.

Within a few weeks the Spanish noblemen were unrecognisable as the men who had disembarked at Titumate. All their finery had become dirty and bedraggled. Like dogs they copulated with Indian women in hovels, drank and played cards against the tedium of the never ending rain. Starving they wandered around in search of something to eat or a place to dry out, straggling off into the woods, eating roots and grasses, until they became feverish and light-headed. Young nobles in silk coats who had pledged their estates in order to come to the New World to make their fortunes dropped dead from hunger while crying for bread in Titumate. Every day a few more of them died, their corpses lying around the town unburied and left to rot. Those who survived were soon disillusioned, watching the rain fall and fall, their dreams of gold oozing away in the quagmire of Indian mud, until they surrendered and chartered a ship back to Hispaniola, cursing the day they had been foolish enough to set foot on this God-forsaken coast.

White Moths

Dom Pedro Felipe's expeditionary force was quartered in the new stone town that had begun to rise over the old palm-roofed settlement of Titumate. Santa Maria de la Antigua began with a whitewashed church, built by Indians under the supervision of Spanish missionaries. The church acquired a monastery, the monastery a fort, the fort an administration, the administration a governor and an imposing residence, all of which was surrounded by a garrison to defend the colony against Indian raids. Fraternisation with Indians provoked Dom Pedro's mistrust. This was the true cause of the charges of embezzlement brought against the factor at the time I arrived in Titumate. So long as the case remained under investigation, Antonio was confined to the governor's residence. Dom Pedro suspected the Genoese of conspiring with the Indians to launch a surprise attack and seize the town, either in order to restore it to Cemaco, the cacique who had ruled Titumate before the Spaniards came, or in pursuit of his own ambitions.

Dom Pedro summoned the old chief to his residence to acquaint him one more time with the provisions of the Requirement, that infamous document which conferred on the Spanish Crown legal title to the lands stolen from the Indians, demanding from him and his tribe a renewal of their oath of allegiance. Cemaco came down from the hills with his Tupi people in a reluctant procession through the rain, filling the courtyard of the governor's residence with feathered and painted bodies. The admiral sat erect in a chair of state, covered with gold and white drapes, on the balcony overlooking the courtyard while the notary read out the Requirement to the Indians assembled below. It was a long document in a convoluted language they could not understand, even when the factor translated it into Tupi. They stood in the courtyard, listening to the notary without stirring or making a sound as the rain smeared the paint on their bodies and ruined their feathers. But when the notary came to an end, and the old cacique was carried up the stairs to the balcony to renew the Tupi pledge of allegiance, kissing the governor's feet and placing the Requirement on his head to show his submission to its will, a swarm of mysterious white moths appeared like a cloud from the gloomy interior of the cloister, settling on Dom Pedro Felipe in a seething mass so dense that his attendants had to beat the moths away in order to extricate the admiral and bring him to a place where they could not molest him.

Tupi stayed, petitioners and scavengers, their hammocks slung up like bats under the eaves, along with soldiers who had killed men in casual brawls and now awaited the admiral's jurisdiction, sometimes for weeks, in the vast hall of the residence, his own entourage of priests, cooks, quacks, interpreters and spies, his most trusted lieutenant Fernandez, as gorged and sensuous in his tastes as the admiral was lean and spare, they all surrounded Dom Pedro Felipe, walled up inside his stone solitariness, watching him for the first sign of weakness. In the garrison his men could do as they pleased, but no women were permitted to enter the residence. A sanctified odour lingered in the rooms through which he passed, compounded of incense scattered by the friars and the sweet smell of rotting that drifted up from the streets. The admiral was marked by an extraordinary pallor. It was said that he prayed every morning with his father confessor and afterwards rubbed ash into his cheeks. More probably he was pale from exhaustion of spirit, brooding on the rain that held him back. Everything was kept ready for the always imminent departure, always delayed from week to week.

The expeditionary force remained confined to the garrison, the camp followers settled into whatever niche they could find, in corners or alcoves or on the slabs of the deep casement windows that ran like shafts into the walls. There was one overlooking the cloister garden where I established myself with Grasshopper after we had been summoned to the residence and had nothing to do but wait, chewing the leaves of a plant the Tupi called coca. The effect of coca was similar to smoking mimosa seeds, which Pig Indians called riding the niopo cloud, but it had a clarity of vision which niopo lacked. I could see the admiral, beneath his pallor, consumed not so much by that venal lust for gold, for mere booty, which sustained Fernandez and his fellow mercenaries through all their hardships, as by a feverish desire for what it symbolised: the incorruptibility of gold, perfection in metal, a holy grail which would redeem the base and worthless quest of life.

Yet the conscience of Dom Pedro Felipe was troubled. I had the evidence for this with my own eyes, peeled back and frozen hard like balls of glass from the coca leaves I chewed day and night inside the shaft of the casement window. Grasshopper and I lay rigid in the darkness as if entombed, staring through the bars into the cloister garden. At noon, when the sun rolled back the clouds, light fell on this courtyard garden like a blindness, wiping it out. We looked into the brightness and saw nothing. It was the admiral's custom to come here alone at dawn or in the cool of the evening, sometimes to walk, sometimes to pray on his knees, bareheaded, splashed by the rain, and sometimes these meditations were accompanied by a curious interlude I was unable to explain.

A small door to the garden would fly open and a Negro armed with a stick sprang out, like a puppet in some cunning mechanical device. It was the silent Negro whose counter I had slept on in Antonio's warehouse. The Negro bowed to the admiral. The admiral removed his shirt, took up his breviary and read silently, his lips moving, while the Negro set to with his stick. He gave the penitent a terrible thrashing, not desisting until his back was covered with bloody stripes. The Negro bowed again, leaving by the door through which he had entered, and had I not seen it before I would not have known what it was, the pale cloud that materialised in the gloomy cloister garden: a swarm of moths, drawn by the scent of blood, descending like a cascade in billowing veils of white and settling to feed on the lacerated flesh of Dom Pedro's back, where the twitching mass of wings darkened slowly with his blood.

Grasshopper saw this as I did, but unlike me he had no doubt about its significance. It was Dom Pedro's sacrifice, his imitation of the warrior-hero who had submitted to death on the crossed branches, his initiation to the godhead. Impatient and pale with inner rage as he watched his great undertaking stall in the mire of Titumate, the admiral gnawed his beard and prayed in turns. Emerging from his self-absorption, he became aware of the accumulation of neglect around him, the correspondence left un-answered, the business of the envoys from Hispaniola unattended to, the cases still awaiting trial after weeks, the droves of Indian hangers-on whose miserable encampments infuriated him, their hammocks draped like cobwebs along the residence walls, until at last he could stand it no more. He went out and tore them down like some Christ among the money-changers in the temple, sending the inmates packing with a warn-ing never to show their faces in Santa Maria de la Antigua again or he would cut off their feet and hands.

The rainy season was now nearing its end, but Dom Pedro would wait no longer, weary of all the administrative matters separating him from his purpose. He sent the envoys home and dismissed the case against the factor. Antonio was allowed to return to his family, but Dom Pedro sent his son Arapásso out with a vanguard of scouts and engineers to survey the rivers and mountain passes. Only now did he disclose to Grasshopper and myself the reason why he had brought us to Titumate. He did not trust the local Indian guides. I did not like the idea of becoming a Spanish spy in order to betray the Indians, but in my sleep my shadow had already passed out of my mouth, I had glimpsed it among the ranks of scarecrows with straggling beards, their hair unkempt, their clothes in holes, standing in the square of a city I had never seen on top of a mountain. Both of my fathers, the Spanish merchant Zarate and my Pig Indian father Guaratinga-acu, were looking over my shoulder to remind me that this was a dreaming from which I could not escape.

I had been swept up by the baggage train of the Conquest, stuck fast to a doom I would have to accept. With Grasshopper at my side I attended the mass that was celebrated in the church of Santa Maria de la Antigua where the Christians prayed to their jurupari for the success of their undertaking and Grasshopper learned how the tsushaúa of the white men bargained with the jurupari to receive from him his strength, and that it was no different from the way the White Earth Indians put their enemies into their mouths. He saw the admiral kneel at the altar to receive the sacrament, eating of the God's body and drinking of His blood, surrounded by the gold chalices and plates which were held aloft by the priests, reflecting a sheen onto Dom Pedro Felipe's face that transformed it into a golden mask.

The Centipede

Wherever the Spanish army went Dom Pedro gave names to the country and I would write them down on the empty maps of the New World. I had passed from childhood to manhood without needing to name anything in All-Creatures-Being-in-the-Forest, but whatever the admiral saw he felt obliged to name and take possession of it for the Spanish crown. He named the gulfs and estuaries, the bays, the rivers, streams, creeks, the valleys, the ridges and the mountains, looking up at night into the sky to name the stars pointed out to him by his astronomer which were still unknown in northern latitudes. What he named became his, the fiduciary of the Spanish crown. Like a god he named the earth and the heavens, like any animal he left his mark to make his claim on the land through which he passed.

In the letters he wrote to the king, which I took down at his dictation, the places that had been nowhere became somewhere the moment the Spanish army arrived. The still nameless water we could see in the distance when we made camp that night became the Gulf of Uraba by the time we reached it the following day. A messenger was sent back to La

Antigua with instructions to the factor to fit out a brigantine and sail in pursuit of us with provisions. We came to a ten-mouthed river, which Dom Pedro named the River of Nets on account of the many fishing nets fastened to poles in the river. The admiral told a notary to go ahead and read the Requirement to the fishermen in the village, but news of the Requirement, and what it meant, must have reached the Indians sooner than we did. The moment the notary took out his scroll of paper the villagers understood what it signified and fled. Their meagre stock of manioc and fish was insufficient to feed five hundred people. But for the prompt action of the factor, who arrived with the provisions on the brigantine after two days, Dom Pedro's army would have found itself starving a week out of Antigua.

Dom Pedro Felipe's expeditionary force moved through the Indian territories like an enormous questing centipede, groping forward, feeling its way cautiously around obstacles. The vanguard ranged ahead, stretching its column of soldiers, while the rearguard with its swollen baggage train remained bunched together, lurching ponderously in pursuit. At intervals the vanguard would stop and wait until the main body of the expedition had caught up before making the next advance. In this way the procession went on, expanding and contracting like a concertina. Standing on a ridge with Grasshopper one day, watching this procession undulating through the coastal hills, we remembered Great White Bird's last dreaming and now understood what it meant. Our tsushaúa had heard the rushing wind caused by the flight of our ancestors from the sacred mountains. He had seen what he described as a giant creature made up of many parts, crawling and ravaging its way through the forest from which the souls of the Indians were fleeing. The centipede drank dry the streams and ate its way through the vegetation, boring tunnels through the forest. It gobbled up man and beast, ingesting entire villages that lay in its path.

Even when they spared the local populations the Spaniards were a menace. Their priests lectured the Indians on God-is-Love. Their soldiers demanded porters and stole wives. Their cacique plagued them with his ceaseless demands for gold. But the coastal tribes did not have any gold. They soon learned that the best way of diverting the centipede was to promise Dom Pedro a hoard of treasure a little further on in the forest, preferably in the lands of an enemy. With every stop it made the centipede grew, acquiring livestock, slaves and an ever lengthening string of inter-preters to filter the dialects of Tupi that became less intelligible the further from Titumate. Thus it became easy for Grasshopper and me to collude with the local guides and deliberately lead the Spanish astray. Even the smallest tribes put up a fight, burning their crops and their villages before the expeditionary force arrived. At nightfall they disappeared into the jungle, ambushing stragglers, and in the morning it was not uncommon to find the headless bodies of their victims dangling from a tree in view of the camp.

Even the slaves taken by the Spanish rose in suicidal revolt. They bludg-eoned their masters with stools, pots and pans. They poured scalding water over sleeping soldiers and threw firebrands among the horses. A ter-rible revenge was taken on these Indians to ensure that their example would not be followed. They were made to run through the forest and the dogs of war were turned loose on them. The dogs hunted the running Indians down like deer and tore them to pieces.

On the edge of the swamps between the coast and the mountains we came to a forest of giant trees, so large that it took eight men touching hands to encircle them. This was the domain of cacique Abibeiba. Because of fre-quent flooding in the swamps Abibeiba's people lived in the trees, descend-ing on ladders which they pulled up at night or in the event of attack. When the expeditionary force came in sight the tree-dwellers prudently withdrew their ladders and sat cackling in the branches. Dom Pedro had a feast spread out beneath the trees and invited Abibeiba to join him. The cacique declined. Dom Pedro ordered his men to bring axes. As the men com-menced chopping at the base of the tree in which the cacique lived, Dom Pedro calmly sat down to eat amid the hooting and cackling that went on overhead. After a while, however, as they saw how efficiently the tempered steel of Spanish axes worked, the tree people quietened down. Their cacique peered over the side of his house, and appreciating how insecure its foundations would soon become he let down the ladder, descending with his wife and two sons. The first demand of the Christians was, as usual, for gold, but the cacique had none, for he was a fisherman. Abibeiba said he knew for certain where gold could be found, however, and he pointed to the distant mountains.

Dom Pedro told him to show him the way, taking along Abibeiba's wife and sons as hostages in case the cacique decided to betray him. But this Abibeiba was a sly cacique. He led the expedition across firm land far into the swamps before absconding during the night, leaving wife and children to their fate. Instead of returning the safe way he had come Dom Pedro pressed on into the swamps. The scouts lost the trail, or perhaps there was none. We sank in up to our knees and floundered on, shedding more and more of the baggage as we went. For days we found ourselves without a dry place to make a fire or even lie down. Dom Pedro's letters to the king of Spain, dictated to me during nights marooned on islands of mangroves and tufts of grass, acquired an increasingly acerbic note. His Royal Highness should not believe that the swamps of this land were such a light affair that we moved along through them joyfully, for we were often forced to go naked through the water with our clothing on a shield on top of the head, dragging our provisions on rafts behind us. No sooner were we out of one marsh than we entered another, and we continued in this manner for many days. But this would have seemed a trivial matter had we been given respite for even a few hours from the bites of insects and venomous snakes infesting these swamps, from which many of the Spanish died.

The night after the centipede reached dry land, dragging itself exhausted onto the shore, a fire attack was launched by Indians fore-warned of our coming by Abibeiba. While the Spanish slept the sleep of the dead they killed the sentries and stole the baggage. Dazed soldiers fumbled with breastplates and helmets as the camp went up in flames. Fire-tipped arrows set alight the straw in the pig-pen and over a hundred hogs burned to death. Streams of bacon grease flowed out over the ground, the smell of roast pork filled the air. Only the piglets were able to wriggle through the bars of the pig-pen and make their escape. Following the direction of the flares coming at them out of the darkness, the Spanish went in pursuit of their stolen baggage.

When day broke they reached a fortified stockade. A hail of arrows such as they had never experienced before drove them back. Realising the determination of the Indians and that they could only be dislodged at the risk of losing too many of his men, Dom Pedro gave orders to set fire to the settlement. The defenders chose to perish in the flames rather than attempt to escape. The baggage we had hoped to retrieve burned with them. On returning to the camp we found that all the saddlery was destroyed too. Most of the metal weapons had lost their temper in the blaze and were ruined. We stood there naked, all our clothes and blankets burned. But the admiral told us how to construct a forge, using bellows made from musket barrels and animal hides, so that within a few days we were able to re-temper all the spoilt sword blades, pikes and armour. Scouts were sent out to scavenge for skins and grass mats, making sleeping bags to keep them warm, for the nights in the foothills of the mountains were cold.

With the loss of its baggage and military trappings, the little Spanish army now revealed itself for what it was — a band of marauding ruffians. All the porters were dismissed, as there was nothing left to carry. The camp followers went with them, as there was nothing left to eat. One hundred and thirty men, with their weapons and the clothes they stood in, were all that remained of the grand expeditionary force that had set out from Santa Maria de la Antigua.

The Speech of Panquiaco

It was at this low ebb of his fortunes that the admiral reached the domain of a young chieftain named Panquiaco. With his army in such reduced circumstances, Dom Pedro proceeded more cautiously than usual. Accompanied by a small following of attendants he went to meet the chief in a long house in the mountains quite different from any malocca I had seen. It was open on all sides, supported by stone pillars with the upper part made of ornamental wood, containing a pantheon in which the desiccated cadavers of former chiefs were preserved. Panquiaco was about thirty years old, well-formed, his face broad, handsome and fierce. The Indians of Panquiaco's tribe had shaven heads, leaving only a comb over the crown, oiled and bound in a coil. Their bearing was marked by an extreme lassitude, the result of eating coca, which they cultivated in terraces on the mountain. They spoke a language that was unintelligible, so that they were reduced to communicating with the Spaniards by signs.

Everything about the long house was spacious, well-appointed and agreeable to look at, a mark of the advanced culture of these people. They wore ornaments of solid gold, rings, amulets, necklaces, even sheaths encasing the coil of hair. Dom Pedro wanted to know where the gold came from. Panquiaco got up and led us to a steep place in the mountains, showing us by pantomimes, which he performed most expressively, how the streams rose in the ravines and subsided, leaving gold behind that had been scoured out of the mountain, sometimes in the shape of flat plates, sometimes in grains as large as oranges. Panquiaco showed us another place where his people set fire to the vegetation at the end of the dry season, collecting the gold dust in the soil that was melted by the heat and remained stuck together when it cooled. He made a show of reaping and spread his arms to encompass all the sheaves, as if to say that what his guests saw here was nothing compared to the wealth of certain caciques further up in the mountains, who had so much gold they stored it like corn in barns.

When we returned to the long house he gave us a cordial to drink, made from pressed coca leaves. At a word of command from Panquiaco, a dozen attendants busied themselves with ropes hanging down from the roof and fastened to the pillars. The men released the ropes and let them slide slowly through their hands. In a state of trance-like composure induced by the coca drink, we sat on the floor looking up at the strange array of figures in the pantheon descending from the roof, the shrivelled remains of Panquiaco's ancestors, covered with mantles of cotton and adorned with jewellery made of gold, pearls and precious stones. They descended with a faint shimmering sound from thousands of fine animal bones threaded on a loop and wound like a garland around the pantheon. The sight of these shrunken, jewel-bedecked cadavers, their skin blackened and their cheeks hollowed out, a barbaric memento mori all the more striking for its appearance in such a desolate place, made a deep impression on the religious sensibility of the admiral. His gaze wandered questioningly back and forth between the young man standing in the living flesh before him with flashing eyes and the ogreish aspect of his ancestors, transfixed in death, hung up on hooks like ghastly dolls with pebbles in the sockets of their eyes. Panquiaco dismissed them with a wave and the pantheon rose creaking from the floor.

If it was gold we were looking for, he said, pointing south, then we must go in that direction. When we came down from the mountains we would view another sea. It was known as the Sleeping Sea because it was continually smooth, and in the smoothness of its sleep it had given birth to many islands rich in pearls. On the shore of this sea lived a trading people who navigated great distances in balsas with sails and who possessed such wealth that they used golden vessels to eat and drink. This speech of Panquiaco, accompanied by a faint shimmering sound as his dead ancestors were hauled up into the roof, provided us with the first intelligence of the Pacific Ocean and the Inca kingdom of Tahuantin-Suyu.

The Possession of the Sleeping Sea

Quarequa guides whom he later killed led the admiral to the top of a nearby mountain where we obtained our first view of the Sleeping Sea. We saw a broad estuary jutting inland, sparkling in the morning light. From the *cumbre* of the Quarequa Dom Pedro Felipe took formal possession of the southern sea, its firm lands and islands, discovered and yet undiscovered, in the name of the Catholic and most serene sovereigns of Castile. The Requirement was drawn up by a notary and presented to the admiral. He kissed it and placed it on his head as a token of his most reverent obedience to the king's commandment, before reading the document to an assembly of the Quarequa Indians.

The Quarequa men were sodomites who lived separate from their women. They wore plates of gold on their chest and arms, with the virile member prominently displayed in a gold tube or an ornament made of sea shells, secured by a cord around their loins. They were distinguished by a stature and physique that was exceptional for Indians. Despite his loathing of the sinful practice of sodomy Dom Pedro could not conceal his admiration for the magnificent bodies of the Quarequa, even as he was reading to them a declaration of war. He called upon them to submit to the Christians and take their religion, and after the priests had found them wanting in their zeal, and had conferred with the military commanders who urged on them the advantages of a surprise attack, particularly when outnumbered five to one, the priests gave their blessing to the enterprise and the Spaniards opened fire. What they began with firearms the Spaniards completed with their swords. Horrified at the sight of limbs strewn all over the ground, the Indians surrendered and were taken prisoner. Fifty Quarequa warriors had their hands cut off on Dom Pedro's orders, as a punishment for those unnatural acts which had brought guilt on them, defiling the grace of their Creator. Those who fled were hunted down for sport and eaten alive by the dogs of war.

Having disposed of the Quarequa resistance in the morning, Dom Pedro's army marched to the shore in the afternoon, accompanied by cacique Chiapes and his few remaining men. We reached an arm of a gulf at the hour of vespers, which the admiral named the Gulf of San Miguel. Finding the tide at ebb, the beach covered with mud, we seated themselves in the shade and waited for the sea to return. The tide rushed in with an impetuosity surprising for a sleeping sea, washing up thunderously under the trees along the shore. The admiral waded in up to his knees, wearing helmet and breastplate and with buckler on his arm. In one hand he held a drawn sword, in the other a banner on which the Virgin and Child in arms were depicted in faded paint above the crest of Castile and Leon. Having read the Requirement to the Gulf of San Miguel, he drew a dagger from his belt and carved a cross in the trunk of a tree whose roots were washed by the sea, marking two other trees with crosses as well, in honour of the most holy Trinity, according to a well-established ritual of conquest and possession which the admiral had already absolved in innumerable other places.

Dom Pedro Felipe looked out to the open sea where the sun hung on the horizon, unravelling bolts of gold over the waters of the gulf, and felt in his heart the stirrings of a desire to carry out one more act of possession. Chiapes put at his disposal three pirogues that had been hollowed out of giant trees, each of which had space for fifty warriors, large enough to accommodate the rump army in its entirety. He watched from the shore as we paddled out into the gulf until the pirogues disappeared, swallowed up in the brightness of the setting sun. We left behind us most of our armour and all our Indian guides, among them Grasshopper, my Taiassu brother and companion, with whom I must have licked more tobacco than the rest of my Pig Indian tribesmen put together. Long after night had fallen the Quarequa waited motionless on the shore for the gods who had descended so suddenly and terrifyingly upon them to return. They dug out the sand on which the imprint of their sacred footsteps had been left and carried it to their village where they built a shrine to worship them, but the gods never came back.

Tumbez

Xiahuanaco, Keeper of the Quipu, had received intelligence of the strangers before they came, pushing out into the sea known to the Inca as the Sleeping Sea, which Dom Pedro had just named the Gulf of San Miguel and his successors would call the Gulf of Panama. Other hands had already written of us long before that, woven reports of our floating castles and thunder sticks into the strings of the quipu, into the knots, shapes, colour and their arrangement across and down the quipu's design, anticipating the Conquest long before it began, leaving a record of it in a world unable to read such records long after the Conquest had come to an end. During the time I knew Xiahuanaco I learned to read the quipu, those strands of wool in which the Inca knotted their history, though only by sight. Half a century would pass before I could read the quipu by touch alone as Xiahuanaco could, distinguishing even colours with his fingers. He wove what he saw, a hand-witness account of the skirmish with the Spaniards. From my later reading of the knots in the quipu it appeared that Xiahuanaco had misunderstood Dom Pedro's act of possession on the open sea when he harangued the western sky, reading the Requirement to the sun and laying claim to all the western dominions on which it set. Xiahuanaco took this for a sacred ceremony performed by sun worshippers like the Inca themselves. This was the last thing the Keeper of the Quipu would see that evening by the light of day, though his fingers continued the knot-writing into the night, recording the first encounter of the Inca with the Spaniards.

When all on board had blindfolded their eyes the sailors manning the balsa raft far out in the gulf uncovered rows of mirrors of burnished silver, reflecting the rays of the setting sun on the approaching pirogues. We were blinded by a brilliance as if we had entered the sun. The admiral, who had stood up in the pirogue to read the Requirement to the sun, lost his balance and fell overboard, toppling the rest of us into the water with him. We clung to the boat, for we could see nothing. When the balsa raft hove to, and the Inca sailors pulled us aboard, I could still distinguish little more than the brightness of the flares held up over the water to search for us and the darkness when they were gone. Deprived of their sight, outwitted and disarmed, Dom Pedro's soldiers resigned themselves to a dishonourable death at the hands of an enemy whom they would not even see before they died.

But in the quipu recording the encounter with the Spaniards in the gulf, which I later read, there was never any consideration of putting the captives to death, for reasons that emerged in the exchange of messages between Xiahuanaco and the supreme Inca, Huayana Capac. The quipu related a voyage of a trading vessel from the northernmost fringe of Tahuantin-Suyu, as the Inca empire was known, down the coast of the Sleeping Sea with one hundred and seventeen bearded white prisoners on board to the city of Tumbez, which lay just south of the equator. They were victims of the *qu'zoa*, the blinding with mirrors. All but two of them suffered from the temporary loss of sight incurred by this stratagem. Yet they were treated well, brought to separate houses in the city where they were lodged. Poultices were applied to their eyes until they gradually recovered their sight. News of their capture was relayed by mirrors from Tumbez to Caxamarca, or The-Place-Where-There-Is-Ice. This was the capital of the Inca Huayana Capac, thirteen thousand feet above sea level, administrative centre of a kingdom whose dominions ran north and south for three thousand miles in a narrow strip between the Amazon and the Pacific.

Long before the appearance of the Inca tribe great civilisations had flourished here and disappeared. The predecessors of Huayana Capac, bearers of a warlike culture whose symbols were the puma and the condor, had already been established in the cordillera during the golden age of Greece. Chavin, Mochica and Nazca in succession were supplanted by another civilisation at Tiahuanaco, whose stone monoliths and gateways to the sun had long become ruins by the time of the Conquest. This was the world in its entirety, past, present and future. Whatever was not of it, did not exist. We who came to it from outside could not be of the living, and according to the official view were regarded as ghosts. When all has been made ready, ran the lapidary passage in the quipu recording the Inca's instructions in a footnote appended to a tax assessment of the wool merchants in Tumbez and knotted by Xiahuanaco himself, bring the ghosts to the city of the dead where they belong.

Our advent was of no more significance than if we had been flies landing on the fringe of the web of Huayana Capac's empire. Captive, unarmed, for a long time without even the use of our eyes, we apparently posed no threat. The web absorbed the Spanish incursion, rebounded naturally, a strong tissue giving proof of its abundant elasticity; or so it seemed. And yet the frisson caused by the impact of these one hundred and seventeen arrivals ran through all the fibres of Inca civilisation. When it closed around us the web was not intact as it had been before we came. In the wake of our entry we left an imperceptible tear.

We opened our eyes to a stone city bordered by the mountains and the Sleeping Sea, with shaded squares, basins, viaducts bringing water through the streets and immense city walls enclosing an atmosphere of emptiness. It was not for a lack of people to inhabit Tumbez. There were markets, crowded thoroughfares, terraces on the slopes behind the houses where men and women were unceasingly at work. Seen through Spanish eyes, all this activity was characterised by some quality more expressive of inertia than motion. Motion in the existence of Indians was circular, ending where it began. Recognition of sameness afforded a guiding principle of life. I knew that all Indians, the Taiassu no less than the Incas, lived within the familiarity of repetition, inhabiting a permanent loop. Thus arose that impression of things resting in themselves which began to make Dom Pedro and his men uneasy soon after their arrival in Tumbez. Stalled in the momentum which had driven them across the ocean and over the mountains, the force behind the Spanish expeditionary force petered out. The inertia of Indian life, the inward pull of its circular motion and the stillness at its centre, made them irritable and caused them anxiety.

As the admiral's secretary and official interpreter, although ignorant of the Inca language, I was quartered with him in the house of the Keeper of the Quipu. Xiahuanaco was a tall, copper-skinned Inca noble with a certain resemblance to Panquiaco. Inca nobles wore heavy ornaments in their ears to extend the ear-lobes, which was regarded as a mark of beauty and distinction. For this reason the Spanish called them *orejones*, the people with large ears. From childhood Xiahuanaco had worn solid gold weights of increasing heaviness in his ears, so distending the ear-lobes that they hung flap-like down to his shoulders. With his bald head and these soft-fleshed, elephantine ears, Xiahuanaco's appearance took on an unexpected gravity, reminding me of the sad-faced ant-eater I used to hunt when I lived among the Taiassu. I followed him now, wherever he went. The mirror instructions from Caxamarca, orders flashed down from above, stipulated that one of the ghosts must be taught the Inca language, as Huayana Capac wished to learn more about the intruders. Until this had been accomplished they were not permitted to leave Tumbez. I was chosen by Xiahuanaco for this task.

Keepers of the Quipu, of whom, as the bearers of state secrets, there were only a few in Tumbez, were known as *quipu camayoc*, or Official Rememberers. Without the immense knowledge of patterns they had committed to memory the meaning of the quipu could not be deciphered, as later happened when Tahuantin-suyu became lost in time and forgot its past. Rememberers went everywhere and were never without their quipu, stringing knots as they travelled, recording all the things they measured. With Xiahuanaco I visited the harbour to record the coral and the crimson shells unloaded from the balsa vessels, to the market where fish, maize and potatoes were sold, to pastures on the hills above Tumbez where herds of llamas and alpacas were grazed. The patterns encoding all these weights and measurements grew ceaselessly out of the Rememberer's hands, and as Xiahuanaco spoke, repeating the Inca word several times, the sound would fuse in my mind with the image of the knots, loops and colours his fingers were tying in the quipu strings.

Sometimes, when his official remembering was done, the Keeper of the Quipu would intersperse splashes of brightly dyed wool, giving expression to a feeling he had for a particular light on the sea, a shadow on the mountains or the sound of bells from the pastures, poems of two or at most three knots, woven just as they occurred to him between measures of grain and some memorandum concerned with public works in Tumbez. His heart overflowed with a poetry which it seemed only his hands could express. In this way I unconsciously absorbed the code of quipu patterns at the same time I learned the language, and in the woven silence of his thoughts I came closer to the person through whom all this knowledge was mediated to me.

Half Moon and Running Wind

It was a city of bells and fabrics that gave colour to the sounds, wind-bells, with cotton streamers attached, fluttering at the windows like children waving their hands whenever a breeze lifted itself lazily over Tumbez. If a breeze tried to slip past unnoticed the streamers flagged it down, drawing attention to it, turning the arrival of the slightest sigh that crept in off the ocean into a jubilant cavalcade. In one of his quipu poems Xiahuanaco compared the coming of the lover in the night to a welcome breeze, rustling the bed-linen with a cool sound when the hot season imprisoned the city in the unendurable stillness of the dark. There was no understanding of privacy among the people of Tumbez. They lived out their lives in the glare of noon, a place without shadows always submitted to public scrutiny. The bed-chamber was as open as the market place. The man came to the woman, the son to his neighbour's daughter who slept in the sign of the river, as the quipu language had it. The sign of the river was three flowing strands, of which the middle strand was shorter than the outer two, representing the sleeping child between her parents. When the lover lay with the daughter in the night her parents heard everything, but they were as still as the stones of the house.

Half Moon was a girl of fifteen when I arrived in Tumbez, knitting her dark eyebrows into a frown of displeasure at the smell of the ghosts who came to live in her father's house. I saw Half Moon and her mother naked the same evening, when they bathed in the basin on the terrace behind the house. Her mother was Quarequa, like many of the women in the city, who were brought to Tumbez as part of the tribute paid to the Inca by local tribes. The daughter was as full-bodied as the mother was spare, with a sensuousness offset by the severity expressed in her eye-brows and by the matter-of-factness in her manner. Since early childhood, as was the fashion with young girls in Tumbez, Half Moon had worn close-fitting bangles below the knee to swell her calves and a girdle worn tightly around her waist to broaden her hips. She was not dark like her mother. She had her father's colour, a warm copper skin. When I came out onto the terrace she wrinkled her nose and splashed me with water, making signs for me to take off my clothes and get rid of my ghost's smell, choosing me for her lover before she knew my name.

Mother and daughter were Xiahuanaco's possessions. He had bought his wife as a slave, and the daughters of slaves became slaves in turn, whom he could dispose of as he felt fit. Xiahuanaco was not a native of Tumbez. His great ears proclaimed him a nobleman of high birth from the capital, Caxamarca. He had been posted here as a young official in charge of levies from the fringe peoples of Tahuantin-suyu, and in this way he had met his later wife. Running Wind was brought to Tumbez in a contingent of one hundred Quarequa women whose fate was to be cut open so that their entrails could be examined for divination, as happened on the occasion of Huayana Capac's acclamation as the Inca. Xiahuanaco redeemed Running Wind and took her for his wife, incurring the Inca's displeasure. It was a breach of etiquette for a flap-eared nobleman to marry a Quarequa slave. Worse, he had defied the Inca. Xiahuanaco was exiled from Caxamarca for life and forbidden to set foot in the highlands.

The Keeper of the Quipu languished in the tropical city on the Sleeping Sea, pining for the Place-Where-There-Is-Ice. His hypertrophic heart and lungs, an immense pump and oxygen reservoir that equipped him to strive at high altitudes in thin air, were as unsuited to a life at sea level as his pendulous patrician ears or his melancholic ant-eater's face to the plebeian customs of Tumbez and the mindlessness of an existence stupefied by heat. He was the sad elephant who had been separated from his kind and sent to live with jackals and baboons in the desert A coastal Indian communism with its origins in collective malocca dwelling, onto which had been grafted the Inca obsession with state control, left little room for individuality or that need for personal expression which the Official Rememberer secretly sought to fulfill in the spontaneous poems he wove into the quipu.

Xiahuanaco was the first Indian I knew who believed in the existence of his inner life as unquestioningly as he accepted magic and all it entailed, the superstitions and cruelties of the cults governing the relations between human beings and the world in which they lived. The Official Rememberer was a humanist who gave credence to the divination of the patterns left by the tracks of spiders, by scattered coca leaves or splashed blood, an astronomer who believed in the personal deity of the sun and the need to appease him by blood sacrifice, and he accepted the necessity of this, just as he did the inevitability of taking for his wife a Quarequa woman whose warm entrails would otherwise have been laid out on a slab for divination. I saw him poised on the edge of a great freedom, of which he had no more inkling than a quipu had of the patterns and the meanings woven into it.

When Xiahuanaco considered I had a sufficient command of the language I undertook the history of the world that later formed the opening string in the famous Quipu of the Ghosts. I began my narration with the Greeks and Romans, as the classical education instilled in me in the free-thinking house of the Spanish Jew was bound to lead me to do, skimming through the shadowy centuries after the sack of Rome, resuming with the crusades in the holy land at the beginning of the modern period and out-lining the developments that had led to the discovery of the New World at the end. I felt this required some knowledge of geometry and astronomy as it had been handed down from the Greeks and the Arabs, for the sciences based on numbers were the indispensable condition of being able to navigate such distances across unknown seas. It required also a review of the history of weapons and shipbuilding, of commerce, cartography and means of travel, and above all of the development of writing and printing to provide a fixed reservoir for all the thoughts that had accumulated throughout the ages, and which would have been lost but for this. My means of giving expression to what I wished to say in a language lacking the words for it were so limited, however, that only fragments of this his-tory of the world had found their way into quipu knots by the time I com-pleted my narration.

Half Moon and her mother, flitting in and out of this narration, stand-ing at the door grooming themselves, oiling their bodies and combing their hair, listened to it as they listened to everything else, to the surf thud-ding on the shore beyond the jangle of the wind-bells or to the tangled cries of the swallows swooping down over Tumbez. They heard it with placid faces untroubled by the effort to understand. What I said was not in their language but in one that resembled it, they heard without listen-ing, for I had my own sound, like the surf or the swallows, which was a sound without meaning. Xiahuanaco, his great ears unfurled in full tackle, had no choice but to listen. He strove to understand. But Xiahuanaco's face remained closed, his hands increasingly still. Knotted here and there, no more than a hurried memorandum, the quipu hung down over his knees, like an old man's beard, in strands sparsely tufted with patterns where something I had said must have made its way into his writing. The heat came that Xiahuanaco hated, settling with the stillness over Tumbez that was only sometimes broken when the cotton streamers on the bells raised their hue and cry over a furtive breeze scudding in off the ocean. Lying with Half Moon in the sign of the river between her parents, I would hear Xiahuanaco sigh, as if were breathing on the flicker of wind to keep it alive, sustaining the relief it brought him just a little longer.

The Quipu of the Ghosts

When a swarm of white moths appeared on the terrace of Xiahuanaco's house Running Wind chased them away, but the moths came back, turning the wall white on which they settled. There were Official Rememberers who claimed these moths had got into the Quipu of the Ghosts Xiahuanaco was knotting at the time, and in this way they must have penetrated the quipu archives in Ki'zak where they caused so much damage that the records could never be pieced together again. Thus the Inca lost their past.

This was one of the many versions I heard accounting for the disorder that overwhelmed Tahuantin-Suyu from the time the Spanish set foot in Tumbez. Certainly it was the case that the arrival of the moths, which had accompanied Dom Pedro Felipe since he landed in Santa Maria de la Antigua, coincided with the spontaneous opening of the admiral's wounds, the self-imposed lacerations on his back and the old wounds he had received in the battles of the Conquest, going back at least a generation. It was certain, too, that when the moths reappeared Xiahuanaco was engaged in knotting the admiral's testimony into the Quipu of the Ghosts after spending a long time on the prologue I had delivered him – years, he said, but this was an exaggeration, for I knew he had worked on it for not more than a few months. There were other instances of Xiahuanaco's lapses of memory which struck me at the time. He insisted that Half Moon had already turned eighteen a week after she had celebrated her sixteenth birthday, or that the swallows would arrive in Tumbez on their annual migration only weeks after they had departed. Such lapses strayed over into the quipu he kept. There was no need of moths to gnaw at the strands, because even while Xiahuanaco was still working on his record there were already more gaps in the Quipu of the Ghosts than the knots they surrounded. The quipu disintegrated of its own accord.

Apart from the many terms for which Xiahuanaco could find no equivalent in the Inca language, there was a more general problem of alignment along that border between what was said by the Spanish and how it could be rendered in quipu writing. The quipu had no tenses, for Tahuantin-Suyu had no divisions of time. Everything flowed back into the immense reservoir of a past in which it was impossible for the unknown to occur since the Inca believed everything had been there already. What was Huanaco Capac to make of the actions of the Spanish, driven across a great ocean to the edge of the world where many of them had half expected to fall off when they reached it?

To him they were the orphans of a civilisation where everything appeared to flow the other way, drawn as naturally into the future as Tahuantin-Suyu was into the past. The force of change, random, slipshod, dangerous and unwise, leaving them to negotiate the unexpected however it came, was always driving them on into the unknown. Like beggars they wandered through the world, spending the night wherever they happened to arrive when overtaken by the dark. Why had they adopted these vagrant habits instead of becoming settlers in the fixed framework of time, part of the unchanging sameness of all things?

The Spaniards said they had set out to find gold. For gold they had taken such risks, endured so many hardships. To an Official Rememberer, who had knotted quipu with inventories of the gold extracted every year from the mountains and stacked like corn in the warehouses of Cuzco, the answer he was given by the Spaniards could not have been intelligible. For an Inca noble like Xiahuanaco, who had visited the temple of the sun in Coriancha where maize grew on silver stems with ears of gold, and who had worshipped the Indians' greatest treasure, the Punchao, a vast golden disc showing the rising sun studded with stars in a mosaic of precious stones, the greed of his guest for his household trinkets was beneath his contempt.

The ghosts had brought with them to Tahuantin-Suyu a sickness for which there was no name. It was not only their fever for gold. From all the

71

strangers, whom Xiahuanaco sought out one by one in Tumbez, there emanated an impatient energy, a restlessness, a permanent disquiet. Lacking a word for speed, he called it the Rushing Wind Sickness. Xiahuanaco recorded that the dogs still barked at Dom Pedro Felipe when he limped through the streets, smelling his difference, long after he arrived and they had become used to him. He was already an old man when he came, his beard was white, he had the skin of an old lizard, the smell of strangeness and of old age. And yet, while for Xiahuanaco the space seemed to become ever briefer between the coming of the swallows and their departure, the shortening and the lengthening of the shadows, the melting snow in spring and the white on the mountains in the autumn, and in this contracted passage of the seasons it seemed to the Official Rememberer that the people of Tumbez aged much more quickly than they had before, the admiral did not grow perceptibly older. Dom Pedro Felipe and all the Spaniards appeared to him as changeless as figures of stone, petrified in the same mould they had when they first came to the city.

According to the Quipu of the Ghosts it was in the spring that we left Tumbez for Ki'zak, the city of the dead. The cavalcade included Inca soldiers and their families, llamas carrying their baggage and the *quipu cayamoc*, who was entitled to ride in a litter borne by slaves, accompanied by his daughter Half Moon and his wife Running Wind. From the sands of the coastal desert we passed through plantations of maize and cotton, following an old Inca trail into the foothills of the Andes, heading inland for the town of Chongoypae. The valley up which we passed narrowed into a canyon, whose steep sides were covered with irrigated terraces. Xiahuanaco noted in his quipu that the fields were no longer cultivated because the viaducts were full of weeds and had unaccountably fallen into disrepair.

According to my own memory of this journey, it took us only a few days to reach Chongoypae, where we found ourselves snowed under in an unseasonable blizzard and were forced to stay for a week. According to the record of the Official Rememberer, the trek up to Chongoypae lasted so long that we spent the winter there, as it was too late in the year to risk continuing up into the highlands. Whether it was in the summer of the year we set out from Tumbez, or in the following year, or even two years later, that we reached the source of the Chancay river and the watershed of the Andes, it was impossible to say with any certainty, for by then it was beyond doubt that the Spanish and the people of Tahuantin-suyu were living according to different times. Time for us had slowed almost to a standstill, while for the Inca it was racing ahead. With my own eyes I watched Xiahuanaco decay in his flesh, from month to month, latterly from week to week. I saw his great ears sag and wrinkle, his tall figure shrink, his shoulders stoop. Overnight his remaining hair turned white.

Our cavalcade did not turn south along the watershed, crossing the tree-less savannah at thirteen thousand feet in the direction of Caxamarca, but east to Ki'zak, the secret necropolis where the mummified bodies of the Inca rulers were enshrined. In the Quipu of the Dead, which he did not live to complete, Xiahuanaco mourned the passing of Tahuantin-Suyu in the rapid disintegration of his own body. Day interchanged with night like a play of light and shadow across his face under a branch moved back and forth in the wind. The Inca kingdom was like a sealed casket broken open. Everything inside it began to shrivel upon contact with the air. What had seemed solid within its own world, and had endured for all time, became ash scattered on a breath of wind.

With Half Moon I built the pyres on which her parents' bodies burned, not many years after we arrived in Ki'zak, but the girl who had been not much younger than myself when we set out from Tumbez had by that time become a middle-aged woman. To her it must have seemed I became ever younger, while she for me inexplicably aged long before her time. Half Moon's body lost its splendour and its grace, its fluid motion, the warmth of desire. Her skin shed its scent and her hair its gloss in what seemed to be the space of no more than an afternoon sleep. It was as if I had closed my eyes with all her youth in my embrace and woken to find an old woman in my arms. There was pity in her eyes, not for herself, but for me, foreseeing the solitary fate that awaited me. Knotting into the last strands of the Quipu of the Ghosts an account of Half Moon's accelerated life and death and her love for one of the strangers who had been her nemesis, I entrusted it to the Ki'zak archives, but when the last Official Rememberer died and there was no one left who could read it I fetched the quipu and took it with me before I departed from the city.

The Quipu Archives in Ki'zak

In a long airy hall the quipu hung, rolled up on poles fitted into racks that rose in tiers to the ceiling. It was like the interior of a great skull, a great barn of memory, in which the harvest of Tahuantin-suyu's past was kept. In the centre of the hall a spiral staircase with passages leading off between the racks provided access to each tier. On my first visit the place bustled with *quipu camayoc* tending the memory of the archive, and they described to me how their work was done. They combed through bales, restoring knots that had come awry, knitting up unravelled strands of wool and replacing those which had become threadbare. Ascending or descending the spiral staircase, the Rememberers went up and down in time. The most recent quipu hung at the bottom, the most ancient at the top. Time was a stone memory warehouse in Ki'zak, arranged in racks and tiers, accessed by a spiral staircase. Maintained throughout the ages, kept in constant repair, the Rememberers said, not a single strand of the original quipu at the top remained intact. New strands were knitted in for old. Filaments of memory in this buzzing hive were ceaselessly being replaced. The barn-like hall was a living mind. Its memory was ever present, passing through generations of *quipu camayoc* hands. But when I visited this memory for the last time the Rememberers had gone. Tahuantin-suyu had lost its mind and the archive was abandoned. Doors had come off their hinges. A cold dry wind blew through the hall. I climbed the staircase and looked down the passages. The memory had fallen into decay. Quipu poles had broken and lay strewn over the tiers beneath. Whole racks had collapsed. I made my way up in time marked off in decades, hundreds, thousands and tens of thousands of years, for such was the measure of what the Spanish and the Portuguese had presumed to call the New World. I had never been in this passage at the top. Animal hides with outlines burned into them hung on the walls. They appeared to be maps of the world, but of a world I did not recognise. Balsa rafts with cotton sails symbolised coastal trading routes from Tumbez to a continent at the bottom of the Sleeping Sea, a place where there was no land known to us in the Old World. They showed trading routes to the west across a great water of unimaginable extent. But the strangest objects in this upmost passage of time were the hides with maps of the world spanned over leather balls, representing the world as round. The land at the bottom of the Sleeping Sea hung bat-like upside down under the belly of the Earth. West of the coastal mountains running from north to south, all the lands between the equator and this continent at the bottom of the world were possessions the Inca had inherited from the ancient days of Tahuantin-Suyu.

Ghost Stories

When they crossed the threshold, leaving a tear in the dome over that airtight chamber which had sealed Inca civilisation, the Spanish created a vortex in which the inhabitants of Tahuantin-Suyu were catapulted into a different order of time and immediately began to disintegrate. The conquistadors, however, caught up in Inca time, entangled in its cobwebs, were gradually slowed down until they had been brought to a standstill and ceased to age. Dom Pedro's trajectory came to rest in the great square of Ki'zak where with all his remaining strength he cried out for gold, but apart from the old priests who tended the necropolis there was no one to hear him. His head was as bleached as a piece of driftwood, his face burned, his body wasted to the bone. The admiral was mounted on a llama, sitting all awry, his shanks jack-knifed in the short stirrups of the Inca saddle, knees almost touching his chin. Around him stood one hundred gaunt survivors, dressed in ponchos and kilts of dried grass or rough breeches made from animal skins. The half dozen cuirasses, helms and bucklers still in their possession after the near drowning in the Sleeping Sea were dented and rusted. The rags of their clothes flapped in the wind that whistled across the square. This was the scene foretold by Great White Bird in his dreaming that I myself had dreamed, the doom in which the spirit of my father Zarate had acquiesced. For a long time we remained in the square of Ki'zak and tried to remember what we were doing there. There had been rumours of gold, Dom Pedro said, but these were vague. Upon asking to be brought to the Inca and the Punchao, the great treasure of which the Inca was the guardian, he was led to a house where the mummified bodies of Huanaco Capac's predecessors lived, and the old men spoke with them, and when the dead had answered their questions we were taken to a small room of cane wattle with woven fabrics placed on the roof as mats to protect it from the sun. The door was studded with corals, turquoises and crystals, but on opening it we found ourselves in a foul-smelling, mud-daubed hovel with a wooden post carved in the form of an Inca god and a pair of crossed sticks mounted over his head. This was all the treasure they had. The admiral scratched his head, as if distracted by memories that would not fall into place. His rump army assembled in the square of Ki'zak facing the rising sun. We marched over the cordillera and descended the mountains on the other side, crossing the ravines by means of cables woven out of rushes, two palms broad and strong and long enough to stretch from one side of the precipice to the other, as we were shown by Inca guides. We arrived in a fertile valley half a league wide, like the plain of Cuzco, with a soft climate in which the maize could be harvested three times a year and the bees made honeycombs in the thatched roofs just as they did in Spain in the boards of houses. The settlement spread as wide as the valley in which it lay, with sweet potatoes and cotton growing in the fields on either side, and an abundance of coca, cassava, sweet cane to make sugar, planted on the warm terraces further down the mountain side. Dom Pedro was in his hundred and thirtieth year when he founded Vilcabamba, about the time that Vasco Nunez de Balboa must have reached the Sleeping Sea. Balboa had a fleet of ships carried in pieces over the mountains and reassembled on the other side to sail the Pacific, but Balboa died and Pizarro sailed in his place. By the time Pizarro arrived at Tumbez two generations had watched the swallows come and go since Xiahuanaco set out with the ghosts for the city of the dead. On reaching the watershed of the Andes, Pizarro and his men turned not east as we had but south, to Caxamarca, where Atahualpa was waiting for them. His watch-towers overlooked the route this second wave of intruders took, but the Inca made no attempt to stop them, for Tahuantin-suyu was already lost in time, and his kingdom had long since begun to unravel along the tear Dom Pedro Felipe had left. Already the Inca knew that its past was as irretrievable as ash on the wind. Thus the indifference of Atahualpa, his careless lethargy after the massacre described by the Spanish-Inca mestizo Garcilasso de la Vega as having been as brief as the Caxamarca twilight, no more than half an hour between light and darkness, during which ten thousand Indians were slaughtered. The bearers of the Inca's litter continued to support it with their shoulders even after their hands had been cut off. Thus Atahualpa allowed himself to be taken prisoner, knowing he had already died. Thus the lofty dismissal for a captor he knew could not touch him. Thus the famous boast to Francisco Pizarro that, in exchange for his freedom, he would fill with gold the great chamber in which they stood, right up to the line which the greedy Spaniard drew along the wall. While Dom Pedro dozed in the sunshine on the terraces of Vilcabamba Atahualpa was murdered and Pizarro's men began the sack of Cuzco, dismantling the walls of temples lined with sheets of gold and silver, disinterring the jewels and the precious vases that were in the possession of the dead and guarded by life-size sentries made of solid gold. In the tombs they found golden crayfish swimming in silver basins; pitchers half of pottery and half of emeralds, inlaid in the pottery so well that not a drop of water escaped; gold and silver bowls on which all the birds and animals known to the Inca were sculpted in relief. There were barns, as Panquiaco had predicted, in which gold ingots were stored, storehouses full of cloth and wool, sandals, bucklers, weapons and breastplates to equip soldiers, cloaks fashioned like dense chain-mail, covered with gold and silver counters and stitched with a thread so fine it was invisible. In the houses of Cuzco they found lofts full of iridescent feathers, the down of tiny birds, threaded together along agave fibres and used for making the finest clothes, to be worn once by the Inca before they were burned. But the greatest treasure, the Punchao, they did not find. The Indians carried it away and hid it, and the quest of the conquistadors for a fabulous hoard began again. The map of the New World took the shape of a tree of rivers along which the white men made their way, the iron armies of the conquistadors, the missionaries, explorers and bandits who were their successors. Juan de Ayolas went up the Uruguay River to find the fabled White King who lived in caves of silver at the headwaters of the river. Jimenez de Casada trawled the streams of the Caribbean for a thousand miles from the source of the Magdalena River in Colombia in search of a legendary kingdom of emeralds. Federmann set out along the Meta in pursuit of yet another Dorado of the imagination, while Juan Diaz de Solis sailed up the River Plate in search of a passage connecting three oceans, the Atlantic, the Pacific and the

Amazon. On the old maps it was not painted in as a river but as an inland sea. It was in search of this sea that descendants of Francisco Pizarro stumbled across the forgotten city on the eastern side of the cordillera. Here the remnants of the first expeditionary force to have explored the continent still lived, with only the most shadowy, brittle memories, rising like dust when stirred by the newcomers' questions, of where they came from and how they had arrived in this place. The older ones among them hunted out some ancient pieces of armour in support of their memories, as quaint and cumbersome as the dialect they spoke, such as might have been spoken long ago at the Spanish court around the time of Ferdinand and Isabella. They cultivated strange fruits and vegetables, lucumas, avocados and potatoes, raising curassows and pheasants and fathering light-skinned, proud-faced mestizo children on women they claimed were their granddaughters, whose mothers they had long outlived, and whose grandmothers, even longer ago, had come with them as virgin wives from Ki'zak, the city of the dead. The newcomers leaned against the door posts, drumming their fingers and smiling at the girls in the gloomy interiors of the houses as they listened to these seemingly ageless inhabitants of Vilcabamba who sat outside on sun-bleached benches, telling their ghost stories in archaic Spanish. Ageing without appearing to age, trapped in my imperishable youth, I listened to these tales and exchanged smiles with the newcomers as if to say I knew better, and I did, I was a young man as they were even if I had the habits of an old woman, sitting with my tapestry, as they mockingly called it, draped over my knee, drawing new strands of wool and sliding knots into the ancient quipu which I had brought with me from Ki'zak. When the descendants of Pizarro arrived on horseback the children of Vilcabamba fled in terror. They had never seen such a creature and believed horse and rider must be one and the same. These were the great-grandchildren of Running Wind and Xiahuanaco, an Official Rememberer whose record of the decline of the Inca empire I knew by heart, including the genealogy of all his descendants. The work I had discontinued in Ki'zak I resumed in Vilcabamba, knotting the years and the tens of years and related summaries of events in separate columns as I had learned to do from the *quipu camayoc* before the first Pizarro had set foot in the New World. When Huayana Pizarro, the mestizo grandson of the founder of Lima, which at that time was still known as the City of the

Kings, led horses out into the plaza of Vilcabamba and challenged me to a race around the square, and I held him off easily by several lengths, I was careful not to tell him how old I truly was and be taken for another teller of ghost stories. After a long stay in the town where the last Inca would seek refuge, living in a painted cedar palace not built at the time I left Vilcabamba, Huayana Pizarro and his men grew tired of the drowsy life in the mountain pastures. They set off one morning, taking me with them as their guide as casually as Dom Pedro Felipe's factors had once removed me from the house of Zarate the Jew and carried me off to the New World. From the cool highlands of the Andes we descended the passes into the steaming forest of the Amazon basin. On reaching what Pizarro took to be an estuary of the inland sea we built a raft to navigate its waters. A priest blessed the raft, and as we pushed off into the stream Pizarro read the Requirement to the jungle. This much at least had not changed since Dom Pedro first reached the shores of Brazil. But after the Conquest, when the Indians experienced all the horrors of the white gold seekers with their war dogs and missionaries, they had lost the will to live. They succumbed to such a deep pessimism that, as word of our coming travelled down river, they deserted their settlements and hid in the jungle rather than face the ordeals they had come to associate with God-is-Love. To some tribes the devil appeared and set them to eating earth until they died. The estuary was resolved to be no estuary but the Napo River, a tributary of the Amazon, which the explorers now began to descend. As the great river carried us east the friars continued to address the shores with their prayers and Pizarro to read the Requirement, as if they had no eyes to see all the corpses of the Indians hanging from the branches of the trees. While the raft floated downstream the friars sung ballads they had composed in the Tupi-Guarani language to the dead Indians who had hung themselves in the forest, telling them of the creation of the world, the fall of man and his exile from Paradise. On such occasions as Indians could still be caught alive they were taught the verses by heart, singing them in a manner pleasing to the friars, who accompanied them on an instrument they called the teplanastle. In time the Indian teplanastle was replaced by Spanish harps and the Dominican friars by Jesuits, descending the waters of the great tree of rivers with boatloads of Indians who had become immune to the white man's diseases that had ravaged their ancestors. They no more knew the myths of creation according to which their ancestors had murdered the toucan and the red-tailed macaw, from whose bleeding plumage the sun first issued as a ball of fire when All-Creatures-Being-In-The Forest began, than they remembered the language in which those myths had once been told. The few Indians to emerge on the far side of the catastrophe of their discovery by the conquistadors, paddling the Jesuit fathers down the many-branched rivers of the continent in their pirogues at dawn, learned to chant their hymns in Latin to the greater glory of God. I was the sole living witness to the crimes of the Conquest, carried out of it on a raft with the descendants of its perpetrators. I had seen Pablito's vision of the unconstrained quality of life, in which the Indians swam as naturally as porpoises swam in the sea, and I had seen it borne out, becoming a river so thickened with blood that it had ceased to run. The friars who came forward with blankets to cover the nakedness of the Indians on board Dom Pedro's ship when his fleet reached the coast of Brazil had in reality been death-bringers, already shrouding the first Indian bodies. These were my rites of passage, a survivor doomed, after all I had witnessed and would be unable to forget, to the solitude of agelessness Half Moon had foreseen. The great river poured me downstream, a hundred year-old man hiding inside a young man's body, carrying me across the continent until at last it spat me out, leaving the raft high and dry on a mud-bank at sunrise as the tide sucked the water off the delta and the river drained into a blood-red sea.

Pernambuco

Father Anselm sat down at his desk and activated the TALK switch on the glass case.

"Good evening, Pablito. Or would it be more correct to call you Pablo by this stage? Pablito hardly seems appropriate for the centenarian you had already become by the end of the narrative I listened to last night."

He flipped the switch to LISTEN. Sea-shell murmur came drifting out of the speaker.

"Pablito, Pablo – it's all one to me. On my passage through the centuries my name has changed many times, as you will see. But for the time being let us stick with Pablo."

"Well then, Pablo. I hope you were able to get more rest in the filing cupboard than I have managed to do in my own bed. What you told me last night disturbed me so much that I was unable to get any sleep. Of course, I have read books about the genocide of the Indians carried out by the conquistadors and condoned by the church. But it is a different matter to be told of these horrors by an eye-witness. The part you played in them yourself, if you have been telling me the whole truth, seems to have been impeccable. Indeed, for much of the time you were almost an Indian yourself. I must admit, I was not prepared for a confession of this nature, nor can I presume to absolve the commission of such sins. No one can. All I can do is to open my ears to a moral history of the New World that I fore-see is going to make for some most uncomfortable listening."

A high-pitched sneeze came unexpectedly out of the speaker. For the first time Father Anselm saw the emaciated little figure in the case move. The index finger slid down over the pad and pressed a button.

"Dust," said the young man's voice. "I don't know where it comes from, but it sometimes gets into the filter system. It may be for the best, Father Anselm, that so much of our past comes to be buried by a collective act of forgetfulness. What else should we do with it? Where would we find room to accommodate all the new horrors constantly inundating us? Who now knows or cares to know what life was like at the beginning of the colonial enterprise in Brazil, where I was washed up by the great river at the beginning of the seventeenth century in my hundred and thirteenth year?"

"I can only speak for myself," said Father Anselm, "but I for one would be very interested to hear what it was like. I just hope that your narrative will provide more encouragement as we move on."

"After my expulsion from All-Creatures-Being-In-The-Forest," said the old man, "I entered a Jesuit seminary, but finding this life not to be my calling I became tutor to the Pilar family in the Big House of the Donatory, His Excellency Dom Pedro Joao, on a sugar plantation in Pernambuco. Between the nun Esperanca and her sister Senhora de Souza, who could turn into a fox, I lost my way in love for the best part of a hundred years, lost the use of my legs, a colonist carried around by slaves in a palanquin to avoid getting dirty feet, dreaming on an opium cushion while the New World grew old and sank into decline. There are perhaps moments in the seminary, characters we shall encounter in the Big House or in the entourage of that great entertainer Porphyry, which you will conceivably find amusing. But any narrative about the conditions of life during times of slavery will have difficulty providing very much in the way of encouragement. We shall see, Father Anselm, we shall see."

Boa Vista

The new arrivals to the continent had soon become its old legends, diffused along the arteries of its rivers, rumoured from coast to coast. Stories of the Pilar family were told to me by fishermen far north at the mouth of the Amazon at Pará where the great river poured me out after a journey of three thousand miles from the eastern cordillera along the Sleeping Sea. They could say where those stories began, naming the three ships making up the little fleet that had brought me to the New World. They knew the *Sao Cristobal*, which had sailed south under Dom Pedro Felipe's command in search of islands rumoured to be full of gold, and the *Salvador*, commanded by Dom Joao, which had carried me up river to the spot where I parted company with the Portuguese, was adopted by Taiassu Indians and lived with them in the rain forest.

Nothing more was heard of the *Salavador*. For a long time the colonists waited at the mouth of the river for the brigantine to return. Among the friendly coastal tribes they learned how to build huts and make farina from the manioc root. They adapted and survived. What they lacked was a harbour. When the *Sao Cristobal* and the *Salvador* failed to return, the settlers embarked on the remaining ship, the *Santa Cruz*. They sailed north up the coast of Brazil until they reached the long reef with sheltered water accessed by a broad inlet where the father of Pedro Joao Pilar was born. His mother stayed on board to complete the birth she had begun at sea before following her husband ashore.

The portrait of Francesca Pilar that hung in the great house her grandson built was commissioned long after she died. It was painted by an artist who had never seen his subject, the picture of a dowager who embodied the colonial ambitions that went with the great house. Certainly it bore no resemblance to the girl in the striped bonnet, Francesca Carvalho, one of the King's Orphans, her trousseau in a trunk, with whom I had sat on deck watching the flying fish leap on our voyage across the Ocean Sea. The thin, pock-marked girl who died at twenty after giving birth to six children was commemorated in the painting as a matron with the alabaster face of a saint.

Pedro Pilar, a landless hidalgo who married Francesca Carvalho at the mouth of the river a week after they had reached the New World, chose to remain alone rather than take a Tupi-Guarani woman for his wife, as Indian *cunha* were the only wives to be had. No sooner had the first Portuguese men sprung ashore than they found their feet slipping among the naked Indian women. The *cunha* offered their bodies to the colonists for a comb or a broken mirror, rubbing themselves against the legs of the newcomers they took to be gods. Pedro Pilar cleared the land with fire and axe and planted maize, millet and corn, but the cane that was already indigenous to the land seeded itself and did best of all.

The first generation lived and died in the squalor of their mud huts. Many became lame or had to amputate their feet before they learned from their *cunha* how to extract a thick red oil from a fruit called the couroq, which could be applied as protection against the torment of jiggers, insects that worked their way through the flesh of the feet unless they were cut out. So long as the Indians remained willing to provide labour for the colonists in exchange for beads, mirrors and metal, they lived side by side on the narrow strip of shore, but when they had enough of these things they stopped working, and the settlers sought to enslave them according to the terms of the Requirement. The colonists attacked the Indian villages, carried off wives and children and held prisoner anyone who came into their land. The Indians disappeared into the forest. Wars fuelled by mutual reprisals began. The Portuguese abandoned their farms in fear of their lives and withdrew behind the fortified stockades on the coast.

Pedro Joao Pilar was a young man at this time, only son of the sole survivor of the six children Francesca Carvalho had borne Pedro Pilar. When his father died he went to live with his grandfather. He distinguished himself in the Indian wars by driving the Tupi-Guarani deep inland and enforcing on them a settlement that would keep them there. In acknowledgement of his services to the Portuguese Crown, Pedro Joao was named Donatory of a vast territory south of the Amazon delta at Pará, still just a fishing village with a few palm huts at a time when the Donatory had built the first house of stone from the quarries outside Lisbon. It was said that the stones of the house had been anointed with whale oil and the blood of murdered slaves whom the Donatory had buried beneath the foundations.

By then a ship a week put in at the deep harbour the *Santa Cruz* had first sailed in to, carrying the stone as ballast on the outward voyage and transporting brasil wood for dyestuff, sugar and cotton back across the ocean. The ships brought livestock and women for the settlers and the first Negro slaves. After half a lifetime as a widower Pedro Pilar married a fifteen year-old girl among the last consignment of Orphans of the King to reach the settlement, fathering a further nine children, two of whom survived. His grandson Pedro Joao, the Donatory, was a shrewd, thrifty man who disliked waste, including the extraordinarily high mortality rate of infants born during the first decades of the colony. Both his taste for their sexual temperament and his judgement of their fitness to survive in a tropical climate made him prefer Tupi-Guarani *cunha* to Portuguese women, but now he was confronted with the Negro woman for the first time.

He stood on the wharf, watching the women come ashore as if they were breeding-mares for improving stock, and pledged the value of a year's sugar crop to the merchants in exchange for their entire cargo of slaves.

The Donatory rode back to his estate inland with two dozen men, women and children in tow like a mule train behind him. His grandfather wondered at this display of extravagance at a time when Indian slaves could still be had gratis by anyone prepared to hunt them down. But Pedro Joao, acting on rumours he had heard among the Jesuits, was anticipating a reform, promulgated as the New Laws of the Indies not long afterwards, by which the Crown sought to regulate the ever-diminishing pool of Indian labour. Epidemics of smallpox, which raged in the Portuguese colonies, wiped out Indian settlements entirely. In vain the Jesuits sought them out in the jungle, administering powdered horse dung as an antidote to the disease. As the Indians died away under the padres' hands the price of African slaves soared.

They were more robust than the Indians, more cheerful, and they worked harder. They had no allies in the jungle, so there was nowhere for them to run away. Pedro Joao noted that the Indians had never truly adapted to the climate. They kept out of the sun, smeared coconut oil into the skin to make up for their lack of perspiration, and plunged into the river to cool off at all times of the day. His African slaves had no need of palliatives to help them endure the heat. They sweated all over the body, not drops of sweat but a complete and continuous film, as if the entire body were shedding oil secreted in the pores of their skin. The Donatory admired the physique of the men and women working naked in the sugarcane and he fed them well, as he did all the animals that worked on his estate and the adjoining plantations. It was in his power to give land to anyone willing to cultivate it and grow cane, which they were to bring to his mill using the labour of slaves they hired from him. Visitors making the journey from the coast to these inland plantations said they were surrounded by so many black people there that it was as if they had travelled in a straight line across the ocean and arrived back in Negroland from where the slaves came.

The Tupi-Guarani woman whom Pedro Joao took as his wife was baptised Maria Conceicao before he married her, and on the advice of the priest, as a prophylactic to counter the spirits she might have brought with her from the forest, he placed a crucifix under her body whenever they copulated. Throughout the marriage she continued to lay crossed twigs at certain places in the house and to place an ear of corn under her pillow at night so that she might see in a dream the person who came to steal it. Whenever she heard the sound of a bell she would hide. She avoided eating or drinking in her husband's sight. Pedro Joao never cured her of these superstitions, nor of her fondness for bathing in the mill stream, however much he beat his wife. But the corn, the cashew nuts and the medicinal herbs the Indian woman also brought into the house never left it thereafter, and Pilar women in the fourth and fifth generation would still treat their hair with coconut oil in just the way their Tupi-Guarani ancestor had done. She was either less fertile or somehow knew how to limit her fertility, giving birth to only four children, all of whom thrived, while most of the children by the white women continued to die. They still swaddled their babies in swathes of cloth as their grandmothers in Portugal had done, but the Donatory's wife followed the Indian custom of exposing infants to the air from the moment they were born.

Reports of the Pilar mestizo girls bathing daily with their mother in the mill stream and running naked with the children of the African slaves scandalised the orthodox Portuguese community. The priest who came to say mass in the plantation chapel on Sundays investigated these rumours and discovered even worse. When Maria Conceicao brought in to the house the son she had given birth to, squatting Indian fashion on the forest floor, she left the second child lying under a bed of leaves. She did so in accordance with the belief of her tribe that it was only animals, not humans, that produced a litter, and whatever came after the first born, being animal, was the work of a demon and must die.

A Negro woman, who had followed the Donatory's wife into the forest and secretly watched her parturition, rescued the second child after the mother had gone. She carried it home to her hut. But Maria Conceicao placed the ear of corn under her pillow, as was her custom, and saw in a dream the Negro woman who came to take it. By this sign she knew that the child had been found by a slave who had hidden it in her hut, and when the foster mother was working in the cane she went there to kill it a second time. The baby lay in a box around which a snake had wrapped itself. In the darkness inside the hut the Indian woman did not see the snake. When she reached into the box the snake bit her hand. Her hand puffed up from the poison and she fell into a fever of which she nearly died.

From her ramblings in delirium Pedro Joao learned the truth of the second child she had sought to suppress and sent her back to her people. In her place the Donatory installed in the house the Negro foster mother who was nursing the abandoned child, and who later bore her master seven of her own children. The older of the twins left by his Indian wife was baptised Duarte Joao. Francesca Carvalho Pilar's portrait had been commissioned by the Donatory and enshrined in the Big House as the icon of the Pilar dynasty. Pedro Joao christened the son abandoned in the jungle Duarte Carvalho, invoking the name of the boy's great-great-grandmother to exorcise the memory of his mother and forbidding his family to speak of Maria Conceicao ever again.

Despite the colour of the women he preferred in his bed Pedro Joao married his neighbour's leftover daughter. A white woman belonged as the mistress of the house on his estate, even if she was an ill-favoured one, just as his dining-table required silver plate, even if it was fetched by Negroes with bare feet in a house so remote and served by such bad roads that there were seldom guests to admire it. As her dowry she brought into the marriage a swathe of cane brake, adding five daughters to the household, a vast assortment of puddings, marmalades and sweets before she succumbed to the inclination of her body to become fat and lazy, pleading weak ankles and dainty feet. She sank into an enormous palisander chair from which she hardly ever stirred thereafter. Four men were required to carry it around the house until it was modified by the carpenter so that poles could be inserted and the chair carried more conveniently by two servants as a palanquin. The massive throne where Sofia Maria da Costa Pilar went into early retirement — sitting in it for her portrait and insisting on its inclusion, complete with the Negro footman behind it, fanning her with a palm leaf — anticipated the habits of a later generation of Pilars who would spend their entire lives in hammocks.

The wife's escape into fatness and a semi-invalid way of life that elicited her husband's sympathy while keeping him at bay behind the screen of her constant attendants was her answer to the neglect she had suffered at Pedro Joao's hands. Women bore the burden, scarcely less so than slaves. She put up with his mountings, performed solely to increase his progeny and aggrandise himself, endured his mistresses and the horde of mulatto children that ran in and out of the house, reproaching him with self-effacement and silence. The Donatory disposed of her as he felt fit, just as he disposed of the daughters of his former Tupi-Guarani wife, marrying the elder one off with a magnificent dowry to the heir of a sugar mill at the age of twelve and entrusting the younger one penniless to a nunnery, pleading that another dowry like her sister's would ruin the family.

This was the feudal estate in which the Pilar family lived at the time I arrived in the Big House. A certain harsh simplicity in the character of the Donatory accorded with the character of his task. The building of his plantation began with the domestication of the forest, the civilising of the land with the suppression of the Indians who resisted its occupation by the colonists. He succeeded at this task by main force, imposing his will on his enemies, his subordinates and associates alike. Force became habit. This was reflected in the treatment of his women, his children and his slaves. All of them were there by his good grace, all of them of subsidiary importance to the family that ensured their safekeeping. The family and not the individual, much less the state or any commercial company, was the force behind the colonisation of Brazil. Even Pedro Joao's own wife had been chosen with foresight rather than according to his personal taste. The cane brake he negotiated with the Da Costa family as the dowry for an unmarriageable daughter secured the produce of the Pilar estate independent access to the sea, a strategic asset he had married her for in a colony where rights of way remained a source of constant feuds.

Ships now called regularly on the journey home from the East Indies, broad-bellied traders rolling in across the swell with the plunging motions of pregnant women, laden with porcelain, spices and silk for the rich planters in the colony. Once or twice a year the Indiamen might be accompanied by an escort of whales right up to the gap in the reef through which Pedro Joao's grandmother had passed as she lay in labour on deck, exclaiming at the beauty of the blue-green water and the flower-crowded shore, sloping up to a wooded headland with a view over the bay. On the cluster of hills at the tip of the inland cordillera perched the settlement they had named Boa Vista for the loveliness of that view. In time it became a town with colonnades and tiled walks surrounding the emporium of commerce, a hospital and a house of Misericordia, convents of Benedictines, Franciscans, slippered and unslippered Carmelites, a Jesuit seminary and the Episcopal palace with a refectory that was thrown open to the town's inhabitants for viewing the spectacle of the whales during their migrations north and south. For a few days each year the bay of Boa Vista was visited by a school of these vast creatures, plunging outside the reef and creating thunderclaps when they smacked the water with their flukes, drawing furrows on the surface as they rippled underwater before bursting out and blowing gigantic spouts, like farewell signals, that were visible far out to sea.

In the Seminary

On board the ship from Pará, at the mouth of the Amazon, to Salvador in the south I met a man who had lived for a long time among the tribes dwelling on the great river. After his experiences in the jungle the Brazilian-born Jesuit was now on his way to the seminary in Boa Vista to devote himself to the creation of a *lingoa geral*, a language that could be used to communicate with the Indians in whatever part of the country. When he realised the extent of my knowledge of the Indian dialects and the contribution I was in a position to make to this undertaking, he asked me if I would help him. I agreed at once. Thus, although it had been my intention to look for opportunities with a trading house in Salvador, my journey ended in Boa Vista, where I was received as a lay brother into the seminary of the Society of Jesus.

I now tiptoed back into a world that, with the exception of my conversations with Xiahuanaco in Tumbez, had been closed to me since I left Zarate's house. There I had been tutored by some of the most learned scholars in Lisbon. Since those precocious studies of my childhood I had regressed to a Stone Age view of the world during the Pig Indian period of my life when I lived with savages. Only later, in the company of men who believed themselves the superiors of the savages they came to civilise by expropriation and killing, had I led a life which truly deserved that description. To serve goodness I now wished to be disembodied and to exist as spirit. This was why I entered the seminary. I felt a need to abase and cleanse myself, to be metamorphosed, I could not say how, into a victim. When Father Eugenio, at my request, agreed to help me with the spiritual exercises that would help me to reach this goal, an indescribable smile hovered at the corners of his lips.

Every day we spent many hours in the library of the seminary where the Jesuits studied diligently at lecterns, frocked and white-faced like women. Goodness, the usefulness of a rewarding task, seemed to soar with the walls of the great white room and to be reflected gratifiyingly back on myself. Yet even the knowledge of Indian languages I brought to this task had been gleaned in the wake of Dom Pedro Felipe's man-eating centipede, which had swum up rivers to devour entire villages, trampled across the isthmus and wrought havoc along hundreds of miles of coast. Even the abstraction of these intellectual pursuits in which I sought to escape was tainted with the blood of the Conquest. That thought did not trouble Father Eugenio. I pointed out to him that a *lingoa geral* was itself a colonial undertaking, a further perversion of the natural state of the country's inhabitants. A general language would be used by the colonists to impose a general government over the Indians. By what right was this done?

Debates of this kind often took place in the seminary. When I watched the frocked and white-faced priests mounting their elaborate constructions as they entered the lists, the memory of my son Earth Puddle (whom I used to liken to a rain drop poised in the great balance of All-Creatures-Being-In-The-Forest) would trickle into my mind. I wondered what benefit he would have derived from the debating tournaments of the Jesuits. I wondered for whom the prayers were said in the long hall and the hymns sung in the chapel. Everything that took place inside the white walls of the seminary reflected back on the inmates. For myself I knew that when I performed my spiritual exercises I was performing in front of the mirror of my soul. No object other than myself was reflected for long in this mirror.

Father Eugenio knew the temptation of vanity and said the purpose of these exercises in solitude was to see beyond the mirror into which the soul gazed, meaning to overcome the self. After vanity came terror. From whatever angle one looked one was looking back at oneself. It grew and grew and filled out one's cell until there was no escape from it. One walked in the garden but did not see the trees or smell the air. The world ended with our skin that bordered it, and our perception of it, blunt to the external touch, would then turn inwards, looking through the infinite open-endedness of the self. The journey into this interior world was no less arduous than the voyage undertaken by navigators across the Ocean

Sea. Not knowing one's destination was what both journeys were about. The journey was a paradigm of our mortal life, in which there was no stasis. All were travellers. The journey in an ageing body was a journey through an ageing world. The house moved in which the traveller lived, going wherever he did, and there was no escaping it, for we travelled through a world that was the creation of our own minds.

The Jesuit father endured a long drawn out spiritual agony over the desolation of the native Indian soul as revealed to him by the untranslatability of Judaeo-Christian ideas into the Tupi-Guarani language. How to bring light into this darkness? For months he had been devoting his nights to a rendering of the Ten Commandments, which bodied out, in the Tupi-Guarani version, as a manuscript running to some fifty pages, not including explanatory notes. I had already encountered translation problems in the attempt to acquaint my Taiassu tribesman Grasshopper with the message of the gospel. It was a futile attempt, and I soon gave it up. There was no way of representing God in many Indian languages except as a female ancestor. This was unacceptable to Father Eugenio. In her place he cobbled together a God compound made up of father-headman, unmistakably male, even as he assured me that God was a neuter, the pronoun He the sexless legacy of a historical convention having to do with Semitic inheritance and property rights, which made God sound rather like a member of the Society of Jesus.

The gospel eventually rendered in the *lingoa geral* left the Indians with no motivation other than the punishment of sin and the reward of virtue. Both of these were alien to them and in practice would have to be administered by Jesuit missionaries in place of God, as He could not be relied upon to carry them out. Love of one's neighbour became a prohibition to eat one's enemy on pain of being eaten oneself, charity an injunction not to throw one's offal in the river and pollute it for tribes downstream on pain of being polluted oneself. The religion brought to the Indians by the priests of the Conquest was perverted by a spirit which led to their extinction even more efficiently than the annihilation achieved by the sword and smallpox that followed in its wake.

One Jesuit father accomplished this immense task almost single-handedly. The labour sucked the juices out of his body, shrivelled and dried him up as effectively as any of the embalming procedures Panquiaco's tribe had practised on its dead chieftains. On the day he no longer needed my services he accompanied me to the seminary gate, a wizened, feather-light man whose body cast a hardly perceptible shadow and whose foot-steps made no sound. Hands as dry as parchment enclosed mine as he thanked me for my help and said goodbye. At last he was ready, he said, and would soon be journeying up river to continue his mission among the Indians in the backlands. I watched him walk back without a sound through the darkening cloisters, trailing what seemed to be a white halo or cloud, inexplicable to me until I remembered where I had seen it before, the swarm of white moths which rose and sank like a fluttering scarf in the wake of the departing priest.

Cake Alley

I told Father Eugenio I felt unqualified to renounce the world. I had no aptitude, no heartfelt longing for spirituality. He said I was free to leave the seminary whenever I chose. I moved out of the seminary and found lodgings with Monsieur Bez, a French dancing master who lived near the house of Misericordia in the old quarter of town.

The Misericordia was an establishment where girls from good families were placed to live chastely and pursue charitable works of a not too strenuous kind. The inmates could push open the upper part of the wooden lattice windows and I sometimes saw them resting on their elbows and projecting their heads to get a glimpse of what took place in the street. This was where the poor went to eat cakes, lowered from the windows in baskets to passers-by in the street. There were many who survived on these cakes, to which the nuns gave such names as Novitiates' Sighs, Angel Sweetness and Heavenly Manna, offering a blessing instead of pay-ment. Scents from the bakery in the Misericordia spiced the air with a fra-grance, reminding me of the flour-dusted arms of the women I used to watch making bread in Zarate's house. Surprised by forgotten memories that suddenly came back to me with this fragrance, I was dawdling by one of the baskets in Cake Alley when a woman somewhere above asked brusquely why for heaven's sake I couldn't get on with it and just put a cake in my mouth. I lied that I wasn't hungry. The woman gave a full-throated chuckle, much too broad to be contained by the narrow window aperture.

Taken aback by this rollicking, least nunnish of laughs, I tilted my head and looked up. All I could make out in the opening between the protruding lattice window and the house wall was the outline of a face. Well, the voice asked, amused, and what did I see? I said the window was too dark for me to make anything out. She could see me very well, the voice retorted, and what she saw from top to toe was the hungriest man to have ever come down the street, which must make me the biggest liar, too. I admitted there was some truth in what she said. Perhaps I was hungrier than I had realised. This might have to do with the fact that I was fasting, for I had taken a vow. I said I was attached as a probationary to the Jesuit seminary, putting to good use my knowledge of the Indian languages and trying to do something better with my life than I had managed in the previous century.

I passed down Cake Alley several times a day and spoke often to the nun at the window of the Misericordia. Her name was Esperanca. She represented my unwillingness to eat cakes from her basket as being so deeply uncharitable in spirit that I felt ashamed of myself and finally gave in. As I had no money and she thought a benediction from a lay brother was a poor exchange for a basketful of cakes she suggested I tell her stories to earn my keep. No subject interested her as much as my life among the Indians. Esperanca already knew something about Indians. She was familiar with their customs and beliefs and possessed a smattering of Tupi-Guarani words, with which she sprinkled her conversation. She listened patiently to stories about tapir hunts, the preparation of the manioc root or the elevation of warriors to the tobacco palaver by presenting them with a rat-skin pouch, but it was my relationship with Lemon Grass to which she always wanted me to return. What had our feelings for one another been?

In the seminary I had already been pondering this question in the service of Father Eugenio's *lingoa geral*. I tended to the view that at the core of the conjugal relationship between myself and Lemon Grass, as between Indians generally, there was not so much any pressing reason that brought a couple together as the lack of a reason keeping them apart. Under the cross-interrogation fired down at me from the lattice in Cake Alley I began to have second thoughts. I wondered if I had done Lemon Grass an injustice. The quite distinct memories I had of returning to the malocca after a week-long hunting expedition and neither greeting nor being greeted by Lemon Grass, both of us resuming our tasks with complete mutual indifference, as was the normal state of affairs between Indian man and wife, began to look different in this light.

Esperanca's concern for my former Pig Indian wife illuminated the concerns of her own life. Her father was Portuguese and her mother Tupi, as she admitted when I asked her about her interest in my Indian stories. She was half Tupi herself. She had not really known her mother, having been separated from her when she was a child. From being a story-teller on a commission of cakes I became listener to a woman with such a hunger to tell her own story that she sometimes forgot to replenish the cake basket and lower it back down into the street. This became a serious matter once I had finished my work for Father Eugenio. Having left the seminary and with it the refectory where every evening I had received a frugal meal, I now had nothing to eat other than Esperanca's Novitiates' Sighs and Angel Sweetness. If these were not freely offered, pride held me back from asking.

Just as I was still in the Pig Indian habit of raising my arms to support the sky on stepping out of the house of M. Bez every morning, I also continued to practise the form of Pig Indian meditation known as guácu when I wanted to escape from my bodily state. Such was the case when I felt particularly tired or hungry. In Cake Alley I often had recourse to guácu. A marvellous lightness rose to my head, and I levitated, or thought I did, towards the unbroken stream of Esperanca's voice cascading to me from the open lattice. In fact I had passed out, striking my head on the pavement as I fell. I came to with a swaying motion, suggesting that I was being carried. I heard the frantic ringing of a bell, surrounded by rustlings and whispers with a texture like cobwebs, which, by virtue of the clarity of the sound, the bell dispersed as easily as the bows of a ship cleaving the surrounding sea. I made out forms scattering like white-crested waves under the keel of the plunging hammock in which I was being carried. The white-capped nuns who had taken vows of seclusion, as I learned afterwards from Esperanca, scattering at the sound of the bell that warned them of the approach of a male visitor.

A light fell on my face and I opened my eyes. Even when she scowled, as she was doing now, apparently dissatisfied with what she saw lying in the hammock, Esperanca was the most beautiful mestizo woman I had ever seen. She stepped up to the hammock and, to my astonishment, assuming I had been brought into the Misericordia to receive its charity, seized my nose and pinched it hard. That was for my low opinion of my wife Lemon Grass, she said. Ensconced as I was in the deep hammock, entirely passive, I had a good opportunity to study Esperanca's face at close quarters as she leaned over and pummelled me with her fists. The exercise put colour in her cheeks and a glitter in the large, slightly slanted black eyes glaring down at me out of a perfectly oval face. She had not taken the vow of seclusion, so her head was capless. Her hair was plaited in a thick black braid that had jumped around furiously while she was belabouring me but now hung quietly, contritely almost, down to her waist. This braid of hair was the weather-vane of her moods. From being a dead thing it could come alive, rise like a charmed snake and stand bristling on end. Having given expression to her feelings, as she couldn't help doing, for this was how Esperanca's nature was, the scowl vanished and her face cleared. She asked how I was feeling, and laughed. I said I was famished and half dying of thirst, maybe a few ribs were broken, I had no money, no employment, no roof over my head, but that otherwise I was feeling very comfortable. I would apply to the master of a ship and work my passage to Salvador to look for opportunities with a trading house there, as had been my intention before I had mistakenly allowed myself to be diverted to the Jesuit seminary in Boa Vista.

Esperanca looked at me thoughtfully and said all my needs would be seen to at once. She sent one of the porter nuns to fetch food and drink. The other was dispatched with a message to a father, a Benedictine, I gathered. One of the Misericordia's slaves was to ride out with it immediately to the estate and hand it to him personally. When the nuns had carried out her instructions she dismissed them, pulled a stool up to the hammock and said she was now going to serve me my supper. I told her I felt quite well enough to sit at a table to eat, and made an effort to extricate myself from the hammock, but she shook her head and pressed me back in. For a wild moment, as I watched a gobbet of fish descend to me on a spoon, I imagined myself back in Pig Indian captivity, and that I was going to be kept in the Misericordia, as I had been in the malocca, in a state of proxy infancy against my will to be fed indefinitely by women whose mothering instincts were too imperious to defy. Protesting, I finally had no option but to open my mouth to receive the spoon. I asked for some wine, which instead of being given to me in a glass was poured into me from a gargoyle of a receptacle with a spout, as if I had been a plant. All the time she was feeding me Esperanca asked me questions about myself, but I had suddenly become so sleepy that I could hardly keep my eyes open. A man came into the room. Two Negroes who accompanied him shouldered the hammock in which I was lying and carried me out. I asked where I was being taken but received no reply, or perhaps I did but I didn't hear it. Esperanca had taken the precaution of drugging the wine before arranging for me to be kidnapped, but I only realised this when it was already too late and I felt myself sliding down into a bottomless sleep.

The Donatory

I awoke in a large room with white-washed walls on which half a dozen lizards sat in motionless anticipation, heads thrust out like old men, staring down at me with obsidian eyes. I was lying in a hammock slung across a corner of the room. About as many children as lizards were perched on the ledge of the window giving out onto a veranda, waiting with curiosity for me to show the first signs of life. I did this by squinting cautiously through half-closed eyelids, evoking a murmur that ran like a single exhalation through the row of children, before it died out.

The room seemed to be on the second floor of the house. I could make out the crown of a broad tree that filled the room with an overpowering scent. I smelled the blossoms from which it came before I saw them, followed by my first sight of the Donatory. For a long time he remained motionless, his head thrust out, peering down at me like one of the lizards. At last he coughed, perhaps to draw attention to himself, and smoothed his moustache outwards with thumb and forefinger on either side. He wore a fantastic feathered hat, a white silk shirt with ruffs, scarlet silk breeches and a pair of mangy slippers. The fingers of his left hand, in which he held up a joint of meat as if exhibiting the subject of the conversation we were about to have, were covered with grease that oozed in slow lines, like congealing candle tallow, down his forearm and into his sleeve. When it had finished smoothing the moustache his right hand moved upwards to remove the hat.

Senhor, he greeted me solemnly. Even if the circumstances of my journey from Boa Vista to the Pilar plantation were regrettable, the journey having been undertaken without my consent, he hoped I had at least had a comfortable one, as I had undertaken it in a state of unconsciousness very conducive to relaxation. He stopped here and seemed to be reflecting with an air of astonishment on the sentence he had just delivered himself of, as if something had escaped captivity inside him whose existence he had never suspected. It had not been his intention, the Donatory continued, to bring me here against my will. But he could not very well ask me, since it had been impossible to wake me, so I had been carried in a hammock, and, well, here I was. He shrugged. The responsibility for what had happened lay with his daughter, Esperanca. She had sent him a message saying no more than that a suitable candidate for the post her father was anxious to have filled had presented himself at the Misericordia. Thus he had gone at once to Boa Vista accompanied by two slaves to escort me back to his home. And found me in the state I was in. His daughter would have to answer for it.

The Donatory took a few steps towards me, blocking out more of the room, and leaned forward as if to get a better look at me. The lizards darted momentarily on the wall and reassumed their monumental gaze. It was almost impossible, he said, waving the joint of meat in his hand in my direction, to find qualified persons, i.e. people able to read and write, who were willing to move inland from the coast. Jesuits came, but — here the Donatory tapped his nose and winked — who wanted a priest in his house? For all that the life out here was not at all bad. Now that the jungle had been cleared the climate was healthy. The Indians kept quiet. There was excellent hunting. The cook was good. The Donatory was a powerful and wealthy man. He was willing to pay me whatever salary I asked. So would I accept the post?

Pieces of the puzzle had already begun to fit together in my mind while I listened to the Donatory talk. I could remember that Esperanca had indeed sent a messenger, not to a father, as I had understood, on the Benedictine estate outside Boa Vista, but to her own father, the owner of the Pilar plantation. Esperanca was the Donatory's second daughter by Maria Conceicao, the Tupi-Guarani woman who had borne him four children and tried to kill the last, for which reason he had sent her back to her people. I asked the Donatory what sort of post on his plantation had such attractions that candidates for it needed to be lured into a house of charity and placed *hors de combat* by a desperado of a nun so that they could be carried unconscious to the interview. The Donatory was amused by this description. He flashed his teeth and his body quaked, going ho-ho-ho as his chest pumped in and out. This noise started off the lizards on the wall, who set up a kind of dry rattling laugh that sounded extraordinarily like the laughter of old men. Ho-ho-ho laughed the Donatory, ha-ha-ha went the geriatric lizards, and soon this racket seized hold of the children on the window ledge too, who chimed in hi-hi-hi with their high-pitched giggles, although they had no more idea than the lizards what they were laughing about. The situation struck me as so absurd that I found my own sense of humour and joined in the laughter. It was in these circumstances that I took up my duties as tutor to an indeterminate and probably indeterminable number of Pedro Joao Pilar 's children, enough at least to fill a barn, on the plantation he had carved out of the forest in the backlands of Boa Vista.

The Big House

Having succeeded Maria Conceicao as the Donatory's wife and given him five daughters, Sofia Maria da Costa Pilar was herself succeeded by his mistress, a Negro woman who bore him seven children and came to be established in the house as if she were his lawful wife. These children alone made up a respectable class for the tutor. When they were joined by a dozen other mulatto and mestizo children who seemed, like the twins Duarte Joao and Duarte Carvalho, to be accounted for more in terms of a loosely self-generating plantation family than as the offspring of particular parents, then they constituted a school which would have done credit to a small town. During the day I absolved my duties as school-master in a vacated granary visited erratically by children, poultry, pigs, frogs and occasionally snakes in pursuit of them. In the afternoon or early evening I was sometimes required to read to Sofia Maria da Costa Pilar in a suite at the end of the house, where she had retired years ago rather than do battle with a slave woman for supremacy in the Donatory's house.

Sofia Maria's body, swelling up like a pear-shaped balloon, filled the solitude she had made for herself. I was involuntarily reminded of what Father Eugenio had said about the self during spiritual exercises in the seminary. It grew and grew and filled out one's cell until there was no escape from it. From whatever angle one looked one was looking back at oneself. The flesh poured down from her shoulders and reached the floor in a cascade formed by enormous white legs, visible through the transparent gown draped like a lampshade over her naked body. She was white with the self-illuminating whiteness of some flaccid deep-sea creature that had never seen the sun. In this extreme state of obesity Sofia Maria had lost her sex. Her breasts were indistinguishable from the tumultuous flesh that rolled down on all sides of the mountain of her body. A Negro stood behind her palisander throne and fanned her with a palm. Wisps of hair at the nape of her neck stirred in this flurry of air with a surprising delicacy of motion.

At our first meeting she informed me she was a cane brake. I thought she might be losing her mind, but I asked her politely what she meant. She said she represented nothing but her dowry, which was a cane brake the Donatory had wanted. Otherwise he would not have married her, and she would not be sitting in his house in this state, a generation machine that had gone wrong and turned into a mountain from eating too much cake. Only with a body as huge as hers did one appreciate the extent of human loneliness, she said. Only the flatness surrounding it defined the mountain. I considered these unusual thoughts for a woman who had been sitting immobile for years in a shuttered room, ignored by the other inmates of the big house in the backlands where nobody thought much about anything beyond the business of the estate, and few people had ever even seen a book.

In the sweltering darkness of the fat woman's room I read histories and romances to her that had been shipped from Lisbon, since for a long time, such was the state of culture in the colonies, there was not a single printer in the whole of Brazil. While one Negro fanned Sofia Maria and the other massaged her feet, I read to her from works that appealed to her romantic sentiments, frequently interrupted by sighs of pleasure so liquid and warm that I found the sound of them disturbing. When the reading came to an end she had her chair carried over and set down by the window, her pet monkey on her shoulder, stroking her hair, and pulled a cord to tilt the shutters so that she could look down into the courtyard below, the market place of the Big House where its inmates came to pass the time of day with gossip, music and dance. Sofia Maria spent most of her waking hours at the window, like a preying deep-sea creature, a sad huntress watching and listening in darkness, her senses attuned to everything that went swimming by outside in the always brilliant flood of daylight.

I became a part of this household, not quite a servant, since I was not black but white, but above all I was a man, to be kept separate from the white women who lived in the Big House. Whenever any mature male entered the house, the Donatory excepted, a servant rang a bell and one would usually hear a rustling of skirts as the female members of the household, even ancient aunts of the Donatory who were still spinsters or sisters who were already widows, hurried away to their rooms. The fact that I was permitted to read to Sofia Maria in her private quarters was an indication of the disregard for his wife. At the cost of her gargantuan fatness and her exclusion from society Sofia Pilar had gained a freedom given to no other woman in the Donatory's house.

In the middle of the courtyard the Donatory laid out a garden with a fountain at the centre, surrounded by flowering bushes, to serve as a retreat for the women of the house when male visitors arrived. The Moorish custom of secluding women, brought over from the old country by Pedro Pilar, was preserved by his grandson Pedro Joao less for moral or religious reasons than because of that jealous possessiveness inscribed in the Donatory's own sensuous nature. The rules to which he submitted the five daughters borne him by Sofia Maria derived from the rapacity of his own imagination. It was a long time before I glimpsed more than a rear view of the three elder girls who already, at twelve or thirteen, were approaching a marriageable age. The younger ones were allowed to attend classes in the granary along with their half-brothers and sisters. These were white girls with all the inherited whiteness of skin of their mother, that monster of flesh, whom they went to visit in her self-inflicted seclusion not more than a dozen times a year.

With the Donatory's black mistress matters were different. She was a slave and her body was public knowledge. She had been possessed by other slaves in the Big House. Esme was a tall, strong Negress born on the plantation, whose parents had been shipped from the Ivory Coast and bought by Pedro Joao at the Vallongo slave market in Boa Vista. She was still a girl when she gave birth to her first child by another black slave, followed the Indian woman into the jungle and took the infant left under the bed of leaves back to her hut, where she raised it with her own child. Sofia Maria told me that the Donatory brought Esme into the big house as wet-nurse for his sons by Maria Conceicao after the Indian woman had gone and before Sofia Maria arrived. He watched Esme take his sons Duarte Joao and Duarte Carvalho to her upstanding breasts and suckle them as her own, a strong, healthy young woman whose black skin with its dark reddish tinge reminded the Donatory favourably of the best farming land in the colony. When Sofia Maria took up residence in the Big House as the Donatory's official bride she found a half-naked slave girl in the kitchen, giving the breast to Pedro Joao's children by an Indian woman and already assuming proprietorial airs from which Sofia Maria at once guessed the nature of the girl's relationship with her husband.

Esme was brought to confinement, if that word applied to the animal parturition of slave women, always a little ahead of the Donatory's upstairs wife. Within ear-shot of the resplendent bed in which Sofia Maria, to her chagrin, was making nothing better than girl children, she successively gave birth to three sons. Latterly the Negress had produced daughters, too, but it was not for these mulattos that their father created the green partition in the house courtyard. It was for the white girls, given to him, as a curse is given, by his embittered wife. From his own experience the Donatory saw them threatened above all by the men closest to them, the male relatives around the house, in particular by their black half-brothers with whom at a precocious age they were already as familiar as animals. It was his own son Duarte Carvalho who first tried to meddle with one of Sofia Maria's girls. The Donatory gave him such a thrashing that the boy had to keep to his bed for a week.

The consequences of that thoughtless promiscuity with which Pedro Joao had sown his wild oats, driving the Indian and black women like a herd of mares before him, bodied visibly forth before his eyes with every year he watched his daughters approaching sexual maturity. Spying at her window, Sofia Maria saw and heard with malicious pleasure the ramifications of Pedro Joao's horror of this plague of incest he had brought on his house. The greening of the courtyard for the seclusion of his daughters whenever they went outside was echoed in the sound of hammering she subsequently heard inside the house. After Duarte Carvalho was caught climbing through a window into the room of Sofia Maria's eldest daughter, Clara, the Donatory installed all five of them in rooms adjoining his own. Masons bricked up the windows facing outside and fitted bars to those facing in. In these suffocating cages the little girls restless for lack of activity grew up into young women who spent nights with sad-eyed monkeys as their bedfellows, worn sleepless by their over-heated imaginations.

As tutor to the Donatory's children I was given my own servant, and it was taken for granted that I would have recourse to the black women for my sexual needs as and when I pleased. When I arrived at the Big House it had already acquired that hybrid atmosphere of tropical luxuriousness and Moorish reticence, reflecting the relationships between men and women, owners and slaves, which was coming to define the culture of the colony. Just as Pilar women in the fourth and fifth generation continued to put coconut oil on their hair, following a custom brought into the family by a long-forgotten Indian ancestor, so they learned subservience and propriety because the Donatory who founded the dynasty had formed women in the reverse image of himself. Murder, rape and pillage, the daily violence the Donatory had grown up with, remained shelved in the back of his mind during his latter years when napkins were changed in the middle of meals, glazed tiling adorned the bath-house and the only sound intruding on his siesta were the waterspouts and the fountains disgorging into the pools in his garden. Buried beneath this elegance there remained a residue of savagery in the Donatory's heart. As he grew older he became a philanderer in slippers and a silk gown, plundering his own household as earlier he had made free with whatever the surrounding country had to offer.

With less and less to do to subject a refractory land and people to his will, his residual energies were latterly absorbed by the conquest of those pubescent mulatto girls who could still sometimes coax out of him a dribble of patriarchal seed. If these objects of his lust were daughters he had sired on plantation slaves, he did not know, because he did not ask. The uninhibited sexuality he expected of black slave women was complemented by free white women indentured as the slaves of chastity. In either case he had dominion over their bodies, if by different title deeds.

This ambiguity ruled the big house. At one end of it was the chapel with the martyrdom of white-faced saints illustrated in chequered panes of glass, at the other end the quarters for the in-house slaves where the Donatory's sons, and sometimes their tutor too, were obliged by black girls who might not find it worth the trouble to close the door. In the dining hall located between slave quarters and chapel the ambiguity surfaced on the long table where the Donatory's extended family took their meals, looking out onto the courtyard with its green island of seclusion. The white daughters who emerged from those thickets as soon as male visitors were out of sight would then retire to the kitchen to busy themselves with forming and trimming sweetmeats in phallic shapes. While the cooks were expected to remain out of sight, the indecent proposals they had baked could safely be set before the guests by a smiling black servant girl with the compliments of the ladies of the house.

As the trees in the park around the house grew taller, concealing the mill house, the refinery, the distillery and the quarters of the plantation slaves beyond, losing the view of the cane fields stretching to the horizon, life in the Big House began also to lose sight of the foundations on which it depended. Silver, snuff, wine, muslin, clothes and furnishings of an extraordinary richness were poured out of a horn of plenty that replenished itself without the inhabitants of the house having to lift a finger. There was peace in the Big House so long as plantation and house were kept apart. When incidents beyond the Donatory's control broke that truce, as happened when the eldest of his five white daughters, the same Clara whom Duarte Carvalho had tried to seduce, became pregnant and gave birth to a black child, the Donatory regressed into a barbarism I had deceived myself into thinking belonged to a past age.

The shame which his daughter had brought on the house was felt by Pedro Joao to be so great that he considered confinement in a nunnery in Boa Vista to be not punishment enough. With his own hands the Donatory drowned the child and banished the mother to life-long exile in Salvador where the Pilar family was unknown. The name of the culprit who had made the girl pregnant was extorted by Pedro Joao with a false promise to spare the child if she told him. The child's father was a mulatto, the son of one of the plantations slaves by a white man who was the Donatory's overseer. The young man's intimate relations with Pedro Joao's daughter had been going on under his master's nose. With the con-nivance of her sisters the girl had smuggled her lover in and out of the house in a laundry sack. The Donatory had the mulatto chained and con-fined in the cellar of the boiling-house while he considered what to do with him.

It was the end of the sugar season. The slaves on the plantation had begun to cut the came. Preparations were made for setting the mill to work and a priest came to bless it, a ceremony that was performed every year before grinding the cane began. The Donatory, the mill manager, the priest and a handful of spectators including myself stood around the works. Some Negroes, whose task it was to feed the mill with cane, waited in case they were needed. Two lighted candles were placed on the plat-form supporting the cane beside the rollers. A statue of our Saviour on the cross stood between them. The priest took his breviary and read several prayers before dipping a small bunch of weeds he had brought with him into a jug of consecrated water, with which he sprinkled the mill and the persons present. The Negroes sprang forward to receive as much of this holy water as possible, rubbing it over their bodies. A piece of cane was handed to the priest and the Donatory. At a signal from the mill manager the flood-gate was opened. Water rushed in and set the huge stone rollers in motion. The cane thrust by the priest between the rollers was the first to be ground, followed by the piece which the plantation owner fed into the mill. When the ceremony was over the priest was escorted to the big house where he was to spend the night before returning to Boa Vista.

No sooner had the priest gone than the young mulatto was hauled in from the sugar boiling-house, matted like a dog dragged out of a kennel, rank with the sweat of fear of a man who knew he was about to die. He was followed by the sons of the Donatory, all male members of his household, black or white and whatever their position, including the overseer whose unfortunate son had done the terrible deed. One by one they kissed the Donatory's hand and touched the blade of the knife he held out to them to show that it had been blunted. The mulatto was seized and thrown to the ground. Six men held him pinned down. Pedro Joao kneeled in front of the naked man spread-eagled before him. The mill house manager stood at the mulatto's head, holding up a lamp to illuminate the scene. The crowd of sweating onlookers moved with a murmur out of the shadows, jostling to make room, peering down into the pool of light. Pedro Joao leaned swiftly forward, seized the man's testicles and hacked them out of his scrotum. The mulatto's face contorted, sweat ran off his body in rivulets, but the whole mill house was shaking from the vibration of the rollers and he made no audible sound. The men picked him up and carried him feet first to the platform with the cane that was waiting to be fed into the mill. For an instant the mulatto must have seen the mill stones revolving in front of him. He must have understood what was about to happen. When he opened his mouth to scream his feet had already been caught by the rollers, but whatever cry came out of him before the rest of his body passed under them was drowned in the thunder of a mercifully never-ending motion.

Rites Of Passage

A stream of magic and maternal tenderness flowed to Duarte Joao and Duarte Carvalho from the black woman who became their mother after Maria Conceicao had gone. She raised them with imprecations chanted over them when they were asleep, reinforced with the spit of her mouth she rubbed into their skin. The younger of the twins, the child she had found and reared as her own, turned away from the nipple when he was a few months old, as if he was impatient to be weaned and have his fortune told. Bem, the Mandingo Negro who placed the snake around the basket to guard the child in Esme's absence, brought her a knife when the boy was weaned. He told her to smear milk from her breast onto the blade, plunge it up to the hilt into a banana tree and leave the knife there until the following day. Esme did as the Mandingo Negro had said and brought him the knife so that Bem could read Duarte Carvalho's fortune by the sap stains left on the blade. Bem said Carvalho would live violently and die young at a parting of ways. She waited five years until his elder brother was weaned. Even before Bem had pieced together the stains of his destiny on the blade she knew from the way he went into a kind of mourning when she could no longer gave him the breast that because he would never be able to love the white woman as he did the black Duarte Joao would not lead a happy life, even if it should be his fate to die in his own bed in old age.

When Duarte Joao still sucked at Esme's breast his brother stood in a clearing in the jungle with snakes wrapped around his body. Bem knew how to call the reptiles from their holes with peculiar noises or tunes. He could make a person who submitted to his charms and ceremonies immune to snake bites. On feast days the Pilar slaves left the plantation and walked all night to Boa Vista, making music with calabash guitars and drums and carrying their canopies with the animals that were their totems, eagles, peacocks, elephants and rams carved on the sides of a wooden box. The mandingueiro headed the torch-light procession with his great dog pacing magnificently like a lion beside him. Duarte Carvalho hid inside the Negroes' totem box and smuggled himself to the carnival at Boa Vista with the intention of running away. Bem brought the boy home, but not before he had seen enough of carnivals and the bandeiras who frequented them, carefree, colourful, lethal men with slouched hats, black moustaches, spurs on their naked heels and long guns on their saddles sticking out from under their ponchos, to have discovered the life that suited him and which he would one day make his own.

Everything tractable, gentle, winning in a child's ways had been poured into the vessel that was Duarte Joao's destiny. In the granary schoolroom he was my best pupil, although I had more sympathy for his brother, Duarte Carvalho. At birth he had been left behind in the forest and there he stayed, his face averted from the people around him, looking and listening somewhere else. He belonged in that Indian world where individuals remained submerged in a tribal consciousness of their place in an order of things known as All-Creatures-Being-In-The-Forest. The younger of the Pilar twins night have been a full-blood Indian, the elder not an Indian at all. While the one looked back into the forest of the mind from which his instincts were hardly removed, the other looked ahead, anticipating the habits of mind of a later, more civilised generation. The murder of the mulatto their father forced them to witness in the mill house had no more effect on Duarte Carvalho than if it was a horse being castrated, while on Duarte Joao it left a lasting impression.

The Donatory observed the tender feelings of his son and saw them as a weakness. Nor did he approve of the bookishness that began to grow on the boy after I took up my duties in the Big House. He took the boy out of school and apprenticed him to the manager to learn the planter's business. Duarte Joao disappeared from the idle round of life in the Big House. He was either working long hours on the estate in accordance with his father's plan of study or asleep upstairs, too exhausted to do anything else when he got home. This was just as Pedro Joao intended. He had no objection to his son's keeping as many black mistresses as he liked. But when Duarte Joao had become so infatuated with a slave girl that he would no longer even look at a white woman the Donatory felt uneasy. His son was too like himself. Sensuousness was a Pilar legacy they shared.

The girl's name was Marta and she was a niece of Esme's. Esme brought her in from the plantation to partake of the easier life in the big house. Marta was older than Duarte Joao, a fully mature girl he fell in love with the day she arrived in the house and he saw her washing under the pump beneath his window. She had a high, small waist and slim buttocks, high breasts that turned and pointed out, blue-black skin with a muted sheen that fascinated Duarte Joao. He stood at the door of his room, no more than a boy and his heart already full of desire, to watch her slender vase-like figure move gracefully down the passage, the white linen on her arm cutting her black skin like bandages, the pitcher balanced on her head with a slight swaying that reflected the oscillation of her hips. During the long afternoons when the house took its siesta Marta filled the hours of lassitude with stories of scandalous love, elopement, furious pursuits. The Pilar girls sat Moorish fashion on a pipri mat in the garden, sewing or embroidering lace-work, while Duarte Joao lay in a hammock. Marta snapped her fingernails through his hair, searching for lice, or keeping the flies away from his face with a fan. The black girl became as familiar with Duarte Joao as his white half-sisters. She was like a sister to him herself; a sister he was permitted to desire.

When the Donatory was absent in Boa Vista one afternoon and Duarte Joao lay asleep in the cot in the kitchen outhouse where Esme took her siesta she called her cousin to her. She washed Marta, rubbed nightingale droppings into her cheeks, an extract of musk and aloes into her throat, breasts and thighs, and sent the girl to the cot in the outhouse. This scented presence filtered into the sleeper's dream, a mixture of Esme's violent perfume with Marta's own *budum*, odour, which slid unawares into his imagination and took the shape of Marta's flat belly, pointed breasts, black eyes as round as moons, looking down at him in the cot when the boy woke up, aroused, ejaculating the instant he opened his eyes.

When Duarte Joao became a young man I rode with him and his father to the plantation of his neighbour, Enrique de Loyola Diaz. The landowner had two marriageable daughters on offer to the Donatory. Duarte Joao saw neither of the candidates because he kept his eyes firmly fixed on the floor as the girls were paraded by the mother through the room. His father whipped him for the insult to the Diaz family and chose him the uglier of the two sisters as punishment for the insult to himself. Magdalena Diaz was a pale, anaemic girl, too burdened with the hereditary melancholy of the Diaz to be anything but indifferent about her fate. The Donatory haggled with her father over the dowry, shook hands with him when the business was settled and rode home with his son. A week later a formal procession set out from the Diaz estate, the bride in white in its midst, her train held aloft by riders on two white mules behind her. The pale-faced martyrs stared down from the windows of the chapel in the big house where she was married to Duarte Joao and took the name Magdalena Diaz Pilar.

Celebrations went on a week. The house became sullen and rebellious under the festivities the Donatory enforced against the wishes of a bridegroom loved by everyone but his wife. The portrait of Francesca Carvalho Pilar, icon of the family, crashed down from the wall in the middle of a banquet. Plates slid over the edge of the dining-table and shattered on the floor. There were rumours of locks on linen chests jamming, refusing to yield up the sheets the servants needed to prepare the marriage bed. Whatever the Donatory picked up slipped from his hands. A stroke had partly paralysed him. Esme stood at the table to feed him. He raged, he was helpless. A curse had been put on his house. Sofia Maria, increasingly short of breath, too fat even to laugh, grinned back out of the gloom when they brought her the news upstairs.

A truce followed between father and son. The real power over the Pilar estate, still wielded in the Donatory's name, now lay in Esme's hands.

Behind her waited the mandingueiro Bem with his giant dog, his talismans and snake-charming incantations. It was Bem who instructed her in the preparation of an aphrodisiac made from coffee, strained through the lower half of a night-gown in which a woman had slept, and mixed with the woman's saliva, sweat and menstrual mucus. Esme selected young mulatto females for this purpose, whom she sent to the Donatory's hammock after he had been given the aphrodisiac to drink and felt his forgotten sexual powers begin to stir. She manipulated the old man's desire, kindled it, fed it, let it die out. Pedro Joao became entirely dependent on her for the remaining pleasures of his life. Africa entered the old man's stomach and pumped with the blood in his veins. In this fusion that nourished the colonial enterprise in Brazil the Pilar masters relinquished a part of their Portuguese heritage and took on the customs of their slaves.

The son of the Indian woman whom Esme had reared and considered her own she kept in the same bondage as his father. She coaxed the reluctant husband into his wife's bedroom by giving him undergarments Marta had worn, saturated with that *budum*, the violent perfume compounded of musk and aloes and the black woman's sweat, which was pungent enough to smother his antipathy for Magdalena Diaz and to arouse a passing sexual interest in his wife. In the aftermath of a passion he displayed for her but felt for another woman she experienced the attentions of her husband for the first time. He came and entered her, urgently and at unexpected hours. Magdalena understood this to be a man's sexual nature, his surrender to an uncontrollable passion the sight of her body awoke in him. She never saw him take the garment from his pocket, how he stood with his face buried in it, breathing in its odours, before he opened the door to her room. Only Sofia Maria saw, who saw everything that happened in the big house. Hurriedly Duarte Joao came and entered and went out, leaving whatever it was that made Magdalena's body swell up. The pregnant girl made her way to the far wing of the house, gliding into the dark room she had first visited in the loneliness of her arrival in a strange house, when the vast woman whom the family shunned had seemed her only ally. For Sofia Maria the little white girl was the reincarnation of herself, the bride who had arrived in the house a generation ago, was neglected and brought summarily to bed to breed white children before being rejected in favour of a black concubine. Here was the instrument of her revenge. The spider woman sitting hunched in the gloom befriended the girl, drawing her into the web she had begun to spin from the day Magdalena entered the house.

Sofia Maria saw with displeasure how Duarte Joao blossomed in the space his latterly much depleted father left, how music other than the sound of the one-string calabash guitar accompanied by African drums came into the house, how books, humanity, the progressive ideas of Europe, flooded the plantation in the backlands. The colony saw its first paved road built by Duarte Joao across Pilar land before he was twenty years old. When the coastal springs supplying Boa Vista were infiltrated by the sea and the town's drinking water turned brackish, the future of the entire colony was at stake. Duarte Joao had freshwater pumped from the inland wells he sank and channelled to Boa Vista in an aqueduct designed and constructed at his own expense. What the citizens regarded almost as a feat of magic was a still working memory for myself, a successor to the stone cisterns and paved conduits of Tumbez, the miles of irrigated mountains in the ghostly kingdom, as it now seemed to me, of Tahuantin-Suyu.

I looked back across more than two hundred years since Dom Pedro Felipe and his companions had arrived in Tumbez on the Sleeping Sea and come under the spell of the Incas, the decay of our bodies arrested, adding to our lives the years we took from theirs as they succumbed to the accelerating time sickness. For every ten years the world around me aged, I had aged by one. My life was like a dreaming, my soul passing out of my mouth to experience the world while my body lay still and refreshed itself with sleep. To Duarte Joao I was an even greater magician than Bem. I had flown on the niopo cloud and ridden on the great river's back from the Pacific to the Atlantic Ocean. These were the stories from the Elsewhere which I had told Duarte Joao as a child, the pictures I had drawn for him, just as I had once drawn them for my Taiassu tribesmen. The artefacts my pupil built through the jungle was the way he reinvented them, the son of an outlandish planter and an Indian woman growing up in the backlands, dreaming again the dreams of the past and scattering a brightness that illuminated everything around him.

The Fox

Since entering the seminary and talking to Father Eugenio I had become aware of my Self, and with this awareness I came to know a solitude I had never known before. I found myself at an extreme remove from the sense of wholeness with my surroundings that had been expressed by All-Creatures-Being-In-The-Forest. I had become part of the Donatory's feudal estate, so fixed in my habits that I continued to live on there long after my duties as tutor had come to an end. For years I had lived as a parasite on the Big House, growing fat and lazy, an addict to all its pleasures, succumbing to all its temptations, in body and mind. I took to wearing a bed-gown all day, and once a Brazilian took to wearing a bed-gown he considered himself a complete gentleman. I had become slovenly in my habits; worse, I had a better opinion of myself for all that.

Latterly I came from Sofia Maria's darkened room, where I read romances to the fat lady with murder in her heart, and walked in the twilight of the garden, drawn to the darker places under the trees from which I watched the lights of the Big House. I saw the inmates strolling up and down the terrace, sitting, talking, trapped in the view of the world they were given from their body and which for ever separated them from each other. Even on evenings when the heat stood like the walls of some invisible maze from which one could never break out, those darker places under the trees made me shiver from an impending sense of my own dissolution. I began to hear only discontinuously now the always running water of the fountain. The sounds that used to fill the courtyard with a sense of unflagging life came to be perforated by holes of silence. Flow, the flow of things altogether, ceased. Day was shut off from night, night from day, with no sense of succession. The glorious unconscious fusing of the world disintegrated. I declined by slow degrees into illness before I fell almost as deep as death.

The collapse I suffered in this illness brought home to my own body the collapse of the colonial life that was disintegrating around me, an illness that only a fever could sweat out of the infected body. For a long time I was confined to my room in a state of feverish delirium shot through with nightmares. After vanity, as Father Eugenio had warned, came terror. From whatever angle I tried to look at the room I always ended up looking back at myself. I saw my Self becoming bloated like Sofia Maria, a monster of flesh. I understood this to be only the outward expression of a deformity of the soul, inflating like a balloon until it had filled out the room and there would be no escape from it. It loomed over me until I turned round to confront it. The face I was looking at was Sister Esperanca's. She was wearing a gown of a soaring azure blue almost painful to look at. The braid of hair hanging quietly down her back showed she was in a tractable mood. Serenely she said: if what you seek is love, you will find it anywhere. The walls of the house of Misericordia are only an allegory of the inaccessibility of woman.

I awoke from this feverish dream purged of the sense of loss that had come with the discovery of my solitude. I understood the dream as a sign that my life should change. Once again I could hear water running in an unceasing flow. The scent of the blossom filling my room was informed with the colour of the courtyard tree that was out of sight. I went in search of the Donatory and found him knee-deep among apples in the still. Cobwebs trailed like streamers from the rim of his hat, undulating silkily in the slanting morning light.

In all the time I had been employed at the Big House, I said to the Donatory, I had not left the plantation. I hoped I had fulfilled my duties to his satisfaction. Now I asked him for leave of absence indefinitely, so that I could attend to some business in Boa Vista that might take a little while to complete. Pedro Joao bit into an apple, and without even turning he waved me away with a greasy hand. I returned to my room to collect the quipu that lay rolled up in a chest of drawers there, for it had become something of a talisman, a genealogy of my previous incarnations, accompanying me wherever I went. There was no trace of the quipu, however, and I could not recall where I had last had it.

The sky had been darkening as I went. On an open stretch of road lacking any shelter the storm blew up and a terrific downpour set in. I came to a bridgeless river that was deep and rapid. The way was obstructed by teams of oxen pulling carts laden with planks of jacaranda wood. A young senhora was in charge of the leading team. Wearing a flesh-coloured pelisse and a broad white beaver hat banded with black crepe, she sat calmly astride one of the planks on the cart, managing the unwieldy team of oxen with great dexterity. Within minutes the river became a swollen torrent. The woman in the hat pulled her team on one side and urged the others down to the river. In the middle, where the current was strongest and the carts almost submerged, the oxen stood up to their necks with only their heads showing above the water. The drivers of the teams had all they could do to just to prevent their carts being pulled under by the current. With the tip of her long whip the senhora flicked the animals' heads, the drivers lent their shouts, and so the oxen were guided through the swirling river.

She called to me to hitch a rope to the tail-end of the team when she went through the river herself. Otherwise horse and rider would have been swept away. As I came up to thank the senhora a bolt of lightning glanced off the river with a tremendous crash. The mare reared, depositing me judiciously in the mud, and galloped off. Looking ruefully up at the senhora, I saw a row of strong teeth fill out a broad white smile under the beaver hat. Climb aboard, she said, giving me a hand and pulling me up beside her.

She asked where I was headed. To Boa Vista, I said. She frowned: that was still quite a journey. There were half a dozen rivers to cross. In this weather the road would be impassable. The rain was doing its level best to drown the senhora's face. A small, shapely but dangerously low-lying nose, swimming bravely in the cataracts pouring down between hat and collar, the tip of it still just showing, seemed doomed to go under shortly. We passed along a mill stream and drove up to a house. Between the trees at the end of a winding track I glimpsed already lighted windows, although it was still early in the afternoon.

Rain pouring from her shoulders, her clothes spattered with mud, the senhora climbed up on top of the jacaranda planks and shouted orders. The drivers lifted the planks off the carts, unhitched the teams and led the oxen through a barn to some outhouses beyond. When she was satisfied that everything had been done as she wanted the senhora went with me into the house. She stood in the hall, shouting as she kicked off her boots. The water was still pouring off her clothes, forming a little lake where she stood. Servants came running from the interior of the house. As she took off her hat and shook out a long braid of hair that had been coiled round her head the senhora gave instructions to prepare dinner and light a fire, to air the bed linen, to show me upstairs and bring me hot water, towels, a change of clothes, wringing out her soaking hair as she talked and flicking the water vigorously from her fingers with an air of still unspent energy, as if she would have been happy for a dozen other things to settle at the same time. All of this struck me as curiously familiar, although I could not have said why. Now that the arrangements had been made, and a refusal became impossible, the senhora turned to me with an invitation to have supper and spend the night at her house, since there was no question of reaching Boa Vista today.

A Negro showed me upstairs into an apartment where servants saw to all my needs. I questioned them about the senhora and learned that Senhora de Souza was a widow whose husband had died soon after she married him, leaving her with two daughters and twenty-four slaves in this plantation house in the backlands. Six black females dressed in white knelt on silk cushions and served me dinner in my apartment as if I had been a prince. When I had eaten, the Negresses made an elaborate show of preparing the enormous palisander bed where I was to sleep that night. Then they withdrew and the house became still. I sat in a chair at the window, looking out into the softly dripping night, became drowsy and fell asleep.

When I awoke I heard a rattling, flailing sound I could not place. There was a curious illumination in the dark. Crumpled beams of light, in which pale-bodied moths the size of bats flitted to and fro, lit up the window outside. I got up and saw the barn below ablaze with lamps. People were threshing millet, beating it so vigorously with poles that the seeds flew about the place with great force. They rebounded off a matted wall and were collected in a heap below. While I stood at the window watching this scene I felt a warm draught glide along my bare arms, as if the moist standing air were being fanned by the huge moths' wings. I could feel the heat of the senhora's body before I turned and saw her standing behind me. Her head was tilted back in a mass of unbraided hair. Her slanting eyes in the shadows were no wider than slits. The light from the barn glanced off the row of white teeth. For a moment it seemed I was looking at the head of a fox on a woman's body. Then her eyes opened wide, the fox-like reverted to a human face.

Imagine, she said. Her hand rested on my shoulder. Someone went out in that storm to catch your white mare and left her tied up at the stable door.

Who can that have been? Who can that have been, I echoed, already feeling her hand in mine, drawing me away from the window. When the senhora undressed me and I heard the garments rustle as they dropped onto the floor I realised that they must have belonged to her husband. I stood naked as her hands moved over my body. I felt whirring creatures brush against my skin in the dark, moths caught in my hair, struggling to get free. The senhora lay on a luminous shimmer of triangular white sheet from which the coverlet had been drawn back, her head and legs cut off by shadow, her breasts and belly alone lit up and somewhat elevated from the dark, like a torso obscenely presented on an anatomising table. When I lay down on her I put out this light. I could hear the threshers pounding away in the barn below as distinctly as if they were with us in the room. The moment I lay down on her a flood rose out of the senhora like a spring divined in a rock, floating me on an outpouring that had been withheld inside her body. The cries she uttered flew all night long around the room, rebounding like threshed grain from a matted wall and collecting in a heap that spread out until it covered the floor, turning white with the dawn, gold with the first shaft of sunlight that came splashing through the window.

There was no sight of the senhora when I awoke. I lay alone on a white bed drenched with blood. I could find no marks on my skin. Perhaps it was she who had bled. I thought of the blood-sucking bats that used to drop from the rafters of the malocca during the night to feed on exposed flesh, and wondered if it was bats, not moths, I had seen in the beams of light. I rang a bell. The Negro appeared who had shown me up the previous night. I called for my clothes and asked for the senhora. He said his mistress and her two daughters had set out early for Boa Vista. I wondered why, but the senhora had left no other message. I dressed and went outside. The white mare was waiting for me, as the senhora had said, hitched up at the entrance, turning her head and looking away with an injured air when I stepped out of the house. Who had brought the mare back? Why had they wanted no thanks? I heard again the voice I had heard when Esperanca, appeared to me in a dream: if what you seek is love, you will find it anywhere. Looking back at the house of Senhora de Souza with a vague sense of unease as I remembered why I had set out on this journey, I walked the mare down the track to the turning on the road. At which junction I met Porphyry.

Teatro do Mundo

I heard bells tinkling in the hills before the vanguard of the procession they heralded came into sight, half a dozen outriders, extremely fierce-looking, albeit in antique costumes and carrying lances with bells strapped on them like bracelets from shaft to tip, which somewhat modified the impression of ferocity. Their mounts were a chestnut colour from the saddle up. From the stirrups down they were powdered white with the dust from the road. Seen against the white cliffs of the pass from which the outriders emerged, they appeared to be astride legless horses accompanied by a disembodied clatter of hooves.

A team of ox wagons and carts rumbled in their wake, loaded with the inventory of what seemed to be a travelling circus. There were caged animals of a kind I had never seen before, followed by wagon loads of Indians whom I had. I identified the cave-dwelling Otomi, who covered their bodies with a phosphorus substance to make them shine in the dark, and the lake-dwelling Uros, a tribe that lived more in the water than on land and in their darting movements resembled fish rather than men. These living Indians were followed by cartloads of their dead — dried corpses shrunk to one third of their size, dwarfish horrors with blackened eye-sockets, staring out at the landscape through which they passed. Behind them trundled carts stacked with huge rolls of canvas, some of them spilled open, showing scenes of erupting volcanoes, battles, disasters at sea and on land, crowds of people dead, maimed or fleeing in terror. Mules laden with household utensils were hitched to these carts and accompanied by perhaps a hundred men, women and children on foot, dressed in all kinds of attire. It was as if I was seeing Dom Pedro and his surviving companions come down at last from the mountains by the Sleeping Sea.

This procession winding its way down through the hills was brought up by huntsmen with poles and greyhounds in leashes. They escorted a curtained sedan, carried on poles between two ponies, and a long-legged gentleman, astride a white mule, whose feet hung down almost to the ground. He was a tall, thin, stately cavalleiro in a large round Spanish hat, turned up at the front, and ornamented with a plume of gaudy feathers. Although the expression on this gentleman's face was extremely grave, it was belied by the fantastic topiary of his waxed moustache. His costume was no less exuberant. He wore a short tattered cloak, large puffed breeches with a pink lining that showed through the slashes, and knee-high yellow boots equipped with enormous silver spurs. Got up in this fanciful costume and astride a mule that was much too small for such a tall man, the cavalleiro might have served very well as a frontispiece for Don Quixote.

Porphyry, he announced as I came alongside, taking off his hat and making a ceremonious bow. I asked if I might have the pleasure of his company on the road to Boa Vista. He inclined his head graciously and requested the honour of presenting me to his wife. Reaching for the curtain of the sedan chair he whisked it aside, disclosing a wrinkled old crone sitting inside. Porphyry shrugged and pulled the curtain back. Putting his hand in his pocket, he took out a snake, which he threw up into the air. The snake disappeared and turned into a stick. Are you there, wife, he called, rapping the sedan chair smartly three times with the stick. A hand appeared and drew the curtain. Instead of the hag I saw a young woman inside with a child asleep on her lap. Putting a finger to her lips to warn us not to wake the child, she pointed reproachfully at the stick in her husband's hand. He tossed it to her. She caught the stick and it turned into a scarf, which she slipped over her shoulders before drawing the curtain and disappearing again. My wife, he remarked thoughtfully, as if struck by a novel insight, adding with a smile: and by all accounts our son, Porphyry the IXth, although I think it wise never to judge by appearances, my dear Sir. Don't you?

A sigh escaped him, and the mule, in a queer act of animal sympathy or perhaps responding to some secret direction from its master, came to a standstill.

We looked down the valley at the dust rising in the wake of the caval-cade. His people had been touring the mining settlements in the moun-tains, Porphyry said, playing to once packed houses in gold and silver bonanza towns that had slowly slipped back out of life and withered away as ghost towns where nothing but memories rustled. They had been so long in the mountains — half his people had been born there, and as many again left buried — that it seemed as though a hundred years had passed. Porphyry spread his hands. One has to adapt, Sir, does one not? Once, so to speak, one has been charged with the task of being in this world. For who are we, dear Sir? And what are we doing here, he asked, addressing his mule. That sage animal twitched its ears and plodded off once again down the track.

We pursued his question on the road to Boa Vista. The Teatro do Mundo's outstanding public success, Porphyry said, had been the presentation of Great Catastrophes of the World, a series of tableaux initiated by Porphyry I at a time when the business was still a small family affair competing with jugglers and dancing bears in the market places of the Old World. The Old Testament alone, beginning with such evergreens as the Flood, the Plagues of Egypt, the Tower of Babel and Sodom and Gomorra, had provided a family of fifteen with a shoe-string living that had stretched from Seville to Constantinople and back. The spectacles of human misery unfolded in the dramatic tableaux conceived by Porphyry I and II had proved to be great favourites with audiences in all countries, and might have remained so, had it not been for the unfortunate intrusion of a state monopoly in the form of the Inquisition. Auto-da-fé had ruined the business, said Madame Porphyry, sticking her head out. It knocked the bottom out of the misery market, explained Porphyry, and when the flames of religious fanaticism began licking at the coat-tails of travelling people in his line of business the family removed energetically to Brazil.

Different conditions prevailed in the New World. His great-great-grandfather, said Porphyry, brought the Catastrophes of the World up to date. He presented misery much closer to home, in a grand series of tableaux depicting the Conquest of the New World. Many of Porphyry's Indians were associates of the Teatro do Mundo in the fourth generation who had learned to bring great art to death: death by impaling with the common sword or lance, death by bludgeoning, by garrotting, by drawing and quartering, by burning and burying alive. There was no way of being killed which they hadn't mastered. His grandfather reckoned that even by his time more Indians had died in the tableaux of the Teatro do Mundo, and certainly with greater emotional nobility, than had been slaughtered in real life.

Our conversation was interrupted by the difficulties of crossing the next river, which was still running unusually high after the storm the previous night. Porphyry drenched his plumage in an ill-considered dismounting manoeuvre. Sitting bedraggled on the white mule, the feathers in his hat wilted, his soaked shoes drooping like bananas, the cavalleiro presented a ridiculous sight, redeemed only by the unfaltering dignity with which he conducted himself. He remarked dryly that he had accumulated more experience in dealing with misfortune than any man with the exception – God rest his soul – of his father, Porphyry VIIth, who had survived his wife and eight of eleven children and drunk deep from the cup of human misery. But the Teatro had benefited from his unhappiness. In order to make a living he put his own grief on the stage.

Imagine, he said, with a wave in the direction behind us as we emerged from the hills, the desperadoes in the saloons of the mining towns in those mountains back there. Imagine them presented with a tableau showing a father mourning the deaths of his beautiful young wife and eight innocent children. Rascally children, in fact, and the wife long past her prime. But Porphyry VIIth knew his audience. His audience wanted angels. He gave them angels. The bodies of the children were painted with carmine and buried in shirt boxes just as they had been in real life. Porphyry VIIth, in the rags worn by miners, wept real tears over them. They had departed to join our Lord, insatiable in His recruitment of angels, and as angels they were resurrected in heaven in the final scene – presto! – emerging from sky-blue caskets with matching silk gowns and silver wings, waving to their father as they were cranked out of sight on wires. Imagine the effect of this at the end of an evening that had seen the Explosion of Etna and Destruction of Pompeii, the Strangulation of Atahualpa, the Sack of Cuzco. Rivers of tears. Tumultuous applause. Voluntary contributions to stage funeral costs from men in the habit of burying their own dead by throwing them over a cliff.

I couldn't help smiling, and Porphyry exclaimed: Yes! My dear Sir, you smile. But you only succeed in this business when you move people, and it is a fact of human nature that people are most readily moved when it is not at their own expense; when it is not the misery of their own reality they suffer, but an illusion of misery, suffered by someone else on their behalf. That, Sir, is who we are, and that is our business here.

The outriders whooped as they galloped across the coastal plain. All their journeys there remained silent in the mountains they had left behind them. It seemed to me that I watched them come riding out of Great White Bird's dream. I saw them standing on the shore, gazing for the first time at an ocean they had never seen and whose existence had remained unknown to Guaratinga-acu in his waking life, and I imagined my Taiassu father had been waiting for their arrival so that his dream could pass up out of the shadow world, and become truth.

The Founding of Boa Vista

Boa Vista welcomed Porphyry and his Teatro as it welcomed any diversion from the tedium of its citizens' lives. In the no-man's-land between the houses of the slippered and the unslippered Carmelites, which had remained unbuilt on in order to preserve the truce between the two establishments, the wagons rolled to a halt, the bales of painted scenery were unpacked, slow fires were lit to produce a pall of smoke and within hours a sizeable area of the town began to resemble Lisbon in ruins after its destruction by the recent earthquake. Within this scenery of devastation, underscored by interminable wailing provided by Indians screeching behind the painted flats, the players of Teatro do Mundo strewed the ground with masonry, blood and severed limbs, and sent out their ragged children with begging-bowls to implore passers-by for alms.

A prosperous, easy-going, good-natured band of citizens, the Boa Vistans came along out of curiosity and stayed out of horror, appalled by the proximity of this disaster which until now had kept a safe distance on the far side of the ocean. The Jesuits saw through what they regarded as Porphyry's cynicism. The French dancing master, M. Bez, applauded the grandeur of the *spectacle* as a work of art. But the townspeople as a whole were overwhelmed by the realism of the tableau of Lisbon in Ruins. In a rush of unconsidered sympathy they parted with large sums of money to the beggar children who ambushed them with tear-stained faces among the still smouldering ruins.

When the smoke cleared the next morning Boa Vista woke up to the disagreeable feeling that it had been hoodwinked by the greatest rascal ever to have set foot in their town. There was an unspoken agreement among its citizens that the town would have liked its money back but felt too ashamed to ask. There were angry calls for Porphyry and his players to be thrown out. Porphyry cunningly forestalled this eventuality by presenting an interlude on a hastily assembled stage in front of the Episcopal palace, where he placated the benefactors of the Relieved Citizens of Lisbon with a generous contribution to the forthcoming festivities on the inauguration of Boa Vista's new bishop.

The municipality decided to indulge the prankster, allowing itself to be amused at least until the new bishop arrived. Boa Vista was still waiting for His Excellency to arrive from the Old World. News was that he had been delayed by baptisms in the Azores, then side-tracked by urgent missionary work, converting a pagan corner of Cap Verde that had hitherto been overlooked. So long as Boa Vista was preparing to welcome the new bishop, its citizens were agreed, they would tolerate Porphyry in the role of municipal court jester on condition that the activities of his troupe were restricted to the neutral ground between the slippered and unslippered Carmelites.

The spectacle of Lisbon in Ruins was dismantled overnight, and a life-size canvas depicting an amusement arcade was substituted in its place, dedicated to Boa Vista's meritorious citizens in recognition of their services by the Teatro's appreciative players. The arcade had painted doors that opened like flaps to admit spectators to the entertainments concealed behind: jugglers and acrobats, contortionists, fortune tellers, magicians, magnetists, a Genuine Carib Feast at which anthropophagi could be viewed devouring their fellow men. Another popular attraction was Porphyry's Amazing Pantechnicon, featuring a magic lantern show of the wonders of the modern world and a grisly collection of heirlooms that had been amassed by the Porphyry' predecessors during the centuries of their extended travels.

In local opinion, the shrunken Indian corpses with blackened eye sockets exhibited in the Pantechnicon amounted to no more than unpleasant curiosities when compared with such marvels as the Turkish hermaphrodite or the headless woman from Samarkand. Boa Vista was quickly delighted with its new amusement arcade. Anticipating a longer stay in the town than was envisaged by its inhabitants, Porphyry and his troupe set about providing accommodation for their considerable numbers. The Teatro purchased an empty lot on the outskirts of the town and within a week had begun to put up makeshift buildings, which the players moved into one house at a time as soon as they were completed until a sizeable community had materialised on the edge of the forest.

Shipbuilders lacking any seafaring experience were meanwhile at work in the harbour, refitting an antique caravel which had been drawn up out of the water for careening, abandoned and forgotten. Porphyry purchased this hulk from the harbour master for a barrel of rum. The whole business was a mystery to the marine community of the town. They watched half-naked Indians, equipped with no other tools than axe, adze and hammer, restore the framework and fit the planks of a seagoing vessel of a couple of hundred tons, construct blocks and tackle to right the ship and let her down into the water with barely a splash. Where on earth those savages had learned to make ocean-going vessels, they asked, and when Porphyry told them in the shipyards fifteen hundred miles inland on the banks of the Rio Negro they thought this was another of his tall tales. Yet for generations the inland river Indians had been building ships for the journey to the sea. They never saw them sail further than the bend in the river and none of the ships ever came back.

To the people of Boa Vista this was another kind of ghost ship, too, when they looked down to the harbour in the dark and saw illuminated figures levitating in the night sky. It was one of the strangest sights the town had ever seen. The illusion was caused by Otomi Indians painted with phosphorus that made them shine in the dark. When they swarmed up the masts to fit the old ship with her new rigging they appeared as luminous walkers suspended in a heavenly night. The name of the ship, too, so faded it had become illegible, was painted across the stern with the same phosphorus substance in dilating silvery letters that expanded and contracted with the harbour swell: *Santa Cruz*. Porphyry had a band of musicians installed in the grandstand that was built for spectators who wanted to watch the launch, and half the town bought tickets on the day the Indians put the old caravel down on the sea.

The tableau of the Founding of Boa Vista, commemorating the first settlers' discovery of the harbour at the tip of the inland cordillera where they built the settlement they had named for the natural beauty of the view, was performed under circumstances approximating so far as was known to the original landfall. The log book of the *Santa Cruz*, diaries and other private records preserved in the municipal archives, reported clear weather and a glassy sea, disturbed only by a school of whales that had been sighted along the coast on their migration to feeding-grounds in the colder offshore waters of a white continent rumoured to lie south. The whales still came, and could still be viewed from the windows of the refectory in the Episcopal palace when it was thrown open to the public to celebrate this spectacle.

While the see of Boa Vista remained vacant because the peripatetic bishop was reported to be still evangelising somewhere in mid-Atlantic, the Teatro do Mundo was granted permission to use the refectory for the staging of its spectacle of the Founding of Boa Vista. While waiting for the arrival of the annual visitors the Uros fish-men had learned from the local Indians how to put out to sea in long paddle boats with eyes painted on the prow to search out the whales. The *Santa Cruz* lay at anchor down the coast with the fish-men on board, their whaling boats in tow, and put to sea as soon as the whales were sighted. After a day's sailing the *Santa Cruz* hove to at the entrance to the passage through the reef, cheered by the spectators crowding the shore while the fish-men did battle with the whales before the windows of the Episcopal palace. Two whales were slaughtered, two boats were lost and a number of the Uros drowned in full view of the spectators who were following the whale hunt from the caravel and the shore. Then the *Santa Cruz* raised anchor, passing through the gap in the reef just as she had done on the day the first settlers arrived at Boa Vista more than a hundred years before.

The arrival of the caravel was greeted with music and fireworks and the applause of the inhabitants of Boa Vista, who had turned out in their entirety to honour the founding fathers of their town. A pregnant woman on board the caravel, whom Porphyry had chosen on account of her condition to play the part of an Orphan of the King named Francesca Carvalho, later Pilar, went into labour and was delivered of a son before she disembarked. Porphyry, in the role of the landless hidalgo Pedro Pilar, presented the woman and her new-born child in the refectory in the Episcopal palace as the last scene in the tableau of the Founding of Boa Vista.

In the great hall, decorated festively with silks and paper streamers, the crowds stood up and cheered. Pedro Pilar went to the windows and held the child up so that the people on the shore could see him too. Then he made a speech, in which he told them that with the help of this son he would clear the forest with fire and axe and plant maize, millet and corn, but the cane that was already indigenous to the land would do best of all. Great estates would one day be carved out of this country. Even by the time of his grandson, who would be named Pedro Joao Pilar and given the title of Donatory in recognition of his services on behalf of the colony, the settlers would live in stone houses with costly furnishings and be masters of cane plantations greater than anywhere in the world.

Carried away by this speech, the people forgot that the speaker was not Pedro Pilar but Porphyry. For a moment they forgot that they were not participating in these events in their own time, but as the audience at a historical play acted out for them by an itinerant showman and his troupe. When the speech came to an end and Porphyry, stepping out of the character of Pedro Pilar, came down from the stage onto the refectory floor, the audience begged him for more, to give them all their history right up to the present, showing them their own lives. Porphyry assured them that more such plays were in preparation. The Teatro do Mundo intended to present an unlimited series of tableaux, Scenes from Life in Boa Vista, showing the entire passage of the colony's history until the present moment in time, the end of history, when the present began to overlap with the re-enactments of the past. They would reach a vanishing point at which it became impossible to tell the difference between the original and the copy, reality and illusion. A gust of wind blew through the hall, the carpets rose along the floor and the long paper streamers hanging from the ceiling stirred. Reinforced with wires formed in spiral coils, the brightly painted streamers began to spiral on updraughts of air, twisting faster and faster as if about to bore through the ceiling, twisting down again and back up, up and down and in both directions at the same time, until it became impossible to say which was which.

Esperanca

After moving into the new colony, Vista, as it came to be known, where the Teatro settled on the outskirts of town, I went in search of Esperanca. At the Misericordia I was told that she could not receive me there. I was to come to a certain house in the evening in three days' time. The house I came to for my appointment, its iron gates mounted with spikes harking back to the conquistadors' lances of a forgotten age, its thick walls adorned with dragons breathing fire to ward off intruders, bore witness to a Moorish-influenced obsession with keeping women apart that now seemed an anachronism in this modern town, even if it was still the rule on the backland estates. I pulled the bell and was admitted by a servant who was unusually self-possessed for a black man. From the way he bowed and gave me a smile I got the impression he knew me, though I couldn't recall ever having met him.

He led me upstairs to a spacious, badly lit room which at first seemed full of shadows. It took a moment for me to realise that the dark forms along the walls were old women sitting in black dresses. I saw only the brightness in the middle of the room surrounding Esperanca as she came forward to meet me. She looked magnificent and still youthful, although I supposed that she was hardly a young woman any more. Why didn't you come, she said at once as she gave me her hand. Why did you wait all these years? Years, I said at a loss for a reply. Has it been years? For me it has been years, yes, she said, and motioned me to sit down. She noticed me looking over her shoulder at the old women in black who were seated behind her. They will always be there whenever you come, she said, those are the conditions. The women are blind. They do not hear too well. You must feel free to talk as if we were alone. For a long time I sat speechless, overcome by the memories stirred up in me at the sight of Esperanca.

My brothers, Duarte Joao and Duarte Carvalho, she continued after a while, are they still boys playing pranks in your classroom? They are grown men, I replied. There you are then, she said briskly with a toss of her head, reminding me of the girl who had once connived to have me abducted to her father's house. She wore her hair up now, coiled round her head. I rather missed that weather-vane braid of hair which used to twitch up and down according to her moods. For a long time we sat in silence. She looked at me steadily, pouring her face into mine, until it was dark and we could no longer see each other and into the darkness I said: I have come here because I would like to ask you to become my wife.

She rose at length to light a lamp. I heard her moving around the room. There is no reason why a nun who hasn't taken the veil should not marry, she said. In the darkness I saw a spark. But my sister, Senhora de Souza, she asked into the sudden incandescent flame, what plans do you have for her? And how is my father's white mare, by the way? Did Francis fetch her after she bolted and bring her to the house?

I watched her moving round the room with a taper, lighting one lamp after another, and I wondered how she knew all these things. I sent you a dream, she said evasively, so I knew that you would have to come, because you are half Indian like myself and believe in the shadow world. Francis followed you on my instructions, to make sure that no harm came to you on the way. Who is Francis, I asked. Francis is the slave my father gave me when I was sent to the Misericordia as a child, she said, who now serves in this house as a free man. But who could have foreseen your meeting with Senhora de Souza on the road? She sat down and smoothed her dress. Poor Pablito! That was your fate. My sister is a witch and put you under a spell. How can I blame you? But you must still do penance.

Esperanca flushed. I want you to tell me about — about *it*, she said. I watched the colour come to her cheeks as her fingers continued to smooth creases out of her lap that were not there. Very well, I said, if that's what you wish. And in a low voice I described to her what had happened on the road to Boa Vista after I left the Big House, how a storm blew up just as I reached the river where a young senhora wearing a flesh-coloured pelisse was about to drive a team of oxen across and told me to hitch my horse to the cart, but for which I would have been swept away by the current when the mare lost her footing. Louder, croaked a voice from the back of the room. The mare lost her footing, someone repeated, and another voice said with a cackle: I'm sure she did, in these stories that's always the mare's part. A sound rather like the cawing of parrots broke out at the back of the room.

Esperanca got up with a frown and spoke sternly to the old ladies as if they were misbehaved schoolchildren. Either they listened quietly or they would go without a story. Still frowning, she sat down again with her back to the ladies and said: so she invited you to spend the night at her house, and naturally you accepted. I nodded. She scowled. And then? And then I was shown into a room, given dry clothes and served dinner, after which I fell asleep in a chair at the window. An old man snoozing after his dinner, said Esperanca with contempt. But then, in the night, she came to your room, and suddenly you were not so tired after all: is that how it was?

There were moths the size of bats, I said, trying to recall the strange events that had taken place that night, flitting in and out of a beam of light from the barn below, where people were threshing millet. Threshing, said Esperanca sarcastically? In the middle of the night? I looked down and saw them from the window, I said, and as I stood watching this scene I felt a warm draught glide up my arms, as if the air was being fanned by the huge moths' wings. Moths! exclaimed Esperanca exasperatedly. And the draught, as you call it — it was that witch flying into the room, wasn't it? I suppose it must have been, I said, because it was when I suddenly felt the heat of the senhora's body against my skin that I turned and saw her standing behind me.

Esperanca jumped to her feet as a chorus of sibilant whispers began to chew up *the heat of the senhora's body* and repeated it in half-audible snatches behind her. She stood white-faced, breathing rapidly in and out, until the colour returned to her cheeks and the whispers fell silent behind her.

So this – witch, Esperanca asked at last. Was she naked when she flew into the room? She had let her hair down, I said, and it covered her body, her hair was all I saw. All you saw — ! Long dark hair — as long as this? She put her hands to her head, loosened the clips and shook out a mass of thick black hair that covered her body almost down to her knees.

Like that, I said. The senhora's head was tilted back in a mass of unbraided hair hanging down just like that. So you saw her clearly, Esperanca interrupted. Not clearly, I said, just an impression: for a moment I thought I saw the head of a fox on a woman's body, but then she drew me away from the window. When the senhora undressed me and I heard the garments rustle as they dropped onto the floor I realised that they must have belonged to her dead husband.

Ah, cried Esperanca, the senhora undressed you! Poor Pablito! Senhora de Souza has been a widow for as long as I have been in the Misericordia. What chance did you have against that witch's spell? So she undressed you. And then? And then, I repeated, I stood naked while she ran her hands over my body. I felt whirring creatures brush against my skin in the dark, moths — Moths, Esperanca interrupted angrily, what are these moths doing here again? Stupid lies! She glared at me. The creatures you feel brushing against your skin with such obvious pleasure can only have been the caresses of the senhora's hands! Why don't you admit it?

I was at a loss for words, baffled by the enraged beauty of my desperado of a nun, the way she was taking possession of the story. Only now was I struck by the marked resemblance between the two sisters. Naturally, I said. What do you expect? I lowered my voice. Naturally the caresses of the senhora's hands gave me pleasure. But one sharp-eared old lady had heard what I said, and soon the walls were writhing with the echoes of the *caresses of the senhora's hands gave him pleasure*, as if a sack of snakes had been released into the room. Esperanca let them writhe. She had regained her composure.

Naturally, she echoed coldly, being the stupid man you are. And so then you – ? Did you – ? What did you – ? Esperanca stared at me and I stared back at her without speaking. You *must* tell me, she hissed.

Lowering my voice a little, I leaned forward and said matter-of-factly: the senhora lay on a luminous shimmer of triangular white sheet from which the coverlet had been drawn back. Her head and legs were cut off by shadow, her breasts and belly alone lit up by a fleck of light from the window and thus elevated from the dark, like a torso obscenely presented on an anatomising table. When I lay down on her I put out this light. I entered the senhora's body like a sword. I could hear the threshers pounding away in the barn below, where they were threshing millet, as distinctly as if they were with us in the room. But the moment I lay down on her, putting out that gleam of light on the senhora's white belly, a flood rose up out of her which metamorphosed into high-pitched cries of pleasure, clawing around the room like bats dislodged from a hiding-place where they had slept for a hundred years. This is what passed between Senhora de Souza and me during the night I sheltered at her house on my way to Boa Vista.

Esperanca slid out of her chair. Before I was able to catch her she lay unconscious on the floor, and the whispers that had risen cautiously from the back of the room were soon buzzing furiously over her like a swarm of flies.

A Package for Senhora de Souza

The nun who formally remained the property of the Misericordia by a contract only her father could revoke assumed power over me as her prisoner of love. On what evenings I was to come to the house where she supervised the blind sisters who lived there in retirement, and whether she instructed Francis to admit me when I did, depended on her whim. This arbitrariness only sharpened my appreciation of her beauty and the excitement of her presence when I was allowed into it at last. I was being asked to persist, to reflect her own worth in the patience with which I submitted to her disregard. I waited in the street, watching swallows swoop through the empty stables behind the house, and would be put in mind of Tumbez, with the sound of non-existent surf in my ears. With regard to my proposal, which in the case of a nun could only be achieved by elopement, Esperanca told me she would have to think a while. Conditions were attached. I would have to prove myself. For how could a woman who had spent her life in a nunnery be the judge of a man's character?

The woman whom her father had entrusted as a girl to the Catholic nuns in the Misericordia was as much a victim of Moorish seclusion as the daughters the Donatory kept hidden in the flowering courtyard of the big house. The cult of chastity surrounding secluded woman celebrated her desirability, her half-way status between lust booty and saintliness. Men were her priests and marauders, her champions and oppressors. In the colony, where everything flourished with tropical extravagance, this ambiguity was exacerbated by conquest and slavery and found a more extreme expression than it did in the Old World. The sexually prized mestizo or mulatto, more than the white woman, came to represent the conscience of her keepers. She did penance for their progenitors' misdeeds. The bones that shaped her face and the pigment that coloured her skin were always present reminders of the sinful nature of the encounter in which she had her origin.

An abstraction called the Love of Esperanca took shape in my soul. Probably no such thing existed in hers. As a woman she was able to inspire me to something beyond and apart from herself. As a man I inspired her to something whose fulfilment would always remain confined

131

to itself. In these differences lay that antagonism between men and women which they were driven to reconcile under the name of love. We lived according to the rituals lovers have, locked in the combat that anticipates the embrace, disguising impulse behind artifice, observing one another, shrewd beneath shows of passion, refined in the pursuit of our sensual needs and cultivating obstacles to defer their gratification.

Esperanca told me that Senhora de Souza had moved from her country to her town house. Had I heard the news? Never again did Esperanca refer to her as her sister. The lady in question was always Senhora de Souza. Then even that privilege was withdrawn and she was referred to simply as the senhora. Surely I would run into her in Boa Vista. It would be surprising if I did not, said Esperanca sarcastically. But I did not live in Boa Vista, I lived in the garret of a house occupied by a Chinese cook and his family in Porphyry's proxy town, Vista. The very name was an echo of the place on which it had settled as a parasite. It had become the pleasure quarter of the town. The bishop whose inauguration Boa Vista had celebrated had never arrived but the celebrations in his honour stayed and became a permanent feature of the proxy town. The Teatro do Mundo staged Scenes From Life in Vista all year round. Carnival and the masked ball were as much an institution there as the emporium of commerce was in Boa Vista.

The religious community in a town still dominated by its Benedictine, Franciscan and Jesuit establishments did not care for the immorality of Vista, but it was not so much this which moved them to take action against Porphyry. It was an episode from the Scenes From Life that purported to show the arrival by sea of the bishop lost en route, a spectacle almost as lavish as the tableau commemorating the Founding of Boa Vista, this time with the phosphorus Indians in a submarine role, illuminating the water beneath the vessel in which his Excellency arrived. A number of citizens, believing this was the bishop at last, hurried to the Episcopal palace to pay their respects and order masses to be sung for his soul. Only when the pageant was over and the bishop took off his mitre and beard was this impressive figure revealed to be Porphyry. Incensed, the church leaders charged him with blasphemy and threw him into jail.

In the room with the living black cobwebs along the walls I reconstructed for Esperanca's benefit the case brought against Porphyry by the

Jesuit casuists in the great hall of the Episcopal palace, where it was followed with keen interest by the public. The journals I read in the emporium of commerce, months or even years after publication, were full of rumours of revolution in the Old World. God-given rights of the feudal estates were being challenged on both sides of the ocean. Profound changes were in the making, which had so far been overlooked in Boa Vista.

Porphyry drew attention to these new terms of business, as he called them, when rebutting the charges of ungodliness, blasphemy and the moral corruption of the people. He knew by heart the texts where the principle of catharsis was set down, quoting the classics at the Jesuits in the original language. The stage held a mirror up to nature and provided an emetic for the passions of the common people. His Teatro do Mundo was an echo in which the world heard itself, said Porphyry. Its tableaux had assisted at the birth of history. I had been struck by the modesty of these claims when I heard Porphyry throw them out at the audience at his trial. Now I lobbed them into the brightness where Esperanca sat surrounded by shadows hunched over their needlework, perhaps with expectations of causing a breath of interest. But the needles continued to weave in and out, drawing silent trajectories through the air, and the serene expression on the face of my beloved was unruffled by any trace of a thought when she said: Pablito, dearest, I have a package I would like you to deliver in person to Senhora de Souza.

The Birth of History

Porphyry compared the becoming of the world to the growth of a child. In the lives of both the earliest events went unrecorded. During the dark ages of infancy there was no evidence that anything had taken place, until recording faculties developed, and reflection on the action became part of performing it. In the world this was the advent of history; in the child, of consciousness. With the arrival of consciousness the pure present disappeared. Present that one was aware of already belonged to past. This was the loss of paradise. The first recording of life thus became the first cognisance of decay and death, as was apparent from the allegory of the Tree of Knowledge and the Expulsion from the Garden of Eden (a tableau that was still in the repertoire of the Teatro do Mundo and a great favourite with the public, Porphyry did not fail to add during the evidence he gave at his trial). Such was the nature of history and consciousness. Truth could only ever be glimpsed in reflections, said Porphyry, such as his theatre attempted to show. The world was a reconstruction of a reality at a far remove from the subject who experienced it, the ghost of itself. The world was only available to us at several removes, the reconstruction of some original we could never know.

Possession

Porphyry was convicted of heresy and banished from Boa Vista, while I was sent with a package to Senhora de Souza. She laid it on one side without opening it. Coffee and wine were served. She crumbled a biscuit, grinding her fingers together until she had disposed of the dust that still adhered to the tips. The senhora's resemblance to her sister was more and more striking. At moments, as I accompanied her around the house, admiring her pictures, her china and her carpets, I felt the same breath exhale from her body that also emanated from Esperanca. We sat in the inner courtyard of the house and watched a column of luminous blue butterflies descend from the sky to feed on the orchids, convolvulus and trumpet flowers. Some of the butterflies settled with their slowly pumping wings brushing her throat and bosom, leaving traces of an iridescent powder, which glittered and scattered lazily across her skin when she blew them away. I left before it grew dark, going straight from her house to Esperanca to report on my mission, as she had asked me to do. My nun was keyed up with excitement, difficult to grasp, all edges and no surface on which to settle. She had been thinking, she announced. She had still not come to a decision. But she now saw her cruelty, as she called it, the impossibility of the position in which she had put me. She wished me to remain her friend, yet I should feel free, since I was a man with a man's unavoidable desires, to resume the relationship with Senhora de Souza if I wanted to do so.

I had made up my mind not to see the senhora again, but I ran into her as I was coming out of the emporium of commerce, and she asked me to pass on a message to her sister. Whatever it was Esperanca had been meaning to give her, she had either forgotten to put it in the package or had never intended to in the first place. For although the package Esperanca had sent her contained nothing, this nothing had been conveyed to her so handsomely by the bearer that it was the bearer she had handsomely received rather than the package. When Esperanca asked me if I had been to see the senhora I told her about our meeting in the street and gave her the senhora's answer. Esperanca seemed displeased with this answer, and at our next meetings she was more capricious than usual, then refused to see me at all. Every evening I waited under the fire-breathing dragons in the hope of being allowed to call on her, only to be informed by Francis that his mistress was indisposed. For a time matters remained like this, until I discontinued my visits and wrote Esperanca a letter, giving her the address at which she could reach me whenever she felt ready to see me again.

The days streamed in an eerie velvet flow, a wide lazy river with patterns of light and shadow rippling across it like a fence, or lying down on it white like a congealed mist on which I could skate with marvellous facility – projections that apparently had no source outside the opium drifting through the labyrinth of my brain. I was introduced to this habit by my landlord, the Chinese cook, who told me he had abandoned sleep and rested for a few hours on the opium cushion instead. It was softer than the niopo cloud I had ridden in the forest, more deeply hollowed out in the trough of the calm it induced than any coca I had eaten in Titumate.

A whole rainy season passed like this. Francis found me slung bat-like in a hammock in the garret towards the end of this twilight, already partially mildewed from the damp, and he came again, and again, until he had slowly nudged me awake. His mistress had been ill, he said. I stepped into the river and bathed for a week, emerging back to front, so strange and new was the feeling of being inside my own body after the absence from it during my opium travels. On my first visit to Esperanca, still weak on my legs, I took a hammock instead of walking to the house and never gave up this practice afterwards.

I had the impression it was not Esperanca but the senhora who came forward and gave me her hand to kiss. Giving me her hand to kiss was not Esperanca's custom, nor the wearing of a square-cut sky-blue gown with a fine silk bodice, nor the flower in her hair. This was an older, a more sumptuous woman. She was working patterns with feathers of gorgeous colours into the fringes of hammocks, white herons, pink spoonbills and golden jacamars, producing the most beautiful effects. I held my tongue, looking past her aura of brightness into the weaving cobwebs along the wall, swaying pitter-patter with the sound of their gossip. The whispering old women were like leaves trembling under drops of rain.

I'm sorry, I heard her say, I mistrusted you. It wasn't your fault. It's just that I'm incurably jealous, particularly of that woman. It makes me ill. This sounded like a familiar tone of voice. When I pulled myself together and saw her in focus, a smile blending irresolutely into a scowl, I was looking at the Esperanca I knew. You've changed your style, I said. You look magnificent. But what use is all your magnificence to me if you're going to remain sitting in this room for the rest of your life? And I quoted back to her: the walls of the house of Misericordia are only an allegory of the unapproachability of woman.

There was something of a flurry among the cobwebs when I said this. After it had subsided Esperanca said serenely: I have heard that my father is dying. The moment he dies I can leave this place and marry you. Is that too much to ask of you? To wait for an old man to die? The needle continued to weave in and out of the feather-work in her lap, drawing silent trajectories through the air. Of course not, I answered, knowing that the Donatory had long since been dead. She looked up sharply, as if she had read my thoughts. And another thing, she said. I can't go on coping with this jealousy. You've given me assurances that you haven't seen Senhora de Souza again. I must believe you. But my imagination sees you together with this woman. I can't help myself. This is what made me ill for such a long time. Rather than be tormented by doubts that you are secretly visiting the senhora, I would prefer to know that you are seeing her. I am asking you to resume the relationship with the senhora that began in her house on the night of the – she scowled – the moths. Do this for me, Pablito. And whenever you have finished your business together I want you to come and tell me about it, because it is my right to know. That is the least you can do after betraying me with another woman. Esperanca snapped the thread savagely with her teeth.

Thus began my proxy sexual life with Esperanca, conducted through the medium of her sister. This was the direction in which she had been moving all along. I had misgivings, but they were brushed aside by the violence of her desires. If I could not do this for her — in the violence of what she threatened to do if I could not do *this* for her she became magnificent in her scorn. Which woman was it I loved? When the blue butterflies descended the shaft into the courtyard garden and settled on the senhora's throat and breasts, their tiny worm-like bodies pulsing, fanning with their iridescent wings the sweat they soaked up through coils of tongues, it was the body of the nun I saw them feed on. When I spoke of these matters in the rooms with the cobwebs it seemed to be the senhora who convulsed in the palisander chair as she listened to descriptions of her own orgasms. I thought the sisters must be in collusion, even that they had some way of changing places. After I had left the senhora with love bites on her throat and arms one evening I rode helter-skelter across town to look for the marks I was convinced I would find on Esperanca's body, but naturally there were none.

In the safety of the Misericordia's retirement house, guarded by fire-breathing dragons, surrounded by her blind nuns, she wanted to be admired from the far side of a line represented by a cord of red silk laid across the floor. Only with my words was I allowed to touch her body. Esperanca began to wear close-fitting gowns in order to show herself off better. Parading up and down the room, she would ask me to compare her body with Senhora de Souza's. She once presented herself naked and told me to memorise what I saw, the better to make love to her in my imagination while I lay on the senhora's body. It was the nun's body which took possession of the language I used to describe the senhora's, her breasts and thighs that left their imprint on these words. The borrowed words came out of my mouth, crossing the red silk line on the floor to become flesh with Esperanca's body again. In the acts performed in the senhora's house there was a sense of fulfilment withheld until they had been described in words that belonged to her rival's body. Imperceptibly, in my telling of those acts, *she* began to be replaced by *you*. Suspicious of the butterflies that came down into the courtyard, perhaps because they were beyond her influence, she moved my lovemaking with the senhora into the house. She determined the rooms and the positions in which she wished the senhora to be taken, the deviant sexual practices to which she must be introduced, the degree of coercion she wished me to use. It was the subjection of the senhora achieved through me that gave the nun the greatest pleasure. Esperanca took absolute possession of her sister. Myself she had already possessed long ago. It was her revenge for the life of which she had been dispossessed herself. She turned us into marionettes. And we performed for her.

People With No Legs

Thanks to the salary that had accumulated during the time I had been working in the Big House, I was now the owner of a substantial sum of money, which I had decided to invest at the emporium of commerce. I was astonished by the ostentation of the town that had become evident during my absence. In the backlands, plantation owners made do with a greasy shirt, a stained pair of drawers, a long bed-gown and a pair of slippers, as if it was their ambition to look as unprepossessing as was possible. If for any reason he left his estate, however, he did so in the usual style of the Brazilian gentry, in a kind of feudal estate. Even men of no apparent account walked the street in breeches of satin damask, while their wives wore kirtles and tunics of silk and were trinketed with gold. I dressed accordingly when I visited the emporium, where I listened to the boasting of the sugar plantation owners, the richest of all, and picked up the gossip of the agents constantly passing in and out. But after I had been down to the harbour and spoken with the factors, from whom I learned that most of the sugar plantation owners were heavily indebted, and had visited the Seminary to ask the advice of the Jesuits, I opened an account with a trading house and gave instructions to invest not in cotton or sugar but coffee.

The asceticism of an age in which men such as Eugenio dos Santos Innocentos had flourished already belonged to the past. These days the Jesuits were not compiling dictionaries but lecturing in casuistry, a lucrative species of moral theology in strong request among Boa Vista's merchants and traders. They hired the Jesuits to solve cases of conscience for them. Armed with affidavits, proving that what they were doing created not merely wealth but good, the merchants were rapidly becoming the most self-satisfied class of people in town, more respected than the priests. However prosperous Boa Vista otherwise seemed there was no mistaking the decline of its religious institutions. The windows in Cake Alley remained shuttered. No baskets were lowered any more to feed the poor. The rubbish at the entrance to the Misericordia had not been cleared in the three days since my previous visit.

Bandeiras frequently passed through town, attracted by the never-ending carnival, carefree, colourful, lethal men with slouched hats, black moustaches, spurs on their naked heels and long guns on their saddles sticking out at each end from under their ponchos. Duarte Carvalho was among them. I got up from the river that flowed through my bed where the senhora lay with her head on the opium cushion, and looking down through the slats of light and shadow I saw Duarte Carvalho come riding down the street in a thin drizzle of rain. It seemed like another of my wreathed visions. I turned from the window and told the senhora that I had just seen her youngest brother, the son whom Maria Conceicao had dropped out of her womb onto the forest floor and left to die, ride past with a band of outlaws on his way to the cross-roads where he would fulfil his destiny.

Vista absorbed the *bandeiras* with their women-stealing, their plundering, casual deaths in gunfights, and when the outlaws had gone the Teatro do Mundo resurrected them in its epic Scenes from Life in Boa Vista. The languid sons of wealthy planters went to the theatre in Vista every day to see what they might have done rather than bother with doing it themselves. The senhora and I were among them. We spent our days on the opium cushion, our nights at the theatre. The world represented on the stage of the Teatro was more real to us than our own, the stage version of colonial life much more convenient for us than attempting to go through the motions of life itself. Theatregoing replaced the evening corso and became the main business of the town. Negroes plied the streets with palanquins. Wealthy citizens vied with one another in the richness of these vehicles and the liveries of their bearers, an opulence which went strangely with the slaves' bare legs and unwashed feet. In Vista the roads were narrow, unpaved and filthy. No person who could afford to do so ever set foot in these streets.

As palanquin bearers slaves took on the function of their masters' legs from the moment they got out of bed in the morning until they returned to it at night. When even this modicum of exercise was abandoned the palanquins became residences vacated by their occupants only in order to relieve themselves; eventually not even for that. Many colonists travelled from estate to estate in this way. When carried in a palanquin from Boa Vista to her country house the senhora and I lay on the opium cushion to relieve the tedium of the journey. For people of fashion on their way about town through shit-bespattered streets there was no alternative. Wearing velvet, damasks, top hats, clothes that were quite unsuited to the climate but showed off their wealth, the rich spent their lives being carried about town in ambulating furnaces. Thick curtains protected the privacy of palanquin interiors where the inmates stretched out in unbearable humidity on piles of steaming cushions. Many thought they suffered from haemorrhoids, in fact from a malignant ulcer of the anus, for which opium was considered the best cure. During the wet season, tormented by gout and an insatiable craving for sweetmeats, they moved around town with deathlike countenances reminiscent of carnival masks.

From their palanquins the rich estate owners conducted their business, dictated letters to their plantation clerks, ate and drank, picking their teeth, smoking cigars, perhaps allowing themselves to be fanned or searched for lice by the piccaninnies of slaves while they yawned and scratched their syphilitic sores. The palanquin shook with master's snores, or perhaps squeaked and jolted while he copulated with one of his moveable possessions he might have taken a fancy to en route. Certainly his hands were less idle than his feet. Hands at least played cards, took snuff, told the beads of a rosary or tested flesh, fondling the genitals of boys or the breasts of girls who leaned into the carriages for inspection.

In the pleasure quarters of Vista there was a greater convergence of palanquins than anywhere else in town. People of fashion went to watch scenes from life manipulated by the Teatro's players. Set down by their bearers on the banked tiers surrounding a space in the middle where the poorer spectators stood, the rows of conveyances with their dark velvet drapes created the atmosphere of a closed theatre in the open air. Scenes From Life were presented there, though there was no theatre as such in Vista. In the town that Porphyry had created to be the echo of another, nothing was as it seemed. Even a slave market had been installed in Vista, a replica of the real slave mart in Vallongo, a long winding street in Boa

Vista where every house was a warehouse for selling slaves, but like everything else in Vista it was no more than an installation. It belonged to that subversive reality with a false bottom which the Teatro had come to represent in the colony's life.

It was in the replica of the Vallongo slave market that a farce entitled *People With No Legs* played to enormous crowds. The part played involuntarily by the audience, filling the spacious apartments where the slaves were exhibited and overflowing into the street, was the role of customers at a slave auction, just as happened at the real Vallongo in Boa Vista. These actor-slaves, it was generally agreed, played their parts with deep-felt empathy. Stowed like so many bundles of merchandise, the women squatted in the middle of the warehouse apartments, their hands and chins resting apathetically on their knees. Their only covering was a small girdle of cotton tied round the waist. When a customer showed an interest in one of these wretches she was whipped up by the auctioneer wielding a long rod, to be handled by the buyer in different parts, just as with an animal. The whole examination concerned her mere animal capability, without the least inquiry as to the moral quality of the slave, which the customers no more thought of than if they were buying a horse. Ladies would be carried in their hammocks through the apartments, summon a piece of merchandise and handle it and take it away to the cashier at the entrance with complete indifference.

Young, strong, male slaves were the objects of the greatest interest and the highest prices. They sat or lay naked on the floor all day and night, doomed to remain on the spot, like cattle in a pen, until they had been sold. Many of these men were more than unusually black. Allegedly soot had been rubbed into their skin, a device often used in the Teatro in order to give slaves the fierce, dark aspect of men who were brooding over untold wrongs. When ordered to come forward they did so sullenly, stamped with their feet, shouted to show the soundness of their lungs, ran up and down the room and were treated exactly like a horse put through its paces. When done with they were whipped back into their stalls. Many of them were disfigured by eruptions of a white scurf, a loathsome appearance like leprosy, an effort of nature to cast off the effects of the salt provisions on the long voyage from Africa. This white-scurf race of Negroes was known for its propensity to eat lime and earth, and whether from a determination not to live or from a morbid appetite for such things they persisted in this perverse habit until they eventually sank under it, dying brain-cracked with swollen bodies.

Earth-eating and scurf were a common condition among slaves. In the case of these theatre slaves, however, it was a moot question if anything about them was authentic. Spectators so inured to seeing slaves beaten that they would not have bothered to visit the *calabouco*, the place of correction in Boa Vista where miscreants were professionally flogged, took a keen interest in the proceedings of its replica in Vista, because it was unclear if the punishment meted out there was genuine. The physical destruction of a man submitted to a couple of hundred lashes in the Teatro's performances certainly looked real enough. Some of the miscreants apparently died as a result. There were witnesses who had seen their bodies thrown into the sea, that useful burial ground for all those unable to afford a funeral in Boa Vista. Sharks disposed of the cadavers within minutes. The cognoscenti, however, said they had sampled the blood off a flogged Negro's black and found that it had quite definitely tasted of red wine mixed with betel juice, while the corpses which bled this mixture had been seen creeping back up from the shore under cover of dark.

Now here was a curious thing. People who had never thought twice about the division of mankind into masters and slaves became much more worked up over the composition of the blood of slaves theatrically whipped than over any real slave blood they had seen shed. They were outraged at the obscenity of pretending to do such a thing in a way they had never been when attending an actual flogging. In *People With No Legs* they watched a slave have the testicles hacked out of his scrotum and his body fed to the mill for having defiled his master's daughter. No question but that all slave-owning spectators at the theatre entirely approved of this action. They watched a love affair develop between a white boy and a slave girl in his father's house, a mature girl whom he began to adore from the day she arrived in the house and he saw her washing under the pump in the outhouse beneath his window. The white youth took her for his concubine. No question but that all slave-owning spectators accepted his right to do so as part of a God-given superiority of the white race over the black. But beyond that he unfortunately loved the slave girl and refused to marry the bride chosen for him by his father. Goaded by her mother-in-law, the spurned bride took her revenge on a husband who was only able to come to her bed while the smell of his black mistress was still fresh in his nostrils. They poisoned the slave girl with a substance scattered on the sheets of her bed and absorbed by her skin when she lay down at night. The girl died slowly in agony. There could be no question but that all the slave-owning spectators who made up the bulk of the Teatro's audience approved of her punishment no less than they had the castration of a slave who had presumed to meddle with his master's white daughter.

Watching such actions performed as a public entertainment was a different matter, however. It was no secret that the Donatory had been embroiled in some such scandal and that *People With No Legs* was a colonial chronicle loosely adapted from the true story of the Pilar family under a different name. It was now remembered in town how the Donatory's son, Duarte Joao, the older of the Pilar twins, had suddenly left the family plantation and moved to Boa Vista, where he still lived, a complete recluse, in the house of one of the Pilar aunts. His wife Magdalena, overwrought by a jealous passion and abetted by a monster of a mother-in-law, Sofia Maria da Costa Pilar, had allegedly poisoned his black mistress.

In *People With No Legs* the background to this affair was bandied around Vista as the subject of a farce. Porphyry, or someone very like him, probably one of his sons, for Porphyry had been banished, impersonated the Donatory and played a number of minor roles besides. He triumphed as auctioneer in the Vallongo warehouse and flogger in the *calabouco*, enraging the audience with displays of sham cruelty, which they took as an insult to the slave-owning class. Like all voyeurs, they were absorbed as much by the scrutiny of their own motives as by the object of their vicarious enjoyment itself. There was a fascinated horror in contemplating oneself in such grotesque caricatures. Despite interruptions and acrimonious debates, this was why *People With No Legs* was allowed to go on. The Donatory was represented as a boorish, bullying hidalgo, familiar as a throwback from the early years of the colony, but now, to an audience that considered itself far more refined, an embarrassing caricature. Here was the nub, the painful dilemma of which Boa Vista's refined leading citizens only became aware when it was presented to them as a play and had already been smuggled irremovably deep into their consciousness. Refinement had dirty feet.

There was a genealogy of refinement, a family tree, or a whole forest of trees, represented by ancestral women who sought consolation for forbidden pleasures, indulged in sweets and ate and ate until their bodies became gigantic. On the stages of the Teatro these women were physically pumped up. Chefs inserted tubes into airtight skirts and pumped and pumped until the ballooning figures lifted off the ground, came swaying to rest and rocked on the points of tiny ballet shoes. Feet, miniature feet, extruding from a distended balloon, was all that remained that could be identified as woman. Insulated from any other contact with the world, a woman's feet allowed her the only access to sexual pleasure, these became her erogenous zones, to be tickled, sucked, chafed or whipped with increasing degrees of severity and increasing degrees of intimacy by the only men who could be expected to accommodate her in this way: her slaves.

It was common knowledge that such depravities went on in those Moorish dungeons purporting to be a lady's private apartments. To see them performed in public was breathtaking, permissible only in the guise of the gross comedy as which it was presented. These women regressed to a kind of giant infancy, ballooning white babies, pampered in a sexual parody of wet-nursing by black men who did full justice to their job description as footmen. The archetype of this colonial matron in *People With No Legs* was easily recognisable as the Donatory's estranged wife Sofia Maria under another name. The Teatro transformed her into a comic masterpiece.

It was all there, the way-stages in the journey of colonial life, the little girls married off to insatiable old satyrs with a scapular of Our Lady dangling from hairy chests, sub-plots involving secret marriages, incestuous relationships or business-like betrothals, which still did not succeed in preventing ferocious family feuds over inheritance and lands, a stretch of canebrake, a woman, a slave or even an ox, the sodomy and felatio described in the Jesuit denunciations in prurient detail, the mothers-in-law plotting to poison their relatives, the pregnant slave girls burned in plantation ovens to get rid of the evidence in their bellies, the foul-mouthed men swearing by the Virgin's muff, the illicit festivals that took place in churches, with merrymakers reclining on the altar singing *trovas* and playing the guitar, while a never-ending game of backgammon was always in progress in the background — all the facts of colonial life, so self-evident they were commonplaces not even remarked, were lit up by the relentless energy of farce, acquiring long, sinister shadows that made the audience shudder even as it laughed.

As the action progressed, the evolution promised by the play's title became increasingly apparent. Normal men and women contracted to dwarves and mutated into a sub-species of human development not previously seen on the planet. The legs of the white people became shorter and shorter until they disappeared altogether. Jokes about black slaves sent off on a wild-goose chase to find master's legs began to proliferate, joke mulattos began to appear on stage, flabby white men and women who were black from the waist down and walked on incongruously muscular legs. Civil wars broke out over the ownership of disputed border areas around the genitals, absurd scenes of auto-flagellation and contortionist acts of self-rape took place as the white upper half sought to establish dominion over the lower black half of its body. Whose body was it after all? This question was squabbled over by protagonists cut in half at the waist and placed on pedestals that ran on castors and were pushed, or not pushed, depending on the way the argument went, by pairs of actors costumed as legs. But the legs got tired of the argument and walked away, leaving the torsos high and dry, screeching on their pedestals like hysterical parrots. Finally they ran out of anything more to say and looked glumly at the spectators sitting propped up on cushions in their palanquins, and the spectators looked back at these stage reflections of themselves in dreadful silence, waiting, praying, that the show would somehow go on.

Miracles

Boa Vista still remembered Father Eugenio dos Santos Innocentos, but he had been away so long that when he eventually returned to the town with a tribe of Indians in tow no one recognised him. From remote backland areas he had been sending Indians back to the Jesuit reservation at intervals, a signal that he was around if not in person — like God, as the more worldly Franciscans used to joke. Now he was there in the flesh, on which the burden of at least a hundred years rested, at a conservative estimate. What could I do but shrug? Age afflicted some more than others, the senhora for example: after prolonged travels in my mind I returned to find her resting on the opium pillow with a drawn and deeply wrinkled face. I asked her what had happened. It's just age, she said, and placed her finger on my lips. Do you know what that means, Pablito?

Soothed by the pipes supplied by my Chinese landlord, or perhaps by his son, I was not sure which, I travelled back into the wreathed windings of my brain, taking the senhora's question with me. It was unfolded to me there with perfect clarity, and I returned joyfully to tell her. But in the interim years must have passed and the senhora lay dead beside me on her pillow, cheek bones rising starkly out of an emaciated face. I was devastated. I sent a message to Esperanca, but the Misericordia would not allow her to leave the premises even to attend her sister's funeral. I brought the senhora's body in a palanquin to the Church of The Blessed Saviour and buried her without a coffin or any other covering, as was still the custom in the churches of the colony, in a few feet of earth under the mud-packed floor. The earth moved and was continually bringing up fragments of the dead from these shallow graves. The skulls and bones of ancestors protruded from the floor and bored into the knees of the living when they knelt for their devotions.

Father Eugenio dos Santos Innocentos came to preach in this church the day after the senhora was interred. A box was placed in the pulpit for the old man to stand on in order that he might see and be seen by his congregation. He was so desiccated he had shrunk to the size of a child. The citizenry of Boa Vista turned out in large numbers. They had themselves carried into the church in palanquins, smoking cigars, drinking and gossiping, as if anticipating another entertainment. When Father Eugenio climbed onto his box and peered over the edge of the pulpit he did not like what he saw, and said so, and once the babble of this fashionable gathering died down his whispered voice reached clearly into every corner of the church, but no one believed their ears. He was telling the congregation to get out of their palanquins and down on their knees or to leave the church. He whispered some more. He was telling them that they were corrupt, that they were useless and gaudy parasites, vermin fit for nothing but to be driven from the face of the earth. He besought God for a great and fiery furnace to incinerate Boa Vista, and then for a deluge to drown it, so that there would be no record of its shame for all eternity. There was uproar in the church. Voices called for the impudent old rascal to be thrown out. It came to blows between the supporters of the priest and his calumniators. This was dangerous ground for the slaves who had carried their masters into the white man's temple. Given the choice of disobedience or blasphemy, they fled.

During the years of Boa Vista's decay old Negro superstitions began to flourish again. Slaves revived forgotten traditions of their ancestors, leaving the outlying plantations on religious feast days and walking all night to Boa Vista, torch-lit processions that were secretly dedicated to their own deities. They made music with calabash guitars and drums, carrying canopies covered with the animals that were their totems, eagles, peacocks, elephants and rams carved on the sides of their tabernacle, a wooden box, which was said to contain the bones of the first black man to have arrived in the New World. One instrument made out of a hollow tree, covered at one end with a piece of leather, was a drum that could wake the spirits. The player-priest straddled it and struck the leather with his palms, producing a sound audible for miles around. The sound of the spirit-waking drum drove Negroes to frenzy. The Donatory had forbidden it on his estate, and it was forbidden by the council of Boa Vista on pain of death, but the players ignored the ban, carrying the instruments from one place to another under cover of dark. A monotonous boom of drums lay siege to the town every night.

Disease-riddled, desiccated, more dead than alive when he arrived in Boa Vista, Father Eugenio took to his bed in the Jesuit seminary. It was as if he had come back to hold up his own protracted process of dying as an example to the town that had deserted its true gods, betrayed his expectations and was now condemned to die with him too. The feet of the sugar economy, the plantation slaves who had borne it, stank in the nostrils of their masters. The market collapsed under mountains of cheaper sugar that was now available elsewhere. New coffee plantations provided a more lucrative trade route to Salvador that bypassed Boa Vista. Unable to compete, too fatigued to adapt, the town sank on the rotting foundations of its sugar plantations.

The gardens of great houses in the backlands with what was left of their family silver, their rosewood, porcelain, ancestral portraits, slave quarters and chapel crammed with images of saints and the mortal remains of former inmates, were gradually allowed to run wild, the town houses of the plantation owners to drift from decay to ruin. Facades of blistering paint no longer renewed, fallen plaster no longer replaced, furniture no longer stained or given a new veneer succumbed to the destruction of the damp climate, rats, bats and ghosts moved into the empty houses.

On the Jesuit estates, stricter precautions were taken than anywhere else to preserve the original colour of slaves. When the complexion of slave children became too light as a result of intermarriage between mulatto and white the Jesuits darkened the colour by reintroducing the aboriginal African strain. Slaves were made to take marriage partners blacker than themselves — for the understandable reason that the holy fathers balked at the prospect of enslaving human beings with skins as light as their own.

In their enthusiasm for the liberation of the indigenous Indian they had tended to overlook the condition of the enslaved Negro. He was not native to the country and did not qualify for the same missionary attention from the fathers. This neglect may have been more to the Negro's good than his bad. In the Reductions, as they were appropriately called, villages that huddled like beaten animals on the ecclesiastical domains, the Indians were protected from plunder by the colonists in order for them to die even more rapidly, it seemed, by their own choice. No one could explain why. Wasn't the Indian more salubrious in these regulated surroundings? Better fed? Closer to God, having been elevated from savagery to a state of grace? And yet large numbers of them were always swept away within months of arrival in the Reductions. No white or black man could travel so far in the wild without rest or sustain such privations as the Indians. But with the deprivation of free agency it seemed as if the main spring of the machine had cracked. Under the shock of a sudden and total alteration of diet, habits and occupations, the Indians died as mysteriously as those Negro slaves who announced their own self-extinction, *banzo,* falling into a kind of atrophy, losing their appetite and turning into a skeleton.

Father Eugenio addressed all these evils in his sermon before he was shouted down from the pulpit and removed for his own safety from the church. Sodom and Gomorra had been resurrected in the flesh in Boa Vista, he proclaimed with his dying breath. There was not a likely-looking black girl in the colony who had not been taken as the mistress of a white man. There was not a plantation where the grandchildren of the owner were not whipped in the field by his overseer. As long as white men cohabited with their black female slaves fathers would continue to sell their own children, and children would murder their own parents to put an end to their bondage.

Esperanca was moved to penitence by the fire-and-brimstone tirades of the old priest. Stricken in the depths of her soul by a sense of the wickedness of her life, she returned to the mother house, took the vow of seclusion and became an anchorite in an isolated wing of the Misericordia. What did I care? Careless from the habitual use of opium, floating above the world, it seemed immortal, while my senhora lay buried in two feet of dirt under the church floor, I drifted on a river of light and shadow flowing through my bed and watched the decline of Boa Vista. Among the shadows closing around the sugar plantations I was rich, they said, a rich man, for hadn't I invested my money in coffee long ago? I couldn't remember. The Chinese cook's son, or his grandson, brought me notes of credits which I signed in a haze, and for opium I would have signed it all away had Duarte Joao not heard of my situation and taken me into his house.

My former pupil lived in one of the fierce old Moorish houses built to withstand the assault on the virtue of a virgin Pilar aunt, but life had quite voluntarily left her unmolested and she died a spinster in the profitless virtue of old age. Duarte Joao inhabited this gloomy fortress with a series of black mistresses and several thousand books, probably one of the largest libraries in Brazil at the time. Nothing could compensate him for the loss of Marta, none of the women he brought to live with him in the house was able to replace the murdered slave he had loved as a boy. Both prophecies foretold by the mandingueiro Bem from the patterns left on the blade of the knife which Esme stuck into a tree had come true. Duarte Joao would love black women more than white, Bem said, and remain unhappy because of it all his life. His brother Duarte Carvalho had learned to be watchful at every cross-roads he ever came to in his life on account of the old Negro's prophecy that he would die young at a parting of ways, but he met his end in the sierra where there were no roads. Ranchers caught him rustling cattle with the *bandeiras* and made an example of him. They tied Duarte Carvalho to four teams of horses and drove them in opposite directions until his body was torn apart.

As soon as Father Eugenio died his canonisation began. Penny pamphlets that told the story of the padre's life in the wilderness, testifying to the many miracles he had performed, sowed the seeds of this hagiography even while the corpse lay in state in the Jesuit chapel. After the Teatro do Mundo had been closed down by the authorities people flocked to a dramatic presentation of the miracles staged in the Episcopal palace. It was a poor sort of play compared with the productions of the Teatro. But fashions had changed. The cloying sentiment of this dramatic homily suited the mood of the time.

No voluptuary ever invented so many devices for pampering the senses as Father Eugenio had done for mortifying the flesh. He looked on his body as a rebellious slave who dwelt within his doors, ate at his table and slept in his bed and was continually laying snares for his destruction. He chastised himself; that is, he beat his slave. This figure of speech captured exactly the new mood of remorse among the citizens of Boa Vista as they watched the tide of their wealth recede, leaving a dirty high-water mark across the town. Slavery, or rather slaves, or perhaps the slave in themselves, must have been at fault. There was an instant demand for purgatives and relics. To be touched with the padre's barret-cap was to cured of all head complaints, to possess a scrap of the clothes he had worn meant to be ensured against impurity of thought. Water poured over his rosary worked over a hundred miracles in Boa Vista. From the surrounding country believers came to the town to kiss the feet of the saintly corpse. They said nothing at first, enduring in silence, for to have acknowledged the terrible smell in the Jesuit chapel would have been an admission of lack of faith. Surely the body of a freshly departed saint should not stink to high heaven like any wayside cadaver. But the stench caused increasing comment, and when a swarm of scavenging white moths descended on the corpse it was hastily buried in the Jesuit cemetery.

Dominion was given to her, too, a second Eve, over mortality so iniquitous that it had corrupted the flesh even of the saintly dos Santos Innocentos. Esperanca reversed the process of nature, becoming younger as she grew older. All over town I heard the rumours of her inexplicable youthfulness, the marvel of Esperanca's undiminished beauty that was

150

nourished quietly inside the Misericordia walls. The nuns themselves spoke of it as a miracle and secretly showed the blessed anchorite to visitors through a window in the door of her cell. All her life she had been working on a piece of embroidery and was reported as saying that once she had completed this work it was her wish for the cell to be walled up. Then she would devote the rest of her life to praising the glory of God. Such were her own words, in the message sent to her brother's house, when she heard from me that I was going away from Boa Vista and that I hoped to see her once more before I left. Esperanca agreed to my request.

I made my way through the cloisters where bells were still rung to warn inmates that a male visitor was coming, passing through a sunlit garden full of oriental spice trees that had long since fallen into neglect. The leaves were still wet from a rain that had just fallen and the garden was shining. It seemed to me that it prefigured the appearance of Esperanca when she opened the slat in her cell door. Her face had the lustre of freshness and youth. Don't stay, she said, I have finished it and you must have it and then you can go away. You left this here when you first came. It was falling apart and I copied it for you, which has taken all my life. She passed two rolls of cloth through the little window, the original quipu, now threadbare, and the copy she had made of it. The quipu, I said. Now I understand. All this time it has been passing through your hands and breathed with the air into your lungs. Don't you see? Esperanca shook her head. I don't understand anything about it, she said, all I did was copy it. The quipu has been passing through your hands, I repeated, next to your skin all this time. Don't you see? The dust of Tahuantin-suyu you have breathed into your body, absorbing it from the quipu through your skin and lungs, is what must have kept you so young. But she shook her head and said Nonsense, how little faith I had, she said (becoming a little angry) how simple the truth was if only I looked, for what else but love could have sustained her in this place all her life, and she asked me to leave without looking back, and I did as she asked, walking through the ruined spice-tree garden, down to the harbour where I boarded the ship, still wondering, but it was not until I had disembarked in Santa Maria de la Antigua and taken passage for New Orleans that I heard the bolts of the little window in her cell finally slide shut behind me.

New Orleans

When he went off duty at midnight Father Anselm hurried down the corridor to his office in a mood of excited anticipation unlike anything he could remember in all the years he had worked at the shelter. He remained on call throughout the night, but only in case of an emergency. Usually he was so tired that if undisturbed he slept through on the cot in his office until he was relieved at six the next morning. During the nights he sat listening to the foundling's story, however, he hadn't slept at all. During the day he only dozed off for half an hour after lunch. Yet he wasn't in the least tired. He wondered if the lack of tiredness might have something to do with the dust. It was this idea that he broached at the beginning of the third night of his conversations with the old man.

"Pablo," he said, having lifted the box out of the filing cabinet, opened the shutters and flipped the TALK switch, "I have been thinking. About the white moths and what they signify, about the Big House and Boa Vista, but most of all about the unhappy nun whom you loved. When you sneezed yesterday you said it was on account of the dust circulating in the system. I wonder if this could be dust that originated from the quipu knotted for you by Esperanca. Breathing the dust of Tahuantin-Suyu rejuvenated her, you believed. And if particles have got into the air conditioning inside your case, it might go some way to explaining your own extraordinary longevity. They might even be passing in and out of the vents and breathed in by me sitting here, keeping me wide awake for days and nights."

For ten minutes he sat listening to the old man's silence, waiting for an answer. Then he flipped the TALK switch and said: "Pablo? Are you all right? Can you hear me?"

Another five minutes passed before he got a reply.

"I have been having....problems....with the voice box. All that talk these past two nights appears to have caused a... a....systems overload, or something of that nature. I suppose you believe I do all that talking myself. Well, these memoirs were recorded long ago on microtape and need only to be retrieved from the memory file and activated. The software works fine. But unless the actual voice box itself is activated quite regularly, it gets clogged up. It's a rather antiquated model, a Sony, you know, and in those days everyone used to believe that Japanese audio systems were the best. Anyway.....you may well be right, Father Anselm. About the dust. The same thing happened to my grandson, Edgar P. Stanton. He too was infected by the dust of the quipu. The last person thus inflicted, I had always thought, until you mentioned your own extreme state of wakefulness, which you attribute to quipu dust. Perhaps it still retains some of those original properties that had such a spectacular effect on poor Esperanca. Maybe, maybe."

"You mention a grandson who will be making an appearance in tonight's narrative. Can I take it that you are about to get married, then? Will things be taking a turn for the better, at least regarding your personal life?"

"Three hundred years old when I reached New Orleans, I married and prospered, till yellow fever took my wife and children back into the serpent river in which all creations flows. Even the steam engines, which on land were put to work as pumps, soon began to travel up the Mississippi as ships. With the arrival of machines our lives changed, our deaths too. The Once and Once Only nature of things was replaced by the Over and Over Again effect of reproduction. Originals were overrun by copies, my grandson Edgar P. Stanton by the photographic plates of him, civil peace by a Civil War in which machine guns killed tens of thousands more than in the wars that had been fought between Indian and conquistador. Were things taking a turn for the better? Judge for yourself, Father Anselm. Judge for yourself"

Rue Royale

After all the wriggling the Mississippi had done — live eel of a river, Mijou said — the bed of the river those French-Canadian explorers had travelled down, not to mention the Spanish before them, ran pretty much over dry land these days, and the sloops that came breezing up the hundred odd miles from the Gulf of Mexico to New Orleans would have stranded in the marshes or run clean aground if they'd been following the course of the river De Soto's men rafted down centuries ago. So it was a fair question where the river ran, one that was frequently asked, matter-of-factly, as if checking on the whereabouts of an erratic and notoriously self-willed horse. Where the river ran, there ran boundaries, dividing the property of states, nations and private persons, which kept shifting back and forth between the French and the Spanish in any case. It was difficult enough to keep track of these property issues without the river repeatedly changing its course, as it had done, said Mijou, the night she was born on a cotton plantation down river from a township on the west bank.

By her mother's account she was already in labour when the river took off. Tired of meandering through one wide bend after another, it wriggled over its banks and took a short cut of twenty miles through the intervening forest. This cut-off had a number of side-effects on the cotton plantation. It was no longer located on the river was one thing. A sandbar as high as a street of two-storey houses now stood where the Mississippi once flowed, and Mijou who had been conceived in slavery in Missouri was born in freedom in Illinois, in accordance with the laws of the state where her mother was deposited along with the sandbar after the river jumped.

Mijou was something of a wriggler herself, with a riverine background prone to short-cuts, and whether she was a quadroon, as she claimed and had to explain to me, or a maroon who had done some conniving in the matter of her birth and status, was as uncertain to me as the trade description of the place where we met. If it was a dance hall, as the women employed there described it, for the clients it was a dance hall that did an excellent imitation of a brothel. Comfort rooms, Mijou said when I asked where the men kept on disappearing upstairs with the girls. She was so taken aback by the question that she took off her mask to see what sort of a fool I was and how I had meant it before she gave an answer.

From the bowie knives and brass knuckles displayed casually by some men with impressive moustaches, the Management, Mijou said, who lounged at the entrance to the ball room and at the bottom of the stairs, I saw fair indications of trouble expected in this area of comfort rooms. But when Mijou took off her mask I liked the look of her and she of me, and nothing else in that place would ever concern us any more. Let's go, I said, and we did, to the best hotel in town. In Spanish Mijou said there was a French phrase for this, I've forgotten just how it went, something to the

157

effect of pouring water into new galoshes prior to purchasing them, a fair summary of my first encounter with a bath-tub, though she wasn't referring to that. I still wonder how she knew what I already had at the back of my mind. Mijou knew it, even if I didn't myself. The smell of loneliness around a man perhaps. The marriage ceremony apart, those comfort rooms upstairs would have done us just as well. Beds remained beds, whatever wriggling was done in them. When we sent out for a minister in the middle of the night they were all asleep. I said I would double the fee to cover the inconvenience of the minister being woken up, and a hungry individual appeared in five minutes. He conducted the ceremony in French, so I didn't understand half of what he said, taking it on faith that I was a married man before breakfast and within twenty-four hours of arriving in New Orleans.

How explain? Describe Mijou. It was what went into the making of the woman, clear enough on her mother's side, straight issue of black and white. Not so clear in the case of the father, who appeared to have wriggled out of all responsibility for Mijou beyond her conception, to which he contributed Spanish-French stock with Indian trimmings such as the slant of her eyes, only visible in the sort of reluctant light available in churches and dance halls. Her face with the luminous quality of pasture steeped in moonlight, darkness lit up, a kind of skin glow along the horizon, an expression that without the least embarrassment one would wish to describe as serene.

When I arrived in town I was a naked animal wanting to cover itself. Such was my feeling of having passed out of youth, losing brashness, the skin that had seemed so resilient between myself and the world all of a sudden become permeable — stepping off the boat into the ambush of middle age, aware for the first time of a feeling of nakedness in the world. In Mijou I found allies, the generations who had been her precursors and were my contemporaries, all the way back into the forest and the first boat to have come over the sea. I surrounded myself with her, the ghosts resurrected in her glints and slants, the whole stock and trimmings, her body a banquet with a generous side-order of wriggle bequeathed by her sometime father upriver. This was not so much love as business at first sight, a deal broached in a dance hall and closed in a hotel, as befitted the makeshift circumstances of the partners.

I bought a house in the Rue Royale, pretty as a picture, Mijou said. Balconies with sensuously rounded wrought iron-work jutted out over the ground-floor shops like imposing bosoms, coquettishly decorated with sprays of pink and white blossom. The locksmith's trade sign creaked next door to the bank, an outsize key, locking and unlocking as it swung back and forth in the light river breeze. Across the way, mendicant-like in the shadow of Garrault's great trading house, squatted the mud laboratory of the mender of broken combs, the glue maker, haberdasher and fitter of wigs, a liquor store and gunsmith. At one end of the street there was a French-style eating saloon, at the other a fencing academy run by the improbably named José Llulla. Dispatched opponents were catered for by another establishment he owned, a cemetery on the south side of the Faubourg Ste. Marie. The appearance of the bewhiskered and sometimes bevizored Monsieur Llulla at his academy door, flexing a rapier and wearing those white pyjamas that seemed to be de rigueur for fencing instructors, gave the Rue Royale a certain edge; class, as Mijou said. On such occasions a frisson would pass down the street that made ladies sigh and the key outside the locksmith's creak.

To my wife the sum of all the appearances she perceived to be myself and summarised as her husband was known under the name Paul Zarraté. I had felt the need to reinvent myself. Somewhere in the Gulf of Mexico Pablito went overboard. The final accent and the double consonant were borrowed from a French commercial gentleman named Barré who gave me his card when we disembarked. I learned to say Paul Zarraté out of the corner of my mouth in the French manner, as if expectorating something with a bitter taste – a characteristic of the commercial gentleman that I had noted and admired. I made these changes to myself out of long experience that had taught me it was wise to merge with whatever background I was placed in. This was to be understood literally, most of my life having occurred in the passive mode, from having been placed in the house of the Spanish Jew onwards; placements by seen or unseen hand, on ships, in maloccas, convents, grand colonial houses and so on, in which my part had for the most part been passive, the better part of a century spent drowsing on an opium cushion. I had not been around in the indicative mode much. I was not sure I had much character. After decades of being carried around by slaves in a palanquin I occupied an untenable moral position, even by the standards of New Orleans.

The time had come to reform myself and I took my cue from Mijou. Who was I in my wife's eyes? A stranger who had made money in coffee in Pernambuco and showed her a magic box containing all her dreams. What was in the box? Money, of course, but Mijou was not avaricious, money was the wherewithal to furnish a small house in the Rue Royale and fill it with a large family. She provided the temperament I lacked; shrewd, humorous, warm to hot-tempered and nothing in-between, a natural wriggler and a born liar like her upriver father who had not in fact gone missing as she claimed, nor even travelled further north than the Faubourg Ste. Marie, but was alive and as well as it was possible to be for a denizen of the malaria-ridden swamps steaming on the south side of the city. All of this emerged bit by bit. Now here was the curious thing about my wife. She could not distinguish between the publicly available facts of life and the private manufactures of her imagination, but she was much more firmly rooted in those facts of life than I was. She had more commonsense in her proverbial little finger than I had been able to put together in three hundred years. For Mijou it was a matter of two creaks from the locksmith's key hanging across the street from our parlour window to see what had been missing in my life and to make up the deficiency. What I needed was a family.

This arrived in the shape of a pale, wizened creature who in my judgement looked prematurely antique, a little like one of those shrivelled Indian heads displayed in the Teatro's panopticum. Mijou assured me it was normal. In the New Orleans parlance of the time, from which the mother must have got the expression, our child was a female octoroon. I protested. Octoroon was not a fit description for a child. It made her sound like something for exhibit in Pommeroy's Raree Show & Zoo on Prieur Street. Octoroon was hotly debated. Unmoved by Mijou's liar tears, shed with the same ease with which she laughed, I forbade the use of the word in my house. Octoroon measured the distance my wife's grandmother's descendants had moved from slavery, but why stop there, with an eighth part Negro blood in the family, why not stigmatise the sixteenth and thirty-second Negro parts, and so on down the line, and give them stigma-bearing names, coons, racoons, macaroons, and keep them in an octoroonery for all I cared.

160

It was as well I took a firm line with this first child, because soon there two more all at once, and then yet another, making a total of four female octoroons, or half a Negro woman in the house, three-quarters if one included the mother, so that as a household we were not so much moving away from as sliding rapidly back towards eligibility for indentured labour on the plantations. And how did I figure in this account, bearing in mind the proximity of Lisbon to the North African coast and all the Moorish blood that must have been squirted into Portuguese veins? Some of the serving women in Zarate's house had been black. I looked at my daughters and saw myself lurking behind their faces, an anxious ghost, purveyor of Old World contraband, smuggling late medieval blood with Jewish-Moorish trimmings into their tiny octoroon veins. I felt surrounded by little bits of myself, acorns shed all around me and beginning to sprout, a lone tree in the process of becoming a forest at last. In the three-hundred year perspective of this particular parent the view of a family naturally took in not merely the father and his daughters but the great serpent-river in which all creation flowed. Pig Indians called this oneness All-Creatures-Being-In-The-Forest, and I had not come across a philosophy that expressed the notion better.

In the Rue Royale and the surrounding Faubourg Ste. Marie there was indeed a density of life which reminded me of the forest in which I had once lived. On stepping out of the house I felt easily threatened by the salient balcony looming overhead, and I found myself reverting to the Pig Indian habit of stretching my arms out to prop up the falling sky whenever I emerged from the malocca; in this case as a precaution against falling plaster. My daughters had already picked up the habit before I could turn round to see what they were doing, eight worm-like arms wriggling aloft in sky greeting, as I defended it under close cross-examination by my wife, when they later filed out of the coop to go to school every morning.

In a Creole neighbourhood there was almost as much ritual involved in saying hello to folks as in an Indian village. The street was an extension of the parlour, and people out there were actually in here. You were expected to convey that familiarity without encroaching, for you were in their parlour at the same time they were in yours. Both sides took care not to impose on this quaint notion of hospitality privately extended in the public domain. It led to a formal familiarity of manner, a kind of courtly dance together cheek by jowl. There was in this manner, despite its expansive friendliness, just a hint of the reserve required to preserve the public character of the street. Thus the Rue Royale, too, joined the great serpent-river in which all creation flowed, the fencing instructor Monsieur Llulla not excepted.

Zarraté & Cie.

This sign appeared in the window in Héloise's handwriting. My eldest daughter had plans for me, or I should say: for us. She was a not very pretty girl, with unaccountable russet hair and a passion for arithmetic. While other children her age were still gnawing their rusks Héloise was working out percentages and compound interest. Her sign, I thought, hit the nail on the head. Late in life I had acquired appendages, become a family enterprise that was clearly a going concern. What could better express that than Zarraté & Cie? I had been pursuing various business options in a peaceful way, but this was more like a declaration of war, reflecting the seriousness Héloise brought to bear on whatever she took in hand. She said: Father, Monsieur Garrault the Elder would be pleased to discuss business with you whenever you care to drop by. What business, I asked. My sharp-eared wife answered from halfway up the stairs. Oh that, she said. I dare say it's just a courtesy call. I met M. Garrault in the street and said that if we could ever be of assistance, you know, as one does. Perhaps Héloise might go with you.

I had never been beyond the front room of Garrault's, but Héloise threaded her way between the clerks at their desks and up the dark narrow staircase at the back as if she had taken this route many times. Garrault the Elder greeted her, indeed, as though they were old acquaintances. I gathered this was where she had learned to calculate compound interest, and expressed the hope that my daughter had not caused any trouble. This raised a little storm of expostulation, a blowing out of the cheeks, followed by a series of popping eruptions peculiarly French and mastered by Garrault the Elder to a fine degree. But no! Out of the question! Absolutely! A shower of spray pitted the soft vellum writing-pad on his desk. Quinze or seize, he said with a weary wave of his hand, inviting us to sit down in old-fashioned, hard-backed elegance as he delivered himself of a tremendous sneeze.

There followed a conventional choice of overtures before getting down to business: good news conveyed with an expression of keen regret, or bad news related with sinister satisfaction. Garrault opted for the latter, enabling him to pass smoothly on to the subject he wished to discuss: the embargo. An embargo was not good for a trading house. But no! Absolutely not! A flurry of explosions scored points on his desk. There were customers, he said, pushing forward a handful of quills, and there were commodities, represented by an inkwell on the far side of his desk. Unfortunately there was no way of getting the one to the other, unless one circumvented the embargo, as the inkwell, guided surreptitiously by Garrault's hand, duly proceeded to do. If only his trading house was on the south side of the street. But yes!

Garrault appealed explosively to me for commiseration, but the significance of this remark was clearly lost on me, so he turned to Héloïse instead. That sagacious child nodded her head with gravity, although I was quite sure she had no more idea what he was talking about than I had. Garrault directed his attention back to me, saw the glum expression on my face and began talking with great animation. How enviable my charming little house, with its convenient access via the Rue Vendôme to the great marshland below the city. What vistas of a wild state of nature untouched since the dawn of time. What solitude. Perhaps some of those advantages, said Garrault slyly as his finger traced a circuitous line on the vellum writing-pad, could be made available to customers with special requests his trading house was regrettably unable to oblige on account of this accursed embargo. He looked at me with his head on one side. A courier could easily come to my house, he said, take the special orders placed with his company, bring the ordered goods by pirogue through the swamps along routes only known to few, connecting marshland and sea without recourse to the river, and deliver them to my house without the Rue Royale having an inkling of the transaction. This would be an inestimable service to the respected house of Garrault, which at all times had its reputation to think about. He bowed, leaving me to draw my own conclusions.

Monsieur Garrault, I replied, this is smuggling, for which the penalty is death. He pursed his lips, as if death were a debatable eventuality, perhaps with a back exit he knew of to give it the slip, then spread his hands to concede the point and said: there would naturally be a commission for Zarraté & Cie. How much, I asked. Ten percent, said Garrault. There was a creak from the other chair where Héloïse had begun to wriggle, no longer able to contain herself. Twelve'nahalf, she said in a rush. Garrault's inflated cheeks popped as if he had been punctured all at once. He got laboriously to his feet and went over to a cabinet from which he produced glasses, a bottle and a biscuit. Pouring a few drops of brandy onto the biscuit he handed it to Héloïse and watched it disappear with alacrity into her mouth. She crunched and grimaced, with rising eyebrows, widening eyes. That girl will go far, said Garrault, and he raised his glass.

The Man with the Tin Nose

Had I known the frequency with which our street flooded I would not have moved into the same house again. Many parts of the Faubourg lay under water, and whatever excess flood was available drained by some mysterious natural inclination into the Rue Royale. Clerks across the road at Garrault's stood on raised platforms to do their work, rather like Pommeroy's performing seals, and passing Monsieur Llulla's establishment one flood morning I could observe an unusual sight, fencers wading, rapiers raised, with a dreamlike subaquatic slowness towards their opponents. In my own house the children remained upstairs, beyond reach of the rats and snakes and other swamp denizens washed in by the flood, including their grandfather Robespierre on the occasion of his first visit.

He paddled his pirogue through the door one evening as I was floating a water-logged chest over to the drier side of the front parlour. I watched him take out a tobacco pouch and silently fill his pipe, and knew without asking that M. Garrault's courier had arrived. Who else could have commanded a flood to tide him over to suit his convenience like that, right onto the premises? Under the circumstances I was also not particularly surprised when this extraordinary man introduced himself as the long-lost upriver father of my wife. He wore a tin nose strapped into the middle of his face, on account of the flies, he said, mentioning almost as an after-thought the lack of a nose that caused the problem with the flies. Robespierre didn't add anything to clear this mystery up, but it seemed likely that whatever had been done to his head might at the same time have done for his nose. His bald head looked as if it had been shivered by lightning. A three-pronged scar burst like a firework over his skull, spray-ing livid trajectories down his face, so that it appeared to have been put together from the salvaged parts. It was a face of extreme violence frozen in a state of death-like quietude. For a professional oyster-gatherer, which Robespierre said he was, he seemed to have had an eventful career in the contemplative solitude of the swamps.

My daughter in, he asked. Out, I said. Grandchildren? Asleep, I replied. Certainly I had no intention of waking them up to introduce them to this tin-nosed nightmare.

The social side of his call heaving been dealt with in two sentences, Robespierre asked what I wanted. Garrault had given me a long list of special requests, mostly of an alcoholic or combustible nature, but includ-ing lace, cinnamon and a dozen Guinea slaves. I read the list to Robespierre. A month, he grunted, declining to take the list when I offered it to him. Incriminating, he said. Couldn't read it in any case. I asked how he would remember it and he grinned, his fingers scampering like mice across his skull in a curious pantomime, which I took to mean he had memorised it.

No stranger to coincidence in the course of my life, I found the chain of events leading from Mijou to the Rue Royale to Garrault's trading house to the swamps to the smuggler who emerged from them and by wonder-ful chance was my father-in-law to be rather more than coincidence could carry. Mijou wriggled for all she was worth, but in the end the truth came out. Her father had been employed by Garrault for a long time. Together they had in fact been conducting their business out of my house years before I came into possession of it, in collaboration with, meaning com-mission paid to, the previous owner, who had unfortunately died under mysterious circumstances. So when they heard that Mijou's new husband was looking for a property – during this confession she wept tears of gen-uine remorse, which I interrupted only to ask if the previous owner of the house had died a natural death, or been murdered, or perhaps convicted of smuggling and sentenced to death. Héloise was summoned for advice. Having listened to representations of both parties, she walked out of the house. Anxiously we watched her cross the road and disappear into Garrault's. Ten minutes later she came back into the house with still widening eyes and said: fifteen percent. Thanks to this intervention my wife and I were reconciled.

There was another matter to discuss with Garrault, an item right down at the bottom of the list between three pounds of fishing-hooks and a bushel of pepper: a dozen Guinea slaves. I told Garrault I wanted no part in trading slaves. He blew out his cheeks and deferred to my better judgement, but not before he had explained to me how slave smuggling was the monopoly of maroon communities in the swamps, escaped slaves who made a living out of trapping and selling slaves themselves. Slaves were a commodity like anything else, only more valuable. I said that for fifteen percent of the sale proceeds I had no objection to my house being used as a clearing-house for any commodity under the sun except slaves. For the consignment of one dozen Guinea slaves Garrault would have to make other arrangements. Coolly he announced that he had already done so. The eccentric doctor whose solitary house stood on the outskirts of the Faubourg, right on the edge of the marshes, was a beneficiary of the free circulation of trade without the incentive of fifteen percent. Slaves came to be treated by Dr Maurois free of charge. He gave refuge to maroons and to smuggled slaves on merely humanitarian grounds. Extraordinary, but there it was. Garrault shrugged.

A month later the empty shed in my back garden filled up overnight with the goods the oyster-gatherer had promised. My father-in-law himself floated in around lunch-time the following day, his nose a little rusty, as he remarked, tapping it with his pipe to make it clang, from exposure to all the damp weather that had come with the flood. The children were completely satisfied with this grandfather. For the time being they were content to study him from a distance, standing on the dresser for a better view of his lightning-struck head as he bent over the craw-fish pie his daughter set on the table whenever he came. She studied him with scarcely less curiosity than her daughters, treating him with that quaint Creole manner, a jocular formality, half-astonished that her vagabond father was there and she entertaining him in her own parlour, listening to tall tales he told late into the night while the children sat like mice on the dresser without so much as a squeak to remind their mother that it was long past their bedtime.

Chief Liar Island

Robespierre said there was a Choctaw chief who told such lies that his tribe got fed up with him and banished him with his wives to an island in the swamp. The chief said he could fly like a bird, burrow like a worm and swim like a fish, claiming to have travelled to the moon, the middle of the earth, the bottom of the ocean, the end of the rainbow, and for telling all these lies he was finally sent into exile by his tribe.

His descendants took root on Chief Liar island named after him, and mixed with the African and Indian slaves who escaped from plantations on the river or from ships sailing up the gulf from the Caribbean. The maroon community made baskets and sifters from willow weeds, fished, trapped birds, collected berries and grew corn and sweet potatoes on tufts of land in the middle of the cypress swamps. The island was ideally located between the river and the ocean. When the wars in the Old World washed over to the New, and French and Spanish, British and American, were fighting for supremacy in the Gulf of Mexico to control the trade and the arms that passed up and down the Mississippi, the swamp inhabitants turned to smuggling and piracy, reviving buccaneer traditions that had been extinct along the Spanish Main for over a century.

The land on which the settlement of New Orleans was built by the French sloped down from the levee, high and dry, but the swamp began only a mile or so from the river. Within a few hundred yards back of my house in the Faubourg Ste. Marie spread a wasteland dotted with cypress stumps, full of ponds choked with pickerel-weed, the haunt of frogs, snakes and rats on the edge of the vast swamp forest that continued all the way to the Gulf coast. A man in there might hear the whine of the mosquitoes or the cough of an alligator and have no idea he was within hailing distance of a city of thousands of inhabitants. I first went out there in a pirogue with Robespierre to hunt water fowl. Robespierre was amazed at the ease with which I memorised the bayous, finding my orientation in the marshes so reliably that I could soon negotiate them on my own. But I did no more than what I had learned from the Taiassu, judging by the sky, the weathered side of trees, the flight of birds, the run of animals, the exudation of sap from a broken twig, the taste and colour of the water.

Surprised by a thunderstorm on one of our hunting expeditions, we put in at Chief Liar Island to wait for the rain to pass. Apart from Robespierre, no whites lived on the island. His wife was a maroon. Many of the women were Choctaw squaws, most of the men still as black as first-generation African slaves. The gleam of dozens of fires, around which these maroon families sat, marked the boundaries of the little island in the night. They sat back on their heels and rocked, talking in soft voices or conversing in signs. On all sides rose the bark of frogs from the swamp, wobbling on the moist air. When this chorus suddenly ceased the surrounding dark seemed to press more closely in on us. St. Malo was coming, a woman said. The pirogue that had driven a wedge of silence into the brawling night scraped up onto the shore, and a huge Negro stepped into the firelight. He wore rings on all his fingers, ear-rings and gold chains that flashed in the firelight with every movement he made. St. Malo was a mute. No one had ever heard him speak. His hands talked as one imagined his voice, a deep bass, with smooth and slow gestures, fluid, unhurried. The maroons who sat around him watching his hands sometimes voiced what the hands said, layers of voices overlapping in a chant.

Yes, yes! They hummed and rocked. Bring the treasure to the Temple! Bring up the bayou to Grande Terre! Yes! Others came from outlying fires and picked up the refrain. Speech passed over into song. St. Malo swayed and began to clap his hands. He stood in frayed britches, the upper half of his body bare, glowing red and orange in he light of the fire.

At dawn we set off to retrieve the treasure on board a Spanish merchantman St.Malo had seized and brought up the bayou to Grande Terr.e. Before the maroons came and took it and jocularly named it Grande Terre, the little island had been a cult place of the Indians. It was still called the Temple, after the great oaks, which spread a roof of solid foliage over the island. It was a graveyard of a place. Cairns of clam shells, marking Indian sacrificial rites, stood on the shore where the maroons had left their own relics, the skulls and bones of people they had murdered here.

The corpses still lay on the deck of the merchantman where they had fallen, three days dead, rain-sodden, abandoned rag-doll dead, not quite real, flies buzzing over them in the early morning heat. Rain had washed the cadavers clean, blood rain had run off the deck, scummy in patches where the blood congealed and ceased to run when the rain stopped.

Fifteen percent of them would in future be debited to the account of Zarraté & Cie. Kneeling in the pirogue and watching the disembowelment of the Spanish ship on which the corpses were still lying, I wondered what compound interest accumulated for the dead who had traded their lives, or why I had sentimentally imagined that dealing in dead men was in any way less reprehensible than dealing in living slaves. Mentally I went through an inventory of services and goods on which I relied in my day to day life. I tried to think of a single one untainted with blood or with the labour of slaves but was unable to find one. Blood and slavery circulated in the entire system of trade, leaving no point untouched. It occurred to me how rightly this ghost-ridden island was named the Temple. Sacrifices were brought here to the god of trade. I imagined all the trade of the world making up one great temple in which sacrifices had constantly to be brought to sustain the commerce of the nations. I realised that trade was an exchange of these blood offerings. All wars between nations were fought on its behalf. Wars were the first acts of trade. All the written instruments, the contracts, promissory notes and letters of credit on which the exchange was based were nothing other than blood pacts, sealing a law that recognised the primacy of commerce above anything else on earth.

St. Malo spread-eagled aloft, arms and legs threaded spider-like in the rigging, looked down on this scene as he must have looked down on countless other divisions of the spoil. When they had stripped the merchantman of its last scrap of value the maroons towed the ship out into deeper water, tossed burning torches onto the deck and pushed off in their pirogues. They watched the ship blaze. Burning timbers crackled with a luxuriant, almost a pleasurable sound, exploding with a whoosh and a wrenching groan that was the sound of wood cracking down the grain, spitting sparks out over the water. St. Malo still stood spread-eagled aloft, watching the flames lunge up and tear down the rigging, as if anticipating his crucifixion by fire, but at the last moment he disengaged himself from the ropes, poised on the tip of a spar and dived in a wide arc over the burning sea.

Vieux Carré

Robespierre said the biggest disservice to the Faubourg Ste. Marie was done by a traitor of a Frenchman, for it was only after Napoleon had sold Louisiana to the Americans that trade turned around and blew in from the opposite direction. It was no longer what sailed up the Mississippi from the Gulf but what drifted down from the river valley in exchange for sugar and cotton on their way upstream that became the source of prosperity of New Orleans. Drifting was what they did, the keel-boats, barges and flat-boats that slipped in on the favouring eddy under the river bank and landed in front of the Faubourg, and this abomination of river craft, as M. Garrault the Younger called it, these huge huddled arks, floating ware-houses crammed with pork, corn and flour, were handled by a new species of savages, jeans-clad drifters who didn't know a word of French.

My wife Mijou and I with her floating origins were well equipped to handle drifters. We made a business of it, enlisting our arm-wriggling daughters in enterprises of the dance-hall variety in the time-honoured meaning of that phrase. It was the time and the place for wrigglers of all description. Zarraté & Cie had come of age. Trade poured in the door, as unstoppable as the annual Faubourg floods. The less the neighbourhood wanted to embrace the newcomers, the more eager the newcomers seemed to embrace the neighbourhood, its food and liquor and above all its women. Even their flatboats poured ashore, broken up for timber that was sometimes laid down in the Faubourg's muddy streets to serve as sidewalks, for no flatboat was ever built that knew how to drift back upstream. The same might have been said of many of the flatboat crews. Hanging on to them until their pockets had been turned inside out, occasionally with the result that penniless drifters got laid down in muddy streets alongside the gunwales of their boats to serve involuntarily as sidewalks, became something of a speciality of the Faubourg Ste. Marie. From the time it was still brand-new people referred to it as the Vieux Carré, inventing tourism way before any place else

Zarraté & Fille had also come of age. Héloise, whose brain-child this new affiliate was, my eldest daughter, thin-armed, flat-chested and spectacles on nose, viewed the brawling scenes of commerce on the Mississippi wharves with unwavering eyes. Having calculated the collective compound interest on the goods handled there in a single day, and this at a time when a guard in a cocked hat still drowsed in the sentry-box in the shadow of the old fort, Héloise had thought of branching out from the parent company in the Rue Royale. She purchased, with my approval and in my name, the empty lots along the Tschopitoulas Road where later the warehouses of Zarraté & Fille stood, before we had even thought of warehouses or would have known what to put in them if we had. It was a whim to please her. Brain-children seemed to me to be as close to the reproductive process as my ugly-duckling daughter was ever likely to get, which was why, in a rare show of independence, I overruled the objections of her mother and her three incomparably more handsome sisters: Marie-Jeanne, Marie-Claude and Marie-Antoinette.

Now these were girls as they had always been bred in the Vieux Carré from the time when it was neither old nor a square but just a few streets between a swamp and a river. Some Choctaw squaws went into their making, along with three score casket girls, so called because of the trunks containing their trousseau, if the city chronicle was to be believed, financed by the French king to be disposed of in marriage under the discretion of nuns. The discretion of nuns left much to be desired, more than flesh and blood could stand. It was at this point in the colonial venture that the wriggling began, of which the upshot, according to the particular shade of connivance, were mestizo, mulattos, quadroons, octoroons, the Marie-Jeannes, Marie-Claudes and Marie-Antoinettes of the New World. These women were the ornaments of the Faubourg Ste. Marie, talking vivaciously in a splash of sunlight on a street corner, shapely women with round arms and throats, the rounder the older they became — Creole matrons like my wife Mijou, all lace and alabaster decoration, still showing off superb torrents of hair, to be dressed two or if necessary three times a day with fast-fading bouquets of jasmine, violets and lady-slipper sold on the streets.

We bought the bistro at the end of the street and called it "Mijou". the girls stood behind the counter selling liquor up front or tickets to the back room where there was dancing with hired girls, rooms overhead for more dancing, and no lack of exits opening directly onto the street without the inconvenience of stairs to eject customers who misbehaved. Mijou had invested in her daughters. She had groomed them. Now they were grown up she said they should pay their way. They were occupied in a "managerial capacity", which included advertising. I never saw much managerial talent in my three daughters but their capacity was never in doubt. They were pretty good at advertising, too. Advertising meant flouncing through the Faubourg and making a bee-line for Mijou's bistro with as many potential customers as possible in tow. Sign-board girls they were called in the trade, the decoy up front, who had vanished by the time the customer was safely inside and the hired girls could start working him over. My youngest, Marie-Antoinette, was sometimes known to disappear upstairs with her beau, bypassing meal, beverage and dance tickets. Like the good managerial mother she was, knowing where such adventures could lead young ladies, Mijou charged her daughter for room service and otherwise minded her own business. Such adventures did indeed lead Marie-Antoinette in the same direction they had led her mother, married within twelve months at the altar of Sacred Heart to a cook from Marseilles, destined to become chef de cuisine at the St. Charles.

Sunday lunch with my son-in-law Gaston, rapidly endorsed by a sprinkling of grandchildren, became a great rallying point for the family. Fifteen to twenty French men, women and children, seated at a long table and all talking at once dined in a narrow glass-fronted room in the Rue Chartres, on display to be envied by people passing in the street. Apprentices of Gaston served at table, moving along the row of guests and ceremoniously affixing napkins the size of shrouds in which they remained interred for the next few hours. At this table France was united with Africa, India and the Caribbean in a potpourri of national flavours, bouillabaisse, callas, congri, patassa, sabotin and jambalaya, richness and sweetness checked by sharp, outlandish tastes. This table at which we were shrouded every Sunday became the graveyard of my wife's youth. She came to it with a light step, still a smooth-skinned, small-waisted woman despite her round throat and plump arms. She got up from it, before the great yellow fever epidemic put an end to these gatherings, with tear-shaped purses under her eyes, barrelled like a ship and plunging with the heavy-swell motion caused by the damp that creaked rheumatically in her bones. Marie-Jeanne and Marie-Claude sailed in their mother's wake, young women in full tackle, triumphant products of Creole cooking combined with the ambitions of a burgeoning middle class.

From about this time there was a new middle quality I became aware of in myself. I had grown plump. My ear-lobes had grown thicker. I was getting heavier around the jowls and had pains in my feet. I had entered my plum-coloured, sententious period, with a lot of scroll-work around my opinions, decorative trimmings at the expense of a clear sense of direction. Side dishes distracted me, the acquisition of knickknacks, the possession of comfort or the comfort of possessions, I was not sure which. I had a consuming interest in food at all hours of the day, ordeuvres without the companionship of a main course, puddings marooned on solitary eruptions of hunger in the middle of the night. I was afraid of emptiness, around me and inside me. Perhaps this was why I became a clubbish man, to be contradicted by the evidence of the reality of life, which at my age seemed increasingly like a dream. I could hear the ghosts rustling in the dark corridor behind me, far longer and better substantiated than the fictitious strip of present on which I precariously perched, a trapeze of light, lurching out into the darkness ahead.

I played cards with my friends every evening, at the St. Louis, at Gayarre's place on Canal Street or Maurois' lugubrious, dilapidated house in an overgrown garden, full of ponds choked with bulrushes and pickerel-weed. It stood by itself on the edge of the swamp, tall and thin, a stark white presence, raised on high pillars and enclosed by some ribbed construction added later to prevent it from falling down. The house looked like a skinny old woman who had been robbed of all her possessions and left standing in the wilderness with nothing but her clasped arms to cover her nakedness. Gayarre thought of the house as a fitting memorial to the late Countess Pontalba, a lady who had been Maurois' sweetheart before she deserted him for a much richer man. Maurois never spoke of the affair. Gayarre said she lived to regret it, but that might have been because he was a moralist, and poor, and what other pleasures did a poor moralist have.

For me Maurois was the sweetness of humanity personified. The bookseller Gayarre arrived at his liberal opinions by process of reason, whereas with the doctor kindness was the ground water of life. Negroes naturally became his concern. They could come to his house at any time and be treated free of charge. He put his head on one side when he listened sceptically to the bookseller's theories about the solution of slavery in the south. Gayarre wrote pamphlets on this subject, energised as much by his own moral indignation as by its cause.

Supposing, his argument went, a slave to be worth six hundred dollars in the present depressed state of commerce. Maurois always refused to suppose anything of the kind, Gayarre always ignored the objection, continuing with his exposition throughout his friend's protests. The bookseller's argument was a simple one and went like this. When the slave's earnings, deposited in the bank, amounted to one hundred dollars, he would be given *Monday* free from indentured labour in order to work for himself. He then had two days in the week, Sunday included, to improve his situation, thus enabling him, by voluntary labour, to acquire the second hundred dollars, with which he purchased *Tuesday*. He now had three days, two of them weekdays at his own disposal, in order to purchase *Wednesday*, and so on, in a progressive ratio, until the whole six days were his own, and the slave was free, entering society with acquired habits of industry and temperance which would make him a valuable citizen. The doctor thought all this preposterous. Liberty was the natural condition of all creation, not a commodity to be brought back in weekly instalments from those who had stolen it.

But that liberty was not the natural condition of all creation — plain evidence of this fact was on display daily in the rotunda of the St. Louis where slaves were sold. The St. Louis hotel was not the slave mart of Vallongo in Boa Vista, where the public came to see naked men and women whipped up out of narrow greasy cages and put through their paces like animals. This was more pernicious, a stealthy exhibition of evil in a civilised setting, the voices of the buyers mingling in whispers reminiscent of a church as they stood sipping their thick chicory coffee and watched wholesome Negroes parading around the rotunda. It did not deter Maurois from frequenting the St. Louis. He might as well have been deterred from frequenting New Orleans or any other city in the New World. He believed in what he called the infusion of decency. It was in the nature of democratic values to spread. It was not possible, he said, to be a

174

guest in the St. Louis for very long and remain insensible to the indecency of slavery. Gayarre and I disagreed. The people who spent most time in the hotel, the sugar planters, having vested interests in slavery, were also those who remained most insensible to its indecency.

So we continued to sit and play cards in the St. Louis, or at the doctor's house, or Gayarre's book store on Canal Street, waiting for Maurois' infusion of decency into the world, and nothing changed. The old mule continued to drag a long lever round and round in an unvarying circle on the grassed avenue where horses were still tethered, goats roamed and lines of drying shirts and petticoats fluttered in the breeze. A tattered Negro in a straw hat was the mule's ring-master and an artesian well was the object of the animal's never-ending revolutions. The mule and the man had been sinking the well for as long as Gayarre could remember, although not much water was ever found.

The Creoles in the quarter remained true to themselves, proud, indolent, illiterate, devoting most of their energies to the pursuit of pleasure. They wept as they stood on the Place d'Armes and watched the flag of a people whose national existence was only a couple of decades old taking the place of the tricolour at the top of the mast, then forgot all about it over the preparations for a forthcoming dance. They had seen their city change ownership often enough, bought and sold, bought and sold half a dozen times within a century. It wriggled back and forth like their river. The Americans, too, would go in their turn. But to the disbelief of the local population, who thought they were so heavy they would sink into the swamp, two granite-paved roadways were installed along Canal Street to make sure it stayed in place, on American soil.

The bookseller's sign on Canal Street still swung in the breeze, although even then Gayarre was being kept alive by apparently the only two customers left in the quarter who still read books in French, both of them by chance his best friends. Between the two roadways was a tree-bordered strip of neutral ground dividing the French and American quarters of the town. Goats and washing-lines had gone, but the long lever continued to creak through the heat of the day, propelled by the same old mule under the supervision of the tattered Negro in the straw hat. One day it stopped. Gayarre said that people on Canal Street had become so used to the mule and the Negro that it was some time before they noticed. Then they realised they had gone for ever, unobtrusively, in the way things go that seem to be there for ever. Some said the mule died, some the Negro, and Mijou said he had not died but fled across the marshes, to join the uprising St. Malo would be leading against the city any day now from the maroons' hideaway on Chief Liar Island.

Flood

The invasion came, not as she imagined from the swamplands to the south but from the lake to the north, where the level of the backwater rose extraordinarily high one night and infiltrated the city. New Orleans was given the choice of flooding from the lake or flooding from the river at least once a year until engineers arrived to deal with the problems. An increased activity of craw-fish, burrowing into the levee, appeared to be at the root of one of them. In the Faubourg there were wisecracks about these burrowing habits of the craw-fish, squirting water into the little tunnel he had made, until the levee was softened up and gave way to the demands of the river. This flood option was smilingly known as a crevasse. It was most unusual, and considered a little unfair, for both options to be exercised at the same time. But on the night in question this was what took place.

River and lake joined forces and sprang an ambush at either end of the city, sneaking up on those inhabitants of the Vieux Carré who happened to be still downstairs. Marie-Jeanne and Marie-Claude both felt their feet getting wet at the same moment, looked down at the floor and saw it flowing. In the room at the back of the street-front bar the revellers noticed that they were beginning to splash, the flatboat crews lying on the ground that they were beginning to float. Bits of boats which had been sentenced to death on land, broken up and laid down as sidewalks, had been resurrected by the river and were knocking around as if seriously intending to get together again. The girls hitched up their skirts, shooed their customers out and told everyone just to keep walking north until they reached dry land.

When Mijou looked out of the window that morning the bottom half of the locksmith's sign across the street was already under water. That was something she had never seen before. She woke me up so that I could see it too. Tiddly, our tortoiseshell cat, sat marooned on the gate-post, watching rats the size of beavers swim by, big enough to have carried her piggyback to dry land. Mijou thought I should rescue the cat and see to our daughters at the same time. So I put on my oilskins and stepped downstairs into the river, recollecting that this had been a conscious choice I had made long ago as a boy on board the *Sao Cristobal*. I was built on water, I had told myself then, my bones were fluid, this river that was life ran through my veins and I would flow with it. So I made slow-motion watery bounds through the parlour, floated up out of the kitchen window and swam over to the skiff lying bottom up in the garden shed. I was getting too old for this game. The cat jumped down into the boat, curled up in my lap and fell asleep, just as everyone else still seemed to be in the Rue Royale. I found my daughters stretched out sumptuously in the same bed, duplicating each other's postures even when asleep. In the Faubourg Ste. Marie, through the inundated suburbs of Gravier and Marigny, I floated down silent, peaceful streets. Skiffs plied back and forth, but for amusement rather than any practical purpose. People sat fishing out of their bedroom windows. They exchanged gossip with their neighbours across the street, saving their energy for pelting rats they saw foraging downstairs and building rafts to host floating dance parties that were popular during the flood season all over the Faubourg in a quite literal sense.

On the third day of the flood I looked out of our bedroom and saw that the high-water mark on the locksmith's sign was no lower than it had been twenty-four hours earlier. I set off in a pirogue for the Place d'Armes to find out what flood measures were being mooted in the hotel de ville. There I was surprised to find my daughter Héloise in a crowd of people listening to a tall stranger, a fine-looking man with long blond glossy moustaches, standing on a table by the wall on which he was drawing diagrams with a piece of charcoal to the accompaniment of a rattling commentary in unintelligible French. The man seemed to be recommending something none of us had ever heard of, machines powered by steam, which could be used to pump the backwater on the northern side of the city via a channel and drain it off into the river within twenty-four hours. Someone wanted to know where the channel was, and the man tapped his head and said here, all he needed were the volunteers to dig it. As for the breach in the levee, he would stop that up with the old three-masted vessel moored upstream. Someone else asked how. By sinking the damn thing in the hole, the man said with a grin, just as you stopped a plug in a bath-tub.

Garrault the Younger, who was the leader of the French council in the Faubourg, conferred with his colleagues and said they accepted these measures. The council authorised him to implement them if the flood had not begun to recede by the following day. The man took a cloth out of his pocket, wiped his hands and said that was most gracious of them, very gracious indeed, there was just one thing he should add. There was his consultant's fee, he said, inspecting each finger and wiping it individually with an air of surprise, as if he had never encountered it before, half of it to be paid in advance, half when he had completed the job. His price was one thousand dollars.

Garrault the Younger's expostulation at the mention of this indecent sum of money followed in the best tradition of his deceased father's explosions. The Yankee's offer was emphatically rejected, Creole self-esteem restored. In the meantime relief committees were formed, boats dispatched to the besieged areas to distribute food to the poor, carnival celebrated in the Faubourg with more than the usual abandon.

After a week the flood had still not subsided. The refuse that swam on its surface began to smell. Less robust houses began to collapse. Old Monsieur Llulla, now retired from his fencing academy and appreciably closer to the cemetery he owned on the south side, where quite a number of his business associates had prematurely found their final resting place, ferried himself over to the hotel de ville in an original Venetian gondola to air his grievances about the flood damage done to his sepulchres. Caskets, he said, and, even worse, their contents, had been sighted swirling down the Rue Vendome, heading across the inundated marshes for the open sea. The city's seventeen cemeteries, many of them privately owned, as in M. Llulla's case, were unique among American graveyards. With the water level so close to the surface, subterranean graves were impossible. In New Orleans, the dead were buried in brick tombs above ground. Terrible epidemics lurked in the wake of this high water, a grave M. Llulla warned. Submerged for too long, scoured out by the flood, releasing the cadavers from their tombs, these cities of the dead would not merely be desecrated. Soon they would threaten the living. Such were the consequences of inaction. All our lives were at stake.

Enter Mr Stanton. Who was Mr Stanton, please? Rumours in the Rue Royale buoyantly described him as a former military adviser to the Vatican who had smart-talked the municipality into paying him one thousand dollars to rid them of the flood. But the municipality denied this. The crazy Yankee who came here last week and scribbled drawings of his steam machine on the wall of the hotel de ville, offering them the use of it for a preposterous thousand dollars, had been sent packing, as everyone knew. There had been no going back on their word. Fact of the matter.

It was equally a fact of the matter for anyone with eyes to see and ears to hear that Mr Stanton had in the meantime set to work. Had already introduced his Trojan horses into the Faubourgs north and south of Canal Street, monstrous machines belching smoke and noise. An army of German and Irish navvies followed into the breach, equipped with shovels to dig a channel and with newfangled watertight canvas tubes of the kind employed for extinguishing fires. The old three-masted vessel, still moored upstream a hundred years after it had brought the last casket girl to New Orleans from France, was floated down and scuttled to plug the hole in the levee. It was a fact of the matter that all these measures took effect exactly as the engineer had said they would do. Stanton's machines pumped the back-water on the northern side of the city via the channel dug by the navvies, draining it off into the river within forty-eight hours just as he had said.

The Faubourg was left with its smell and the worst wreckage in history. The smell lingered on through the onset of the warm weather. With the advent of swarms of green bottle-flies, tagging it like a marker dye, it seemed even to have become visible. Not only the remains of the more recent dead, crumbling like waterlogged cake in M. Llulla's tombs, manured the Rue Royale. A hundred-year record of ill-managed human waste surfaced in the streets. The Faubourg was a latrine. We lived in a shit-spattered house. Walls still damp and sticky with unidentifiable substances dried out in the spring heat and cracked.

Mijou sprayed them with eau de cologne. Perfumed excrement was the smell with which we lived. No one mentioned it, but the same smell embalmed Gaston's table in the Rue Chartres, where the family assembled for their first Sunday lunch after the flood. Marie-Jeanne and Marie-Claude complained that business was slow. Visitors stayed away from the quarter. In the course of the afternoon the smell rose with the heat pumping up from the floor. My son-in-law walked up and down, spraying the air with perfume, too late to prevent Héloise from fainting.

She excused herself and left early, crossing the smell boundary marking the aftermath of the flood two blocks south of Canal Street. My friend Gayarre mentioned he happened to see her come past his bookstore at the early evening hour when he was accustomed to take his aperitif. Héloise crossed the roadway, walking rapidly north. She had been living in her own apartment in the American quarter for some years. The maid put out lavender water, rose petals and a fresh set of clothes before she took the evening off as instructed by her mistress. Héloise barely had time to wash and get ready before her guest arrived. He followed her upstairs into the bedroom. He tore off the clothes she had only just put on, his knees gripping her wriggling body, a skinny spare-ribbed bone-house in which she had so little confidence that she submitted herself naked for his inspection only in a curtained light that showed off her meagre body to less disadvantage.

Fever

Héloise, ah Héloise — she had nothing but her civic duty in mind, although that was a great deal, given the intense seriousness of her nature, when she first sought out Mr Stanton at the St. Charles. She went to offer him the thousand dollars to save the city which the city had not wanted to pay. Very much to the forefront of her mind were the arguments he had so convincingly presented at the hotel de ville despite his bedraggled French. Somewhat to the side, fleetingly acknowledged, as she confided in a diary she later gave me to read, was her susceptibility to the idea of saving or being saved, she was not sure which, that had preoccupied her daydreams she since was a child. Mr Stanton's sheer animal handsomeness, let alone those luxuriant glossy-golden moustaches which filled her with distaste, played no part in her decision whatsoever.

She knocked and heard a voice say enter; was convinced, at any rate, that she had. To her surprise the room was dark, although it was past the middle of the day. Mr Stanton, she asked with a slight quaver in her voice. It took her a while to locate the occupant of the room. He lay sprawled in a chair with his feet on the bed, emitting an occasional snoring growl, which explained how it was possible for her to have heard him answer in his sleep.

Mr Stanton, she said more firmly, but he only growled again in his sleep. She stepped forward with the intention of taking him by the shoulder and shaking him awake. Instead she froze, aghast at her own resolution and the quandary into which it had led her. Mr Stanton, having made himself comfortable when he lay down, sprawled in the chair with his shirt unbuttoned, his breeches shockingly open. For the first time in her life she saw the male organ, semi-erect, pulsing with inexplicable self-motion, released like a living creature from its place of dishevelled secrecy. She stood as if hypnotised by this revelation, unable to move. She had no idea how long she had been standing there when Mr Stanton opened his eyes and asked: may I be of assistance, Ma'am? Héloïse handed him a purse. Once she had found her voice she told him how deeply she had been impressed by the demonstration of his engine and that she would pay him one thousand dollars to implement it. With pleasure, said Mr Stanton.

Héloïse's passion for Stanton began with a payment. She offered him her purse, and he took it. Sleepwalking where she had never been before, enabled by her lack of experience, she dared what none of her coquettish sisters would have dared. Finding herself on the brink, perhaps because in her circumstances and at her age there was nowhere other than the brink, she jumped. It was done, simple in the innocence of her desire. From then on she became Stanton's mistress.

Lying awake after he had gone, scrutinising in her memory every moment of his body and face for something she might have missed while she lay with him in her bed, she heard the latch on the door when the maid returned at dawn. Later she was woken by groaning, got up to investigate and found the maid retching in the closet. The girl was sweating and feverish. Héloïse put a compress on her forehead and told her to stay in her cot under the stairs until she came back. That was at noon. She found the girl asleep. She was turning restlessly in the cot when Héloïse returned at night. Stanton arrived soon after. She turned into his arms the moment she reached the top of the stairs, her hands rummaging inside his shirt, clawing his skin as he pulled up her dress and hoisted her onto his waist. Stanton made love to her in the corridor, holding her up against the wall.

He carried her into the bedroom, where he undressed her and made love to her again. Between caresses she slipped downstairs to see to the maid and found her vomiting blood. I have to go, she said to Stanton, as he settled her astride his lap, I must fetch a doctor. He ran his tongue along her collar-bone and put his finger on her lips. The maid is ill, she said, putting her arms round his neck, squirming as she felt something move inside her, I think the maid is dying.

I arrived with Maurois in the grey light when the night was already over. Héloise showed us to the maid's sleeping-place under the stairs. The girl sweated and rolled her eyes. Muarois asked Héloise about the onset and symptoms of the illness. She told him it had begun with vomiting twenty-four hours ago. The girl was already feverish then. She had complained of headache and pains in her back. Maurois asked us if we had seen these symptoms before. We both nodded. Holding up the candle and pointing to the yellowish whites of the eyes, Maurois told us it was yellow fever we were looking at now. Every couple of hours Héloise must change the cold compresses to keep down the fever. That was all she could do.

Warm weather turned to heat. Héloise lay in the stream of silk her lover poured over her body. Leaving the door of her room open all night to hear whatever sounds might come, she caught the dawn breeze that crept through her window while she made love with her lover and the girl under the stairs lay dying. From time to time she heard the fever in her call out. She got up and dried the naked girl with a towel. Stanton rolled her over while she changed the sheet. He fetched cool water from the well in the yard, knelt by the cot, soaking the linen cloths, which he wrung out and passed to Héloise to place on the girl's burning body. The heat ran off her in rivulets, her skin bubbling as she perspired. Héloise covered this steaming black oven of a body with linen swathes from the feet up, loins, stomach, breasts and throat, leaving only her mouth and nose free, a dark cavity in the bound white mummy that lay on the cot.

When the heat in the cubby-hole became insufferable they brought the cot upstairs and put it under the window at the end of the corridor. Swathes of linen ran from the cot to the bed where Héloise deliriously wound the girl's body into the thickets where she lay entangled with Stanton, the broad hips, big breasts and glare of skin she imagined as the body her lover had seen and was still caressing when he made love to her in the curtained light. She cried and heard her cry out at the same moment. It seemed to her that the girl convulsed in the cot had been seized by the same fever and sweated with the same love, that she had died from an exhaustion of ecstasy when the fever became too much. Héloïse wouldn't let Stanton go. She wouldn't let the body out of the house. Only here were they safe. By the time Stanton persuaded her what must be done, the body had begun to stink. She sent out for a bale of linen from the warehouse in the Tschopitoulas Road to embalm the girl's body. She reeled out the linen, soaked it in spirits and reeled in the corpse, and Stanton carried it out to the yard where he burned it.

Temporary infirmaries were opened throughout the city, even the work-house, the parish prisons and insane asylums were used. The ballrooms in the St. Louis and the St. Charles were converted into hospitals. The nurses and nuns who cared for the sick soon lay there themselves, victims of a disease no one knew how to cure. Some suggested taking quinine, avoiding the night air and the rays of the sun. Others kept the patient dosed with liquor or drugged with opium. At the beginning of the epidemic the city fathers still had cannon fired regularly and tar burned in the streets, as their predecessors had done generations ago, to clear the air of unwholesome spirits. The epidemic burned throughout the spring and flared up with the onset of summer. More than a thousand people died each week. Immigrants crowded together in boarding-houses, where the dead, the dying and convalescent frequently occupied one bed, perished like flies. Families of three generations disappeared overnight. The city turned into a lazar house, a stinking tenement of the dead.

One of the most experienced physicians in New Orleans, Dr Maurois, set out the aetiology of yellow fever in a newspaper article at the time. From the accumulation of filth in large cities, a poison was generated, which in the form of a volatile oil was inhaled by human beings, taken into the circulation and thus poisoned the system. The population was dying, in effect, of its own dirt. White or black dirt, it was all mixed up together and made no difference. The claim that black people were immune to yellow fever stood in the service of a cowardly convenience that justified delegating slaves as body-collectors and grave-diggers; the equivalent, said Maurois, of sentencing them to death.

At the height of the epidemic private persons were not even permitted to enter cemeteries to bury their dead. At determined gathering points in each district carts rolled by to pick up the bodies, driven by slaves or by the only teamsters who could be obtained voluntarily for this work — criminals released from the city jails. For the few weeks they might be expected to remain alive they were paid exorbitant wages. These teamsters were drunk when they did their work, usually to the accompaniment of ribald mirth and profane expressions of contempt for the dead they tossed onto their carts. They drove as if they had the devil aboard, challenging the silent streets with curses and shouts, the clang of whip thongs and a rattle of wheels we heard with dread as they raced each other to the cemeteries. The corpses of the poor lay piled by the hundred, exposed to the sun and rain before they were covered with quick-lime and buried in the communal graves permitted for the duration of the epidemic by special order of the city. Swollen by corruption that was exacerbated by the heat, those affluent dead who were privileged with a coffin sometimes burst their coffin lids, surrendering, as if by physical effort, the ligament that bound their hands and feet, and extending their rigid limbs in every outré attitude they had been at pains to avoid in life.

My youngest daughter and two of her children were overwhelmed by the fever in the first week of the epidemic. Her husband Gaston and their one surviving child contracted the fever but recovered. Héloise and Stanton seemed to have survived on love. To live was the exception, to die the rule. Marie-Jeanne and Marie-Claude passed away within an hour of each other in their own comfort rooms. They reverted to children again, babbling as they were nursed back into nothingness by their mother who had brought them out of it. Our friend Maurois, as a physician, had access to the cemeteries. Mijou asked him to see the interment of her girls more gracefully managed, not in one of the mass graves but "in Llulla's parlour" on the south side where they belonged. St. Malo was coming, she said, the same evening her girls were bricked up in their tombs. He was as surely on his way from Chief Liar Island to save the maroons as she was sitting here on her balcony fanning herself. But no St. Malo arrived to save my wife, no amount of fanning could keep the fever from wasting her body, no amount of wriggling would ever help her again, only the river, the great serpent-river in which all creation flowed, took her in swiftly and carried her away.

The Stanton Line

Héloise closed up the house in the Rue Royale, kept her apartment but took me to live with her in the house she bought in the less flood-prone quarters of town north of Canal Street, a new commercial and residential area established upriver to cater for the growing city. We were joined there by Stanton. As soon as the murderous summer heat gave way to a mild fall, New Orleans began to buzz with newcomers, anticipating the opening of the business season with the cotton harvest. No one talked now of leaving the city. To a stranger arriving on the waterfront that fall, the harbour whitening with canvas, the levee crowded with sugar, tobacco and cotton for export, there was nothing to indicate that a few weeks earlier it had been the scene of a scourge unparalleled in history. The whole great valley above New Orleans began to fill up with wonderful speed, pouring down into the city the wealth of its agricultural produce. Bales of cotton and casks of molasses, hogsheads of sugar, tobacco, butter, hams, rice, peltries, indigo, lumber, beans, hides, staves and cordage, barrels of beef, pork and flour ran bickering down from the levee's top into the warehouses along the Tschopitoulas Road. Tens of thousands of people were astir in the streets. They overran the old bounds, pulled up the old palisade, shovelled the earthworks into the moat of the Spanish fort, made broad ways out of narrow ones and pushed them into the fields, thickets and swamps. Kitchen gardens vanished. All the streets were paved with cobblestones. Day and night the buildings continued to rise — halls, churches, schools, stores, banks, theatres and hotels.

On the site of a former cabbage garden stood a hotel, the city's finest, with a white dome reminiscent of a cathedral: the St. Charles. In the rotunda of the St. Charles a new man held court, a type, an index of the city's great wealth: the Mississippi cotton planter. Slave-driven, it was a species of wealth that was unchangeable and fictitious as paper money, although it still generated an immense volume of business, filling up the city with people and with the thousands of dwellings to accommodate them. The planter in his turn was made possible by the speculators who had preceded him, now intoxicating an entire Indian tribe, seducing it with presents or simply buying it out, now corrupting a state legislature or erecting a new state where they found none ready to serve their purpose.

In their wake followed the gamblers, merchants and lawyers on the make, quacks, con artists, adventurers of every description lured by their common fascination for quick money. They arrived in the city to live off seasonal killings during the winter months, stunning the wealthy upriver planters in the hotels with flash-and-smoke routines while they turned their pockets inside out, skimming the queues of mystified immigrants waiting for the privilege of being hog-tied in the bars. Some of the swindlers were transient, floating down river, up river, according to the season and the risk their scams involved, which might make advisable a long absence from town. Some of them stayed, succeeded, escaped detection, for success legitimised their past activities and opened a future for them as impeccable citizens.

Those who got out and those who stayed, all stood in one line and could be charted along the same moral meridian. There was this curiosity about Stanton, or with how I perceived him, or it was just something which coincided with his coming: that from the time I set eyes on him in the hotel de ville I always saw him as one of a large crowd of people. When he joined the household I set up with Héloise it was as if a crowd of a hundred, more, of thousands of people, had moved in to live with us. Stanton the individual was defined for me by the large numbers of him that seemed always to be available. No particular degree of noise accompanied him. No particular rush characterised his presence. And yet I still felt as if I was surrounded by an ever-growing mass of human beings, both living and dead.

After the death of my wife and children I lost the sense of the indivisibility of the self. I no longer felt defined by any borders, neither of my body nor of the consciousness that inhabited it. I was not bound anywhere and had no sense of belonging. I felt as if my self had been distributed in many small parts informing everything around me. I was re-entering the Pig Indian stream of All-Creatures-Being-In-The-Forest in which I had floated as a child. Abandoning that narrow enclosure of the self, I was rid of the constraints of aesthetics and morality. Nothing on earth was strange to me. From the inside of a spittoon, spattered with mucous, I meditated on the taste of metal in my mouth as impartially as I quivered on my haunches and shat with the dogs in the street, or clambered with an ant up the thigh of the maid and foraged with my ant's tongue in the reeking swelter of her private parts.

In the street I would sometimes approach a group of women who suddenly turned to face me: my wife and my three dead daughters, dissolving
within seconds like the image seen behind closed eyelids. The ghosts I saw
arose from the state of transparency in which I was left by my grief, sensitised, like the specially treated plate Stanton brought to my attention
soon afterwards, to record not otherwise visible images left on it by the
light. But the ghosts who began to appear at about the time Stanton first
came through the door seemed anxious to correct an imbalance between
the living and the outnumbered dead. Hitherto I had thought of people
coming into the world as replacements for those who had gone out of it.
People used up were replaced. But now more were coming in than had
gone out. It was unlike anything I had experienced in three centuries of
All-Creatures-Being-in-the-Forest. The population trebled and quad-
rupled within years of an epidemic that had killed most of the inhabitants.
Tens of thousands streamed down the Mississippi valley into New
Orleans, a flow of humans like migrating pirati, in swarms so dense they
shook the river's banks. They poured through the door in the wake of
Stanton, his human slipstream, wiping their feet ten thousand times as
they took off ten thousand hats.

Each new arrival had a name and a history and claimed no less individuality than his predecessors, but it was an individuality blurred by the
rapidity of succession. This was the first law of the new age represented by
Stanton's arrival. The nature of a thing changed according to the number
in which it was present. There was a sense of crowding, soon of over-
crowding — and ghosts hampered in their freedom of movement put in
an appearance in order to complain of harassment by the overmighty
living. Sitting at the window with a view of the river, while the smallest
parts of life in me, irrepressible constituents of a poplymorphous universe, streamed out of the window like filings drawn into a flow of magnetic energy, I witnessed the arrival of a sky-blue thing with a long
bowsprit at the landing in New Orleans, one of Stanton's ventures, to all
appearances a ship, certainly built after the fashion of a ship, with port-
holes on the side and a cabin in the hold and her name painted across the
bows: *New Orleans*. She was the first steam vessel on the Mississippi.
Stanton's traction engines, in the water or on land, were invested with
magic when they first appeared. So was the man who designed them. The

amorality of his intellectual curiosity, of his uninhibited imagination, of the means he employed to get financial backing from a plain-looking woman with independent means and a never admitted fascination for lux-uriant moustaches — with his methods he hog-tied not only the daughter but her sceptical father too.

Nothing could not be done, nothing was impossible — possessing the steam-powered machine, and believing he was thus in possession of the Archimedean point that lay outside the world, with which to move the world, Stanton abrogated the treaties existing between man and nature. The machine enlisted in the man a superhuman confidence, becoming an extension of his mental and bodily powers. Here was a man who made hubris the foundation of his charm. The eagerness to gratify people's wishes followed from his belief that everyone could have everything they wanted. This was the banner he carried through the world. Héloise agreed with it, adding in small print: at a price. He was all invention and pleasure. She was all book-keeping and business.

Their partnership floated a fleet of steamboats which became known as the Stanton Line. In the early years it was still as perilous a journey as the passage through the Gulf, subject to Spanish-armed extortion, hijacking by white marauders and attack by vagabond Indians, the rem-nants of extinct tribes. They boarded boats that steered too close to the bank and slaughtered all the passengers. Paddle steamers blood-washed by these massacres were still in service a generation later, moving Indian tribes from territory absorbed by the westward migration of settlers. The government paid for the Indians' enforced passage, their silent retreat from the plains along with their malodorous spell-binding chat-tels, their curs, wigwams, feathers, sacred bones that crumbled to dust, souvenirs of their spiritual devastation. They were accompanied by white-man supplies intended to set them up in a white-man life they did not want – barrels of flour and lard, salt, pork and ploughs, which the Indians traded for liquor.

This blood-soaked riverine history was covered up under layers of white paint, already illegible for the next passengers who embarked. The paint blistered, the gunwales rotted, the machinery began to rust. When the engine eventually blew up, the old hulks were pulled out of service and all their history with them. The engineers and designers replaced them with prototypes that were a shade sleeker, faster, more luxurious every time, river-boats with the tonnage of ocean-going vessels, which nonetheless lay so shallow in the water that the Stanton Line boasted their ships would run on a heavy dew. Stanton set the benchmark himself in a low-water clearance contest to which he invited all his competitors. Personally he piloted a steamboat carrying ten tons of freight in ten inches of water without a drop of champagne spilling from the glasses supervised by the judges in the saloon. Stanton won the contest. Thereafter he had a watering-can mounted on the flagstaff of all the boats of the line, as a sign that he could supply his own water to float the vessel should the river run dry. Héloise didn't care for these exhibitions, although exhibition, as she knew, was the point at which everything between herself and Stanton had begun, a purse for an engine exhibited to her in a dark hotel room, for sweet river traffic floated on silky white dew, a fleet of dreams transported to delirium and back by the engines of the Stanton Line.

Moveable Parts

Edgar P. Stanton was born in something of a hurry as his mother was leaving the house. She tripped on the threshold and a minute later the child slipped out. The birth was as unobtrusive as the pregnancy, the baby as complete, neat and self-sufficient as the mother, who seemed surprised rather than pleased by what had come out of her body. After the interruption caused by Edgar P. Stanton's arrival she handed her son to the maid and left for her bureau in the Tschopitoulas Road, her only concession to the circumstances being that she took a carriage instead of walking as she usually did. Héloise was already a middle-aged woman, old to be giving birth for the first time. Outwardly there had been no sign she was pregnant. The child had been smuggled in and out of her without her full consciousness of what was going on, naturally she still resented the intrusion, Dr Maurois said in defence of this inexplicable coldness. The mother had no milk for her child. A wet nurse was found for the baby, an Irish woman with a well-nourished appearance, but the woman drank and when Héloise smelt whisky on the baby's morning breath it was time for the nurse to go. The only replacement who could be found at short notice was a Negress, a huge woman with a formidable swell of bosom on which the tiny white child bobbed up and down like a castaway at sea.

Wet nurse with child were the first black-and-white studies undertaken by Stanton, using a device that fixed pictures on silver-plated sheets of copper made light sensitive by exposure to vaporised iodine. How much of Edgar P. Stanton may also have been exposed to the chemistry of these early daguerreotypes, the fumes of iodine, mercury and silver iodide that wafted liberally in and out of his bedroom, was hard to say, but Maurois attributed the boy's early anaemia in part to their influence. As an infant his skin had such transparency that one could sometimes glimpse the organs encased beneath. Another detail arrested in these images of the new-born child were eyes that remained open in sleep. Later images of Edgar P.Stanton were created not on metal but paper. The paper image process yielded a negative image from which an infinite number of identical positives could be produced by putting chemically sensitised paper in contact with the negative and exposing it to the light.

Stanton believed that with the invention of photography man had discovered the moral if not yet the mechanical principle of how to stop time. The moments of the passing world, a running spool exposed frame by frame to a flash of light in which it was registered by our perception, were no longer obliged to vanish back into the eternal oblivion from which they had appeared. All thinking based on the premise of originality, the Once and Once Only Effect, needed to be modified in the perspective of machines that were able to manufacture copies independently of time and the individual human manufacturer. The Once and Once Only Effect of what he called primary reality was something we would lose to a secondary reality increasingly characterised by the Over and Over Again Effect of reproduction.

Edgar P. Stanton was the living example of this prediction. For the first few years of his life he was the most documented child in the history of the world. His father moved the nursery into the attic of the house to have more room for the images that copied the childhood. They surrounded the child on the walls within which he suckled, slept and played, copies of himself suckling, sleeping and playing over and over again. There Edgar P. Stanton acquired his first impressions of life on earth, impressions of himself, living at one remove, the inhabitant of a secondary reality that was at least a hundred years ahead of its time. The child was lifted to and fro, positioned, illuminated in flashes of saltpetre and fixed in solutions of sodium chloride and silver nitrate without many of the attributes of primary reality, the hugs and kisses and all the affectionate nonsense usually exchanged when a father took his child in his arms.

Life in the house a few blocks north of Canal Street might have been going on a thousand miles from the Vieux Carré. For the rest of Stanton's household – he had imposed his style on it, his it had become – time in this secondary reality seemed less to stop than to accelerate. New phrases buzzed between breakfast and dinner, meals that now took place minutes apart. I have no time, said Stanton at least once a day, or: I need more time, or, in particularly urgent circumstances: there's no time. I had no understanding of the meaning of this phrase. In my dreams I saw him sprinting though the house, moving the hands of clocks forward, advancing time, and I wondered why he wasn't putting them back if time was what he lacked. In my dreams I travelled back to Tahuantin-suyu and saw the conquistadors sacking the palace where the Indians kept their greatest treasure, the Punchao, moving forward the hands of the massive clock of gold while the inhabitants shrivelled in the streets of Cuzco and disintegrated before my eyes.

The camera moved downstairs from the attic into the master bedroom, where it began to peer at Héloise. With accessories, without, unadorned, plain as she was. Soon she had taken off all her clothes, posing naked during the long exposures to a machine behind which her husband had vanished. Was he still there, looking at her? The nude portraits of her hung on the bedroom walls. Héloise hated them, the exposure. She took them down and burned them. Stanton laughed. He had the negatives, he said, the negative images of his wife, and showed them to her, the thin-ribbed, black-and-white corset constructions that were the negatives of her body. She seemed to be looking at her skeleton at the end of a tunnel. Stanton told her he could make an infinite number of identical copies from these negatives. The language scared Héloise. The idea terrified her. Where is love, she asked him, what has happened to the passion, why aren't we happy any more? She didn't want these pictures. She refused to pose for him any more.

Stanton made pictures of her from the material he had, cutting out parts and switching them around. Heads sprouted out of shoulder-blades, feet grew out of arms. He pasted picture parts onto wooden squares and took them upstairs for Edgar P. Stanton to play with. Making Mama from Moveable Parts, the game was called. Mama could be made up and down in any number of different ways. Stanton declared rearrangement to be the logical consequence of all mechanical processes of reproduction. Within secondary reality things no longer needed to be arranged as in Nature. Things could be rearranged to make more time.

In a warehouse on the levee he began to build his dream. There was a steamboat that ran through the warehouse on an iron river, said the water-front packers hired by Stanton to install the machinery brought down river, and a freight loader running upside down from the ceiling that could shift weights of many tons. The steamboat on the iron river was an indoor steam locomotive running on 6-foot gauge, the freight loader a steam-powered crane operating from an overhead rail. The warehouse backed onto a coal yard that stocked the fuel for the three huge boilers supplying the factory with steam. Stanton planned all the functions of the machines in his factory to be interconnected by means of moveable parts. The coal that fired the boilers would be conveyed along a moving belt from his steamships moored on one side of the levee to the coal yard on the other and from there into the boiler furnaces without the intervention of a human hand. A system of gears, chains and cog wheels could be implemented to co-ordinate the locomotive on the factory floor with the crane moving along the rail overhead. Energy would come in at one end of the factory and a product leave it at the other. In the middle was what Stanton called the energy transformation space, a temple dedicated to secondary reality for the purpose of manufacturing perfectly identical interchangeable parts, ideally: the creation of machines by machines.

Stanton addressed audiences at the chamber of commerce and the civic education society on this subject. He used methods of production as a paradigm to talk about a change in society he described as the departure from primary reality. Individual, sensual, whole working methods to make Once and Once Only things were giving way to mechanical methods of production for the manufacture of Over and Over Again things. The essence of production was reproduction. Having become the inhabitants of a world we were now in a position to see not as a singular act of creation but as a continually modified copy of some original matter, claimed Stanton, we would find our relations to each other, to Nature, to God, had changed.

Only the fact that people did not understand what Stanton was talking about prevented them from denouncing it as blasphemous. The president of the civic education society himself had recently presented a paper demonstrating that the world had been created six thousand years ago at a quarter past four in the afternoon. There might be disagreement about the precise time of day, but by and large this represented the still orthodox view. Members of the city's business community were more disturbed by what they saw when invited by Stanton to visit his factory. If all the work there, as he proposed, was to be done by machine, what implications did that carry for the class of people whose whole existence was defined in terms of indentured labour? Who were themselves nothing other than working machines? What became of slaves if they were deprived of labour? They became free to do nothing, argued Gayarre and Maurois on behalf of the abolitionists. Their opponents said that if that were the case they would blow Stanton's factory up.

I did not believe anything would ever come of his factory. Stanton was a man inspired by possibility. A system of interconnected chains and wheels and moving belts continued to be aesthetically satisfying to him so long as it remained undecided what it was for. The factory in its unfinished state of possibility held up to Stanton a mirror of his own mind. He rummaged in it, tinkered, experimented without end. The undecided project metamorphosed, as the years passed and time for Stanton was running out, into an insoluble one. Fuel came it at one end of the factory and set wheels in motion and still nothing came out at the other. But the inventor had got so caught up in his own system it no longer let him go. He shut himself up in the factory. Solitude turned his charm stale. His appearance was unkempt. Inside that vacuum he called the energy transformation space nothing was ever transformed but Stanton, a youthful, vigorous enthusiast who became a cranky old man corked up in his dreams. Héloïse discovered him sitting on his own doorstep one morning, house key in hand, muttering he was unable to find his way back in, and she took him away from New Orleans, to give him a change of air, she said, for a long time.

The Passage of Edgar P. Stanton

The child was late learning to talk, and to the best of my knowledge the first words he said were not Mama or Papa but Edgar P. Stanton. This was his name and he demanded the full measure of it on his birthday and for thirty years after, without abbreviation or anything so familiar as a nick-name. I was his grandfather and I had a stake in his name, the P. that was never permitted to unravel, a hieroglyph, a secret to which we were all sworn. The life he proposed for himself might have come out of a fairy tale. He would find a fortune in an empty field and the woman he would one day marry, he announced when he was five, would reveal herself to him by knowing his middle name without having to ask. The family called him Edgar P. Stanton as a matter of course, Edgar P. only in moments of special intimacy. Children who wanted to sail paper boats with him in the drain outside the house either deferred to his full title or were not allowed to play.

What more natural for a grandfather sensing a special affinity with a child than to share with him the secret of his life? A secret never told to Mijou and only once broached with Héloïse in the vaguest possible manner. When would have been the moment to take Héloïse on one side and confide, even to this daughter I most trusted, that I was born before the discovery of America that was now on the verge of civil war? And what, on the other hand, could have been more natural for a grandfather with responsibility for a child during his parents' frequent absences from the house than to embark on a long story beginning "When I was born some three hundred and fifty years ago"? Or for the child to believe the story, taken down at his grandfather's dictation and recorded by a *quipu camayoc*, an Official Rememberer, no less, in a rolled cloth book called the Quipu of the Ghosts that had been examined by the antiquarian bookseller Gayarre and testified to be of great antiquity?

I rolled the boy up in the quipu and let the colours rub off on him while he lay in it asleep. He absorbed patterns of experience through his wide-open eyes and transparent skin, watching the patterns, in his clairvoyance, intensify in colour and form until they took shape as ghosts he could see in the room as clearly as I was evoking them in my memory — Lemon Grass, who was my Taiassu wife, and the tsushaúa Great White Bird, Dom Pedro pursued by swarms of white moths, desiccated, bleached to the bone, run out of dreams in the empty square of Ki'zak, the Donatory Pedro Joao Pilar with greasy fingers, surrounded by his wives, mistresses, mestizo children and slaves, the Senhora de Souza, who could turn herself into a fox and change places with her sister Esperanca the nun, whom I had courted in Boa Vista until I awoke from a hundred-year opium dream.

Until the river reached the bend where it jumped on the night Edgar P. Stanton's great-grandmother was giving birth, placing mother and child on the slave-free side of the state border, the events that flowed through the quipu down to the boy wrapped up in them ran without interruption across hundreds of years of enslavement. When the boy was free Stanton took Edgar P. Stanton in a carriage down to the waterfront, rattling away through the narrow dirty streets of the Faubourg, among grimy old stuccoed walls, the high arched windows and doors, the balconies and entresols of the Vieux Carré with its pungent French noises and smells. The carriage turned onto a broad place, covered with bales of cotton, casks of sugar and weighing scales, opening up a view of an array of steam-boats, moored bows to stern in a line so long that the end of it was lost in the mist. Across the street from a landing stage for local river traffic Negroes were standing in front of a New York clothing store while their owner was inside, settling the bill for the outfits he had just purchased them. Edgar P. Stanton counted twenty-two men as the carriage moved along the line. Each of them wore a suit of black cloth and a black hat, each held an additional bundle and a pair of shoes. The Negroes were silent and serious like a file of soldiers standing at ease before going into action, waiting for the general to come out of the store and lead them to the steamboat which would convey them to the plantation where they lived and died for him. We can't wait, Edgar P. Stanton heard his father say, there's no time — the boy saw the twenty-two Negroes in their identical black suits and hats disappear into the mist, walking away from the store while their owner was inside settling the bill, because they could no longer wait, there was no time.

In the factory his father had built in an empty warehouse on the Tschopitoulas Road he watched a complicated system of interdependent parts grind into motion when Stanton pulled the lever, going round and round and up and down until Stanton pulled the lever again and the system stopped. His father explained to him that the moments of the passing world, a running spool exposed frame by frame to a flash of light in which it was registered by his perception, were no longer obliged to vanish back into the eternal oblivion from which they had appeared. That was the achievement of the camera. Then I am a camera, Edgar P. Stanton whispered to himself, who had recorded everything he had ever seen and much more that he never had. There was no need, his father assured him, to know what was at the ends of the chain or on either side of the frame exposed on the running spool. Machines could do that. Then I am a machine, said Edgar P. Stanton, not loud enough for his father to hear, and wondered who had ever thought this thought before.

He grew up into a dandy, a sybarite, who by the age of sixteen had acquired a *placée* and installed her in an apartment off the Place d'Armes, now a public garden bright with orange and lemon trees. Fronting it was still the old Hotel de Ville where Héloise first met Stanton, still the city courthouse, a quaint old building with a scaly, worm-eaten surface, deep-worn sills and smooth corners scoured by legendary floods from a time before Edgar P. Stanton was born. In the Faubourg he was still importuned by the ghosts of his mother's family and their neighbours, his grandmother Mijou, her daughters and her grand-children in the sky-blue satin suits in which they were buried, by the creaking Monsieur Llulla and his lightning-struck great-grandfather, even by the bogey-man St. Malo, who might still be summoned by nurses when putting reluctant children to bed, Edgar P. Stanton among them, who had seen more clearly than anyone the maroon buccaneer crucified by fire, spread-eagled in the rigging of a ship burning above him in the dark.

These childhood apparitions could still terrify him, and since he was most likely to succeed in escaping them at the Merchants Exchange adjoining the St. Charles, that was where he often came. I was a founding member of the Exchange and had my own booth. There were traders on the floor whose grandfathers I had known. The grandsons put about rumours, not in my interest either to confirm or deny, that Paul Zarraté was a hundred if he was a day, even if he looked much younger. I remained inscrutable, smiling, smiling, of infinite patience. I had learned trading from the Jesuits in Pernambuco when New Orleans was a Choctaw huddle of dwellings in a swamp, a mere surmise on the colonial horizons of Louis XIV. Edgar P. Stanton visited me almost every day in the exchange and took lunch with me in my member's booth, chatting gaily, never discussing the business of the Exchange or showing the slightest interest in it.

When he tired of the city he reserved a permanent suite for himself on one of his father's riverboats, the *Maid of Orleans*. Edgar P. Stanton came to know the Mississippi like the avenue of a great city, the landmarks, back alleys and signs for almost a thousand miles on either side of the river. He crossed one of its great intersections, at St. Louis, a hundred times on his journeys north and south. It was in St. Louis, at the end of a three-day game of poker while the engines were being overhauled, that a wealthy local businessman, the Chinaman Fong, was accused of cheating and shot by the man who owned the life lease on the steamboat's saloon bar. Edgar P. Stanton wrested the gun from the man before he managed to kill the Chinaman. Fong sold his business in St. Louis and came aboard as bar keeper, introducing to the *Maid of Orleans* gilded dragons writhing on the ceiling of the saloon, paper lanterns illuminated by fireflies, and a twelve year-old girl with bound feet, his daughter Wai On.

In gratitude to Edgar P. Stanton for his timely intervention Fong offered to make Wai On over to him as his concubine. She could prepare lark's tongue in plum wine, breed silk worms and fireflies. She had other rare and useful accomplishments besides, such as the art of drawing horns out of a snail. Edgar P. Stanton expressed interest.

Locking the saloon door one evening, the Chinaman placed five silver dollars at intervals along the bar and lifted Wai On up. The girl pulled her dress over her hips and squatted with parted legs as she slithered sideways, toes in toes out, along the polished counter on tiny silk-covered feet until she positioned herself over the first of the silver dollar pieces. By some process of muscular contraction, mysterious even to Edgar P. Stanton watching from immediately beneath, she picked up the silver dollar piece and gripped it with her vagina. Her sex was hairless, the smooth orifice of a young girl, but this unusual exercise had given it wadded, protuberant lips. Wai On repeated the performance with each of the five dollar pieces, one after another, until she had stacked them in a neat pile at the end of the counter. Fong said a man's snail could shrink into his belly, but Wai On would still find it and know how to draw it out.

197

This was why men in his country, at an age when they lost their sexual vigour, placed a high value on wives possessing the accomplishment known as drawing the horns out of the snail. So there they stood, father and cut-purse daughter, the giver and his gift, drawer of horns with that scandalous snatch between her legs, and the daughter of Fong came to live in Edgar's stateroom as his concubine.

When my grandson learned from Wai On to chase the dragon — just as I had learned from the Chinese cook in Boa Vista, where I lay with my head on the opium cushion for the better part of a century — he perceived in the serpentine folds of the great river a quipu unravelling the flow of history. So long as people remained on the move, nomadic tribes that flowed with the river, carrying their encampments with them, they owned nothing but motion and the things of motion, no man owned any other man or woman. But then Dom Pedro Felipe read the Requirement to the mountains, forests and oceans, and they became the possessions of the Donatory Pedro Joao Pilar, with every living creature they contained, passed down and divided through generations, maroons of fixed possession but uncertain belonging as Edgar P. Stanton's own great-grandmother had been at the time the river jumped.

These were the patterns that flowed in the river from the Old World to the New. In a light-headed opium haze through which he saw cotton plantations blooming like flower gardens in June, their creamy fleeces sometimes still white late in December when slaves wandered up and down the rows of plants in the setting sun, culling the year's last fleeces and carrying them to the gin-house, Edgar P. Stanton was hypnotised by the blood-red river snaking out behind him, an endless bale of unravelled cotton dyed and printed with a pattern in black and white, the same pattern woven into the quipu in which he had been trussed up as a child and rolled around on the floor. The river had only one mouth where all this snarl of meandering water could disgorge. The Negroes waiting outside the store while their owner was settling the bill would no longer wait. Claimed by an inevitable progression, the possessed would claim self-possession. While their master continued to haggle in the store, they would walk on down the line of steamboats that had evolved from the ocean-going caravels with slaves from Guinea in their holds as they sailed up the Gulf to the Mississippi, defining the moment of their extinction from history when they disappeared into the morning mist. There was still the bill to be settled. The southern states would dispute the bill. It was too high a price to pay. They would demand compensation, secede from the Union. There would be war.

My grandson's thoughts on these subjects, floated on a combination of opium and steam power as he ploughed up and down river, were conveyed in electromagnetic telegraphic bursts into my booth at the Merchants Exchange in New Orleans. *Buy Baltimore & Ohio, Marietta & Cincinnati now!* I bought, cautiously, as was my habit, until another clairvoyant message arrived from St. Louis. *Scroungy old man, mean hoarder of centuries, buy more!* A precocious young man who was already rheumatic, his collar green with mould from the moist river air, Edgar P. Stanton now disembarked from the *Maid of Orleans* for the first time in years, shooting off on the railroads intersecting the river at tangents, skimming out across the flowers of the trembling prairie. Cities along the Atlantic seaboard were soon bound by railroad into the central system of the Mississippi-Ohio valley and the Southwest as far as Mexico and California. Baltimore-Santa Fe. Names which had meant nothing in the remoteness of their mutual isolation were brought together in our consciousness, separated by no more than a hyphen, a union from which it had become impossible to secede. The continent I had been washed across via the rivers Napo and Amazon in a couple of years would soon be transected in as many weeks. Merely by reading the railroad advertisements, let alone contemplating the journey, I felt as inundated by this rush of time as the Indians must have felt, disintegrating when the slow revolutions of Tahuantin-suyu's civilisation were harnessed to the traction of the furious Spanish advance, spinning ever faster until the centre collapsed and everything flew apart.

Discarding the river, the opium cushion, the slow reflective Mississippi habits of his past, Edgar P. Stanton became an addict of the new speed. He hung his head out of carriage windows, risking death by smoke congestion, flying sparks and decapitation more times than I could count. In Cincinnati he parted company with Fong, who acquired a controlling interest in the pork processing industry after visiting a model factory where a disassembly line, as my grandson called it, enabled twenty men to slaughter and dress six hundred hogs a day. Hogs were herded in at the roof, spiked, went sliding along on overhead rails, propelled by their own momentum, and as they slid downwards from one floor to the next by the force of gravity they were dismembered and processed in moveable parts. *Buy Fong & Sons, meat packing, Cincinnati.* Until this trading instruction there had been no word of any son of Fong, but now the moment was ripe he rubbed a lamp and the sons appeared, all six of them, arriving in Cincinnati for their sister's wedding feast, complete with lark's tongue in plum wine sauce served by the bride under garlands of firefly lanterns, swarms of light that Edgar P. Stanton said he heard rustling like silk, their glowing whispers illuminating the dark.

Wai On divined his middle name in a tea cup, he said, or maybe he confided it to her while he was riding the dragon, or she came astride him, snatching it between her legs. His Chinese wife must have put a spell on him, stolen his name and hidden it in her body. He was obliged to reach inside her, inside her cabin, he wrote, to remind himself who he was. He had been unable to keep from her the secret of his middle name and she had acquired power over him, because I had neglected to give him another name to protect him, he said, as the tsushaúa Great White Bird had done for me. Her stunted feet had crippled him with pity. He wrote deliriously of riding in a steam-powered cockle shell under a snow white sky across a vast golden sea, then of changing ships in mid-ocean and embarking on a prairie schooner. All the world stretched away in a sea of short grass. Here was the empty field of his destiny. From his letters it appeared that he had bought all the land around him as far as he could see, establishing himself with his teenage Chinese wife in a middle kingdom of nowhere where they had fallen out of the sky.

Shipwreck

The ten-inch mortars that opened the American Civil War, even if they had been shelling Fort Sumter right across the river, would not have been heard above the blast of the explosions that ripped apart the wharves of New Orleans on the same day. There was nothing left to bury of Stanton, who had apparently been in his factory on the wharves at the time. All that was left were images in black and white, which Edgar P. Stanton came across in his father's archive years later. He recognised in these pictures the principle of the Cincinnati hog-dressing factories that had been antic-ipated, and surpassed, by his father's invention of a mechanised assembly line far ahead of its time. What Stanton had invented was a system, but he had been searching for a machine, not a system, which was why he failed to see the discovery to which he devoted the second half of his life. On the widow's instructions the funeral cortege set out from the hotel de ville where she had first met Stanton. She had not been south of Canal Street in years. It seemed to Héloise, as the carriages rattled through the cold, wet, foreign-looking streets of the Vieux Carré, as if she was burying her own past. The coffin containing her husband's hat arrived at the vestibule of the cathedral accompanied by a small group of mourners. A bolt on the main entrance doors had jammed. The cortege had to wait for them to be opened. She took my arm, listening to the gloomy cadences of the dead march inside the cathedral until the doors were thrown open, revealing an interior bright with candles and empty of a single person. For the last ten years of his life Stanton had led the shy existence of a recluse. Many of his former business associates no longer knew he was alive.

Edgar P. Stanton did not arrive until a month after his father's funeral. He had left his wife with relatives in Memphis, food vendors on the steamship pier. Not doubting for one moment that the South was doomed, he joked to me that the time had come to put one's mouth where one's money was. He could not tell his mother this, however. Instead he told her that now summer had come — yellow fever season in New Orleans, which still hadn't improved on its reputation as the least healthy city in America — there was reason for a responsible father with family enlargements on the way to leave the city for a more salubrious place. Héloise, the grandmother-to-be, stalked loftily round this gobbet of news like a cat offered a morsel, looking sideways at it from all angles. The sur-viving proprietor of the Stanton Line, a widow still maintaining girlish airs about her, unable to repress a little skip when she crossed from the gang-way onto the boat, as if to make sure she didn't fall in, boarded the St. Louis packet departing at noon.

It had been raining for weeks prior to our departure. The river was car-rying so much water that its surface seemed to curve downwards at the edges. Familiar banks had been effaced, the river's contours changed, in parts gone altogether. The Mississippi was a vast, shoreless lake. No sign of the pier when the *Queen of the South,* the flagship of the line, steamed in to Memphis. No sign of Chinese food vendors or of Edgar P. Stanton's wife either. At dusk he went ashore in a lighter that came alongside to disembark passengers and returned at midnight with a bundle in his arms. I first saw Fong's daughter then, rain-wet sparkle glancing off round cheeks, two chocolate smudges, one at each corner of her purse-shaped, crimson-painted mouth, riding out on the smile that spread across her face. She was followed by an unmemorable young lady with mouse-brown hair and a snub nose who gave a hand to a hefty dowager of a female in black, her towering hair-do ravaged by gusts of rain, as she stepped from the rocking lighter onto the main deck of the steamship.

The pilot leaned out of his cabin on the texas roof and shouted to the boatman in the lighter to pull off, he could no longer hold the ship steady in the current. Seconds later they had gone, the whole spook of wind and wet and rocking lights, blotted out by the blackness on the other side of a pane of glass. This side warmth, brightness, the comforts of a saloon with chandeliers suspended from a mass of curved filigree woodwork on the ceiling and reflecting the coloured glazing of the skylight. The saloon had a double row of columns on either side, supporting elaborately gilded arches and flanked by the staterooms of the first-class passengers. It served as our dining-room and lounge, here we waited curiously to see in what transformed state the passengers who delved dripping into their staterooms at our ports of call on the stages up river would reappear from them for dinner.

At Natchez the most interesting transformation had been undergone by a pale young man, swathed in yards of rain cape, who appeared for dinner in décolleté and displaying enough bosom to qualify him as a woman, perhaps in flight from some terrible fate. All ended well for the young lady in Vicksburg, where she was joined by a young man with such a striking resemblance to her that wagers were being offered around the saloon as to whether the young lady's companion would turn out to be her brother or sister. The newcomer didn't oblige with another sex change, however. Fellow introduced himself blithely as Galloway, and to the grudging envy of the male passengers on board declared himself to be her husband.

At Greenville we were joined by a missionary couple, very quiet in black, on their way to do God's work in Africa. Quiet in black they went into their stateroom, quiet in black they came out of it. There could only be improvement when we took on new passengers at Helena, and there was, in the generous shape of Madame Cagliotti, an Italian prima donna singing her way up river from New Orleans to St. Louis, from there by railroad to the east coast. Accompanied by a poodle, she was handed aboard by an old-style silver-haired rascal, all smiles and silk shirt ruffles. Mr Chemin de Fer, as Edgar P. Stanton dubbed him, already had the deck of cards out of his pocket when he stepped out of his stateroom and took stock of the passengers sitting in the saloon.

Memphis saw the arrival of Wai On, child transformed by her husband into a grotesquely bloated wife, biggest with child, a bound-foot roly-poly now unable to walk at all, plus the hefty dowager in black with a rain-ravaged tower of hair which would remain dismantled under repair for the rest of the voyage. She brought into the saloon her unobtrusive female companion and a long-tailed macaw. The macaw was soon attracting the lethal attentions of Madame Cagliotti's poodle and the ship's cat, and for its own safety had to be confined to a perch near the ceiling.

There was a general feeling that this was enough zoo for one ship. No one had reckoned with Mr Pardy, however, who came aboard in Cairo blazing with side-whiskers and a red check coat, a hundred hogs, two score of geese and a dozen goats; an extremely hazardous embarkation, owing to the high water. The animals went to join the cargo stacked inches above the water line on the boiler deck, sharing it with two hundred human passengers, Negroes for the most part, a few white people and a deputation of Indians on their way to Washington. While the rain came incessantly down and the river continued to rise, the smells and noises of the various animals on board competed for our attention. Inspired by the river in flood all around us, the African missionaries' interrupted their silent prayer vigil and broke out into a joyous hymn comparing the *Queen of the South* with Noah's Ark. They were heard out by a captive audience in the saloon with mixed feelings of exasperation, hilarity and a gloomy foreboding.

During dinner the night the ship left Cairo a message came down from the pilot house for Edgar P. Stanton. The pilot would appreciate a second opinion. My grandson sent a message back that he would be up after dinner, and invited me to accompany him. It was some time after midnight when we climbed up into the pilot house. Its main component was a giant wheel, which must have measured twelve feet across. A man with a cheroot in his mouth and his hands folded behind his back stood peering out into the night, moving up and down on his toes and creaking audibly as he did so. This cherooted gentleman was Mr Shannon, who had piloted the *Maid of Orleans* during the last years of Edgar P. Stanton's Mississippi odyssey.

Now from your extensive knowledge of the river, he said after the introductions were over, where would you place Cape Girardeau, Mr Stanton? My grandson poured himself a glass of champagne and said, after glancing through the window rather cursorily, I thought, that he reckoned they must have passed it on their left about half a mile downstream. Mr Shannon inclined to that opinion too. He just wondered then, and this was more of a rumination than a question, what had happened to the promontory with three trees. Edgar P. Stanton wondered as well and fell short of an answer. Mr Shannon savoured the situation for a while before remarking that if they *had* passed Cape Girardeau it hadn't been there, no more than the promontory with three trees half a mile on, right *there*, said Mr Shannon, stabbing a finger at an empty space in the dark. The moon came out from behind a cloud as if in confirmation of what he said. River looking exceptionally wide to me at this point, Mr Stanton. The latter agreed it looked pretty wide to him, too, and Mr Shannon said he was damned if there was any river there at all, they were running a mile west of the usual channel, he was damned if they hadn't steamed clean over Cape Girardeau and the promontory with the three trees.

Edgar P. Stanton poured another glass of champagne and let this observation rest before beginning to wonder out loud, in a purely speculative manner, why the ship hadn't run into any snags. He considered that the inhabitants of Cape Girardeau, a few thousand at least, who might be expected to have drowned dead when their town went under in such a hurry, and whose corpses now ought to be littering the river, would constitute an appreciable snag, one unlikely to have gone unnoticed even by the diners in the saloon, with the paddles churning bodies up out of the river and tossing them back in again right outside the window. But dinner had been exceptionally smooth. He pointed at his glass balanced on top of the compass. Not a tremor disturbed the level surface of the champagne. This was Edgar P. Stanton's polite way of indicating that the pilot didn't have the slightest notion where he was. The *Queen of the South* had slid off the river with the flood and was now some place shipping had no business to be, most likely steaming over wide-open cattle grazing spaces in the direction of Kansas City.

Day broke over an unearthly landscape, no solid ground anywhere in sight. The pilot steered north-east in search of the river, doubled back south-west, then steamed around in circles until the boiler-men told him they had fuel for another twenty-five miles, enough to make it to St. Louis if the boat drove there in a straight line. But Mr Shannon had no more idea than anyone else did where St. Louis was. He had last seen it only two weeks ago, still a sizeable city he thought it would be difficult to misplace. He told the boiler-men to cut the engines and they would see what happened if the boat was left to drift with the flood, but the boat showed no inclination to do anything other than stay put where it was. After a while we asked Mr Shannon if he registered a movement in any particular direction, and Mr Shannon said he was damned if she was going anywhere but down. I agreed with the pilot's opinion. The downward motion of the ship as she prepared to lay her broad bottom down in the mud was unmistakable. There was hardly a jolt, just a creaking of timbers, not at all ominous, more like a sigh of relief, when the flat-bottomed hull finally came to rest on the ground. Then the boat began to tilt. The clamour of terrified geese, hogs and human beings was capped by Madame Cagliotti's shriek, hitting the perhaps highest note in her career. The boat leaned twenty degrees out of the perpendicular and then stopped. Having jettisoned the *Queen of the South*, the flood lost interest in her. It drained away under the hull, leaving behind a greening delta landscape, coursed with fine-veined rivulets already drying out in the sun while the water line receded and disappeared under the horizon.

The Landing of the Ark

The steamboat came to rest at cross-roads, or rather, a place where two tracks met in the wilderness, scratched out of the dirt. One track led from a deserted homestead on the edge of a copse to a ghost town a couple of miles through the wood. Homestead and former riverside town, both appeared to have been abandoned after a cut-off had shifted the Mississippi east and with it the source of their livelihood. The other track headed west in what was presumed to be the direction of Kansas City, or east to the Mississippi if you were going the other way, in the direction the flood waters had retreated. This was the direction taken by almost all those who clambered out of the boat as soon as it had settled in the mud. Héloise made clear she had no intention of abandoning ship. If the boat could not be brought to the river, the river would have to be brought to the boat. Returning from a reconnaissance, the chief engineer reported there would be difficulties doing that. It would mean digging a ten-mile channel to float the *Queen of the South* back to the river. Then she would wait for the next flood to raise the boat, Héloise announced. Mr Shannon said there was no telling when that might be. Another flood like that might not come along in years. Héloise folded her arms and said nothing. I knew her stubbornness. She wouldn't budge.

Passengers who had booked staterooms on the main deck decided they would wait with her until they were provided with alternative means of transport to continue the journey to St. Louis. Mr Pardy was not one of them. Mr Pardy reminded us he had a hundred animals to worry about, which he had to get to Davenport pretty quick. The hogs and geese down-stairs had been weighing on Mr Shannon's mind, too. He took Héloise on one side and suggested buying the animals. Héloise didn't think she wanted to do that. She was terrified of animals. The pilot told her how much they had left to eat on board, and how much they could expect to eat while waiting for a flood to lift the boat back onto the river. A hundred hogs would cover a lot of meals on the way there. Put them down in the field and they would fend for themselves, walking, root-grubbing, self-sustaining dinners that could be transformed into pork on a plate at the swish of a knife. That was an awful lot of pork, Héloise thought. But she took the point and approved the purchase, and the last we saw of Mr

Pardy was his flaming figure, striding through the hog-grunting landscape in the direction of the river the same afternoon.

A week passed, and still nobody had come along the road. Mr Chemin de Fer became restive. He had played cards against the rest of the boat all week, taken everyone's money and now had nothing to do. He hummed and hawed for a day or two while he flipped a little silver coin between his fingers and back and forth over his knuckles, then returned everyone's money, announcing he was giving us a second chance. The missionaries kept themselves to themselves and would have no part in this satanic work. A stupendous thought had struck them. Was this shipwreck to be understood as a sign that God did not intend them to go to Africa? Had He re-routed them here? Was their Arafat in Missouri? They prayed for another sign. A muttering of voices could be heard from their stateroom where they sang hymns when they took time off from praying. Irritated that anyone other than herself should presume to sing in her presence, even these humble singers of hymns, Madame Cagliotti launched into a series of grand operatic concerts, thunderously reinforcing her prima donna supremacy.

The missionaries were crushed. Even the raucous long-tailed macaw was silenced. The macaw's attention-seeking owner, Mrs Pereira, became jealous. She stood up in one of the concert intervals and made a speech. Here we all were, fooling around in this stranded boat with sing-songs and such-like while our country was at war. All because the management of the steamship company, in default of water, was too stingy to fork out for alternative transport to get its passengers to St. Louis. This was breach of contract. On her return to civilisation she would sue the company for damages. Héloise had been confronted with similar demands and shrugged them off, but the threat of legal action reached her right in her penny-pinching core. She reacted at once. A messenger was dispatched with written instructions from the proprietor to the company's St. Louis office, authorising the purchase of horses and wagons to relieve the passengers stranded in the prairie. Madame Cagliotti never forgave Mrs Pereira her *sing-songs and suchlike*, an insult so appalling it made her speechless. I have lost my voice, she announced, and for this reason her concerts would be discontinued until further notice. Secretly everyone was relieved.

For the peace of the ship I was assigned Mrs Pereira as a difficult case.

I was to woo her and flatter her, do anything to distract her from thoughts of prosecuting the Stanton Line. It was half a century at least since I had engaged in any serious campaigns of flattering a woman. How did I appear? I took stock of myself in the mirror, bringing in my grandson, my sole confidant, for an honest second opinion. How old did I look? Edgar P. screwed up his eyes and peered at me. Well, I asked. Just very, very old, he said, inde*fin*ably old, and rolled around on the floor, cackling. I felt fine, I said coldly. I still walked upright, had a healthy appetite, most of my hair was in place, even if none of my teeth were.

Edgar P. frowned and asked: what is this, old fellow? What is this vanity? Not vanity, I said, but loneliness. I was trapped on an island of old age drifting far away from the mainland that was the rest of mankind. My grandson had never considered it from this point of view. He looked thoughtful, and asked me to roll him up in the carpet on the stateroom floor. He still occasionally had this craving, ever since I used to roll him around in the quipu when he was a child. It gave him a feeling of snugness. I got down on my knees to oblige him. Don't forget the rhyme that goes with it, he said. I rolled him around the floor, reciting *roly poly pudding and pie* as I did so, until I ran out of breath.

While Edgar P. lay there wrapped up in the carpet, with his eyes shut for a change, I explained to him that since the Spanish conquest of Tahuantin-suyu my biological rhythm had changed. All the functions of my body had slowed down to such an extent that for every ten years other people aged I aged only one or two. I had little hope of dying until well into the next millennium. This was an appalling prospect, to exist as a living memory with an ever-growing backlog of past while I watched the lives of all those close to me burn and go out in what seemed to me no more than a flash. To keep abreast of the times I hoped I looked the age I proportionally now was, to have 'more or less' the appearance of a man in his early fifties. Edgar P. heard me out in silence, did some calculations, opened one eye and asked with a grin if the old fellow who was my client would settle for early sixties.

While waiting for the wagons to arrive from St. Louis I strolled with Mrs Pereira every day to the ghost town through the wood. Her companion always came with us, the freckled young woman with the snub nose, a silent shadow on the far side of the garrulous Mrs Pereira who was her employer. I tried to engage Miss Littlewood in the conversation, but once Mrs Pereira discovered that she and I had a common language in Portuguese Miss Littlewood was doomed to silence. I wondered why Mrs Pereira invited her to join us at all, until I realised this was the ploy of a vain woman's nature. The silent, plain-looking employee was retained by the older, more artful employer for the purpose of showing herself off to better advantage. She had a florid charm, the sensuous, overripe good looks typical of Brazilian women who succumbed early to a tropical cli-mate and spent the rest of life in search of their mislaid youth. I amused her with stories of the country's colonial past, told in such archaic Portuguese that she began to grow suspicious. There might have been something else about me, stale air, a reptilian smell in uninhabited rooms. You describe that as if you were actually *there*, Mr Zarraté, she would say with a funny look.

Around the corner of Mrs Pereira I noticed her companion taking a peek at me from time to time. She who understood nothing of the stories I was telling Mrs Pereira was amused by this other story she watched unfolding right beside her. Nothing awaited Miss Littlewood in St. Louis. The contract as her employer's travelling companion ended there. Perhaps this was why, when the wagons eventually relieved our stranded Ark, the young lady with the snub nose decided that she would stay. Here at least she had bed and board. The Africa-bound missionaries agonised until the last moment, but even as their valises were being loaded onto the wagons a rainbow appeared, an arc plunging down and striking the wilderness where they stood. The missionaries remained rooted to the consecrated spot while the wagons lumbered off down the track with the rest of the passengers. It was the last I saw of any of them except Mr Galloway and his transvestite accomplice, whose faces on Wanted posters would follow me around America for a long time to come.

Pawfrey's War

Lee was born on a saloon table with a list of twenty degrees south, taking full advantage of this natural inclination to slide into life as if on a chute. There was a degree of hurry about this exit from Wai On's womb that reminded me of the circumstances of his father's birth. Sometimes it seemed to me I could see Stanton there watch in hand, superintending his son's and his grandson's births like a factory manager, exclaiming impatiently: I have no time! Only two months later and the boy would have been born on the level, minus all the repercussions of a lopsided birth, after the carpenter adjusted the furniture to the ship's starboard list by sawing a couple of inches off the hind legs of the tables and chairs. A timely act of carpentry might have provided my great-grandson with a better angle to enter life. This assassination of the furniture, as Mr Shannon, the pilot, described it, was carried out against his wishes on the orders of Edgar P. Stanton. My grandson reached his decision about the amendment to the furniture the morning after announcing that he had just seen his destiny through his stateroom window. The *Queen of the South* had not merely brought him to that empty field in which he would find his fortune, it had jettisoned him there with a new-born child, effectively making it impossible for him to leave.

A piece of Missouri so nondescript it had discouraged even the Mississippi from staying thus came to be contested by three parties. Both Edgar P. Stanton and the missionaries claimed a mystical significance in the land, though they didn't yet know what. Only Mr Shannon envisaged pork actually fattening on the land, coaxing the soil to yield a crop or two during the ship's stay. Seed, a plough, a few other farm tools and supplies brought out by the wagons that had transported the bulk of the passengers to St Louis gave evidence of the pilot's farming ambitions for the land while my grandson and the missionaries continued to ponder its meaning. Bit by bit the pilot moved ashore. He fixed the barn and began to repair the house. When he took more or less permanent shore leave, spending not only the days but the nights on land, he was followed by the rest of the crew. A division between boat and shore people gradually became apparent, widening until it reached a degree of animosity.

Mr Shannon's view of a boat lying around on dry land was that she didn't deserve to be considered a boat at all. At the back of his mind he harboured a sense of betrayal: by the river, by the boat, even by those who remained on board and adapted to a lopsided life the shore people considered unnatural. Here was a child growing up with feet on edge from having learned to walk at a permanent slant. Here were people who slept on a slope with their heads a foot higher than their toes. Here were dreamers tilted out of balance with the rest of the world, who claimed a God-given right to their life of leisure. The shore people cast the boat people in the role of slave-owning Confederates. Like the majority of people in the South we owned no slaves, however, and as far as I went back in living memory, which was quite a bit farther than anyone else, we had held emphatic views on the Peculiar Institution, as slavery was known, ever since the embargo of New Orleans. I recalled that when asked by Garrault the Elder, our neighbour in the Rue Royale, to act as a receiver for slaves smuggled through the swamps and offered for sale by his trading house, Zarraté & Cie had felt unable to oblige on principle. On the question of slavery, the root cause of the war igniting like bush fires all around us, the policies of the two warring governments were more similar than people realised. A Confederate constitution leaned one way, expressly granting the abolition of its peculiar institution, and the Federal government leaned another, taking pains to say nothing to jeopardise the loyalty of the four slave states that had chosen to stay in the Union. Meeting in the middle, they found that where they agreed lay the cause of their quarrel. It hardly seemed we had stranded by accident in Missouri, one of the two-timing states that had managed to retain the peculiar institution of the South while remaining loyal to the Union.

Porphyry came from St. Louis and was headed south. I saw dust rising while his wagons were still below the horizon. Slowly, through a hundred-year cloud of vagabond memories, past rolled into present and came to a standstill at the cross-roads where the *Queen of the South* lay stranded in a stubble field of wheat. The name and the profession had been adapted to his new country. Pawfrey & Sons, Raree Show, Diorama, Greatest Travelling Exhibition on Earth was painted in yard-high letters along the sides of the wagons. A long-legged man in a sombrero rode out in front of the wagon train. At the sight of our steamship, belly up like a dead whale, vines creeping out from under the hull, he reined in his horse, puffed out his cheeks and exclaimed admiringly to himself: now how in hell did they do that? By my reckoning this must have been Porphyry XIIth or XIIIth. If I exchanged the sombrero for a Spanish colonial hat ornamented with a plume of feathers and the horse for a mule, then the grave-faced rider with the exuberant moustache I now saw before me was the spitting image of his ancestor Porphyry VIIIth, the greatest showman ever seen in Brazil, exiled for blasphemy from Boa Vista more than a century ago.

As presented in Pawfrey's diorama the current standing of the war showed a slight advantage for the Confederacy, which tended to get more pronounced, he said, the further the show travelled south. A dozen wagons had been converted into peep-shows that gave remarkably vivid impressions of the war. They used photographs of famous persons as backdrops, sometimes as montages to show events that nobody had witnessed or which perhaps had not taken place at all. Pawfrey justified his preference for invention rather than strict adherence to historical truth on the grounds that showing what might have happened would be about as close as one ever got to showing what actually had.

Confederate troops under Stonewall Jackson repulse the Federals to Washington, read a caption, or: Battle for the Confederate capital Richmond, or: Second Battle of Bull Run — Generals Lee and Jackson rout Federal troops. In the foreground of scenes depicting the carnage of battle, live bodies, gored and bloodied and uniformed to accommodate local prejudices, were used to great effect as tableaux morts. Burnside, Fredericksburg, Salem Church. Tens of thousands of men died in battles named after places nobody had heard of. Pawfrey said his show had not been equipped to deal with the scale of such carnage. At first he had presented live spectacles with horses and riders carrying cards that read: two thousand Federal infantry, fifteen hundred Confederate light artillery, five hundred cavalry and so on. Thirty or forty men galloping back and forth had been able to account for a full-blown day of butchery by means of this device, but it lacked verisimilitude, he said. Audiences had objected to mestizos and mulattos representing the slaughter of their soldiers and impugning their dead white honour. Then corn for the animals became scarce. In parts of the country they had charged him over a dollar for a bushel of wheat. One dollar, Pawfrey repeated, rubbing his head in disbelief. This figure seemed to trouble his memory more than the tens of thousands slain.

Greatest Travelling Exhibition on Earth struck me as something of a misnomer for this huddle of dusty wagons littering the wayside. In my mind I saw the stylish figure of Porphyry VIIIth tossing his cane to Madame Porphyry in a sedan chair, where the cane turned into a snake and then into a silk scarf. I recalled his epic recreation of the Founding of Boa Vista, complete with the arrival of a Portuguese caravel and half-man, half-fish Indians, riding the whales they hunted in view of the spectators at the windows of the Episcopal palace. Where was all Porphyry's glory? What had happened to the scores of extras, the mestizos and mulattos his much diminished successor had mentioned? Disbanded when he could no longer pay them, Pawfrey said, soaked up in two shakes by this dry sponge of a country, gone to dig canals or build railroads or whatever, and this had been his good fortune. Which stood right there in the last wagon.

Progress, he told us, was minimising effort to maximise effect. That applied to the entertainment business as it did to war, to the crank-operated multi-barrel machine gun recently patented or to his own invention, similar to a kaleidoscope but more sophisticated, of an infinite mirror system. This was the installation waiting in the wagon, which at last he had perfected. We stepped up into the wagon one at a time and peered through an aperture at a scene showing tens of thousands of soldiers engaged in battle under the caption: Federals hold off Confederate advance at Gettysburg. Pawfrey explained it was based on illusion, no more than a dozen figures on either side modelled to his specifications and reproduced in apparently infinite numbers by the arrangement of mirrors in the cabinet. Either you saw it here or you didn't see it at all. This was the most superior representation of war, said Pawfrey, ever devised, powerfully affecting the imagination, without the need for men and horses and wagon-loads of costly supplies, which were still no more than fractions of a whole that could never be perceived, even if you had been on the battlefield at the time.

Who was winning the war? Judging that was not his business, Pawfrey said with a shrug. Slight advantage, if advantage it could be called in view of the enormous casualties on either side, for the Confederates. But their forces had been checked. Maybe the tide was turning. He said he would let us know when he brought his show back up this road. After a week of repairs to wagons and wagoners he got up into his saddle and the Greatest Travelling Exhibition on Earth moved on.

The flood came at the end of a long wet fall. It stole up in the night, floated the *Queen of the South* an inch or two and set her down the other way round, listing some twenty degrees to the north. The boat people adapted to the new inclination, sleeping with their heads down now and their feet up. It seemed to shift around the arrangement of the ideas in some heads, too. The missionaries learned humility. Their place was among the suffering in this war, which had surely been sent as a visitation on their countrymen for their pride. They descended from the ark one morning and set off in the direction of the river. Edgar P. Stanton was still chewing on an item he had picked out of the litter of ideas left by Pawfrey's visit, the notion of the dollar bushel of wheat. In spring he watched it green around him, in summer turn to gold. He wondered what if it hadn't, if it had been taken by a late frost, blighted, dried up or been rained out. Buy green and sell gold. There were gilt-edged profits in the margin between the two. This was the significance of the empty field, not a place for him to weed and hoe but to irrigate with capital investment. My mind wandered as I listened to Edgar P., but unless I was mistaken I had clearly heard him say: there's love to be made in the margin between the two.

Littlewood

How? This was nonetheless a margin of three hundred and fifty years. Margin? More like an ocean slopping around between the two of us. Still, the evidence: my susceptibility to plain words like margin, which enveloped me in the hitherto unsuspected sensuousness of their nature. Margins of flesh at midriff, left uncovered for a moment between garter and hiked skirt. Searing visions of these in the night. Speech impediment, obstructing my otherwise smooth tongue. An unspeakable beauty lighting up inside myself. Unruly thoughts, a sensation of rising on tip-toe, a wound spring at full chock, released to leap for the unattainable. I allowed none of this, not the faintest hint of it, to show in my behaviour to her. It took a year of swilling trough by trough aboard the ark before I dropped the formal Miss. She suggested a name, Eliza, but I preferred Littlewood, to call her plain Littlewood.

She was all in the landscape of this name, pine bark, clear water, valleys of freckled green ferns on moss, a grove rather than a forest: littlewoodish. In my three hundred and seventy-five year-old brain a woman of twenty something was taken apart and put together again in the images I made of her. What was this mysterious process? These mirrors in which it seemed she must be reflected in order for her to be seen at all, the projections of the camera obscura that was myself? Pawfrey had reflected a world in mirrors, believing that one either saw it as an illusion or one saw nothing. Porphyry had called his Teatro an echo in which the world heard itself.

In these constructions, or reconstructions, enacted on some proscenium of the brain, a blind world learned to see itself, perhaps through the kind of landscape looking-glass fashionable at the time. The glass had a pinkish tint and the world one saw through it took on a softer complexion. Through the looking-glass that was Littlewood I regained a scattered sense of self. Littlewood put me together again. The ghosts who had remained at my side since I lost my family withdrew into thin air. Becoming tired of life, I had been half way towards joining them. Now I turned back. The world around me grew denser again, solid with objects, colours, sensations I had felt growing weaker and weaker. This exorcism of my ghost-ridden world, sharpening of focus, recovery of appetite, quickening of the blood, a restored sense of gravity pushing me firmly back into the world — all this was attributable to the Littlewood effect.

Curious, in the face of it. The face was round and unremarkable except for the freckled nose tilting up out of it, a nose suggesting a contrary streak behind an inoffensive demeanour in which I read competence, reliability, a brisk out-door manner if need be. I agreed with Mrs Pereira. Out of a hundred job applicants one would choose this girl for a travelling companion.

Littlewood invited decoration because she provided so little herself. That was the deep inspiration a plain woman could give to a man. He gave her the beauty she did not possess, this gift she gave him to give. She was the plain linen table-cloth as much needed by all embroidering imaginations as these were unneeded by her. Plain linen table-cloth described

Littlewood's quality of thingness that resisted the embrace of an idea. The plain matter of Littlewood tapped a slow sap concealed in me, set flowing a youthfulness congealed in me, inside my fossilised brittlewood state. I felt it rush into my extremities, thawing out bloodless feet and hands, spurting with a sharp tingling sensation into my old man's husk of penis. How shameful! An unexpected resurgence of life, a stump greening and flourishing inside my pants, shamed me even as it enflamed, battered me with a cudgel of desire that had stayed quietly in its drawer for the better part of a century at least. The old man put out his brightest feathers, despite himself, and preened. Héloise noticed. When I sunned myself with Littlewood, a gaping lizard motionless on deck, she skulked in the background, hissing. She sounded her way around the ship like a trail of steam escaping from a valve. Sssssss! She slid notes under my stateroom door. Shame on you, lecherous old goat! Down, Sir! My implacable daughter's jealousy caused me distress. I felt ashamed for the miracle of my old man's love.

The Floating of the Ark

All of this babble flowed past Littlewood. She went back and forth between boat and shore, mediating between shore and boat people with her quiet impartial presence. She taught Lee to walk and his mother to speak a language resembling English. She darned for the ship's crew in their womanless house, grew vegetables, sang lustily and leaned sideways for us to play the piano lashed down on a 20° gradient in the saloon. Even Héloise was unable to prevent herself from being befriended by Littlewood. Among the temperamental, eccentric Zarratés and Stantons she seemed extraordinary in her ordinariness. Here was a woman more concerned about others than both those families put together. A self-serving instinct made them look closely at Littlewood and inquire: why is she doing this? What's in this for her? The interest on pumpkins and rows of beans in Littlewood's kitchen garden? Her laundry, cooking and other services supplied free of charge? They waited to be disillusioned, to be presented with the bill, to get bored at least with the character of this woman.

Her trustingness was such that even Chemin de Fer's sleight of hand became fumbling when faced with Littlewood at a card table. She believed in people's good intentions. This made it such a temptation to tease Littlewood and play practical jokes on her. At three years of age Lee Stanton was finding snakes in the bed, falling from the boat and pretending to be dead — Littlewood's shrieks were guaranteed genuine. Edgar P. Stanton told her hair-raising tales about dust clouds he had seen on the horizon, marauding Indians sighted in the neighbourhood that afternoon, scalping parties, blood rites, the Indians' very particular resentment of stranded Mississippi steamboats obstructing their hunting grounds.

Héloise poked fun in her waspy widowish way. She invented a figure called Mr Vag, an acronym standing for Very Antique Gentleman, referring to myself. How do you put up with Mr Vag, she would ask. Don't you find his attentions comic? Ridiculous? Slightly disgusting, in fact? How patient you are, my dear. I'm very fond of Mr Vag, Littlewood would say, giving my hand a squeeze. Ugh, responded Héloise, and pulled a face. Héloise, who had been so reserved in her rational judgement, prudish, modest to a fault, became vicious and obscene in her senile ramblings, castigating imaginary lovers who had disappointed her, bandying with those who satisfied her in the most obscene terms. Mr Vag was only one of many fictional people inhabiting her mind. Littlewood indulged them all, inquired after their health, allowed herself to be drawn into conversations with non-existent third parties and offered condolences when informed by Héloise of their deaths.

Lee flourished like the wild vine that had grown up all round the boat and transformed it into a green wedge of a house, while his mother played with dolls the assistant boiler-man made for her before he decamped, his father dreamed and muttered among fields of wheat, his grandmother raved wherever she was, Littlewood spread commonsense, rounding out on a diet of bread and pork, Mr Shannon manufactured tobacco to roll his own cheroots, and herds of hogs, Pardy's porkers in the twentieth generation, now roamed through the fields and woods. I felt affection for these animals. Whether they were indigenous North American hogs, or the descendants of Portuguese pigs, or perhaps a cross between the two I couldn't say, but they seemed to have been my loyal companions all my life.

Snouts to planks, they had rooted around for whatever was edible in the hold of the *Sao Cristobal* on my voyage across the Ocean Sea. They had been the totem animal of the Pig Indians and for years we had lived amicably in one house. At short notice they had been transformed into bacon, liquefied as knee-deep rivulets of fat when Indians set fire to Dom Pedro Felipe's expeditionary force on the peninsula and hundreds of them had burned. Those that escaped had gone forth and multiplied, following their noses north up the peninsula in search of food, only to become food for others. Pigs had been a source of considerable wealth to me after I bought stock in Fong & Sons, Cincinnati, on the advice of Edgar P. Stanton. They had sacrificed themselves for the pork-processing industry on an unprecedented scale. It was their cadavers that had set in motion the world's first assembly line. I didn't know of anyone else with a record of such loyalty to the human race. I watched the *Queen of the South* gradually deserted by everyone but her pilot, the proprietor and her family and her pigs. The geese had flown, the goats gone wild, even the chief engineer had sneaked off. A deep somnolent peace settled on the community of survivors who remained with the ark.

Records of them were preserved in the daguerreotypes Edgar P. Stanton made with his father's equipment. Time was stopped in these pictures, as his father had predicted. They showed the desert islanders of the civil war. Bad exposures on bad paper contributed to the impression of dirt ingrained in the unkempt figures lined up by the photographer. He posed them in too much light on the deck, too little under the hull of an ark that lay dry-docked on an empty horizon, bristling with vines, wind-dropped seeds which had lodged in cracks and become flourishing plants. Brightness flared around the borders of Edgar P. Stanton's pictures, as if the scenes they showed were about to disintegrate in an explosion, moments ripped from the continuous flow of time.

My own images of these years, retrieved from a landscape looking-glass with the Littlewood effect, featured a sensible woman in a plain blue dress with a pinafore who was always turned out spruce, swore by soap and water and kept the boy in trim too, running a comb through his wildness from time to time, scrubbing his face and patching his pants. The brightness around these images was just in the air. Flow never ceased. We inhabited a tideland, a margin between the rise and fall of the river. To me it seemed brief, our occupation of this tideland. The flood would come and the flood came, lifting our settlement up, trailing vines, like a water-logged plant, and floating it back to the river. Beneath her layers of camouflage the *Queen of the South* remained a steamboat miraculously in working order, even if she seemed to recoil with a shudder when reminded of the sound of her engines. On her way upstream she began to break apart, timbers cracking with sharp reports like gunshots. It was the dead of winter, bitterly cold. We encountered ice floes just south of St. Louis. The pilot decided to run her aground on a sand-bank off the Missouri shore so long as she still remained afloat. Ice was already enclosing the *Queen of the South* when we went ashore in a rowboat, freezing the wild vine to cables of hoar frost, gripping the trailers and drawing them tight, as if the winter had anchored her there. We went along the river bank through vineyards withered white in the moonlight until we saw the city glowing with a thousand furnaces, showering sparks, like a hell-fire apparition in the night. At St. Louis the Mississippi was frozen with a thick layer of ice. Teams with sledges, silent as ghosts, made the trek across the sealed river, and in this way we passed over to the Illinois shore.

Reconstruction

So long as the winter sat tight we sat tight with it, occupying two suites that took up the top floor of the Grand Southern Hotel. On the top floor there was less likelihood of Héloise causing inconvenience to other guests. Littlewood stayed on as my daughter's nurse without needing to be asked. Lee Stanton hung all day at the window, disbelieving this mirage of a city spread out below. There were so many things he had to figure out. The steep-floored home in which he had grown up, the only home he had known, had suddenly levelled out, floated away and been abandoned in the night when the fire-eating city appeared at a bend in the river. His arrival in St. Louis was acomplished by walking over inexplicably solid water. I sympathised with my great-grandson. Lee's situation was not so different from mine, surrounded by things I had never seen and for which I had no name.

To me this urban scenery was as mysterious as it was to him. Acres of close-packed houses rising on ridge after ridge from the water side. Vast manufactories and magazines of commerce riddled day and night with the clang of machinery. Two miles of steam-boats solid white along the levee. A spider's web of railway tracks, slung from the city centre and hurled out over undulating prairie. Within three-quarters of a century all this had materialised out of nothing and already it looked as ancient as any city in the Old World. Illinois coal had tinged the buildings a venerable brown colour. Age came instantly to St. Louis with the patina of industry that seemed to cast a shadow across the city. The industrial contractors, arriving in that empty space and filling it with their machines, had succeeded above all in contracting time. They condensed time and built decay, brand-new towns which began to disintegrate as soon as they were complete, the cities of a new Tahuantin-suyu, crumbling to ash on the fiery wind that came blasting through with a new breed of iron-clad, rail-shod conquistadors.

Returning to the world after a long absence, I realised how well it had managed without me, so quickly had old things disappeared that I would have recognised and new ones appeared in their place. The most uncompromising of these was news. What used to concern us, in a warmer climate, a more intimate society, was slow-moving gossip. Less happened. There were fewer of us. Our day to day lives made history. On a few rumours we would get by for a decade or two. Those who made news, those who passed it on and those who chewed it over until history came out belonged to the same small group of people. Between stepping onto the boat in New Orleans and getting off it in St Louis a gap seemed to have opened out between the makers, the producers and the consumers of news. It was the last time I would live without news. It became an all-pervasive medium, as inescapable as air.

I became aware of something called the general public. It seemed to be so vast that even had I climbed onto the high roof of the temple the people of Missouri had dedicated to the god of insurance I would not have been able to see it in its entirety. I would have seen thirty incoming railroad lines converging on the central depots of St. Louis, and following each of these in my mind's eye, and extrapolating the population of all the cities along all of these lines for many thousands of miles I might have arrived at a rough approximation of what made up the American public. It was the conclusion, one might also have called it the invention, of the country's new transport system, the mass human parcel the railroads had knitted together and bound up, some of them people who were fast asleep in remote backwaters of the country and had no inkling of their good fortune — members, whether they wanted it or not, of the great American public.

Southerners would not have wanted. They had seceded from the Union, fought a war, lost it, and now they were back in again. But the war and the politicking were skirmishes, side-shows to that other great federal advance of wagon trails, railroad, telegraph and trade seeping unstoppably as blood through a spontaneous proliferation of arteries which made one living organism of a country stretched too far to be able to sustain continuous life: transformed a country into a nation. What the war did was to enable retroactive legislation acknowledging the existence of this great American public. In the moment of its creation began the process of its disintegration. Thirteenth, Fourteenth and Fifteenth Amendments were issued in an attempt to halt this process of disintegration while they only reaffirmed it, the crack that opened up as the great divide in the nation's consciousness the same instant the "Union" had been accomplished and that irrevocable, doom-laden word was spoken.

A general public required a general news. Its reach was so wide that as one part of the public got its news behind it and went to bed another part of the public was already up and about and generating more news. News required constant priming, nowhere more so than in St. Louis, a turntable city bringing news in with the railroads from one direction and sending them off in another. What they called the Mid-West was mid-nowhere, not so much a place as a receiving station for goods and people in transit. Those who described themselves as local residents were individuals like my son-in-law Stanton, perpetually coming or going, wiping their feet and taking off their hats ten thousand times as they crossed and re-crossed the thresholds of their revolving turntable lives.

In the foyer of the Grand Southern Hotel, where the flood survivors took refuge to consolidate their position in history and find their bearings in the future, broadsheets with the latest news were being touted two or three times a day. There was a new president whose name I didn't know, new words such as copperhead, carpetbagger and scalawag, whose meaning I didn't understand. What was called Reconstruction looked to me like re-entrenchment. The North had the principles and the South had the niggers. Even as we sat in the foyer of the Grand Southern, sipping coffee and considering what to do, a late edition of the *St.Louis Herald* was canvassed around the hotel aisles. News was that blacks had been murdered by embattled whites in riots in New Orleans. This would be the end of the line for a never counted, never published number of the new class of the reconstructed American public: black but free, free enough to swing from the nearest tree, faces still dazed with the suddenness of their hurried departure from life.

The Hog Trail

I felt affection for these animals. Whether they were indigenous North American hogs, or the descendants of Portuguese pigs, or perhaps a cross between the two I couldn't say, but they seemed to have accompanied me all my life. I started out with them on board the *Sao Cristobal*, snouts to planks, rooting around for anything edible in the hold, and my great-grandson started out with them too in the hog-grunting landscape surrounding the ark where he was born. When his mother Wai On died unobtrusively one grey afternoon in St. Louis, clutching the assistant boiler man's dolls as if she intended to continue playing with them in another life, it was Lee's hog-dressing uncle Goh who arrived the next morning from Cincinnati to supervise the final rites. She was buried, to all appearances, in accordance with Christian custom, but it was the coffin, not his mother, that the boy watched lowered into the ground. Goh brought the body to a countryman from Shanghai who ran a funeral parlour out of a back room of a restaurant.

Reports of quite what happened there were a little vague, partly because of poor communication between Goh and Edgar P. Stanton. He had acquiesced to the Fong family's request that his wife's remains should return to the Middle Kingdom without realising that remains meant literally what it said. Corpses were buried by the Chinese in America only because it couldn't be helped, an interim storage, until a relative arrived to dig them up, bake the bones dry and scrape them clean and take them back to the old country. Goh obviated this lengthy process with the help of the Shanghai restaurant owner and his cauldrons in a back room overlooking the Mississippi. My guess was that the river was where the leached tissue of Wai On not destined for burial in China must have been launched on another post-mortem journey back to the Gulf of Mexico via New Orleans. Lee's uncle returned to Cincinnati with Edgar P. Stanton. When we said goodbye to them at the station Goh was carrying a brown paper parcel he had not had with him on his arrival in St. Louis two days before.

Hogs had been friendly food on the hoof throughout four centuries, from the day they were embarked in Lisbon to victual the voyage to Brazil until they trotted through the gates of the Union Stockyards in Chicago, first opened, one might say christened, for mass slaughter on Christmas Day the year the Civil War ended. From my perspective, I saw the Union Stockyards as the apotheosis of the colonial enterprise in the New World, centuries of killing livestock, whether hogs, Indians or runaway slaves, to satisfy the different appetites of different conquistadors. A vast colonial body required a vast amount of fodder. Before and after the making of laws and the blessing of churches there would always remain the darker primary activities of hunting, herding and blooding those animals man fought to the death to supply him with life.

Lee Stanton's childhood had relied on hogs not only for food but for sport, just as mine had among the Taiassu when I stalked the capybara with my blow-pipe or sat with Grasshopper in a tree all night to kill the tapir in the Mud Indians' manioc patch. With a sense of familiarity, even nostalgia, I followed the boy's barbarous years on the ark. I was an accomplice to his natural cruelty, his desire to meddle with dirt and death. I taught him how to make bows and arrows tipped with poisons concocted from vegetable alkaloids and the juices of decomposing animals. My own primary needs had ebbed away in the course of a hundred blood-soaked years before I returned to civilisation and went to live in the big house in Pernambuco, but Lee Stanton stepped straight from the wilderness into a modern city. He didn't belong. Surrounded by buildings, machinery and traffic, the child remained isolated in his own savage space.

There was a question of who belonged at all, in these instant towns that felt as if they had been designed for people passing though. The buildings looked provisional and hasty, the avenues, intersections and railroads immense and built to last, because the residents had drifted here and stayed rather than done anything as deliberate as arriving. They still remained travellers at heart, and the traveller always had right of way. It was an interesting proposition, building towns for this nomadic tribe, putting down stones, like anchors, to keep people from drifting away. Once we had abandoned New Orleans, or been abandoned, because the South had withdrawn into its unforgiving past, I realised that if we belonged anywhere it was to the travellers. To be on the move, between places, was the natural state for an unbelonging Lee Stanton and his unquiet grandmother Héloise. They were conspirators in the new restlessness.

I advised Fong by telegraph that his grandson was coming to see him. We travelled by the railroad in which I was a stockholder, the Marietta & Cincinnati. It had prospered, and its shareholders with it, not least on account of the business provided by the hogs it had hauled to Cincinnati. The Fongs owned and occupied a three-storey structure called a tenement. We had been expecting to find Edgar P. Stanton there, but he had moved on soon after he arrived in Cincinnati, said Fong, and gone to live in Chicago. Fong was considering moving there himself. Business was no longer expanding as it had in the decade since he started up in the meat-processing industry. With the opening of the Union Stockyards the challenge from Chicago competitors had become too strong. I knew that speculation on the Chicago grain market was what had lured Edgar P. Stanton there. We sat in Fong's back-room parlour in silk-covered chairs carved with dragons, sipping tea as we talked, interrupted by Fong's sons putting their heads in to ask his advice or by a flight of grandchildren with Lee in pursuit. The sight of the wispy Chinaman in his Shanghai robes mustering this Stanton addition to the house of Fong filled me with a greater sense of wonder than anything since Lemon Grass brought our son Earth Puddle to my hammock in the malocca. It was the diversity of the ingredients which had gone into the child's making, the utterly fortuitous nature of the encounter in which he had his origins. The boy incorporated the shot-apart country where he was born. The restless genes from Europe, Africa, China and Brazil, coming together at the intersection of Edgar P. Stanton with Wai On, were like the travellers on their way through all those instant American cities. I realised that Lee did belong.

We set out to find them, the spaces between the places, the between places where Lee belonged. They had the names of the railroads that joined them, which was why they came in strings, connections rather than locations, the Pittsburgh, Cincinnati & St. Louis, the Wabash, St. Louis & Pacific, the Missouri Pacific, the Northern Pacific, the Atchison, Topeka & Santa Fe, the Union and Central Pacific. There was no escaping this terminal ocean. It pulled people across an intervening land mass in just the way their ancestors had been pulled across an intervening ocean. Lee memorised an ever lengthening litany of railroad company names whose tracks drained into it, which he chanted during our journey west. Three hundred years on, when the first transcontinental rail route opened, I crawled back to the Sleeping Sea.

My view of the landscape between Cincinnati and Sacramento was obstructed by a film like a fine rain of sand, a side-effect which Fong had warned me about when he handed me the medicine. This was a powder ground from a rock-like substance, reputed to be dinosaur penis. In particular it had the effect of reinforcing limp erections, more generally a hardening of tissue in other parts where this might not always be desired. I would gradually slough off my old skin, which would be replaced by a tougher, more sinewy epidermis. The substitution took place more quickly than Fong had claimed. When she saw my skin beginning to crack like the bed of a dry lake, flaking from my scalp, neck and face, Littlewood treated it for sun-burn and applied essences of oil as often as the locomotive stopped to take on water. As soon as this film evaporated, the fine drizzle of cutaneous dust from my forehead resumed. Something that was already rather scaly, even reptilian, in my appearance was undoubtedly reinforced by Fong's dinosaur powder. This ailment may have been responsible for my impression that so much of America was a desert. The need to bathe and change my clothes made frequent stops unavoidable, but wherever we did so we seemed to be surrounded by nothing but dust, as if dehydrated travellers with similar skin complaints had been shedding cutaneous matter along the same route for thousands of years.

Héloise scrutinised my condition with suspicion and not the slightest sympathy. Because of this mistrust I had married Littlewood secretly in St. Louis and led a morganatic marriage with her since. I had used the opportunity of acquiring a new wife to acquire a new name, too. Zarraté pronounced in the French style and tainted with a Southern accent was not how I wished to identify myself in the post-bellum Union. When spoken by Americans the name was mangled beyond recognition in any case. We began our married life as Mr and Mrs Straight. My first name Paul underwent a transition from pole to pall. Pole to pall was not necessarily an improvement, but I thought that Straights and Stantons read very well in hotel ledgers. When spoken with Littlewood's Boston twang, Straight sounded as if it might have a pedigree. My wife was Boston-born and had natural grace. For all that she was the daughter of a Dublin coster. I supplied her with more impressive antecedents, tried out without risk on forgettable travelling companions west of Omaha, Nebraska. In conversations we struck up with strangers in the dining-car of the Union & Pacific an English duchess dabbled, a Scottish laird lurked in the greenery of the family tree. By the time we headed back east I had her story pat and felt confident I could appropriate it myself.

In the name of Straight I purchased a house in the dunes overlooking the ocean. There was so much water out there, such surf and sucking and swirling, that it seemed to absorb the noise made by my daughter Héloise. She ceased to hear the barrage inside her head and registered something like peace. She came to terms with her flaking, newly-wed father. She no longer, thank God, walked around hissing — a vicious habit that had not been improved by association with steam locomotives for months on end. I was too exhausted to cope with anything but my change of skin. I was shedding my life.

Fong's medicine evinced so many side-effects that they cancelled out the effect I had taken it for. Sometimes I became delirious with fevers from a previous age, deep disorders, forgotten but still there, that rose to the surface as the scarf-skin was unwrapped from my body. I lay naked on the bed, exposing the suppurating sores of my past to the sea breeze. I listened to the boom of surf and the snap of air when swallows dived through the room and hallucinated I was back in Tumbez. Pus stained the sheets, fritters of rejected skin curled up like dying caterpillars on the floor. When Half Moon swept the floor and changed the bed linen I was ashamed to look her in the face. What's this mushy stuff, she asked. It's your people, I said. When the centipede came up the river they hanged themselves rather than face God-is-Love. Walk through the forest and see the ripeness of the foliage. Indians have taken to rotting on trees. When the centipede came down the river the tribes ran out and hanged themselves in the forest. Did you see the mulatto castrated in the mill house before they stuck him between the rollers and he was ground to death? What put the knife in the Donatory's hand? Who bore the priest's sword and heard his prayer? Whose word was in our ears, whose mission in our hearts? We have invented God and He is evil, I said to Littlewood where she once again took shape after the ghost of Half Moon had receded, but Littlewood merely rejoined that He had given us good times too, and she went on sweeping the floor.

She put a rocking-chair out on the porch and there I sat getting better. Convalescence or a process of consolidation, membrane of scarf-skin knitted together, memory closing the gaps.

In the watery-eyed osmosis of my fabulous old age I was rediscovering the truth of All-Creatures-Being-in-the-Forest. Strength became evident in my weakness. The notion of isolated selfhood was an illusion, for the world was a single flowing organism. There were no divisions beneath the appearance of individual things. When the walls of my skin broke down and I became too weak to resist, I absorbed everything around me and was absorbed by it. I was the centipede that devoured the Indians and the Indians devoured by it, I was the knife, the hand that drew it and the blood that was drawn. A river jumped and became dry land, earth to water, water to earth, shifted borders around and changed the ideas of people living on its banks, mingled their blood, white blood flowed in black veins, black blood in white. My great-grandson Lee was latent in me as his quadroon great-grandmother Mijou was in him, as the spaces were in the clusters of human habitation punctuating them and the habitations were in the spaces between them and both of them were in the strings of railroad names interconnecting them. All the constituents of the world were constantly being shuffled around to form new appearances like the patterns formed by pieces of glass in the kaleidoscope Pawfrey had given to Lee when he visited the stranded ark.

Sums of addition and subtraction, inevitably of compound interest too, showed up in giant figures Héloise drew in the sand. Lee capered into arithmetic with flying shirt tails, his lessons occasionally mobbed by gulls and erased by an inrushing sea. He came to me and asked for the quipu, the wool writing, he called it, which his father had told him about. The quipu lay in a drawer, sealed in a leather sheath, but I lied and said I hadn't brought it with me, because I had decided to keep it under wraps forever. Not because the scroll was falling apart, moth-eaten, damaged beyond repair. Some life-prolonging essence remaining in the quipu had been breathed in by Edgar P. Stanton, along with solutions of sodium chloride and silver nitrate, during exposure to the various recording processes of his childhood. The effects might be weakening but were still unmistakable. They had retarded his natural ageing. My grandson in early maturity looked like a freak youth of twenty.

The quipu was a curse I would not wish on anyone; least of all on myself. It was a moralising myth that old people ceased to feel desire. If it did not trouble them they merely made a virtue of weak appetite. Thwarted by lack of performance, an old man might try to ignore desire, make a habit of abstinence and in time forget it. But few old men, except perhaps in China, where they could benefit from an art called drawing the horns out of a snail, had to compete with the appetites of young wives. More than once since her death Wai On had crossed my mind, smiling with sideways glances, giggling into her deep sleeves. In treasure-seeking dreams she consented to come astride me and salvage the wreckage with her snatch. Erect on the bed of the sea I looked up to see her bottom descending, a smooth round hull, her name in undulating letters along the side: *Wai On*. I thought of this when I was pick-pocketing Littlewood with sedulous hands, using persuasions on her body with gentle abrasions, inserting callous-worn fingers tipped with dinosaur horn to paddle in channels between thighs, navigating puff-like sighs across a gradually deepening sound until she reached the sea. We were Beauty and the Beast. I was the ugly old man whose sensuality could still fascinate despite age, an ambiguity answering to a humming-bird quality in Littlewood's secret feelings, which I observed hovering between attraction and repulsion, sympathy and aversion.

Edgar P. Stanton was running his first corner in wheat on the futures' market in Chicago while his son's calculations were being scratched in sand and erased by forgetful waves that came washing up out of the Sleeping Sea. Scratched and erased, makeshift communities adrift from time cropped up on the shore, came and went with the flotsam disgorged and retracted by the sea, the bareback Indian riders on ponies with soft hooves, castaways of life from the far side of the continent, the rims of their hats thick with brine, their garments sun-bleached, dazed from the seemingly endless journey, the wagon-stopping, brain-jolting halt when they came up smack against the ocean. It all came to an end here. This was the border finalising emptiness. It stopped travellers in their tracks. Nothing happened. No more place. Lean-to houses creaked on shifting foundations. Wind blew through shadows. Sand drifted across the porch and buried the rocking-chair runners, slowing down the old man's rocking sleep until he reached a complete standstill and woke up with a start. He saw a herd of half-wild hogs sniffing the sea air, turn back from the shore and come trotting up past the house. They were small, amiable, quick-footed black porkers with corkscrew tails, squealing with delight when Littlewood leaned out of the window and threw them a handful of corn.

Encased in a new skin that felt like a suit too small, I moved a little stiffly these days, even in California's loose-fitting climate. My body seemed to be made of glass. We moved to San Francisco and lived in a hotel near the House of Fong. These were cousins of Lee's, tailors and drapers. With their tradition of extraordinary medicines – dinosaur powder, tiger extract, scorpions and venomous snakes in liquor – and their faith in the extraordinary results their medicines could achieve, the Chinese surmised the true extent of my antiquity and treated me with a deference I was never shown by westerners. The West had little respect for a man who was smaller than his wife. Never particularly tall, not by the beef and beer standards of modern times, I had been about the same height as Littlewood when I met her and had shrunk considerably since. She dispensed with her bonnet, encouraging me to wear a high-domed western hat, but I looked like a side-show midget in the hat. Besides, what did I care? I was the great-grandfather of Lee Stanton, son of a man rumoured among his purse-eared relatives in Chinatown to be worth over a hundred and fifty thousand dollars. Edgar P. Stanton was alleged to have earned that fabulous sum on a corner he had run in wheat.

A week away from Lee's tenth birthday we passed through Promontory, Utah, gliding east across the desert. When we reached the Iowa state border the evenings were already much cooler. We descended from the Union Pacific to change trains and waited an hour for the cars of the Chicago, Milwaukee and St. Paul Railway to be shunted into the station. Lee counted over a hundred cattle cars of the Chicago and North Western. Livestock lowing, the long train lurched slowly through a siding and trundled out over the prairie. The tail-lights were still visible when we boarded our car half an hour later. Lee and Héloïse shared one compartment, Littlewood and I the other; two berths, a water closet, an escritoire at the window through which we watched the scenery being carried past. We admired the sun coming up, had breakfast in Des Moines, lunch in Cedar Rapids and crossed the Illinois border late in the afternoon.

The car attendant said we would be in Chicago the same evening. He was a Negro from the South, with an old-fashioned obsequiousness that Littlewood found strange after the years we had spent out west. For want of any other particular place to go she had decided Chicago would be our home. For myself, home would be wherever Littlewood was. I listened to her as she got carried away by the furnishings and colour schemes of a house already built in her imagination. Littlewood was planning the children's room. I was touched by her faith, stirred by her impossible desire. I fondled her through her clothes as I watched the sun go down over her shoulder. The Negro attendant knocked softly with a light supper. Later, she said. The sun went down on the horizon and came up again burning more brightly. I stood behind her, looking at the phantom sunrise in the east, flickering on her bare arms. Between myself and this strangely refulgent horizon Littlewood's body stretched out, naked but for her stockings and garter belt. What is it, she asked. She kneeled on a stool, bending over the escritoire, on which she rested her elbows as she looked out of the window. I ran my fingers down her back, watching her breasts sway with the motion of the car, and saw a long scaly penis, so remote from me it could not have been mine, pitched at her like some fossilised, horn-clad spar, inching its way laboriously into her body. The city, I said, the city's on fire. Littlewood gasped. The train came to a halt some miles outside Chicago, lit up by the blaze, the shadows of the cars jigging in a crazy kind of motion, and the seedless husks of my barren heat, all the provender that was left in me, finally spurted inside her while the city burned and a spark storm flying out over the tinder-dry prairie set fire to the night for miles around.

THE FOURTH NIGHT

Chicago

"The fire," prompted Father Anselm after he had activated the LISTEN switch and waited in vain for the old man to resume his narrative. "When I left you this morning we had just arrived in Chicago on the night the great fire broke out that destroyed the city. That must have been in 1870, if my memory serves me correctly."

There was still no reply to this gambit. Father Anselm tried jogging the old man's memory once more.

"Paul, you had just arrived in Chicago with Littlewood, your new wife, your daughter Héloise and your great-grandson, Lee. Approaching the city by night over the plains, you must have found the sight of the horizon in flames an unforgettable one."

A dry rustling sound drifted out of the sea shell of the old man's case.

"It was in 1871," the voice began at last, "on the night of the eighth to the ninth of October after a long spell of dry weather. Unforgettable? One thing is much like another in the great tide of events when you have been programmed to make no distinction and to forget nothing. "

"You sound a little hoarse tonight. Is there anything I can do for you, Paul? A glass of water? An aerosol tablet? A circulation of fresh air? "

"I am touched by your solicitude, Father Anselm. But such refreshments have no meaning for me. In due course a couple of new Everbright batteries for my sound reproduction system might be beneficial, perhaps, but not for the time being, thank you. I arrived in Chicago with my third wife, as you say, to begin a new life, making a home for children broken by Leviathan, gobbled up by Cannibal City, spat out by the Machine. My grandson, Edgar P. Stanton, you will remember, had a vision of a field of wheat. He traded in futures and made a fortune in the pit. Watching how our orphans grew, my wife and I had a vision too. We would beat the Machine. For my four hundredth birthday celebration Chicago hosted a World Exposition in what was called a White City at the Summit of Time, as if time could have such a thing as a summit. Such is the vanity and pride of man in his timebound achievements. Believing myself immortal, I ventured all in the futures market, lost all, and thus I was punished for my hubris — the Machine beat us."

"I am from Chicago myself," said Father Anselm. "My grandfather emigrated there as a boy from the city of Cork in Ireland."

"Then he is to be congratulated on having survived the experience. In those times, in that city, where it was said that the poor made a living dying for the rich..."

"Is that what they said?"

"Keep your ears pricked, Father Anselm, your eyes skinned. Somewhere in the crowds of Chicago's immigrant poor you will perhaps catch a glimpse of your grandfather. Perhaps you will hear it in the background, a long noise of masses of people on the move, tramp-tramp-tramp, like the cattle herded though the gates of the Union Stockyards. Perhaps he is among them. I can already hear it far away. Tramp tramp tramp....listen, Father Anselm. Do you hear them coming?"

Union Park

To me the sight of the burned-out city resembled a human being with the skin removed but the functions intact, all the physiological processes still going on inside. Railroad depots, grain elevators and the stock yards in the south-west, sheltering behind the ribbon of the Chicago river, escaped the flames. Undeterred by, perhaps even unaware of the fire, never-ending streams of new immigrants poured in unchecked at the terminals on the East Side. They made their way on foot into the city, swelling the procession of refugees from the gutted east bank of the river, a grimy concourse of men, wagons, lowing animals, bottle-necked at the few unburned bridges still spanning the Chicago River. On our way north up Halsted Street, through shells of buildings the fire had picked clean of their masonry, we had glimpses of the lake to the east in places where it could not have been visible a year before. In the aftermath of the fire the city functioned like a stripped-down machine, processing input and output, arterial flow through conduits laid bare. Food on the hoof brought into the city on one set of rails was processed and eaten by human consumers coming in on another. The by-products were sent back out over the same tracks that shipped in whole animals for dismantling into their component parts, canned meat, glue, fertiliser, soap, oil and tallow, manufactured in the stock yards from blood, bone and hoof. The waste of men and machines discharged into the river, into the open cesspools behind the houses, the city's running sores, its dank, overflowing, putrefying sumps. Purged by fire, there were no adornments to hide the primitive mechanism on which Chicago ran. The lid was off the city and the city stank.

West of Halsted, a great urban artery, perhaps tracing an old Indian portage between swamp and lake, which ran north-east for thirty miles, the Straight family moved into a rambling old patrician house on the fringe of a once well-to-do area known as Union Park. Over the few bridges that were still unburned we watched the homeless trek night and day, wagons piled with household goods, families trudging empty-handed on foot with long shadows of children in tow, a procession of the destitute that within a year had transformed itself into rows of squatters' huts where wild onions used to grow. These were thin, elusive, squirming people who could beg their way through cracks in the door, a breed of unstoppable human seepage on whom Littlewood took pity, countrymen to whom she first gave refuge, then charity to tide them over, then provisional keep for a modest charge, until she found herself running the kind of boarding establishment that transformed the geography of the house, the street, the neighbourhood. This was her family, surrogate for her own she would never have, which she first took to herself on the ark, lost in St. Louis and assembled again in Chicago. She could listen into a passing crowd, identify freckled individuals tossing their freckled Irish brogue in the smattering of tongues that rose above the sounds of the wheels in the street, still varieties of English, for the most part, followed by German, then by a rapidly broadening spectrum of eastern European languages, squeezed past our windows and eavesdropped on by our house, from Poland up the coast of the Baltic Sea to the inland steppe of Russia.

Houses in Union Park lost their claims to gentrification when they started having to earn their keep, or maybe it was having to earn their keep that brought the genteel tone of the neighbourhood down to the level of the crowd passing through on its way to work in the city. Squeezed from both sides, Union Park downgraded. The gentry left and the retail stores departed with it. An old avenue of leisure and pleasure, a business-afflu-ence axis that took care of its own kind, running west from lakeside offices where money was made to the houses set in American-Gothic parks where it was spent, screened by trees to preserve the atmosphere of fan-tastic unreality pervading such oases with their gazebos, grottoes and artful ruins — one day I saw this toy world gone. Wholesalers moved into the former retailers' premises. Streetcars on Madison and Lake were still connected to the central business district now running north-south along State Street. But these days the tracks ran through a long gauntlet of buildings with barred windows, factories warehouses shipping depots and lorry stations. Through the relics of what had once been Union Park's orderly commercial streets stretched block after block of men drinking in makeshift bars, of prostitutes and rag men and women and their ragamuf-fin children scavenging the sidewalks.

To all appearances the city was the triumphant market place, the great Machine. It brought in the raw materials and sent out the finished goods, generating unprecedented wealth that was very unevenly distributed among something like half a million inhabitants. But these were almost incidental effects of what to me seemed a still more extraordinary devel-opment, the runaway growth of leviathan, brute physical self-assertion of city as such, a hypertrophic environment beyond control, a pitch-dark, bottomless, cannibal locker into which a never ending supply of people was tossed and gobbled up in as short a time as possible. It was said that the poor had always been with us and that they always would. But in four centuries I had never seen so many of them or living in comparable bondage. On the eastern fringe of Union Park, slums with as great a den-sity of human misery as any place on earth were well established within a few years of the post-fire immigrants' arrival in the promised land.

If the poor made a living dying for the rich, as these new immigrants said, the slums where they worked at their dying might have been regarded as the most efficient of all our factories. It was a long noise of masses of people on the move, like cattle, a long drawn out conveyor belt of motion shuddering between places of work and places of sleep, clattering down a corridor between one dark room and another, human energies, sweat, muscle, always straining hope that were bundled like bright filaments, passed through spools and transformed into products, until the worker had been worn out and was thrown away. This was the pig-human whose bones were converted into fertiliser and glue, a new industrial breed, disposable in all its parts but the groan when it was knocked in the head and died. Standing armies of these pig-humans, raised out of unproductive idleness by the discovery of artificial light, could be heard marching through our streets at all hours of darkness, clattering along long drawn out corridors of sound between tenement and factory, preserving energies sustained by an absolute minimum of food and sleep for the machines to which they would be harnessed ten, twelve, sixteen hours a day.

This was the great discovery of the age, the pig-human stripped down to the essentials. Men and women were dispossessed of unproductive human requirements, refashioned on the analogy of a machine, machine traction power, the manufactures their pig-mould served to produce. They were flayed in the likeness of the city, their skin removed to facilitate the working of the moveable parts, and the city was generated in this image, flickering day by day with frantic motion as the streams of raw human material poured in through the railroad terminals and splashed their imprint on the pavements of the city.

Poverty was at the same time the most individual of all experiences and the most general. Poor people in the mass, how the poor collectively lived and died, this was something abstract, and Littlewood turned away from it, knowing that the individual poor was as much as she could cope with. The poor lived and died by the grace of God and minded their own business, in so far as they had a business to mind. They were herded together in columns, the columns trimmed into blocks of statistics, cities in which a new class of social workers accommodated them. There was nowhere else to put them. For the poverty of the immigrant poor was unimaginable. This was the new quality of urban life, a daily proximity of death so familiar that it fell short of comment, a silent starvation of tens of thousands, the accumulation of dead people every day, the defeated armies of the poor lying down to die in windowless rooms. A week of hot weather and foul water in the most overcrowded tenements back of the yards accounted for a death toll exceeding the slaughter in the greatest battles of the Old World. These horrors were unremarkable. They didn't make news.

But splashed an imprint on the pavements of the city. A fleeting image formed on the floor across which so many people in so short a time had passed. It might have been worn in by their desperation, a shadow left on a stone, a soiled outline on a discarded cloth. It was the abstract of the unimaginable, a montage of a thousand glimpses: a composite photograph of mankind that emerged from the Chicago West Side of these years.

Straight House

Littlewood took possession of her first boy on Christmas morning as he scrambled out of a coal chute from the sidewalk to the boiler room in the sub-cellar of the post office on Madison. Ragamuffins made use of the chute as a toboggan slide to a snug berth in cold weather, raising the cover in the street, sliding down in single file and snuggling up to the boiler where they spent the night out of harm's way. When it was time to begin the day's work they would surface by the same route. Work for Littlewood's first boy was beer-running in the Bohemian quarter for thirsty cigar makers, taking mugs and pannikins to be filled at the nearest saloon and returning them to their owners for a few coppers. When his head popped up out of the man-hole and he saw Littlewood looking down at him his natural instinct to flee was already weakened. She confided with a wink that she had just seen a Christmas dinner all set up at a table and no one there to eat it in a nice house down the street. The ragamuffin stood thoughtfully for a moment on his considerable dignity before dusting down his sooty coat and declaring that if Christmas was a holiday in any case he might as well give himself the day off to help the lady out with her dinner.

He offered us a choice when we asked his name, Sheeny, Mockie, Shonniker, Kike, but Littlewood didn't like any of them and said she would call him Matthew if he didn't mind. Where did Matthew belong? Matthew wasn't too sure, but as far as he knew he belonged to the post office. He spent the winter in the cellar there along with a few other boys he knew. In summer he belonged to the shore end of Armour's pier at the waterfront on the lake. That was the extent of the personal history to be gleaned during his first visit. After some impressive throat-clearings and statements concerning the various business obligations still awaiting him, not a word about the three-plate dinner he had demolished, he got up from the table, Littlewood opened the back door for him and he slipped out like a cat.

Sometimes I doubted that anybody knew just how many street children there were around. The bodies of children were found who were not known to be missing. Drowned children often turned up whom no one seemed to know anything about. When workmen moved a pile of lumber on Armour's pier at the end of the winter and found under the last plank the body of a boy crushed to death the previous fall — inadvertently no doubt, perhaps in his sleep, God only knew — no one had missed him, though his parents turned up afterward. Small, desiccated corpses, children dried out like the flattened pelts of starved mice, were discovered in pipes and drains, refuse trashed in the crannies of the city. More dead children were found in Chicago than the authorities could account for as living in the city. It was known to them that half the children in the city died before they reached the age of five, but they couldn't explain so many children dying in Chicago who were not known to have ever lived there.

Littlewood took to hanging around the Madison Street post office early in the morning with pies for the coal-chute urchins, nabbing them when they came up for air. She didn't preach. The pies were good and had no strings attached. There were four regulars, all beer-runners, two for the Bohemian cigar makers, two for the Lithuanian tailors in the sweat-shops along Maxwell and Jefferson. A night down in the coal bunkers in the close anthracite air required a good deal of hawking and throat-clearing on the part of these boys before they were ready to speak. Once they had found their voices it was usually to announce that they were busy right now, business was their always pressing concern, it was a wonder they found time to address the question of the pies at all. But business came and went in the tenements the way that it did, roaring for three months and slack for six as the world adjusted to commodity markets which had nothing to do with tailors or cigar makers needing to make a living every day. If the market went into a tailspin and crashed, beer was the first thing they let go, the beer-runners with it. This may have been the reason why when a pie unfailingly available every morning throughout the winter was one day accompanied by Littlewood's suggestion, Well, boys, so why don't we call it a day and head back home, not too much was needed in the way of throat-clearing before the coal-chute gang agreed to give it a go.

Mick, Lugan, Bohunk were the generic names by which these boys went, but Littlewood continued firmly along the path she had set out on with Matthew. She called his successors Mark, Luke and John, invoking the four evangelists as the boys' patron saints before they even got a foot in the door. There will be no swearing in this house, she said, no spitting, no chewing tobacco or drinking beer. Yes 'm. Otherwise they were free to come and go as they pleased. She charged two cents for bed, two for breakfast and two for dinner of pork and beans. Credit was negotiable for those who wished to attend trade school or who had a sensible business proposition that needed start-up capital. All of these practical sentences flowed out of Littlewood while she and the maids engaged quantities of soap and water to contest the issue of onion-like layers of dirt that peeled off the evangelists, accumulating in a slick half an inch thick on the surface of four baleful zinc tubs, lined up in the kitchen like coffins.

Self-help was the shibboleth of our complacent age, the password distinguishing the deserving from the undeserving poor. It wasn't my wife's style, however. When I challenged the wisdom of two-cent dinners, credit arrangements for twelve year-old boot-blacks contemplating launching out as independent businessmen, and I asked her if she had her heart in such talk, Littlewood said no of course she hadn't, but the boys did, and that was what counted. Listen, she said. These children had been put out on the streets because their families couldn't afford them. Life was *business*, dollars and cents the only language her evangelists had been taught. Maybe I should bear that in mind when making the reading selection for our boys. Take a leaf out of their book. Ease back on the Danny Boone and bring modern business adventure to the fore, Swift's refrigerated cars for example, which were now coming through against all the odds, backing up while someone sawed off the eaves of the wider-body refrigerated cars to squeeze them through the tunnels. They were shipping meat fresh from the yards right into butchers' stores on the east coast and even across the Atlantic.

Naturally Littlewood's heart was in what she did. She cultivated matter-of-factness to save her from sentiment. The evangelists respected her and said Yes 'm, but they ran little gauntlets on the other side of respect when they bandied with her as she did with them, and in the play of words I could hear undertows of a strong mutual affection.

All of these boys suffered from instant loss of history. None of them could say for sure if they had been born in Chicago. Couldn't remember a journey here either. This was America's purpose, the reinvention of people. Straight House, as it was nicknamed in the neighbourhood, matched new identities to nameless boys whom the first forage through the streets of pig city had stripped of any belonging to any place but the Madison Street post office. Glue, soap, tallow, the reconstitution of pig — Chicago was about the so-called by-products of industrial waste, which until recently had gone down the drain. Within these twenty, thirty, forty square miles (the city grew so fast it was never quite there at any one moment) reality could be reinvented. This was where they made it new, where the world could always be made to happen again. City burned down – so build it new. Boy flattened on Armour's pier and got broken – so start again. More where that came from. Trash the old one. New pier, new boy. Disposable and interchangeable. Machine metaphors had taken over. Half a century on, the assembly lines and moveable parts that had been shipped out of Stanton's visionary New Orleans warehouse had broken and entered our language, our lives, our view of the world.

Boys remained boys, this was our view, the commonsense point of view. Even after Bohunk, Lugan & Co. were restyled by Littlewood as her evangelists and became Straight boys they played stickball, shinny and buck-buck, prowled the side-walks, stole bottles from back porches, foraged for junk in garbage heaps and stripped pipe from vacant buildings, which they sold for a few coppers to junkmen. On a bad night it might come to breaking street lights and throwing rocks at moving trains. This was required background. How else could they be expected to make good? This was it, the reinvention America required, not gave as an opportunity but demanded of its immigrant raw material, if not voluntarily then by force. Boys did not remain the boys they'd been. They grew up. Weighed on average twelve pounds more. Measured five foot one inches within a year of transferring from the post office coal cellar to Straight House — and overtook me on their way up. This was the difference made by regular two-cent square meals and doses of cod-liver oil. They attended school, learned rudiments of hygiene, acquired, by God, prospects of a better life. Their own mothers wouldn't have recognised them, as Littlewood tearfully remarked.

St. Luke was interested in electricity, St. Mark in clothes, St. Matthew in streetcars, St. John in nothing particular at all. I saw piling up behind the boys their discarded, might-have-been lives, the immense forfeit of what they would not be in order to be what they were. There were ready-to-go versions of small-town life in Lithuania, on farming plots in Galicia, God knows where. They continued to amaze me, these boys, along with the hundreds of thousands of other people in the city with ready-to-go alternative lives they had abandoned someplace else. Nothing on this scale had ever happened to the world before. In Straight House we counteracted the dull materialism that was inherent in all notions of improving one's situation by encouraging Straight boys to live in the imagination some of those discarded, might-have-been lives they had forfeited for the life they now had. Instead of reading from the lives of Danny Boone, Christopher Columbus or Philip Danforth Armour I would sometimes ask the boys to report from their might-have-been lives.

John was terrified by such an idea. He had trouble with boys he wasn't. Didn't take kindly to them. He was worried that while he was being them someone might slip in behind his back and take his place in Straight House. Of the four evangelists it was this boy who was the most attached to Littlewood. He liked to hang around in the kitchen, had a penchant for hiding in laundry baskets where he fell asleep. She overheard a conversation in a laundry basket between John and his alter ego, who turned out to be none other than old Bohunk. She heard him tell Bohunk to quit following him around. Bohunk told him to roll over and make room for him, and John broke into tears. She asked me to exempt him from further journeys through his might-have-been life. John might be a little dull, she said, but he had the best character of them all. She said he sometimes left sandwiches on the doorstep, little offerings to appease Bohunk, because he felt bad about having left him in the lurch. One day she showed John a letter with a Liverpool post mark. Greetings from Bohunk! the letter said. It said Bohunk had been taken on as ship's boy in Boston. He wasn't planning on coming back to Chicago for a while.

Our clot of collective dirt from the coal cellar, wearing one indistinguishable face of immigrant misery, emerged from the crucible of these early experiences as four individuals, each of them as clearly distinct as the Chicago that emerged from the Fire. The living climbed over the dead to reach the light. Debris of the city disappearing in the flames the night Littlewood and I arrived was dumped in the lake to push out the shoreline and make room for more buildings. Within six months real estate sold at advanced prices and the volume of trade was already greater than at the time of the Fire. Within a year there were the makings of a wholly new city. Within two it was being boosted for its marriage and divorce rates, for its house-raising, its rats, its pigs, its stink, the lavish celebrations the citizens held to mark the anniversary of their city's destruction. The new citizens of Chicago had emigrated from the past and gone to live in the future, people like the Straight House boys who had left behind them their previous lives in the Old World.

The Education of Sophie Stanton

Edgar P. Stanton had already been dreaming of wheat futures when he told us as a boy that he would find his fortune in an empty field. The empty fields were the Great Plains. My grandson purchased an enormous territory before the Civil War, in his days of feverish railway travel with Wai On. He sold land the settlers were moving into to plant wheat, and exchanged it for real estate north of Chicago after the Fire. On twelve acres of swamp along the lake shore he laid out a park. He had the frog-pond in the middle filled in and built over it a French chateau, a Marquette brownstone in late Renaissance style. A butler's pantry contained a sink with three faucets, hot and cold water and on occasion champagne. The world's then largest mirrors, as the *Tribune* claimed, were imported from Paris and installed in the chateau's lake-view rooms. They could be unfolded and pulled across the long windows at night, throwing back into the interior the extraordinary reflections of itself. The decor mixed all places and periods, Moorish with Romanesque, English-Gothic with ancient Greece. This was not so much Edgar P. Stanton's ignorance of good taste as his rebuttal of it. It was his intention to make what was familiar seem strange, an aesthetic harking back to his father's notion that nothing was ever original, reproduction being the essence of production, strings of endlessly repeated parts whose only novelty lay in the way they were arranged.

He married, or rather: he acquired a wife. Sophie was the only daughter of a leading family that had lived in Union Park before its decline. A governess for Lee was hired from the East coast. Tutors from Europe came and went. Edgar's mother was installed in a wing of the house designed to his instructions, with *trompe l'oeil* scenes from the Mississippi along fifty yards of lakefront, so that she would feel at home, but then Héloise changed her mind. She decided she didn't want to live with her son and came to live with me instead. Gorgeous social displays unfolded in Edgar's house. For some reason he had dropped his middle initial. He called himself Edgar Stanton now. After he arrived in Chicago he reinvented himself. He invented a life that was dedicated to perfect artificiality. Anything natural Edgar abhorred. He lived to make money, and he made it in the most artificial way the money market put at his disposal, which was trading in wheat futures at the Chicago Board of Trade.

Before the old building burned down in the Fire he had run his first corner and was reputed to have cleared two or three hundred thousand dollars. He was forty now and looked twenty-five. To spectators in the gallery of the pit, the figure in the old-fashioned long black coat buttoned up to the collar was an intriguing anachronism, a youthful relic of the ante-bellum South. To other traders on the floor of the Board of Trade he was a menace. There was nothing old-fashioned about his methods. Edgar Stanton was a scalper, buying one minute and selling the next, feeling the market with a passion tempered by restraint that was never other than judicious. He shimmied in and out of the market, changing his position from short to long and back again with every fluctuation. He dealt in small quantities, but they added up. Although rarely long or short more than ten thousand bushels at a time, he was accustomed to scalp two or three hundred thousand bushels a day.

In any one year three times as much wheat was sold in the futures pit at Chicago as was grown in the entire world. The actual grain might be handled six or eight times, and if each transaction was hedged by a purchase or sale, then the actual grain and its hedge accounted for the handling of thirty-two times as many bushels as there was actual grain out there in the real world. Edgar was the living embodiment of Chicago. He speculated in the future. He bought and sold and made his profits on a commodity that didn't exist. This was the nature of the money that fascinated him. He danced in and out of the market but never allowed it to embrace him. Edgar was a pimp and the market was his whore.

Perhaps a sense of invulnerability lingered on from that attic room where Stanton had instilled in his son the notion that decay could somehow be suspended, that the images of life passing now and now could be preserved on mercury and silver iodide plates as ineradicable daguerreotype memories. I was to blame for having rolled him up in the quipu when I played with him as a child, but how could I have known? Whatever residual dust from Tahuantin-suyu remained in the original quipu had added an aura of eternal youthfulness to the acuteness and phenomenal powers of retention Edgar already possessed. As an adult he continued to sleep with his eyes open, a seer dead to the world, absorbing by transparency whatever was around him, landmarks on the river bank he passed while he slept, rumours in the dark, a faraway noise of the world: whispers of money.

He told me that on the night be brought Sophie Stanton home to her marriage bed he initiated her in all the sexual practices he had learned from Creole women. Hunnish practices, she called them, shocked by the animal nature of her husband and humiliated by her complicity in such acts. She couldn't touch his heart, wouldn't believe he didn't have one and never gave up her search for it. On the social side of her husband she encountered a gentleman of the old South. He deferred to her with impeccable courtesy whenever they had company. But the prospect of guests about to arrive or the memory of them after they had gone, the sofas, where he took possession of her, still warm from the company that had just vacated them, infused her husband with a sexual excitement that made his lovemaking barely different from assault. Protesting that company was about to arrive, she knelt at his insistence on the scrolled ottoman, her legs apart, her gown hiked up to her hips. I didn't marry you for your looks, my dear, he told her on the first occasion he inserted into her orifices a slender Chinese vase he had bought that afternoon and would later pass around for the company to admire, I married you for your virtuousness. The French chateau in Marquette brownstone was a mockery, the envied life he led there with his gracious wife nothing but a charade, entertaining the assiduously rich whom he thought of as merely the better thieves and liars.

Sophie believed her husband was wicked. She came to Straight House and poured out her heart. Unable either to resist or to abandon herself to his wickedness, she was tormented by pangs of conscience as his accomplice. What could she do? Two hundred years earlier in Pernambuco, faced with the demands of the Donatory, she might have sought refuge, like Sofia Maria da Costa Pilar, in impregnable obesity, or in the sanctuary of the Misericordia, like Esperanca, pressing her lips impeccably into the sweet lap of Christ. A hundred years ago, in New Orleans, she might have been a casket girl, sent out by the grace of the French king to breed subjects in his colonies, or a slave who had even less say in the matter. But in Sophie's age, marriage had become a Noble Institution, man and woman raised up out of their animal natures by chaste ideals. An ideology was at stake.

She sought refuge in good works. Charity became an atonement for flawed ideals, for unpardonable acts of vice hidden away inside her marriage. She lived in a city of sin and, like many others, bore her share of it in secret. Had she but known what she later knew! Despite the confidence that was finding expression in a vast new city hall and a Board of Trade more like a cathedral than a derby-hatted jobber's place of work, there was a sense of contradiction in the air, the unmistakable smell of hypocrisy. It hadn't escaped the bishop either, who commented on the number of single working women in the city and wondered what so many of them were doing walking the streets when they finished work at night. Preaching men came from all over the country and preached against unruly women in this den of vice. Sophie told her husband what the preaching men were saying and wondered quite what the bishop had meant. Edgar laughed. Let the preaching men copulate instead of preaching, he said.

He took her in a cab to the nineteenth precinct, to a district between Harrison and Polk, walking her down Custom House Place and Fourth Street where the whorehouses stood wall to wall for a quarter mile. The whorehouses backed up onto saloons where the procurers touted custom, onto pawnbrokers' where men would trade their wedding rings to buy an hour or two with a girl. From a window at Carrie Watson's establishment on Clark Street she watched the privileged customers who passed in and out of premises where they could fornicate more conveniently on credit.

Sophie thought she had seen enough, but her husband told her there was more to come at another place on Dearborn. He had an arrangement there with the management, he said. It was a brothel with a salon in the florid style of the old South, velvet drapes, silks screens and potted palms, where all the women sitting around in more or less degrees of undress were black and all their clients were white. She followed Edgar into a narrow passage behind the rooms of these Negro whores. She stood there in silence, the tall blonde woman whom Edgar had married for her virtuousness, looking through a spy-hole at men of substance as they were called in her circles, some of whom she knew by sight, committing sodomy and felatio and taking a switch to the bare black butts upended like some obscene offering the better to provoke the whipping appetites of white clients.

If traditions were honourable and practices that had continued for hundreds of years could be counted traditions, Edgar told his scandalised wife, then what Sophie had seen in the Dearborn establishment might claim to be as honourable as anything conducted in private between men and women. What did honourable have to do with it in any case? These whores were not slaves as his great-grandmother had been and his grandmother Mijou would have been if the river hadn't jumped the night she was born, delivering her from an enslaved womb into freedom on the other side of the border. She had been about as free as these women at Carrie Watson's when she went to work in the brothel in New Orleans. There she had met his grandfather Paul Zarraté, as he then was, straight off a boat from the West Indies and married him in a hotel the selfsame night before the old rascal changed his mind.

None of this could look acceptable from a woman's point of view, thought Sophie, but there was no mistaking the drift in the crowds on Madison and State any evening you cared to go down there and look. The drift was made up of single working women from the country, walking out alone for the hell of it, to see the stores and the crowds and maybe to have themselves admired a little by single young men before they went home to the boarding-rooms where they lived, which was about as much entertainment as anyone got on five dollars a week. Sophie Stanton should stop and think about it, Edgar said, because in the history of the world there had probably never been anything like single women who were not prostitutes walking out in the city at night just for the hell of it. As for the bishop — and here Edgar completely lost his temper.

If the bishop wondered what they were doing there maybe he should direct his inquiries to the offices and the dry goods stores. Maybe Marshall Field would open his ledgers for the bishop to figure out the connection between a department store's profits and the less than a living wage paid to his female staff. There would be no escaping the conclusion that Marshall Field was indirectly being subsidised by female staff working part-time as whores, not for the hell of it but because they weren't being paid a living wage.

Meanwhile they might consider themselves lucky. The unlucky assembled on winter nights in the Pacific Garden Mission, the Grand Junction Temperance Association, the women's charities subscribed to by the robber merchant barons who had forced them there in the first place. A thousand drifters a night slept on the floor of City Hall alone. Every night you could look into the police station in the nineteenth precinct and bribe the guard with a few coppers to be shown hundreds of the most dissolute men and women penned up in underground cages. The homeless hid in the basements of saloons, slept coiled up in the breweries' outhouses or kennelled in empty cattle trucks on the railway sidings back of the Yards. Edgar said that the only difference between them and us was money. Sophie shuddered at the thought of it.

In the spring, when she became pregnant with her first child, her husband gave instructions to the maids that whenever they drew their mistress a bath they were to add essences he bought from a Chinese apothecary. On emerging from her bath she knelt down on all fours to be groomed by her husband, much as if she had been his mare. He applied a pumice stone to her body to disperse a camomile lotion and brushed her afterwards with soft brushes, supplied by the same apothecary, up and down and back and forth until it felt indeed to Sophie as if her coat shone. Then he rubbed a sweet smelling oil into her breasts and belly. What's this for, she asked. Edgar said it was to encourage her to enjoy the feeling of her own body. Luxury, he laughed, pure and unashamed.

It was while grooming his wife that Edgar became aroused as he hadn't been aroused for years. He came over to Union Park and told me he was feeling bullish about wheat. I can feel it in Sophie's body, he said as he was leaving, and then I heard a thump on the stairs. A moment later Littlewood came rushing up and said Edgar had suffered a fit. For two days he lay dead to the world, his eyes stark open, listening to faraway rumours, whispers of money in an empty field.

Circumspectly I was introduced to the Board of Trade. Paul Straight was my name. No connection between myself and Edgar Stanton was known. I was a mysterious stranger with an American or English name but an accent that was neither. I had never been seen in the pit before. I stood in the second-storey trading hall for the first time, looking up at the frescoed walls and the stained-glass windows high above, and had the feeling of being in a place of worship rather than of business. Gradually, a little at a time, then a lot at a time, I began to accumulate grain for September delivery with funds supplied by my grandson.

Throughout the spring there had been unusually heavy rainfalls in the wheat belt that year, with the result that planting had been delayed. Accordingly there was a possibility the crop would be damaged by frost before the harvest came in. Edgar was banking on that. It was not a gamble, he said. He had seen it positively in a vision of a devastated field. He told me to start buying at the depressed price of fifty cents a bushel. Over the next few months it rose to ninety-one and a quarter. Even at this price I was still amassing millions of bushels, in accordance with Edgar's instructions to buy as high as one dollar.

A dry, temperate summer followed the wet spring. Reports from some wheat states indicated that contrary to Edgar's forecast a bumper crop might be on its way. Prices plummeted to sixty-five at the end of a single disastrous trading day. When the gong signalled the close of business I saw my grandson laughing as he joined the brokers, traders and clerks who were putting on their hats and rushing out for corned beef and whiskey in neighbourhood dives as usual. I remained ruminating in the pit, surveying the emptied trading floor, littered with grain samples and thousands of crumpled yellow telegraph forms in which I already saw the wreckage of our doomed enterprise.

In August Edgar left town as usual for a vacation with his family. At the end of the month a cable reached me from Minneapolis with instructions to buy immediately to the limit of a two and a half million dollar short-term credit he had arranged with New York financiers. Two days later, news of an early frost in the Red River Valley reached Chicago. A large part of the spring wheat crop had been ruined. At the beginning of September crop failures reported from Europe combined with the poor harvest at home to create a wheat deficiency of some two hundred million bushels. By the middle of the month one lot of cash wheat had changed hands at the magical figure of a dollar a bushel. By now the brokers had got wind of the huge loan to Stanton and cottoned onto what we were doing. I disappeared from the pit as mysteriously as I had shown up in it. My job was done and my partner stepped in.

The bears kept hitting the market, selling in the belief that Stanton wouldn't hold up to the pressure. They waited for prices to break when he found himself forced to sell his corner of wheat. But Stanton hung on. On September the twenty-third wheat opened at a dollar five. By the close of trading it had risen to a dollar twenty-eight. From the gallery I witnessed tumultuous scenes in the pit. Small-time traders caught on the short side of the market begged Stanton to sell wheat. He offered them a dollar fifty, telling them it was a bargain price, because by the end of the month a bushel would cost them two dollars. They reviled him. They would have done better to accept his offer. It turned out as he had predicted. Wheat eventually went to two dollars five. Brokers and trading houses were wiped out. Edgar Stanton made four million dollars.

He was hailed. He was hated. There were calls for the Board of Trade to exercise control on its members, and a strong attack on grain futures erupted in Congress. Asked in a *Tribune* interview what he intended to do now that he had carried off his coup, Stanton said that he still had a little side bet to see through before considering that his ship had reached its home port in safety. Edgar was understood to be speaking metaphorically, but he wasn't. He was referring to the *Thelma Louise*, a cargo ship that had taken three thousand tons of wheat aboard and sailed from Adelaide for Liverpool. Edgar paid sixty-six shillings and seven pence a quarter for the cargo the day the ship sailed. When the *Thelma Louise* reached Ceylon a couple of weeks later British agents in Colombo offered sixty-eight shillings a quarter. Edgar refused. By the time the ship reached Cairo the price had gone up to sixty-nine shillings and twopence. As the *Thelma Louise* sailed along the North African coast and rounded Gibraltar, news of the advance of wheat to two dollars five in the Chicago market was cabled to London. Before the ship arrived in Liverpool her cargo had changed hands for seventy shillings and threepence a quarter. Edgar's profit on this transaction was negligible by comparison with what he had made out of his corner, but when the scoop was splashed over the Chicago papers it appealed powerfully to local pride. The saga of the *Thelma Louise* and her cargo proved to our citizens how the Chicago market dominated the world.

Even Sophie Stanton, with her inbred old-money disregard for the new fortunes being made by upstarts like her husband, could not remain unimpressed. She caught herself thinking of the respectable businessmen she had observed through the spy-hole at the Dearborn establishment, and she now understood that the source of their pleasure was the secrecy of their hidden lives. All the more enthralling to take a whip to a woman secretly when in public you paraded as a do-gooder, a God-fearing family man. Her own husband was one of these delinquents, a whipper after his fashion, thrashing the daylights out of the market and driving up the price of bread and being loaded with public adoration for his pains. Sophie squared her conscience in order to become her husband's accomplice. Their poverty is your luxury, Edgar said as he rubbed sweet essences into her skin, and now she thought she knew what he meant, the mutual dependence of those giving pain and those receiving it, and the great moral conspiracy concealing it, and the thrill of living on the edge, of showing one thing in public and doing another in private, the deep purr of pleasure when she yielded to the caress of hypocrisy. She laughed when they both said it at the same moment, the girl's name that had independently struck each of them as the name they wanted to give their child, for in that family, in that city, at that time, what more did one need to do to bring a daughter good luck than call her Thelma Louise Stanton?

Illuminations

Under the ministrations of John P. Barrett, a direct current was induced to arc across a small gap between two carbon rods, demonstrating a continuous spark of electricity. The effect was perceived by a large crowd of spectators including Luke, Matthew, Edgar and Lee Stanton and myself, as an unsteady but very brilliant light, which turned the darkness into day at the Water Tower on Chicago's North Side. Luke told us that just two of Mr Barrett's devices generated a more intense illumination than six hundred and fifty of the standard gas lamps installed in many factories and private homes. The purpose of Mr Barrett's stunt, the first public display of electricity in Chicago, I believe, was to promote the superiority of the arc lamp over traditional gas lighting.

In Union Park we had gas lamps installed soon after our arrival. Littlewood and I saw no need for a change. I also had little desire to invest in Mr Barrett's company, as Luke was urging me to do. The boy was full of a new professional jargon that got on our nerves. He was a live wire, our batteries were run down and we needed recharging and I don't know what else. Luke had just completed his apprenticeship with Mr Barrett when the company went bust. He went to work for Westinghouse. This was at a time when practically everything was a candidate for being electrified, including humans and leisurely streetcars that until now had been drawn very satisfactorily by horse power. Matthew was hired by one of these new electric streetcar companies. Mark learned the dry goods' business and was employed at Leiter's emporium. All the evangelists lived at home, and John stayed in the family business, working as a caretaker at Straight House.

With two to three dozen children there at any one time, a family business was what it was. Straight House had become a forwarding station for homeless children off the streets of Chicago who were adopted by families out west. Littlewood was the children's link between past and future, the unchanging heartbeat of Straight House. In our malocca in Union Park, she was the tsushaúa, dreaming us all into right lives, orphans into solid families, evangelists into sound careers, foretelling a heartening outcome for them all. Only for Lee Stanton was she unable to dream a right life. Rather than dream him a wrong one she chose not to dream him a life at all.

Undreamed, slant-footed, Lee Stanton limped between the North Side and the West Side. He seemed to change colour whenever he stepped into Straight House. I sometimes wondered about the nature of that direct current induced to arc across a small gap between two persons, how it elicited the spark and a sudden illumination in the darkness of Lee. Littlewood's trust in the boy gave him trust in himself, but the effect was limited to her immediate presence. There was a deficiency of selfhood in my great-grandson that turned him into a reflector of his surroundings. A rough diamond, Littlewood called him years ago on the ark. It was a long time since she had last said that of him.

When Lee was still just a boy a governess used to accompany him on the streetcar ride to Union Park, to protect him from mishap in the rougher parts of the neighbourhood. When he was growing into manhood it was his father's coachman who went along for the ride, just in case, as Edgar once wisecracked, the neighbourhood needed any protection from the rougher parts of Lee. There were pranks that Littlewood tolerated when Lee went out with our boys, but she drew the line at looting freight cars, throwing switches to derail streetcars and cutting Western Union cable. The slum neighbourhoods on the West Side, so different from the uptown area where Lee lived, exerted a fatal fascination on the boy. At fourteen he could go into the yards behind the tenements with a fistful of dollars and buy whatever depravity he wanted, some of it criminal, like the incident in Hell's Half Acre, a run-down area between South State Street and the river. I heard rumours rather than facts and I chose to dismiss them. Lee paid a gang of youths to rape a prostitute and cut her with hog-dressing knives while he stood looking on. He was held by a constable and remanded at the police station. Edgar sent his son to a boarding-school on the East Coast. We didn't see any more of him in Chicago for a long time.

Lee's banishment from town caused an irreparable break between Littlewood and Edgar Stanton which made it impossible for him to visit Straight House any more. It was a crime the father had visited on the son, Littlewood said. The son carried it out in the father's name and had to pay the price. Privately, Littlewood blamed herself for not having taken Lee into the family at Straight House. After Lee's departure she became closer to John than ever, as if to say: this one is mine and I shall never let him go. He was her right hand in the running of Straight House. Frailer, smaller now — four foot and a half, even among a crowd of children I tended to be passed over — I looked up to both of them.

I did not begrudge John a relationship with Littlewood that was more conjugal than filial. He was nearer to my wife than I was by several hundred years. The slow, good-natured boy who had left sandwiches for an imaginary Bohunk remained in the sandwich-leaving business as a man, the caretaker of innumerable children who arrived famished at Straight House and left it overfed. He sat down with the rest of the children who listened eagerly to the stories I had to tell about St. Malo and Chief Liar Island, about the man with the tin nose, mandingueiros who called snakes out of the jungle, time travellers to Tahuantin-suyu who fell out of rhythm with the rest of the world. Héloise sometimes sat in the audience too, snapping her fingers and interrupting whenever I departed from the versions of stories she had grown up with. For the children she must have been a very strange old lady, as ineradicable a memory as the fabulous flow of stories carrying them away to places which they would probably visit for the rest of their lives.

Bound into the community of Straight House by her book-keeping duties, as much an institution in Union Park as Littlewood was, Héloise came back into possession of mental faculties which for the most part had been mislaid since her husband died. She read two or three newspapers before anyone got up in the morning, and when she took out a lengthening list of figures to work out the progression of compound interest on the total wealth of the nation her eyebrows would still rise and her eyes widen, just as they had done during business negotiations with Garrault the Elder. Héloise declared that compound interest, if left undisturbed, would concentrate the wealth of the country in the hands of an ever smaller number of ever richer millionaires. It would be the ruin of America. This was an extraordinary conversion for someone to whom compound interest had been an undisputed article of faith throughout her life. Before the war, twenty percent of the families had owned fifty-four percent of the wealth, she said. Now it was more like fifteen percent of the families and sixty percent of the wealth. Her mannerisms, at least, remained unchanged. My daughter still did a little skip when she thought nobody was looking. Was still inclined to harangue invisible persons when she drifted back into her own world. But miraculously our world had reclaimed her. That is, the evangelists had. Addressing the child in Héloise, they succeeded in restoring a distempered, severely flaking old woman and refurbished her as a gleeful accomplice to their schemes. The most memorable of these were the Illuminations.

Since the evening when Mr Barrett set up his arc lamps at the Water Tower an electric landscape had begun to mushroom in patches across the city night. The three evangelists outlined to Héloise an idea for a mobile illumination service, bringing generators and lights to customers who wanted their premises illuminated at night. The capital needed for this venture was beyond their means. At her suggestion they formed a company called Illuminations & Co., in which Héloise and I, as the sole shareholders, provided the entire capital under terms that could be considered extremely satisfactory by the management. The task of drumming up custom was left to Héloise. She set about this task less as a petitioner than as a sergeant major making battle dispositions for her troops. The advantages of illumination were presented to business owners as so self-evident, their good fortune in having her arrange it for them so exceptional, that they agreed to everything Héloise said if only because they were afraid they would look ungracious if they didn't. In obstinate cases she was not beyond putting on her grandest Southern air, commandingly rapping store counters with her umbrella to get her sales pitch across to the shopkeeper.

At first the premises wanting to be lit up were confined to the central business district along State Street or to private houses on the South and West Sides hiring light displays for celebrations. The rapid spread of an electrified streetcar system changed the dimensions of the city. It pulled people into offices and department stores downtown and took businesses out to the city outskirts. The company Matthew worked for was among the first to figure out that once you had people in your depots at either end of the journey you had customers. You could make a lot more money out of passengers by entertaining them while they waited at the depot, and you only needed to take a street-car track, pull it and twist it and toss it out into the yard like a coil of scrap metal and run miniaturised cars up and down it and call it a roller coaster in order to give customers the thrill of their lives.

Matthew moved into the amusement park business while it was still being born. He learned about advertising. He learned about the importance of image. It occurred to Matthew that Illuminations & Co. should pitch a light at something so commonplace that people would wonder what they were lighting it for, drawing attention to the lighting rather than what it lit. We were sitting around the supper table one night, discussing how best to do this, when Littlewood asked in her diffident, trailing-off tone of voice that didn't make it sound like a question at all: why don't you boys illuminate the poor.

Through several weeks of hot summer nights Illuminations & Co. set up their generating machines, their cables and arc lights at locations between Maxwell and Jefferson Streets. Basement sweat-shops, illuminated through air-shafts surfacing at street level, were seen for the first time ever under hard electric light, and they sprang up out of their permanent twilight existence like scenes from some underworld city of the damned. The boys took their illumination into the halls, gang-ways and backyards of the tenements, into the queues for the water tap and lines for the can. Squatting with the tenement dwellers on porches and stairways, they illuminated roofs where life moved up with the rising heat, mothers with babies and lovers with each other, and people lying on parapets and window-sills for a breath of fresh air sometimes fell off and were killed when they turned over in their sleep.

At dawn they set up an illumination at an empty lot on Thirteenth Street, putting a spotlight on a ragged old man, reputed to be one of the wealthiest Jews in the ghetto. He rented push-carts for a quarter a day, three hundred of them, and he recognised every one of them. Push-cart and back-pack peddlers swarmed out in their hundreds from Canal Street, peddling junk and vegetables, notions and light dry goods, at corners and in streetcars, waiting outside cigar stores and barber shops where the swells held forth who liked to count for something in the neighbourhood and might give them a quarter on the way out. Illuminations & Co. put arc lights on girls jumping rope and playing jacks in the street, on the dingy tide of bums streaming through saloon entrances for the free dinner they got with a beer, on the poolrooms and dance halls and the toe-scuffing, garlic-reeking, dime-clutching crowd queuing to get into the Saturday night show at the Bijou.

Whatever objective Littlewood had in mind when she suggested illuminating the poor, the stunt attracted a lot of attention from the newspapers. Our boys had discovered night, one editorial said. They used light to take pictures of things that had never been seen before. They had given beauty to unprepossessing streets, lifted commonplace scenes from the banality of the streets, shown them as something which could be admired. Put light on anything and you transformed it. Electric light would prove to be a

panacea for urban dinginess and squalor. Soon there were calls for continuous flows of light in the business sections of town. Illuminations & Co.
were commissioned to install arc lamps along a quarter mile of store
frontage shared on both sides of the street by Leiter's emporium, banks,
offices, a variety of new-fangled fancy goods shops, all of which were
eager to advertise themselves in the best modern style to the nine percent
of the families who already owned sixty-seven percent of America's
wealth.

Light washed the pavement and flooded out at either end of the street
like a cataract pouring from a gorge. On winter nights, when the air
seemed to thicken with the cold, an effulgence hung over the White Way
like an explosion arrested in mid-burst. Spectators who came to admire
the spectacle walked up and down and saw nothing outside a cloud of
brightness. Newspapers styled it the White Way. Other White Ways soon
followed the first. They reminded me of strips of chemically sensitised
paper, placed in contact with the dark negative of the pavement and
exposing it to the light. These exposures showed up the imprints left on
the pavements of the city, images formed on the floor across which so
many people in so short a time had passed, worn in by their desperation,
shadows left on stone and rendered visible at last, the composite photograph of mankind.

Twelve of Diamonds

When Lee Stanton came of age his father bought him a railway. Lee went
West, in a Pullman car designed to his specification, to take over the management of the company and improve its fortunes. The rest was pretty
much legend. Lee's idea of managing a railway was to turn his Pullman
into a mobile gambling establishment, attach it to the regular cars on the
Topeka-Santa Fe run and give high-rollers a free ride. The idea caught on,
particularly among an ardent Chinese gambling community that seemed
to be made up largely of Lee's relatives. Bandits hit the train three times
on three successive runs. At the fourth attempt they were met by a crank-
operated multi-barrel machine gun mounted on a hydraulic turret that
appeared from the roof of a fortified companion car. Six bandits were

killed in five seconds. The massacre made headlines across the West. A dime novel celebrated the exploits of Lucky Chinee Lee. The hated sobriquet stuck. Years later it was still remembered in a popular ditty, cranked out on a pianola in a saloon in Sacramento. Lee was walking out of it when stabbed by a brother of one of the men he had killed and was left to bleed to death on the boardwalk with the tune of his legendary triumph in his ears.

A mysterious Indian woman with whom he had arrived in Sacramento nursed him back to health in the hotel across the street. No one knew who she was, when or how she had entered his life. She never spoke. He was never heard to address her. She accompanied Lee like his shadow on a small-town odyssey that ended south of the Mexican border a year after the stabbing. She was his accomplice when Lee kidnapped his assassin, rolled him up in a carpet and drove him back over the border. In a sinister throw-back to the cooking of his mother's bones in a restaurant overlooking the Mississippi, the Indian woman fetched the water and stoked the fire when Lee borrowed the kitchen of one of his mother's countrymen in Santa Fe, squeezed his assassin cross-legged into a cauldron and boiled him alive.

An account of this macabre cooking lesson, which in a nudging reference to the local town was described as an auto-da-fé, appeared in the *Santa Fe Inquirer* under the heading VENGEANCE IS MINE SAITH CHINEE LEE. It was dictated to the reporter by Lee in the courthouse where he turned himself in, but the would-be murderer's confession was disregarded, the case dismissed for lack of a corpse. During the days it took for the judge to reach this decision while Lee was held in the courthouse jail, the Indian woman settled on the pavement outside with her chattels, half a dozen woven bags containing among many other souvenirs the dead man's finger and knuckle bones. These details of his earlier life were confided by Lee to my great-granddaughter Thelma Louise and recorded in her memoirs half a century later.

Lee returned to the Pullman car with his reputation as the meanest man on wheels established beyond doubt. It caused gamblers to treat him with respect but did nothing to improve his game. His life as a mediocre poker player was prolonged well beyond its natural term by the assets of the Atchison, Topeka and Santa Fe Corporation, which, whether they were liquid or not, certainly showed a high rate of circulation in the form of IOUs, handed out by the president of the Corporation and passed back and forth among the gambling fraternity as if they were as good as printed money. Within a year of his return to the seat of management the Corporation's remaining assets had become liquid enough to be seen draining away through the floor, leaking paintings, carpets, chandeliers, the entire inventory of the Pullman car and the rolling stock on either side of it, until the proprietor was left riding on a threadbare magic carpet with nothing more to his name than the shirt on his back.

Insolvency didn't include the Indian woman and her woven bags, Lee's shadow with appendages Lee lacked, to all intents his possession, even if in reality it was the other way round. Among the other things the woven bags contained were the reserve assets, paper trash the Indian woman despised. She had it in one of her bags when they stood on the banks of the Chicago River one morning, looking across pools of tar and gravel shimmering on the roofs of the low-level houses in the foreground at a building that impossibly filled out the sky. From the beer-hall in the basement to the barber shop under the roof the Camelot Building stood eighteen stories high. Hundreds of windows on the lower three quarters of the building glittered with lettering in silver and gold, advertising business premises. Above, like birds hovering over window embrasures with fluttering wings, blue and white awnings signalled from the front doors of private residences parked in the sky. Ten elevators, which on first acquaintance reminded Lee unpleasantly of vertical coffins, facilitated the daily cliff-climbing for the Camelot's population of four thousand. This was made up of capitalists, bankers, lawyers, boosters, brokers in bonds, pork, oil and mortgages, a host of principles, agents, middlemen, clerks, cashiers, stenographers, errand boys and a hundred-strong force of engineers, janitors, scrub-women and elevator hands who stood at Lee's service from the moment he handed over to the superintendent the wads of hundred-dollar bills which the Indian woman fished wordlessly out of the depths of one of her woven bags. Lee bought the apartment under an assumed name. No one in Chicago would ever learn where he lived.

Lee slid back easily into city ways, but the Indian woman in the poncho and the hat with a drooping feather maintained a sense of desert space around her even in downtown Chicago. She needed to have impressed on her the necessity of making use of hygienic amenities only in the places set aside for this purpose and repeatedly had to be restrained from lighting fires on the apartment floor. She showed not the slightest surprise on her first encounter with elevators, telephones and electric lights, whereas brass door-knobs completely fascinated her. Otherwise, as Lee had fore- seen, living surrounded by the vast presence of the sky, even if on the eighteenth floor, was as natural to her as in the Nevada desert where she was born and had grown up with her now extinct tribe. The city out of which the skyscraper had grown, the pinnacle of its technology and ambi- tion, all this the woman passed over with a magnificent disregard. Out of the woven bags she produced sticks and coiled switches and leather thongs, made circles with them, one after another like ripples becoming broader as they fanned out, until she had constructed a mesh resembling a spider's web. She consecrated it with burning resin and week-long prayers and hung it up over the bed in which Lee slept. Once it was in place she had her peace. Her magic was strong and would protect him. This was what mattered in the Indian woman's life. The dream-catcher was the labyrinth in which her soul resided. While Lee slept on the bed, under the dream-catcher through which dreams passed into the sleeper and the dreamer's emanations passed back out, the shadow woman unrolled her blanket at night and lay down across the threshold of his bed- room door.

With meat-packing money from Cincinnati my great-grandson opened Lucky Chinee Lee's Original Western Saloon, a gambling club off State Street, half a mile from Custom House Place. The location was convenient enough to attract serious business money and to draw windfall customers from out of town, for whom gambling and whoring were twin vices that came together and preferably left together in one humdinging sinful night. The Cincinnati backers sent meat-packing minders to make sure that Lee stayed away from the tables. The proprietor was a celebrity and his place was at the bar entertaining his guests. Many of them who would never shoot anything other than craps came to the club to shake the hand of the man who had shot six bandits in five seconds, returning home to tell the tale as told them in Lucky Chinee Lee's Original Western Saloon by the man himself. He led a regular life, without guns or knives or gam- blings. His touchy digestion settled down. He ate well and filled out his expensive suits. In the streets he could pass for a solid businessman. Lee began to get bored and wondered if he was still a young man. Sometimes he brought girls home from the club, stepping in the dark over the prone figure stretched out across the threshold of his bedroom door. His dreams were placid. The Indian woman sifted them in the dream-catcher in the morning, picking through the dream droppings she found and sniffing them as if they were pellets of dung.

One night at the club, in the middle of telling the story of the train massacre for the five or maybe the six hundredth time, Lee walked out of the Original Western Saloon and never went back. He was wandering through the streets with nothing in mind when he was hailed by a tout, standing outside a theatre giving away tickets. Lee took one and sat down inside as the curtain went up. The auditorium was half empty. On stage, nymphs and sylphs with silver wings were flitting in and out of dark green panels representing a wood. In the pit below the stage juvenile musicians were sawing away at their instruments, providing some kind of an accompaniment for the dancers on stage. It was a children's ballet. Lee was susceptible to children's ballet, even if he had never seen one in his life. He was touched by the innocence of the protagonists and felt himself moved to corrupt it. There was a girl with swan feathers and a rather moping appearance who immediately caught his attention. She was a human in a swan's form, waiting to be redeemed by a prince who went gliding by in a boat. After many confusions and protracted delays, which had Lee impatiently kicking the seat in front of him, the swan's transformation into a human being was finally realised. Out of the feather costume stepped a pretty girl of twelve or thirteen. When she took her bow she blew kisses at a man and a woman in a private box to the side of the proscenium. Lee's eyes followed the air-borne kisses. He felt a little squeeze in his heart when he recognised his stepmother Sophie Stanton sitting in the box beside his father. The girl he admired was their daughter Thelma Louise.

When Lee called on Edgar his father had no idea that his son had been back in town for a couple of years. They lunched together in a restaurant near the Board of Trade. Expecting to meet an outlandish figure with a brace of pistols under his coat, Edgar was impressed by his son's judicious manner and the conservative cut of his suit. Lee spoke circumstantially about the losses incurred in his railway venture and was diplomatically vague about his current occupation. He did not mention the Camelot Building or the Indian woman who lived there with him. Not a word on the subject of the exploits of Lucky Chinee Lee. Boy's a reformed character, Edgar told Sophie as he was brushing her down that night. The prodigal son was invited to an illuminated evening in the gardens of Stanton House and stopped over for the weekend.

Thelma Louise grew up in Lee's absence convinced of her half-brother's wickedness. This was her mother's view, a view of her husband and her stepson in particular but broad enough to cover men generally, which was painstaking instilled in Thelma Louise. She variously and thrillingly heard him described him as a killer, a gunman, a gambler and a fugitive from justice. This last phrase had a kind of poignancy that stirred the girl's sympathy for Lee. In the dime novel which told the story of his life he was cast in the role of a hero on the run who still represented the traditional values of the West. Thelma Louise devoured this little book again and again until she knew it by heart. Without consciously thinking about his appearance she knew she would recognise Lee if she met him in the street. Thus the shocked fascination when she saw him for the first time.

Her brother was an Oriental. He was not in the least like anyone in her family. He had uncompromisingly slanted eyes, his mother Wai On's sensual red lips, which seemed all the fuller for his small, unobtrusive nose. She noticed his long finger-nails and wondered if he put rouge on his lips. There was something feminine about his appearance, a puffiness around the eyes, little commas of malicious discontent at the corners of his mouth. The fugitive from justice had perhaps done dreadful things, but all she could find in her heart was a desire to console him for the injuries that must have been done to him to provoke such deeds.

Instinct told Thelma Louise to say nothing to her parents when Lee began to show up at the stables in the park where she went riding every afternoon. She trotted round the paddock and Lee stood watching by the fence. She cantered out of the paddock to Elwell's Folly at the end of the park. Lee dwindled to a speck in the distance, gradually acquired a hat, coat and face as she came galloping back. She felt his eyes on her when she dismounted. He always seemed to be shifting back and forth like this from far away to very close to her. At first he used to ask her if she wanted an ice-cream or soda. Then he didn't ask any more. It became a routine.

She linked her arm through his and they just went. There was a streetcar depot on the way from the stables to her parents' house. When the roller-coaster went racing down and hit the dip at the bottom Thelma Louise shrieked and hung onto her brother, and her brother held Thelma Louise tightly in his arms, to prevent her from falling out.

Once a month Lee visited Stanton House. These were official visits. He took tea with her mother and made an effort to be cordial. He stretched out the little finger of the hand that held the teacup, imitating a former landlady, a cultured woman with whom he had once boarded on the East Coast. After dinner he retired to the smoking room with her father. Who was also his, as Thelma Louise reminded herself with a twinge of confusion. She watched him play a part. He hid himself and she covered up. She grew into the habit of collusion with her half-brother against her parents in her own home.

Surrounding Lee was something Thelma Louise had never met and didn't quite know how to describe. She thought of it as a bit like a halo that surrounded a saint, only a fugitive from justice couldn't have a halo and wouldn't want one in any case Her half-brother was conserved in the fluid of his fame, imperishable through all change even unto death, an image reflected ten thousand times over in the many-surfaced diamond which was the legend of Lucky Chinee Lee. Being together with the owner of that diamond, eating ice-creams with him, taking roller-coaster rides in an amusement park, nourished an ambition in Thelma Louise. She wanted a diamond like that for herself.

Lee was walking through the park from the streetcar depot after a rendezvous with his sister when three Chinese appeared out of the shrubbery and escorted him to a nearby hotel. Lee's financial backers from Cincinnati wanted to discuss business with him. They felt they had been let down. Lee had not fulfilled his side of the deal. This was dishonourable and had to be punished. While Lee struggled and the three meat-packers held down his arms a fourth appeared with a pair of butcher's shears and cut off both his thumbs. The backers said they would be back in a week's time. They expected him to have resumed his duties at Lucky Chinee Lee's Original Western Saloon. Failing that, they would turn their attention to his little girl friend in the park and when they had finished with her she would wish they hadn't left her alive.

Lee made his way to a saloon on Polk Street. He met there with an Irish syndicate that had influence in City Hall and a controlling interest in the vice trade of the nineteenth precinct. Leaders of the syndicate looked at Lee's bandaged hands without comment and surmised his intentions through wreaths of cigar smoke. Lee told them that a group from out of town were muscling in on their territory. If the local bosses let this happen the Cincinnati packers would be back for more. They had to take a stand now. Lee said the syndicate could take over the packers' fifty-percent share of Lucky Chinee Lee's Original Western Saloon if the syndicate helped eject the intruders. The syndicate said eighty percent. Whisky bottles passed back and forth. Lee said he didn't drink whisky. He didn't like liquor at all. The syndicate leaders commiserated. They asked him what had happened to his thumbs and Lee said they had been sliced off by a roller-coaster. The bosses nodded and offered seventy-five.

It was business as usual at the Original Western Saloon when the packers returned to Chicago a week later. There was a good crowd in the club. They were manhandled by some of the prettiest whores in town. Heavy betting went on all evening at the tables in the pit. Lee leaned against the bar wearing black gloves. The Chinese wouldn't touch the girls or take a drink. A couple of look-outs were posted at the entrance. They were suspicious. They watched the swirl of money and people. After a couple of hours they began to relax and told Lee they wanted to see the accounts. He showed them down a passageway into his office behind the club. Seconds later the door burst open and two men opened fire. Two of the Chinese were shot dead, the third wounded. A couple of guests who had been lolling drunkenly at the bar when the packers escorted Lee to his office stumbled out of the club seconds later. The moment they heard gunshots they stepped up smartly and quite soberly behind the two Cincinnati men posted at the street door and slit their throats.

Five bodies left the premises through the rear entrance that opened onto an alley. They travelled in a hearse to a railway siding back of the yards where the syndicate's butcher was waiting. Lee asked him to step down so that he could take his place. He took the cleaver from the man's hand and set to work without bothering to take off his coat. Hog-dressing was a skill he had learned from Mr Shannon during the years on the stranded ark. He was quick, precise, avoided unnecessary loss of blood. The butcher put the chains on the legs and swung the naked bodies aloft by their ankles. Lee slid meat-hooks along the rails and skewered them through five pairs of feet. With a few strokes he cleft the bodies from crotch to breastbone, ripped out the intestines, stapled tickets with the name of the consignee to each of five pairs of ears. The gutted cadavers swung there as soft and pale as deer, creaking in the cold blue light. Hog-dressing and tickets stapled to ears, a production-line design for the ambush, murder and disposal of the packers, put forward by Lee to the syndicate, had all been his idea. The syndicate was impressed. A refrigerated car containing five human carcasses in a consignment of chilled beef and pork arrived at the Cincinnati yards the following day.

A week after the closure of Lucky Chinee Lee's Original Western Saloon a new club opened on the same site under the name Twelve of Diamonds. Lee was prevented from attending the opening by pressing business obligations out of town. People wanted to know about the club's name. Old name was too long, the syndicate said. Gamblers liked diamonds, so give 'em more. Word got around that twelve was the sum of six one five, twelve scores which Lucky Chinee Lee had settled in his life.

Lee disappeared, for his father and Thelma Louise, for his associates at the former club, for the syndicate representatives who in his own best interests had seen him off on the train to St. Louis but never received confirmation he arrived there. He never did. Lee got off at the first stop after Chicago, took the next train back and holed up on the eighteenth floor of the Camelot Building. If he could have gone any higher he would. The city had erupted like a geyser, shot him up into a lonely sky with no place to go but down. The longer he stayed up there the more he dreaded the journey back. The Indian woman studied frozen dreams, dreams like broken ice where the dreamer had fallen through, disfigured dreams, lacerated dreams: dreams like hands without thumbs. She swept the broken pieces out of the dream-catcher and turned them over in the palm of her hand. Dry-eyed she watched him trying to button his shirt, weeping with rage, frustration, remembered pain. The man came and lay on her and she licked her spittle into the places on his hands where his thumbs once used to grow. Her magic could not protect him in a place where there was no longer night. The silent pursuit of dreams, the darkness in which dreams were tracked down and caught, had been obliterated by a brightness outside as bright as day. The man lost sleep. Sat all night long at the window looking down. The woman rummaged through the dream-catcher and found it empty in the mornings.

Day and night construction work continued along the lake shore. They were building a city within a city. Thousands of arc lamps lit up the construction site so that the builders could work throughout the night. It looked to Lee like a stage set. Imagining a gigantic children's ballet, he floated on wet dreams of Thelma Louise. He wondered how it happened that a man who did not feel on the inside the way he looked outside, who neither thought of himself as Chinese nor considered he had had much luck in life, came to be given a name like Lucky Chinee Lee. He watched white buildings rise out of the swamp on the lake shore. He imagined himself a swamp and how a swamp might feel about being pumped dry and turned into all the dry places it was not. Then they switched off the lights. Lee fell asleep and dreamed. When he looked down at the white city, sparkling like God's own creation in the morning sun, he felt something akin to pity for it, trapped in the image of its own perfection, doomed by the very hopes and longings the image epitomised, the millionfold expectations which the ideal aroused but the reality would never be able to fulfill.

Birthday Blues

Leaving aside those uncertainties as to the exact year and circumstances of my birth, the four hundredth anniversary of my arrival in the world coincided more or less with the arrival of the world in Chicago. The birthday party the city wanted to give the nation was conceived as a pageant of American history. As the commercial interests began to thicken the history got thinner, and the World's Columbian Exposition that eventually opened in the White City on the former marsh land of Jackson Park brazened out as a celebration of modern industry. *Tribune* reporters unearthed a young fellow who only sixty years ago had arrived as a settler at the desolate trading post where thirty souls eked out a living between a swamp and a sand-choked river. Beyond this horizon the curvature of the earth's surface dipped away and the rest of history with it. The present had become a teeming planet with not much space for the past, swept away by the Rushing Wind sickness of which Xiahuanaco had long since written.

A million people now lived in Chicago. Perhaps because there were so many of us we began to live by numbers. Fascinated by the rate at which we had multiplied and accumulated collateral mass, we counted the things around us. We counted the boys who came in and out of Straight House. They entered the ledgers kept by Héloise, columns of children in double-bookkeeping columns, the soap, shoes and sandwiches they consumed. We in Chicago measured and quantified everything. We might not be certain what all the things were for but we were damn sure how many of them we had. On the editorial page opposite the story about the settler who had once herded swine on the present site of the Board of Trade we were informed that in the decades since the Union Stock Yards began business a quarter of a billion hogs had been driven through the slaughter-house gates. The most obtuse observer, as the editorial went on to assert in the wake of this funeral of a statistic, could not fail to perceive that the path of humanity had been upward from the beginning of time; that every century had been better than the preceding one; that man had advanced more rapidly in the past fifty years than in the past fifty centuries, and was now standing, yes, on the Summit of Time.

That summit might as well have been the roof of the Camelot Building as anywhere else. The organising committee of the Exposition had its offices on the fourteenth floor and took visitors up for the best view of the miracle that had been created in Jackson Park. On the other side you could see the site of the trading post where thirty souls had once eked out a living between swamp and sand-choked river. A generation or two before the white settlers came, a Negro by the name of Du Saible had been a trader on the same site, but trade had been slow and the black man moved on. There was no mention of Du Saible in the *Tribune* and no black people had been invited to the opening of the Columbian Exposition. Du Saible's predecessors on the shore of the lake were Indians who had been dwelling there for thousands of years, and the *Tribune* did run a story about them under the banner *Return of Freaks*. A ragged group of Potawatomi whose ancestors had been expelled from the trading post of Chicago sixty years before were invited back to the smokestack and skyscraper city to take

269

part in the Indian exhibit on the Midway Plaisance. The pecking order of the travellers on the path of humanity leading upward to Chicago from the beginning of time was thereby clear, even if it wasn't the same as the order in which they had set out. Big Bill Broonzy might have said it then if he'd been around, but in that spring when the first visitors streamed through the gates of the celestial city Big Bill was still applying for permission to come into a white man's world, and we would have to wait a while longer for him to come to Chicago to sing us his birthday blues.

They say if you's white, you's all right.
If you's brown, stick aroun'.
But if you're black,
Mm, mm, brother, git back, git back, git back.

The Love Song of Mark Alderman Straight

Littlewood and I were naturally proud when the job of publicity assistant to the chief of construction at the World's Columbian Exposition went to the most polished and outwardly assured of our evangelists. Mark Alderman Straight was as good a name as you could find. It would go well with a celestial city, even if he had learned deportment in a department store.

Ten years at Leiter's emporium had given him a feeling for the right things in the right place. Apprenticed to haberdashery, he had dealt in thread, tape, ribbons, collars and hats, going on to drapery, curtains and covers of all kinds, the fabrics that covered women in particular. He acquired tact and an impeccable sense of style. He rose to become a senior manager at Leiter's, responsible for the store's advertising. Mark decided how the public should see Leiter's, as a place of beauty, harmony and order, an oasis in a world that was all the things the emporium was not. He introduced regular seasonal changing of the store window displays. It was our Mark who created the profession of the Chicago claqueur, better known as Leiter's Window Gazer. For three dollars a day men and women were hired to impersonate gentleman and ladies of wealth, strolling up and down outside the store and periodically standing transfixed before the new displays in the windows of Leiter's emporium. The changing of the window at Leiter's became a social event, like the opening of a new show.

Naturally he was attracted to Mr Burnham. Against Chicago's chaos and savagery Daniel H. Burnham set symmetry and civilisation, the neo-classical values of design, order and balance. As a metaphor of moral order the White City described an inner space of controlled, civilised experience, centred in Will, surveyed by Reason, organised by Memory and Foresight into temporal and spatial coherence. For Mark, the White City was more simply the greatest department store the world would ever be privileged to see.

In the fourteenth-floor office of the Camelot Building, overlooking the real thing, long before the real thing was there and long after it had gone, a scale model of the White City was built that took up most of the room. Littlewood and I toured the Exposition with the help of this model and the flow of information provided by Mr Burnham's personable young public-ity assistant. The model city should ideally be viewed in the surroundings of a model office with comparable aesthetic standards. Typewriters, machines, were specially ordered for this office with white instead of black keys. Typewriters, female operators delivered with the machines, were interviewed and chosen by Mark Straight in person. White faces matching white keys were a self-evident prerequisite. Light grey skirts, blouses in the lightest pastel shades, replaced the standard black skirts with white tops that were the uniform of the office woman. The haberdasher still in evidence inside the publicity consultant provided his typewriters with small straw hats, which contrived to look both rakish and demure. Women with ample busts were passed over in favour of slender figures. Mark desired an effect of the feminization of the traditional male office, but beginning with the superfluous intrusion of breasts he wished also to eliminate from it the slightest reproach of sexuality.

Filing-cabinets in the sky were the paradigm for the modern skyscraper office, one identical with the next, piled tier on tier. Mark set about reforming what had been a deeply conservative male province, a small, cigar-scented place of polished dark hardwood and brass furnishings, the clerks in shirtsleeves and visors as they hunched over their ledgers, the manager dressed in a frock coat and seated at a high roll-top desk, a gilded cuspidor within spitting distance. Merely the presence, the smiles, voices and scents of the straw-hatted typewriters in pastel blouses undermined this old-fashioned institution.

The underpaid, ill-equipped, ink-stained clerk was got rid of. His functions were shared out between file clerks and billing clerks, mail handlers, typewriters, smart stenographers and telephone operators, many of them women. The frock coat vanished with the obsolete cuspidor. Mark furnished the Exposition display rooms in shades of grey and off-white. He ordered glass-topped desks and glass-columned chairs apparently without legs, forerunners of the cantilever steel-tubed chair. Traditionally heavy office furnishings with their centre of gravity somewhere beneath the floor seemed, as a result, to move an appreciable distance in the direction of the ceiling. The furniture acquired a floating quality. It gave to the office, surrounded as it was by glass and light, an ambience of transparency and effortlessness.

Visitors to the Columbian Exposition office, receiving a favourable first impression of light, were well disposed to appreciate the *amenities* of the White City. Mark rose and balanced on his toes, fingertips pressed together, to give this word its due emphasis. There were many things that enabled the Exposition without being part of it that were no less important than the things on display. It was equipped with its own electricity, water and, indeed, sewage plants. Miss Lavinia Manning moved in at this point with swift and silent grace, armed with a long white cue, as if to deflect any suggestion of unpleasantness. She stood charmingly on a dais, directing the cue at the amenities named. They were indicated by differently coloured pipes exposed in cross-section that somewhat resembled the tendons and arteries in an anatomical guide to the human body.

Designed to handle crowds of up to half a million a day, perhaps the greatest single mass of humans in history, Chicago's public transportation was today the most advanced urban system in the world, with amenities capable of moving one hundred and fifty thousand people from their lodgings in the city to Jackson Park each morning and bringing them back at night. Walkways and miles of watercourse connected the various exhibition halls on site, so that visitors could board an electric launch or battery-run ferry to be conveyed to the next spot on their agenda. Miss Manning pointed her cue at these amenities as they were named. To avoid accidents, a railroad encircled the White City on elevated tracks, the first in America to use electricity for the operation of heavy high-speed trains. Guards patrolled the streets, ensuring they were not only safe but free of litter. A model sanitary system — thank you, Miss Manning — converted human waste into solids and burned it, the ashes being used as fertiliser or to cover roads on the outskirts of the city.

One hundred thousand small willows had been planted on the shores of the lagoons, which the landscape architect Olmstead had sculpted out of the swamps on Chicago's South Side. They bordered the main exhibition area, the Court of Honor, with its chief buildings all executed in a neo-classical style. Along the avenues leading off from the Court of Honor all the individual exhibition sites were located, the Fisheries Building, the Agricultural Building, the Electricity Building and the Machinery Building, where two gigantic Worthington pumps pumped twelve million gallons a day from the well sunk beneath the building, supplying the entire Exposition with water. The Manufactures Building was the largest roofed structure erected in the history of the world, three times larger than St. Peter's in Rome. It seated three hundred thousand people. The entire army of Russia could have been mobilised on the building's floor space.

But what did even these figures mean in comparison with the marvels displayed in the Electricity Building on the Court of Honor? Electric kitchens and calculating machines, incubators for hatching chickens, electric brushes for relieving headaches and electric chairs for executing criminals. The teleautograph, a machine for transmitting facsimile writing along wires. Or the Kinetoscope, a peep-show device for viewing motion pictures on celluloid film. The world's first nickelodeon would shortly open in Pittsburgh, Pennsylvania. Fairgoers could see demonstrations of long-distance calls over Bell telephone lines. As they walked about the building they were treated to live orchestra music, transmitted over wires from New York and broadcast through a giant telephone suspended from the roof. At night they saw the outlines of ghostly palaces etched in fire against the blackness of the night. Huge searchlights swept the basin and settled on the electric fountains, illuminating jets of coloured water, while hundreds of electric water craft strung with threads of lights glided like fireflies over the waters of the lagoon.

When Miss Lavinia Manning pointed her eager cue at model buildings, model sewage amenities and boats it sometimes seemed to Mark as if they were returning the compliment, reversing its direction and pointing Miss Manning's cue back at herself, saying "This is the chief of our amenities, our crowning accomplishment and glory". The dais on which Miss Manning stood placed her physically above everyone else in the room, so that the young lady whose job it was to attract attention to the objects Mark was talking about not unnaturally attracted attention to herself. A few wisps of hair which had escaped the severity of the back upward combing from the nape of her neck escaped Mark's rigorously impersonal view of Miss Manning too. These were the culprits that crept in to undermine his professional relationship with Miss Manning. When she leaned forward with outstretched cue to indicate the Court of Honor and said "The Court of Honor is the heart of the White City," he became aware of her figure and would never succeed in becoming unaware of it again. It would never again be extricable from associations with court and honour and heart.

When he sang the praises of Chicago's manufactures, parroting advertisements about Armour's corned beef cans that littered the banks of the Ganges and of the Amazon, the desert and Nile routes to Khartoum, he was surprised by the vividness of his descriptions and realised he owed them to Lavinia Manning. Images of corned beef cans disappearing under desert sands or drifting down tropical rivers astonished him with their poignancy. He sang to her of the twelve-million-gallons-a-day Worthington pumps, the illuminated Westinghouse electric tower, live music transmitted long-distance over Bell's wires as if these were his own accomplishments, personal offerings he was making to Miss Manning. He courted her and honoured her between the lines and Miss Manning responded obligingly with her deft cue but remained unaware of his song. Between the lines of her figure he identified a court of honour to which Mark Alderman Straight aspired, if only to stand there and wait, if only in an attendant function. But where Mr Burnham had surely envisaged an empty space, a neo-classical plaza circumscribed by severe professional lines, Mr Olmstead had improperly planted a luxuriant forest. Uneasily anticipating the obscenity he would find, he leaned forward to inspect it more closely, even directing his audience's attention very particularly to it with his cue. Too late he remembered with horror that the white city was Miss Manning's naked body, the fern-floored, dark-branched forest

274

which had sprung up uncontrollably in the thwart of honour was Miss Manning's mossy pudendum, and he awoke from this awful dream with a cry.

Sons & Brothers

Matthew told me he was often awake and heard his brother's cry in the night. He knew he must be having a nightmare, guessed the nature of the terror in his brother's dreams, for he still had such dreams himself. I could talk to Matthew about these things, but Mark kept to himself. The woman raised her head from his arm the first time she heard the cry from the next room. She shook her head and went back to sleep. When she heard the cry again on one of the following nights she sat up in bed. What is with your brother? What has he? He is back in the coal cellar and can't find his way out, Matthew said. He listened with pleasure to the woman's deep melodious voice, strange English, Lithuanian accent. He wondered if he had himself once spoken with an accent like that when he and Mark lived in the coal cellar.

He remembered such accents from a time before then, spoken in vague dark rooms by women who resembled his landlady, big women with big voices and far-off rumours of peasant smells beneath skin-deep layers of soap. Sometimes she produced soft booms of laugh, which seemed to come up to him from the bottom of a well. He wondered if the woman beside him in bed was someone he had once known, if the stranger who crept upstairs into his bed at night was in fact a friend, a relative from the old country, an aunt, perhaps, or an elder sister. He thought of the brother in the room next door who was the other way round, not a blood relative but only a brother by name. In the arms of the lover-sister-woman he fell asleep. Whoever she was, when he woke up in the mornings she had always gone back to her own room.

Continuity, or rather the lack of it: the discontinuity of existence was his theme. He had once woken up somewhere in the dark. That was the beginning. Every time he woke up he found himself somewhere else. Found himself: this was how he experienced life: as found. He inhabited exteriors: and interiors. Mind and body: pursued: different lives. I told him how similar my own experience of life had been, the many places where I had woken in the dark and not known where I was. It must have been the same for his brother Mark, too, only he never talked about it.

They rattled together on the elevated railway, heading downtown to Jackson Park to see the fair. The El skimmed the second-floor buildings on either side: skimmed, did not touch: but still exposing: all for the interval of the briefest glance. Mark talked and he listened. They stood in the car facing out, snatching bits of street life as they passed and Mark told him about his girl. They got off at the corner of Michigan and Madison where the girl was waiting with a parasol in a pastel shade of blue that perfectly matched her blouse. May I introduce Miss Lavinia Manning.

The girl twirled the parasol and they walked through pastel shades of summer evening that perfectly matched the girl's name. Matthew was still thinking about something he had seen on the way and the name didn't register until they were standing in front of the Panorama of the Chicago Fire. She didn't remember the fire, but they did. What was her name? One thing about that Chicago Fire, he said. I guess it does put a date on you. Lavinia twirled her parasol and tinkled a laugh. Even before she broke surface with those twirls and tinkles he surmised an outline of the young woman swimming up to him through a now deeper blue shade of evening — which must have been on account of reflections off the lake — and with no forewarning he arrived at the conclusion that if Miss Lavinia Manning liked a guy enough she might go home with him the night she first met him.

What was with his brother? What had he? He had the cellar. Miss Lavinia Manning he had not. That was with him, fear of the unknown, of the opposite sex, worse, of his own, pumping it feverishly in his hand and scaring the hell: out of himself: blindness, impotence, syphilis and deeper than that the unspeakable shame branded on him by a coarsely contrived mating arrangement he shared with animals. Until the woman came upstairs into his room that night, three months after the brothers went to board in her house, Matthew had glimpses of that terror himself. But for his brother Mark Alderman Straight, fastidiously cultivating surfaces to protect himself from what lurked underneath, he supposed that the terror must have been much worse. All he needs is a woman, he said to the woman, squeezing her breast and putting his hand between her legs in reply to her question.

They walked up Wabash Avenue to see the Battle of Gettysburg Panorama. The girl hadn't seen it. It was extraordinarily realistic, his brother said, and right opposite there was a Niagara Falls Panorama, which was even better. They should take it down the road to put out the Fire, Matthew said, and Lavinia Manning tinkled. He stood with his hands in his pockets, the straw hat with the black and white ribbon tilted over his forehead, smiling back at her. He had taken a liking to his brother's girl, and for this reason couldn't stay near her. He said he wasn't coming with them. No? What a pity. And she meant it. Why not? Matthew substituted another engagement. Arranged to meet Luke, he lied easily over his shoulder, turning, waving, losing them in the deepening blue.

In Jackson Park they built a city as fair as fair could be. A picture palace city. Classical Rome on the shore of Lake Michigan. So beautiful and so clean, cleaner than classical Rome and without the slaves. People came in their hundreds of thousands, and they believed it. Mark believed it, who knew better, that the White City was made of staff superimposed on lather, an unstable combination of fibres and plaster of Paris. In a year it would begin to warp. The year after, unless it was demolished, the Court of Honor would begin to sag and droop in the rain. Matthew looked down a fairy-light vista swarming with visitors to the black space of the ocean lake beyond. He was full of admiration, not at all for the grandeur of Burnham's neo-classical perspective but for the genius of the illusion. Welcome to fake city, folks! Come and meet the true America!

In the Hall of Dynamos

He stepped out of the main darkness into a side-room of the night, a huge hall under a high ceiling, mysteriously lit with a soft and fleecy effulgence like some self-illuminated cloud. As he saw the scene he imagined it. What he imagined was not the same as what he saw. Practically-minded men who took an interest in the exhibits in this hall visited when they could inspect the moving parts by daylight. The much smaller number of spiritual worshippers of the machines came to pay their respects at night. Artificial light inside the building created the atmosphere of a cathedral. This was when Luke liked to come, to listen to, or as he said: to be recharged by the organ music after he had finished work. Motes of dust floated in the shafts of light falling slantwise from lamps mounted on the girders. There was a sense of quivering in the air. Echoes sprang up from his heels as Matthew struck out across the enormous floor, quickly muffled in the obscurity encircling a dome of light.

The dome enshrined a gallery of machines where twelve great wheels were turning. Stairs leading up to a platform gave access to the gallery. Luke leaned against the rail up there, arms folded, statuesque in the frieze of shadow and light. Matthew saw him the moment he came into the hall. What had been a lie to Miss Manning turned into a truth. At this moment the two brother-friends, the one standing, the other walking towards him, seemed to be the only visitors in this part of the hall. His heels sparked sounds from the floor. Echoes trailed through the air like shooting stars and were snuffed out in the surrounding darkness. Luke raised an arm in greeting as Matthew ascended to the gallery, his feet sounding muffled gongs on his way up the iron staircase. When he reached the top he stopped. The quivering in the air became audible as a faint humming, the whirr of the great wheels, dynamos forty feet in diameter, revolving at vertiginous speed. He could feel the tremor as the gallery vibrated under his feet. Luke stood only inches away from one of the huge dynamos, eyes closed, head cocked, as if he were listening to the pitch of a tuning fork.

For a long time they stood there in silence. Luke listened to what Matthew watched. Luke had said that when he stood here long enough he began to feel the forty-foot dynamos as a moral force, much as he imagined the early Christians might have felt in the presence of the Cross. Matthew didn't feel this. To him the dynamo was an ingenious means, no more, of converting the heat stored in pieces of coal in the bunker of an engine-house into an electric current that passed through a wire. Luke had explained to him many times how the miracle of electromagnetic induction was done but Matthew had never understood. Luke showed him pieces of iron that pulled toward or away from each other. When he described to Matthew how there were positive-negative forces in the magnetic field generated by permanent magnates in nature, it reminded Matthew of the Lithuanian woman who was pulled upstairs into his bed at night. He could understand the forces in the magnetic field because they were no different from the forces generated by human beings in nature. But here was the great divide between himself and his brother Luke.

Between the spinning coils of wire in the hall of dynamos and the engine-house with the coal bunker outside there was a connection Luke grasped and could guarantee which for Matthew required a blind act of faith. Had he gone back in time and taken this knowledge with him it would have served at best as the basis of some hugger-mugger cult in dark places, consecrated by the blood of slaughtered animals. Here was the great divide where time stopped. Rooted in the old country where the workings of the world were still explained in terms of magic, he remained behind with superstitious women and children on the shore from which his brother had departed for the future. The tribe of Matthew and the tribe of Luke would hereafter live in different worlds.

Out of respect for Luke's feelings he stood with him in silence, watching the great wheels spinning for a while before he brought the matter up. Matthew said he didn't know when he'd see Luke again. Just guessed he might be here in the hall of dynamos: knowing he had a hankering for these machines: just happened by: on the off chance. Difficult to catch Luke these days, proprietor-manager of Illuminations & Co. Barely able to keep up with all the work that the Exposition had brought him. He had come to say goodbye, Matthew said. He watched the words being pulled like teeth out of his mouth, sucked into the magnetic field of the dynamo beside which they were standing. Luke asked him where he was going. New York he said, lying when Luke asked if he'd got a job there. And when was he leaving? Any day now. One of these fine mornings I'll just, you know, get up and go, Matthew said. Luke thumped him on the back and wished him good luck.

They stood in silence again for a while, tuning in to the humming of the big wheel spinning beside them. I want you to say the prayer, Matthew said, and Luke frowned: prayer? Time you were apprenticed to Mr Barrett, you used to stand in the kitchen and recite to us the principle of electromagnetic induction, and to us it sounded like a prayer. When placed in a magnetic field a wire carrying an electric current experiences a mechanical force. Remember? That's how it began, and that's how we felt, like we were the wire experiencing a mechanical force, we didn't the hell understand why. I want you to say that for me one more time. I want you to put your hands on my head when you say it and make it kind of a blessing, so that I'll never forget it, Matthew said.

At intervals the humming from the twelve revolving dynamos came up louder again like a light colour looming out of a darker one. Luke placed his hands ceremoniously on his brother's head and said: dear Matthew, never forget that magnetic forces provide the fundamental motive power in electromagnetic machinery. How is this? When a coil of wire is situated in a magnetic field that is increasing or decreasing, an electrical voltage proportional to the rate of change of the field is created in the coil. Have you got that? He removed his hands and declared solemnly: this is the phenomenon of electromagnetic induction that forms the basis of the dynamo, and explains how powerful forces can be generated by comparatively small machines. Now go forth and multiply in peace.

It's a beautiful principle, I'll never forget it, Matthew said, and shook his brother's hand.

Jim Joyner's Yawn

The blazing mile of the Midway Plaisance leading down to Washington Park ran together into a single band of light, side-shows, roller-coaster rides, dancing girls, jugglers, medicine men, acrobats and sword-swallowers spouting fire, three thousand costumed inhabitants from fifty nations exhibiting at the fair, a Street in Cairo, a Cafe in Vienna, an Island Village in the South Seas. Matthew hurried on past all of this. He reached a small enclosure with the words EDISON'S KINETOSCOPE printed along the sides and a banner OUT OF ORDER hanging across the entrance. A small man wearing a soiled Derby sat outside smoking a cigar. Matthew asked to see Mr Dickson and the man jerked a thumb down a passageway leading to the back of the enclosure.

Mr Dickson had his head in a cupboard full of spools, levers and wires. His voice came out muffled, irritated. No more Edison's kinetoscope than it was Dickson's, the Englishman said. Dickson invented it. Edison patented it. So whose kinetoscope was it? He withdrew his head from the cupboard and shut it. A whirring noise came from inside. Let's have a look, said Dickson.

280

He pulled up a chair, squinted though a peephole on one side and signalled Matthew to sit down and look into the other kinetoscope. Matthew
told Mr Dickson that in his opinion the machine Dickson had invented
and Edison had patented was the greatest thing to be seen at the
Exposition. Greater than Mr Ferris' wheel, the Englishman asked mockingly, his eye glued to the peephole. Matthew thought that the sheer size
of Mr Ferris' wheel made it the most spectacular exhibit on the Midway,
but it had no complexity, no soul, no future, only its unchanging iron self.
In a hundred years it would be just the same as it was now. Forces much
more powerful than those which motivated the Ferris wheel could be generated by the much smaller kinetoscope. The picture machine invented by
Mr Dickson, transporting so many notions other than itself, had infinite
possibilities.

Dickson merely glanced ironically across and asked him if he had seen
the belly-dancer performing just down the way at the Persian Palace of
Eros. Matthew said he had. Now there was a case if ever there was one
said the Englishman, pausing as he pulled out a handkerchief. He began
to laugh in breathy flakes, as if grating cheese with his mouth, before he
continued: case of a pretty small engine: generating a pretty powerful
force, doing some transporting in the pro-, pro-, pro-, process too, and his
laughter disintegrated in a cavernous yawn simultaneous with the yawn
they were watching in the kinetoscope.

Matthew yawned too and looked across in astonishment. He asked Mr
Dickson if he had noticed a similar reaction among visitors to his kinetoscope. Sure, when they saw the policeman chase the Chinaman in the
laundry they probably laughed, and when the girl died some of them
maybe cried. Matthew could understand that. But yawning? Catchy as
hell, but come on, did anyone yawn to please a machine? Had Mr Dickson
observed yawning among viewers in response to the man yawning on the
moving strip of celluloid?

Not an uncommon reaction at all, the Englishman said. He must have
watched Jim Joyner yawn hundreds of times and reckoned he'd become
immune to him, but he hadn't. Still very yawn-prone himself. Catchy
thing, yawning. Jim Joyner yawning into the camera had customers yawning one after another all down the line. And Jim's yawn hadn't even been
real. Just seeing the next fellow yawn was enough to start customers off

while waiting their turn at the peephole to see the yawn that wasn't even real. Dickson rose and said prophetically as he switched off the kineto-scope that in his mind he heard the hinges of Jim Joyner's yawn creaking all the way down through generations to come.

Moving Picture

At Washington Park he took his leave of Mr Dickson. They agreed to meet at noon the following day on the roof of the Manufactures Building. From that vantage point they commanded a complete view of Chicago's downtown skyline. Mr Dickson invited Matthew to assist him. He proposed to install his kinetograph on the roof and take a series of panorama sweeps, an additional item to splice onto the growing loop which contained the Chinaman chased by the policeman round a laun-dry, the death of the poor girl and Jim Joyner's yawn. Matthew was elated. He stood looking back down the Midway, jostled by the home-bound crowds of fairgoers flowing off the Plaisance into the city. Kilauea, the Hawaiian volcano, erupted for the last time that evening and sputtered out. The Ferris Wheel came to rest. In accordance with the safety guidelines of the Exposition fire department, the sun had already set on the Panorama of the Alps at half past nine. The afterglow that bathed the mountain peaks in a last lingering light had been punc-tually switched off at ten. Two hundred thousand people, turned out of paradise, swarmed into the restless city night.

A breeze came up off the lake, ruffling the flags, rocking the festive paper lanterns strung up over the streets. The breeze brought with it an unexpected scent of resin, memories of a deep green shadow on a distant forest shore. On the border between park and city the crowd massed and seemed to tread water, reluctant to go on. The aftermath of high spirits surrounded him, jostlings, shouts, smells, in the midst of the crowd's stirring he shared its pleasures, as reluctant as he was to let them go and leave this day behind. A sense of oneness with the crowd flowed through him. He looked around at people he was part of and who must be part of him. Limbs of the same leviathan. Crowd incorporated, fusing wherever shoulders rubbed, hands touched, words stitched up intervening space, ravelling loose filaments into the skein. Here all came together. Here was the city in the flesh, markets cheek by jowl, tenements pressing, saloons out walking, rows on rows of boarding-houses, stores and factories personified, bound up into a single tissue by the arterial flow of traffic, blood, guts, sewers, energy in sinews, strands like wires, the common appetites and desires of a subliminal urban state of mind. On the border between the park behind them and the city in front the crowd hung for a moment like a mass of water. Then plunged, streamed out on separate ways into the night. Crowd was gone.

Matthew boarded a car going north up Halsted for a few blocks, alighted at the intersection and changed to the El. The El skimmed the second-floor buildings on either side: skimmed, did not touch: but still exposing: all for the interval of the briefest glance.

He rode up a mile through the sweaters' district and looked through a moving window into illuminated interiors. They were so close he felt he could reach out and touch. Every lighted window in the big tenements was like an opening in the solid brick wall that continued on either side. It gave him a glimpse of the life that went on behind the wall. He looked into one shop after another as the train sped past, took in entire scenes at a glance, families bending over machines in cramped rooms, half-naked men and women ironing clothes at open windows to get away from the heat inside. He observed individual faces, hands and arms blackened to the elbow with the dyes of the cloth they were working up, floors littered with half-sewn garments, votive pictures hanging on a wall in the background. Sometimes, when the train stopped, he could hear the whirr of the machines coming out of these rooms. Smells of fish frying, onion and cabbage drifted out of air shafts leading down into windowless landings where people were cooking in the middle of the night. The elevated railroad track was like a gangway threading through a city that was nothing but a workroom for people who did nothing but labour. Window after window repeated these scenes, and his eyes began to glaze, the windows slurring into frames of flashing light interrupted by bars of dark.

Suddenly he saw the similarity with the celluloid strip passed between a lens and an electric light bulb in Mr Dickson's kinetoscope. But here the strip was stationary and the lens moved. The camera moved, his eye tracking with the train. Put a kinetograph on the El and ride up through the sweaters' district just as he had done. Film through the windows and record their interiors on celluloid. Images of the city were what millions of voyeurs riding on the El each week glimpsed through second-floor windows skimmed but never touched. Banalities of everyday life that became poignant in an intimacy surrendered to public scrutiny. It happened all the time. But use a kinetograph to register that process on a celluloid strip and hold it up to the light. The kinetograph as an object lesson in the human machine and how its perceptions worked. Different families and different scenes in adjacent windows separated by a bar of darkness. One might tell more real stories by dispensing with the continuity that was always being interrupted in life. Mr Dickson and Mr Edison favoured the notion that forty-eight frames a second reproduced the natural speed of life, but in Matthew's view this was quite arbitrary. Matthew stuck his head out of the window. The El had stopped at an intersection and the brake man was climbing down from the car to clear an obstruction from the track.

A defective light bulb flashed on and off in a hotel sign attached to the wall of the corner building. There was a saloon on the first floor. On the second floor was a hotel bedroom. In the room a man and a woman were engaged in what crime reporters of the *Tribune* would have described as an obscene act. They were so close he felt he could reach out and touch. They appeared and disappeared in the intervals of light and dark as the hotel sign above the window flickered on and off. Matthew imagined a situation where they would be invisible in the room when the light was on but visible when it was off. The woman was kneeling on the floor with her back to the window, a girl rather than a woman, perhaps a boy, judging by the straight figure lacking feminine contours. The man whose penis she had in her mouth stood facing the window. His face switched on and off with the light. Matthew watched the obscene act with impunity through his imaginary kinetograph. He felt the pleasure of an illicit thrill experienced without risk. The man was looking at him, staring right up into the lens, but the viewer felt protected behind the apparatus. Matthew knew him. He hadn't seen him in a long while but he recognised his face.

It seemed that Lee Stanton recognised Matthew too. As the El moved forward across the intersection his face turned with it, following the observer in the car. A bridge girder came between. Then Lee was gone.

Matthew didn't even wonder that he was back in Chicago or what he was doing accompanying a whore to a trashy hotel in the sweaters' trashy area of town. He was already thinking back to details of the scene his eye must have caught but his memory had dropped. Was the girl a brunette or a blonde? Had he witnessed an obscene act or had he imputed it, filling in the missing details? Wasn't this how the mind worked? Suppose not only that something moved inside the frame, but that the frame itself moved. There was no discontinuity between frames that the mind would be unable to follow, no gap it could not bridge. A moving image imputed an obscene act in a stationary room. Stop the train. Take the kinetograph back into the room and film it as a self-sufficient place defined by the man and woman occupying it. Reduce to a man and woman with room blurred in the background. Reduce down all the way to the man's penis in the girl's mouth. Splice these images together and to hell with the disrupted flow of an orderly sequence in time and place. Here was a new expression of reality.

With a rising sense of excitement Matthew got off the train. A film of his life. Disjointed series of frames showing the dark places in which he had found himself when someone switched on the light. He wondered if he had spoken with an accent like the Lithuanian woman's when he lived in the post office coal cellar. He remembered it from before then, spoken in obscure rooms by women who resembled his landlady, big women with big voices and far-off rumours of peasant smells beneath skin-deep layers of soap. (The images appeared like magic. Rub the word and the image would appear. A magnet pulled his landlady into his bed upstairs. Shot of the woman awake in the room with her children. Shot of the man in the solitary dark place of his bed. Shot of the stairs. Naturally the viewer would locate the stairs between the man and the woman).

Attribution was everything. It was the motive power behind the revolving wheels and whirring spools that transported the strip of film physically. The motion picture perfected the illusion that one image had anything to do with the next. It was the reassurance that between frames one didn't fall into nothingness but continued within the same film. That one woke up the next morning inside the same life. The motion picture connected one dark place with another, a woman with a man, an obscene act in this room with a sensation in the room next door, a sensation with a shout heard in the middle of the night, his brother's cry, no longer of terror but of relief when the Lithuanian woman, taking pity on him, became waking flesh in his bed and drew him into her arms, shutting the ghosts out of his dreams.

Falling Bodies

Before Matthew left Chicago for New York he came and told me his ideas about motion pictures. He spoke of the reassurance they gave him that between frames one didn't fall into nothingness but continued within the same film. This was something he didn't see in life. A couple of days before he left, two bodies fell from the sky. They fell into Mr Dickson's slow panoramic sweep across the Chicago skyline from the roof of the Manufactures Building. What the hell was that, Mr Dickson asked, when he saw something streak across the viewfinder of the kinetograph. Fixed on celluloid, the bodies were only visible as a blur which one might have taken for a technical fault in the film if one hadn't known better.

Independent observers confirmed an object falling from a window near the top of the Camelot Building. One or two objects? Newspaper accounts cited eye-witnesses who found a smashed body on the pavement beneath. Disentangled by the pathologist, one body was separated into two. Such was the force of the impact on landing that an arm of the woman was thrust up to the elbow into the stomach of the man with whom she fell. Her fingernails were embedded in his intestines. Clutching his heart, the newspapers would make of this. In the light of facts which only became known after the event, eye-witnesses who had seen one body falling from the window remembered two. The smash hit people queued to see at Edison's kinetoscope show was entitled Falling Bodies, although they were visible as no more than a single blur on the film. Attribution was indeed everything, as Matthew said.

When Lee Stanton and the Indian woman were falling out of the sky Thelma Louise Stanton was waiting at the railroad terminal, according to her own account, which I would read in her autobiography half a century later, with eight hundred dollars in cash she had stolen from her mother's strongbox. Lee had told her not to worry. They would go away together, everything would be all right. When night came and Lee still hadn't shown up, Thelma Louise checked in at the station hotel under an assumed name.

A janitor of the Camelot Building opened an apartment on the fourteenth floor and admitted the police. They found a smashed window through which the couple had evidently fallen. They also found a network of hoops, concentric rings tied together with leather thongs, forming a mysterious canopy over the bed. The structure was apparently of Indian origin. No one knew what it was for, but it suggested a link between the apartment and the unidentified persons who had fallen. The woman was Indian, the man an Oriental. From the wreckage of their bodies that much was clear.

How had the man and the woman fallen through the window? The coroner's court brought in a verdict of accidental death. The *Tribune* favoured the theory of a double suicide, the *Post* suspected foul play. Thelma Louise, reading the newspapers in the station hotel after Lee Stanton's death, suspected the *Post* had got it right.

She knew that the mysterious canopy over the bed was a dream-catcher. She knew that the Indian woman who watched over Lee's life rummaged through it in the mornings and extracted from it the gist of his dreams. I have to be careful, Lee said to Thelma Louise in the hotel in the sweaters' district where he hid her the night before they had planned to elope, because the woman can find out what is in my mind. Her brother had told her about these things only the night before he died. Why did he have to go back to spend the last night in the apartment? She found no answer to her own question. I must put all this behind me, Thelma Louise told herself in the mirror where she admired a new expression on her face, a pale, drawn look that made her look older than she was. Tomorrow she would leave Chicago and begin a new life with that new look, a waiflike look appealing to strong men's protective instincts.

The Negro car attendant had already stowed the folding stair when Matthew ran onto the platform. As he jumped up onto the moving train the attendant gave him a hand. Matthew took a seat in the car opposite Thelma Louise. He asked her where she was headed. New York, she said. Matthew said he was headed there, too. That was the last thing either of them said for the next two hundred miles. For the next two hundred miles neither paid much attention to the other, both of them being preoccupied with the past lives they were putting behind them before beginning the new one.

For Thelma Louise it had already begun, a lurid life of adventure, crime, celebrity and passion. Lee Stanton, or so she would later maintain, had been murdered by a jealous Indian woman, and Thelma Louise already carried inside her the fruits of the moral crime she had committed with her brother. That was not acknowledged until the career it might have jeopardised was already behind her. Already at the age of sixteen she felt herself conserved in the fluid of her later fame. She thought of it as a bit like a halo that surrounded a saint, only a fugitive from a moral crime couldn't have a halo and wouldn't want one in any case. Like Lucky Chinee Lee, Thelma Louise wished nothing more fervently than to be conserved in the fluid of her fame.

Whatever she became she would always remain someone else, imperishable through all change even unto death, an image reflected ten thousand times over in the many-surfaced diamond which was the legend of Thelma Louise Stanton. The legend surrounding her brother was what had attracted her to him and now she began to create one for herself. She could feel the aura like a cascade of gold spreading around her in the car where she sat, a pale young moral delinquent with a drawn look on her face and eight hundred dollars she had stolen from her mother in her purse. Some of the cascade splashed onto Matthew's lap, gold-flecked spume visible in the afternoon sunlight that streamed through the car window. Why was a girl so pretty and so young travelling alone to New York? What connected the girl arriving in New York with the girl who had departed from Chicago? What hidden continuity lay behind the images of Lee Stanton committing an obscene act in a hotel room one day and falling from a skyscraper the next? Thelma Louise could have told him, only it wouldn't have interested her. She knew the things that mattered about her brother and this wasn't one of them.

What mattered in the end was his death. The Once and Once Only Effect of what her grandfather had called primary reality was being lost to another reality that came into being with the Over and Over Again Effect of reproduction. Less and less would be reproduced more and more. Lee and a blur of an Indian woman would literally go down in history as the first people to die falling from a skyscraper. Their death was the first to be recorded on celluloid in forty-eight frames a second. It would be re-enacted on copies shown all over the world. Over and over they would fall, rewind, fall upwards, reverse the laws of gravity, the flow of time, remain suspended in free fall for all eternity.

Mammoth Sensations

Was it real or was it humbug? This was the question. Pawfrey maintained that people enjoyed having the wool pulled over their eyes. Tickle the public's belly. Reach in where you shouldn't and tickle their fancy. Amid all that serious practical business of life there was a craving for humbug. Folks had such an appetite on them they couldn't get enough hogwash to put in their belly.

The shyster had a snitch on him, his detractors said, you could tell him apart in a crowd a mile off. The humbug in the man was advertised by the improbable nose on his face. If a rumour stirred within a hundred miles that bulbous apparatus was the first thing to break the air in its direction. Nose travelled independently, if need be, as advance man for the show. A knob of a nose as irrepressible as a cork in water. A nose in the round with a notorious three hundred and sixty degree faculty for smelling a rat. It may have taken a few knocks from people he had hoaxed. Quite some drinking had surely gone into it, too. But Pawfrey's nose was an independent creation entirely thanks to its own exertions. Wherever he went and whatever he saw he would appeal to his nose: is there money in this? Will the public like it?

When Daniel H. Burnham asked him to tender proposals for an avenue of entertainment at the World Exposition Pawfrey suggested a Tower of Babel. It was to be forty stories high, built using the new metal-frame structure that had been pioneered in Chicago, with a different language spoken on each floor representing the nationalities of the immigrants who had recently settled in the city. But Burnham already had his neo-classical city on the drawing-board and rejected the anarchy of such a tower. Instead he offered P. J. Pawfrey & Sons space on the Midway Plaisance for a pantechnicon to display the marvels of the age.

Pawfrey delighted in the sales pitch of showmen demonstrating ingenious electric toys. He inspected the phonograph and the kinetograph and listened to the live transmission of an orchestra thousands of miles away in New York. All these achievements were extraordinary, but he reckoned they were only the beginning. Men would travel, as Chief Liar had long ago dreamed in the swamps of New Orleans, to the end of the rainbow and the bottom of the sea. They would invent machines to fly through the air and allow them to visit the planets. He didn't doubt it. He acknowledged these as the true marvels of the age. Yet Pawfrey was confident that the great American public would continue to be more intrigued by a collection of freaks than by any such technical wonders.

Thus he looked on with equanimity as work on rival exhibits at the Exposition continued all around him. Even the spectacle of the giant wheel, the landmark of the fair, provoked no pangs of professional jealousy. George Washington Gale Ferris arrived in person to supervise the construction of the hundred and forty foot towers immovably embedded in concrete. Hoists lifted the wheel's 45-ton axle, the largest piece of steel that had ever been forged, and lowered it into the sockets of the twin towers. Despite these massive foundations the wheel still looked frail. Pawfrey was among the sceptics who were persuaded of its strength and safety only after Ferris, his wife and a *Tribune* reporter rode out a gale blowing in from the lake at a hundred miles an hour. Pawfrey looked up appraisingly at the enormous wheel revolving against the sky, wondered if it got his vote as the supreme marvel of the age and in all impartiality decided it did not. His vote went to the Three Kentucky Mammoths, a sensational new acquisition he had himself put under contract and conveyed in complete secrecy to a hotel outside Chicago where they were being fattened up for the fair.

The Mammoths were presented to the public at a reception at Palmer House, scooping by several days the rival presentations of Pawfrey's competitors, including Ferris and his wheel. In fact the boys hailed from Wisconsin and Virginia, but to Pawfrey's ear these states sounded unsatisfactorily thin. He had taken the liberty of exchanging them for Kentucky, a corn-brimming, fuller-bodied sounding state with the suggestion of hearty eating tucked into the lining of its name. The boys he had hired from unrelated families at $50 a week were transformed into brothers, reinforcing the kinship of flesh, a trinity of fatness from the same extraordinary horn of maternal plenty. It had taken his scouts two years to find them. At the time of stepping onto the world stage when they entered Palmer House the smallest of the Three Kentucky Mammoths, seven year-old Vantile Hodge with an amazing sixty-one inch chest, tipped the scales at two hundred and sixty-three pounds, while his ten and twelve year-old brothers Randolph and Horatio Hodge weighed in at four eighty and six hundred pounds respectively. Pawfrey billed his boys as the fattest siblings on earth, offering a hundred dollars cash down to anyone able to beat them.

By a stroke of genius, Pawfrey cast his presentation at Palmer House in the form of a charity dinner, the proceeds of which would go to poor children. Charity was the business of the rich and the virtuous, and it was Chicago's rich and virtuous who turned out in great numbers to see the fattest boys on earth. Littlewood, our John and I went along by invitation as the representatives of Straight House. In the hotel's gorgeous dining-room the Three Kentucky Mammoths presided over a seven-course dinner that included boned quail in plumage, moose and buffalo cuts served with blueberries in porter sauce. The boys dined on a raised podium where their eating could be seen and admired by all.

John, who had spent most of his life topping up undernourished children with sandwiches, was dumbfounded by the splendour of these appetites. Littlewood's impression was one of workmen getting down quietly and efficiently to their assigned task. The banquet was not so much eaten by the Mammoths as dismantled course for course, stowed away down to the last crumb. Smoothness and unruffled placidity characterised the performance. It was eating as a form of somnambulism. Piles of food vanished from the table like ships mysteriously gone down in a calm sea. To Littlewood it seemed to get up off plates of its own accord and be conveyed to the boys' mouths under the influence of a magnetic attraction not easily explained. The Kentucky Mammoths undoubtedly possessed magnetism, an aura. All the women present agreed on that. Mothering instincts were aroused, even an urge to self-abasement to do anything to care for these enormous boys. The Mammoths were imbued with a spiritual calm that moved the assembly to feelings almost of adoration.

After the banquet was over the audience was permitted to come forward and touch. I was fascinated by the disappearance of all contours from the human body. Flesh had been recreated here in a novel form, a continuous gliding and intermingling of parts such that it was impossible to say where one bit ended and the next began. The sheer skin lacked a single blemish, stretched taut over the subcutaneous tissue like hide spanned over a drum. The bodies didn't bulge. They appeared rather to be hemmed in by the air surrounding them. Touch these boys and they seemed to reverberate with vibrant implosive sounds.

The Mammoths wore tunics that left mountainous shoulders free to pour flesh down into gradually narrowing estuaries identifiable as arms. The tunics hung down in straight lines like curtains drawn round a cubicle ending six inches above the floor. Viewed from nearby, no legs or even feet were visible. The cubicles appeared to run on castors. From a distance the legs showed up startlingly in tartan socks that matched the tartan caps topped off with a jaunty feather. The green and red check gave the Mammoths a vaguely Highland air, extracting from their grossness the improbable promise that if you looked long enough at these boys you would begin to discover they were cute. There they stood in a line, rotund, globe-like figures, broadest at the equator and tapering off steeply towards the poles. Balancing rather than standing on their tiny feet shod in pale blue ballet shoes, the boys resembled gigantic spinning-tops that miraculously managed to remain upright even when at rest.

At the sight of these stupendous children, poignant despite their grossness, even beautiful in their helplessness, the inclination of the audience was not to laugh but cry. Prepared for this moment by Pawfrey, who remained discreetly in the background looking on, two hundred and sixty-three pounder Vintle Hodge trundled cap in hand between the tables to do a whip-round among the audience. Women wept outright as they stroked his expansive cheeks and patted his chubby head. Grown men who cast a cold eye on the starving ragamuffins in the streets blubbered into their handkerchiefs and gave reckless donations when the cap came round. Was it real or was it humbug?

Oh, undoubtedly real. But as an ancestor of Pawfrey's had formulated long ago in an archaic Portuguese I could still quote more or less verbatim: you only succeeded in this business when you moved people, and it was a curious fact of human nature that people were most readily moved when it wasn't at their own expense; when it was an illusion of misfortune, undertaken by an intermediary on their behalf. Pawfrey put it more succinctly: genuine feelings could be elicited by humbug. In the course of the years he refined this dictum. So long as they got their money's worth nobody gave a damn whether it was humbug or the real thing.

The Dream Factory

There were white men like the old fellow unearthed by *Tribune* reporters, who only sixty years ago had arrived as a settler at the desolate trading post of Chicago where thirty souls eked out a living between a swamp and a sand-choked river. There were black men like Du Saible, who arrived there before the white man, and there were red men like the Potawatomi, who had been portaging canoes between river and lake long before that. None of them arrived at the White City in the order in which they set out. Most of them never made it back at all. The only place native American participants in the Chicago fair had an opportunity to be anything like themselves was as performers at Pawfrey's emporium. The red man with his feathers and his curs, his wigwams, sacred bones and malodorous spell-binding chattels was included in the show along with the Elastic Skin Man, the Bearded Girl and the Horned Woman of Cyprus to illustrate alternatives to that forever self-boosting white race which had only recently arrived at the Summit of Time and made itself at home there to the exclusion of everyone else.

Although Pawfrey had never heard of the Yankee engineer Stanton, who was blown up in his factory the same day that ten-inch mortars shelling Fort Sumter opened the American Civil War, these two quite different men had thought along not so different lines. Stanton's notion, that the Once and Once Only Effect of what he called primary reality was being displaced by another reality that had come into being with the Over and Over Again Effect characteristic of machine reproduction, was pretty much the kind of thinking behind Pawfrey's emporium. It exhibited Once & Once Only items collected by Pawfrey or his ancestors because they were irreplaceable, unique. Pawfrey reasoned that people surrounded by processes of mass manufacture, and who learned to live with the mass products generated by those processes, would acquire mass habits, tend, in the long run, to become Over and Over Again people themselves. Once machine mass production had been established as a factor of evolution this was the logical outcome, that more and more would be produced of less and less. Thus the acquisition of irreplaceable items as the mainstay of the emporium ceased to be merely a business, the trade in sensations it had been for his predecessors, and became for Pawfrey the expression of a philosophy of life.

Visitors to his emporium of marvels at the Chicago Exposition passed down a walkway through a series of side-shows before entering the main exhibition, passing under a banner that read: IS IT REAL OR IS IT HUMBUG? Between the Headless Trooper and Pygmalion's Dream, a marble statue of Galatea that came alive, Pawfrey distributed human and animal freaks, everything, as he put it, that was monstrous, scaly, strange and queer.

Spectators laughed outright when they saw the duck-billed platypus and called it a hoax, but they were ready to believe in the Horned Woman of Cyprus. With the Wild Australian Children, first discovered by explorers who had taken them for kangaroos, they weren't so sure. Billed as the off-spring of a distinct race, hitherto unknown to civilisation and displayed in a side-show as the missing link between ape and man, the microcephalic siblings from Ohio with their capers, moans and their queerly uptilted cone-shaped heads were a tremendous hit with the public. Stretch the truth. It didn't matter if they weren't what they were claimed to be. Truth was elastic.

Pawfrey said he believed in a moral obligation to exhibit human freaks and his detractors cried: humbug! Didn't the public pay him money to boo and throw bananas at the Wild Australian Children and call them a cross between niggers and baboons? This was always rather tricky ground for the showman-crusader. As a showman he made money from freaks, while as a crusader he wanted to make morals from them. He had a penchant for freaks, he was fond of them, but there was never any question of standing up for freaks' rights or respecting any such thing as their dignity. Pawfrey exhibited his freaks not merely as sensations but as human beings who put the case for a minority. So like ourselves and so different! Here lay the fascination of freaks, and in Pawfrey's view the moral benefit, for the majority of his customers who had all been made the same way: to contemplate on the drawing-board of creation an alternative draft of themselves which, in the infinite wisdom of the Creator, had been found wanting in the final event.

This interpretation of freaks converged with Pawfrey's changing estimate of himself on his passage from showman to crusader. From the latter point of view the lies or exaggerations he had perpetrated in the course of his earlier career could be seen as alternative versions of the truth, in much the same way that a freak with two heads could be seen as an alternative version of a human being. At bottom the purveyor of humbug, the teller of tall tales, didn't believe in a single version of the truth. At bottom Pawfrey didn't believe in an exclusive version of anything.

In the Dream Factory visitors never saw the same place twice. Repeatedly they found themselves back at the entrance, or so it seemed. Had they been there before? There were differences every time. Distortion mirrors lined the passages between chambers. There were mirrors that made people very small before they arrived in the Giants' House. General Thunder measured eight feet and a half. Elevated shoes and a raised floor made him look nearer ten. His wife Eliza made pastry with a rolling-pin big enough to brain an ox. Little Frederick Thunder was already given it to play with from the age he began to toddle. After the Giants' House came the Dolls' House. This was the residence of Duke Malmesbury and his duchess, Minnie. The stage on which the twenty-eight inch Duke acted out his life represented the Store, the exact miniature replica of a gambling establishment at the corner of Clark and Monroe Streets.

His Grace was the dealer, manager and waiter in one person. All the props used, the cards and coins, glasses, matchboxes, ashtrays, were twice to three times the normal size. When he dealt the cards the Duke humped them around the table on his back like a builder carrying sheets of panel. He used a miniature electric hoist to lift cigars out of their box onto the table, rolling them like carpets over the baize to the player who had ordered them. In order to refresh a player's drink his Grace climbed a ladder with a pail of liquor and poured it into the glass. If a player won a large pot the Duke would oblige by trundling across the table with the winnings in a wheelbarrow.

Side-shows were arranged in rooms tipped ninety degrees or furnished the wrong way round. The public groped its way through these rooms horizontally along the walls or upside down across the ceiling. They saw bearded infants, aquatic Indians who lived with sea creatures in an aquarium, a phosphorous tribe living permanently in the dark where they communicated all their needs by semaphore. In an empty cell brilliantly lit they viewed the Human Skeleton, a very thin man whose legs and arms were hardly thicker than his thumbs, wearing a codpiece and a feathered hat, muttering to himself as he paced up and down. Nonsense displays in Higgledy-Piggledy Home showed familiar objects out of place — a garnished typewriter baking in an oven, a melon with an implanted ear-trumpet, a spruce tailor's dummy offering his arm to a standing lamp in an evening dress cut seductively low over two illuminated pear-shaped bulbs.

In the long-established tradition of his house, Pawfrey was moved to his greatest heights, or depths, in his rendering of human misery. The public was ushered along a gloomy subterranean walkway past a series of animated tableaux unfolding the Flood, the Plagues of Egypt, the Tower of Babel, the devastation of Sodom and Gomorra. A grand series of tableaux depicted the Conquest of the New World. Many of the Indians butchered in these tableaux were the descendants of Indians who had brought great art to the verisimilitude of death in their performances for the Teatro do Mundo; death by impaling on the white man's sword or lance, death by bludgeoning, garrotting, drawing and quartering, burning and burying alive. By the time their successors were being wiped out in twice daily shows of the Sand Creek Massacre probably more Indians had died in the tableaux of Pawfrey's emporium, and certainly with greater emotional participation from the public, than had been slaughtered across America during the conquest of the West.

Pawfrey's original diorama of Gettysburg, which by an ingenious arrangement of mirrors showed the decisive battlefield of the Civil War strewn with tens of thousands of corpses, was flanked by the Lynching of Negroes in New York that occurred just before and the Sand Creek Massacre just after. This triptych brought an already fabulous seeming American History series to a close. Thereafter the depiction of disasters moved much closer to home. Railroad Accident at the Crossing, Explosion in the Mine, Tragic Mishap in the Union Stock Yards were titles that read like newspaper headlines. They led on to interiors of domestic squalor which affected the public even more profoundly: consumptive immigrant families living in windowless rooms, queues of ragged women and children between cesspool and tap in tenement yards, low life in saloons, fallen women in Hell's Half Acre, street bums huddled on the sidewalk round a warm air shaft during a snowstorm on State Street, their plight underscored by the actual sounds and even the smells of the environments depicted.

Was it real or was it humbug? Visitors to whom such scenes were not familiar from life dismissed them as gross misrepresentations. Others were more sentimentally stirred by these tableaux than by anything they had seen on the streets of Chicago. Distraught women were consoled by ushers who moved in at the first sign of fuss with the soothing reminder that it was only a show. If the ladies and gentlemen went on into the future, just round the next corner, they would find things improving beyond recognition. The ground began literally sweeping visitors off their feet as they found themselves conveyed along an automatic belt. Mawkish gas lamps that had accompanied them all their lives suddenly gave way to a glorious spread of incandescent light. Hurrah, electricity had been invented! As if at the touch of a wand, happy domestic interiors, clean and bright, sprouted in the tableaux they passed. The moving belt gave way to an escalator that took the public up and up through galleries of space and light. As a grand finale, Pawfrey added a wing of the Manufactures Building to the Dream Factory tour, incorporating the White City itself into the show.

If the future was identifiable as anything then as a residential department store. Here was the dwelling of the future, and it capped all the illusions the public had seen so far. Life in this twittering place of brightness seemed to operate according to some inexplicable principle of self-motion. Objects moved, gadgets started and stopped, people exchanged written and vocal communications without any outward sign of cause and effect. Well-educated and well-nourished workers supervised the labour of machines. They lived in highrise buildings just like the gallery of light and glass through which the time travellers were transported on the final stage of their wonderland tour.

In this light and airy world man's struggles ceased. When commodities were available in unlimited supplies, thanks to the unlimited energy of machines, all people became equal. There was no longer a reason for dis-crimination between individuals or even races. Due to the amazing advances in nutrition and medicine the inhabitants of Pawfrey's wonder-land began to resemble each other physically too. Men, women and chil-dren wore identical long gowns. They looked healthy and clean. Harsh realities didn't intrude on this place. It was a Garden of Eden with all modern amenities, including a roof to keep the inhabitants dry. They were free to do as they liked, even if there didn't seem to be much choice of things for them to do. Fleet of foot, dressed up as jockeys in racing colours, they ran round and round a hippodrome under the roof of the crystal palace where the grand finale of the show was housed. They ran for their lives. They ran and ran. Under banners reading Running For Eternity they lapped circuit after circuit. They were running for immortal life. The general public could join in. What a romp!

Everyone ran. Oh how they ran, following signs directing them to the World's Greatest Living Wonder. Unbelievable but true! For only a small additional charge they could take an elevator to the crow's nest in the tower of the Manufactures Building for proof of what all had dreamed but never dared hope. Run for admission before it was too late! Ladies & Gentlemen, P.J. Pawfrey & Sons proudly presented to the public, in a lim-ited number of appearances exclusively at the White City, the Living Proof in Person, the one and only Paul Straight, born in the year Columbus discovered America, still going strong and with fair expecta-tions of living forever (or thereabouts) —

The Summit of Time

Nothing bound Pawfrey more to me than the fact that while almost every-one took me for a hoax he was confident I was real. From the moment I presented myself at his office and told my story the celebrated snitch on him began to quiver in a state of intense excitement. This was the greatest challenge his rat-smelling faculties had ever faced. During the ten hours it took me to give the bare outlines of my life from the day I was kidnapped from the Spanish Jew's house Pawfrey carried out a prowling circumnav-igation of my person.

Sometimes he pulled off and surveyed me with a telescope from the far end of the tent, sometimes came swooping in to inspect me from only inches away. Muffled explosions, half-suppressed cries of astonishment, pleasure, curiosity to hear more, betrayed to me his whereabouts in the room. This crop of involuntary noises grew particularly dense when I reached the point on the road to Boa Vista where I had met Porphyry VIIIth a hundred and fifty years ago. When I described how his own father's dusty wagons had rolled to a standstill at the Missouri crossroads where the *Queen of the South* lay stranded in a stubble field of wheat during the Civil War he broke into sobs. After I had come to the end of my greatly abridged story, leapfrogging over the backs of Du Saible and the Potawatomi to arrive in Chicago at the summit of time, Pawfrey slammed his hand down with an exclamation, reached for his check book and asked me how much I wanted.

For one thousand dollars a week, a fabulous sum that had only ever been equalled by the Swedish Nightingale, Jenny Lind, I was hired as the star attraction of the Dream Factory. According to his mood of the moment, Pawfrey wanted me rigged out in one of my incarnations as the son of a Renaissance merchant prince, as ship's writer on board the *Sao Cristobal*, as a Pig Indian warrior or secretary to a *quipu camayoc* in Inca dress. I resisted all such vulgarities, persuading him his business interests were best served by allowing me just to be myself. Wearing a frock coat and top hat, I would be available for inspection every day from ten to six in a glass-walled compartment at the top of the Manufactures Building tower, with the curtains closed for lunch between one and two. The compartment would be furnished as a ship's cabin, with various features relevant to my four-hundred year life, such as maps, pictures, books, quipu, which I would refer to in my twice daily lectures. Questions from the public would only be permitted at this time. In order to spare me the journey from Union Park every day I would be provided with an apartment in the Dream Factory where I would live with my wife for the length of my engagement. For my part, I agreed to submit to examination by whatever specialists Pawfrey chose to present, to waive all rights arising from our contract in the event that any of my claims were disproved and to desist from making them in public ever again.

A week later I donned my frock coat and top hat and rode the elevator up to the crow's nest where I was to be exhibited. Seizing on the *Tribune* phrase, Pawfrey had labelled it The Summit of Time. He stood outside in the rotunda with hand-picked guests invited to the unveiling of what advance billing already described as the greatest sensation the world had even seen. It was a hot day, and Pawfrey sweated with the same vigour he applied to all his activities. I could tell he was nervous by the sound of his voice. This was audible to me inside my glass cabin thanks to an ingenious Edison device which by means of wires made communication possible even through solid walls. I had not been prepared to be literally unveiled, but this was what happened. The curtains surrounding the cabin opened without warning — and there I was, surrounded by faces peering down at me through the glass.

What did they see? I quote a description of me that appeared in the London *Times*.

"A dwarfish, hunchbacked figure, perhaps a little over four foot tall, bald as a billiard ball, with mottled skin discolorations on the head, face and hands. When the face turns and looks up at us it presents an appearance hardly different from the ghoulish disclosures familiar from the opening of Egyptian mummies now in fashion. The impression of the doll-like physique is one of extreme fragility. It has been put through the wash at a high temperature, shrunk and slow-baked in an oven until the last drop of moisture evaporated. If this is what immortal life looks like, God help us die."

For what seemed a very long while my audience studied me in silence. I knew I was no longer prepossessing, but here I found myself being looked at like some unidentifiable creature risen from the bottom of the ocean and left stranded by the outgoing tide. The unspoken feeling seemed to be that wherever I had come from it might be best for me to return there as soon as possible. It was so long since I had ventured out of Union Park and been exposed to strangers that I didn't realise just how unappetising the sight of me had become.

Perhaps to get over this mutual embarrassment someone remarked that it was a very warm day and everyone was suffering from the heat, but I didn't appear to be in the least affected. I said that impression was correct. I had been born a mammal just like them, I had lived like a mammal for most of my life and sweated my way through three or four tropical zones and as many centuries. But latterly I had undergone a metamorphosis, becoming reptilian in my old age. Reptiles were cold-blooded animals, I said, adding a quotation from St. Augustine about those beasts of the field whose head man bruised with his heel, and I performed swaying motions I had learned among the Pig Indians that were highly suggestive of a snake.

My audience gave murmurs of astonishment, as much at the discovery that the mummy could speak at all, I think, as on account of anything it had said.

After a few more general exchanges of this kind the representatives of the press were asked by Pawfrey to refrain from further questions. He wished to proceed with my examination by the various experts he had engaged to test the veracity of my claims. The first of these was a professor of the classical languages whose pronunciation of Latin and Greek was so impenetrable that I requested him to put his questions in writing. Then he asked me to translate unseen from and into both languages. None of these childish exercises gave me the least problem, more the professor, whose irregular use of the subjunctive he was unable to substantiate when I asked him to cite authorities for it.

Other professors followed, Portuguese linguists and historians of every description — medieval, ecclesiastic, naval, colonial, experts in pre- and post-Columbian studies. They asked me to describe Lisbon at the turn of the fifteenth century. They showed me drawings of churches, chamber pots, caravels, medieval coinage and weaponry and asked me if they were accurate or not. They pestered me with questions about Dom Pedro Felipe, a figure for whom there was no historical foundation, they said. There were no records of the discovery of the Inca civilisation before Pizarro. I said that was to be expected. Within a generation of Pizarro's arrival almost all Tahuantin-suyu's records had been destroyed by the padres in order to suppress its heathen past. But I had taken care that *my* records had been preserved. And so saying I whipped out the Quipu of the Ghosts.

This was not the roll that had been begun by the *quipu camayoc* Xiahuanaco before he succumbed to the accelerating time sickness the Spanish had brought to Tumbez. It was the copy to which my beloved nun Esperanca had devoted her life in the Misericordia of Boa Vista. The quipu was full of her errors and my knotted corrections, tattered, moth-eaten, kicked out of shape by Edgar P. Stanton in the days when I used to roll the boy up in it, letting the colours rub off on him while he slept with wide-open eyes and dreamed his clairvoyant dreams. Knots had come awry and were no longer aligned in the proper order. I stumbled over these inconsistencies as I deciphered the quipu, and perhaps this lent my account an air of authenticity. My audience was impressed. But even the professors of South American history had never seen a quipu, let alone heard one speak. They doubted if there was anyone left alive who mastered the art of knot-writing and could verify the truth of the history I claimed to derive from it.

More and more evidence I adduced to substantiate my story was rejected for the same reason. There was no way of proving it. The missionaries brought in to examine me in a variety of Indian tongues all spoke bastard forms of the *lingoa geral*. They seemed unaware that it was an artificial language created to serve colonising ambitions of the Church no better than the rapacious schemes of soldiers, traders and planters. I could tell them the names of the men who had invented the *lingoa geral*, for I had been one of them myself. Annoyed by the ignorance of these missionaries, I embarked on a lecture to illustrate the tree of Indian languages that had been chopped down and the bits fitted together to make the common language. I cited examples from half a dozen Indian tongues, Taiassu, Tupi-Guarani, including dialects of the northern forest tribes such as Boti, Curao and Wahininamba to demonstrate the common elements on which the synthesis had been based, but it was all to no avail. With the exception of Tupi-Guarani, the missionaries hadn't heard of any of them. When I was asked to show them on a map the regions that had been peopled by these tribes, and did so, the missionaries smiled and said that during the last three hundred years these regions had been cleared to make room for plantations, factories, towns. The tribes that had spoken these languages did not exist any more.

Pawfrey intervened to suggest a break for lunch. I had no appetite, but that, as I explained to six eminent Chicago physicians, had been the rule for three-quarters of a century. It was the turn of the medical profession to examine me in the afternoon, which took place behind closed curtains. Pawfrey hoped they would be able to date me. They peered into my mouth, anticipating teeth or at least a small portion of one to grind down to powder and submit to forensic analysis. Their naiveté amused me. All laughed heartily when I told them I had parted from my last tooth at about the time their great-great-grandfathers were acquiring their first. With the exception of the Civil War years, when by force of circumstance I had eaten an uncommon amount of pork, I had not eaten any meat since the Declaration of Independence. Lack of teeth in a man made him a natural vegetarian and advocate of soups. To old codgers in my amolar condition the sight of nice soft fruit was much more mouth-watering than a beautiful woman. I directed the physicians' attention to the scaly rim on the inside of my lips where a bone-like callous had formed after decades of pulverising food with them. I had the hard mouth of a turtle — and something of the snap of its jaws. In their day they had masticated agouti, tapir, alligator and human flesh, too.

At the sight of my naked body the medical men were filled with dismay. The discolorations on display in my face became the more dramatic the further they went down, from navy blue around the groin to dark purple shins and feet that were almost black. Pawfrey later passed on to me a copy of their report.

"Like the charred remain*s* removed from a fire" was one phrase used to describe my body. My eyes were watery, my sight dim, but my hearing and sense of smell were rated good. More similes crept into the clinical prose on the subject of my reproductive organs. Withered raisins was an unsurprising choice to describe my testicles, small and hard as a cactus thorn an original comparison for my penis. Since the days when I had taken Fong's dinosaur aphrodisiac it had remained in a state of semi-erection. It had become necessary to attach a rubber hose in order to pass water the considerable distance, as it now seemed to me, between the interior of my clothes and the receptacle outside, which effectively meant wearing one of these fixtures the whole time. But much the most intriguing discovery for the physicians was that I had a pulse rate of only twelve.

I told them this was quite normal for me. Since coming down from the high plateau of Tahuantin-suyu some three hundred years before, my pulse had beat at an average rate of ten times a minute. Lovemaking with the passionate senhora in Boa Vista, which had imposed sometimes strenuous demands on a man of my age, might raise it to fifteen but not a shade more. At the ebb of my life, as an opium addict living in a palanquin, it had sunk to four or five, perhaps as close to ground level as was humanly possible. In the vastly slower dilations of the pupils of my eyes, with their incomparably more subtle range, I had once been able to distinguish not only shades of light and dark and colour not perceived by the mundane living but shades of events and the fractions of time within which they occurred. I had been able, I told the frowning medical men, to see the senhora ageing when she lay asleep on her opium pillow, the burned exhaust of the lives of strangers, dissipated energy, trailing like the tail of a comet in interstellar space when briefly their paths had crossed mine.

When I suggested that it might be worth financing an expedition to Vilcabamba, the settlement founded by Dom Pedro Felipe in his hundred and thirtieth year, in order to search for other survivors from that first expeditionary force of one hundred men to have reached Ki'zak three and a half centuries before, a gleam lit up in Pawfrey's eye but the medical men only frowned more deeply than ever. This was precisely the point, said the leading physician sternly. There was no physiological evidence for a condition connected with what I had called accelerating time sickness, nor for its reverse, the decelerating time sickness, from which I claimed to be suffering — much to the benefit of my health, it appeared. It was beyond doubt that I had lived to an extraordinary age. One hundred and twenty, perhaps – grudgingly he opened his hands a bit wider – even thirty, maximum thirty-five years. Such cases were rare but possible. In consideration of such an age I appeared to be in phenomenally good health. But four hundred......in the face of the unspeakable the physician shook his head in silence.

Pawfrey chimed in with a question. If an impossible pulse rate of twelve, measured here in this room by these physicians themselves, was not phys-iological evidence of a condition connected with the decelerating time sickness or other hitherto unknown factor, then how did the physicians explain it — the impossible?

The Impossible

Yea, oh yea!

Voices uplifted, the deep murmur of ten thousand voices rose up from the Midway below us as if in support of Pawfrey's question. In the tent tabernacles surrounding the White City's satanic amusement park the evangelist Dwight Moody opened each revivalist vigil with the exhortation to Christ and his saints to appear verily in clouds of glory at the Second Coming. Loudhailers carried his plea to the heavens, passing us on the way up. The physicians flinched. The question challenged them to declare themselves. Were they to be the legislators of the impossible? To tell us whether or not the dead would rise from their graves to meet Christ and his saints in the air? The hosts of the Lord had already pitched their moody tents in the plain between Jackson and Washington Park and were waiting for an answer. The White City held its breath. In the blue light of evening the Ferris wheel, the dynamos, all the frenetically pitching, spinning, leaping machines stood still and waited for an answer.

What certainty did we have about the impossible? The certainty of a seafarer before there were sextants, clocks to calculate the longitude? Of someone living before the discovery of steam power? Before electricity? Before motion photography had been invented? Mr Dickson's certainty inside the kinetograph, with no inkling of what was to come in another twenty, fifty, one hundred years? The certainty of Stanton inside his New Orleans warehouse, with no inkling fifty years ago of what was then impossible but had come into being since, the self-excited generator Westinghouse had built on the principle of electromagnetic induction? Increasingly powerful forces, as my brother Luke said, which could be generated by increasingly small machines – how certain would Stanton have been of that impossibility?

Wherein lay certainty for Great White Bird? How did it apply to the view of the world from within Corócoró's spirit-teeming head? Or to the *quipu camayoc* in the archives of Ki'zak where I had seen navigation charts of the Sleeping Sea, drawn by the mysterious master builders of Tahuantin-suyu long before the Inca stepped into history, showing the ice-free coast of a sub-tropical continent not rediscovered by whalers until the present century, a frozen waste they named Antarctica?

The Impossible was nothing but a line marking the provisional frontier on our journey into the interior of an unknown continent, a line obliterated in the moment of drawing it. The frozen continent melted behind us as soon as we passed over, and the solid land under our feet became sea.

An Empty Field

Even if the *Times* denied that I was all I was made out to be, calling me the most scrupulous hoax ever perpetrated, and this opinion was shared by the rest of the press, no one denied my status as a freak. Acceptance by my peers was what mattered to me most. The warm reception my colleagues gave me when I moved into the Dream Factory compensated for the slights I had received at the hands of the experts. Pawfrey wept profusely when he welcomed me into the company. He was an emotional man. Only Littlewood seemed unhappy about this venture into show business. She was even less happy that I had taken the step without consulting her. She couldn't understand why. Rather than make worse a situation it had been my intention to keep from her altogether when I first approached Pawfrey, I took her into my confidence and told her the real reason for what I was doing.

For quite some time now my grandson Edgar Stanton had been attempting to run a wheat corner at the Chicago Board of Trade. It had been a good time to buy wheat futures in the spring of the previous year. There was less wheat in store in Chicago than there had been in a decade. At the high point of the market Edgar could have pulled out and cleared ten million dollars.

I had been caught up by the excitement of what my grandson was doing and invested my entire fortune. I was drawn back into the pit as if it possessed the secret of restoring to me the pleasure I had once taken in life. In the sweltering days of August, when many brokers reeled out of the pits in exhaustion, panting with sweat, I stood on a stool among stalwart rural visitors in the gallery who would kindly lift me up and down so that I could see better, quite literally caught up by their excitement, cheering like schoolboys the day that wheat futures hit the magic $1 mark. One final fling! We scalped foreign markets, mortgaged our houses, sold all the moveable property we owned and took up credit to bid at auctions in the European capitals. Forecasts across Europe all the way into Russia predicted a poor harvest, sending up the price still further. This was to be the corner of corners, and all the goodness of Littlewood, all the things we had fought for in the running of Straight House, fair distribution, taking up arms against that cold-hearted leviathan, the Market, to correct the naturally unequal course of the world – all was forgotten. In the suspense of this terrific money-making game I became a slave of the Market myself. We were now buying cash wheat, moving it out of Chicago at a furious rate. Stocks in a city with storage capacity for thirty-five million bushels sank below three million bushels, lower than they had ever been. There would be a global wheat deficit. It was a certainty.

No one had contracted to deliver us more wheat than the pork baron P. D. Armour. It was a certainty the pork baron would be crushed. Philip Danforth Armour, he whose biography in the contemporary hero series I had read aloud so many times I knew it by heart, hero of the tenements' two-bit boot-blacks and its pip-squeak beer-runners. When workmen moved a pile of lumber on Armour's pier at the end of the winter we arrived in Chicago they found the body of a boy crushed to death the previous fall. Small, desiccated corpses, children dried out like the flattened pelts of starved mice, were discovered in pipes and drains, refuse trashed in the crannies of the city, nowhere more so than in the cesspool of the pig city known as Back of the Yards. Many of them had worked there, stripped of their usable parts and thrown on the trash heap to make P. D. Armour an even richer man. That grim reaper of the poor, that crusher of street boys, would now be crushed himself.

Gleefully I contemplated him ransacking his empty grain elevators when it came to meeting his contract, and took pleasure in the prospect of his failure — letting my judgement slide, as if I didn't know the stuff Armour was made of or why he had Danforth for a middle name. His huge grain elevators, ten stories high and capped by tower-like attics, stood near the south branch of the Chicago River adjacent to the railroad tracks. They were the largest and most modern in the world, equipped with chutes to receive grain from the cars, with elevator buckets to deposit it, with bins to hold thousands of bushels and hoppers to move it to the shipping elevators. Grain was still leaving the city but none coming in. It was certain that P. D. Armour, who had sold us millions of bushels of wheat for December delivery, would be unable to meet his contract.

But around the middle of the month Edgar was told all at once by his informers on the Chicago & North Western, the Rock Island & Pacific and the Milwaukee & St. Paul that shipments would reach town within the week. Armour had sent out emissaries to scour the country. They had orders to stop at every grain elevator in the Northwest and buy wheat whatever it cost. Some of the biggest stores lay along the Canadian border in areas serviced only by steamship. Armour charted the fleets of all the major lake carriers in the North. Edgar reckoned Armour could buy the wheat and charter as many boats as he liked and still not be able to deliver because it was already too late in the year. The lakes had frozen over. But Armour hired convoys of tugs to break the ice, ploughing a hundred-mile channel and keeping open water for the ships. The first wheat transports arrived at Armour's pier on the lake on Christmas Day, the twentieth anniversary of Littlewood's encounter with Matthew as he came up from the coal-chute of the Madison Street post office. It was the last Christmas in Straight House for which all the evangelists would be at home. Within a year of the anniversary the institution of Straight House as it had been known and much loved would have ceased to exist.

Bakers that Christmas were making bread with rye, refusing to pay the price for wheat to which Edgar's corner had pushed the market. In freezing weather Chicago's poor turned out in droves to cheer the steamships arriving at Armour's pier. At his massive elevators, freight trains were backed up for miles while lighters in the ice-snarled, jam-packed river stood bows to stern and waited their turn for unloading. No more than irritated by the passing inconvenience he had been caused, P. D. Armour escaped the wheat corner, shaking off his pursuers as a dog shakes off his fleas.

Edgar might yet have kept an edge on the market if a number of trends favouring this corner had not all been reversed at the same time — much better harvests in Europe than had been forecast, an outbreak of wars simultaneously in various parts of the world, which first drove up the price and then caused it to plunge when peace settlements were reached unexpectedly soon. Armour's emergency wheat supply during the critical weeks when Edgar Stanton owned two-thirds of the wheat in America held the corner in check until news of a bumper harvest of winter wheat pulled prices sharply down.

Edgar hung on by the skin of his teeth as he tumbled into the second year of his corner. In January he took up more credit, paying the cash price of eighty-one and five-eighth cents for No 2 spring wheat. Spring came, and the market rose with a momentary swell, lifting Edgar with it, sustaining the illusion he controlled the forces that controlled him. I had nothing more to give, was resigned to irrecoverable losses, in the worst case destitution, and on the chance of an engagement at the Dream Factory to tide us over had secretly made an appointment to see Pawfrey in person.

This was the situation I described to Littlewood at the time we moved into our apartment on the Midway. She took the bad news quietly, said I was an old fool, worse, I had broken my word and with it her trust. She mused over this for a while, dabbing at the table from time to time and raising her hand to look, as if some particle of what had been smashed might be found adhering to the tips of her fingers. Into this vacuum stepped a messenger from Straight House, one of our boys there, with the news that John was dead. The messenger came out with it cold, just like that. There had been a streetcar accident. A flange projecting from a streetcar track had wrenched a wheel off the axle and hurled it into the crowd. John had been killed. Littlewood withdrew a dabbing finger and stared at it with a puzzled air.

We buried John in Union Park cemetery in a coffin covered with a white and gold cloth embroidered by Littlewood. A large crowd made up of former inmates of Straight House followed it to the grave and attended the wake afterwards, paying tribute to the man they all remembered as an indefatigable maker of sandwiches. We had no news of Matthew, no address, but Mark and Luke came home to support their mother. Littlewood spent the night after the funeral going through John's things. At the bottom of a trunk she came across a letter she had once written to John in the name of Bohunk, telling him Bohunk had taken ship in Boston and didn't plan on coming back for a while. She looked up from the letter at breakfast and said Well, boys, he did, you see. Bohunk came back for him in the end.

She stayed at Straight House while I went off to fulfill my contract and entertain the public. I thought I had no choice in the matter. Something must have given way inside Littlewood which might have held or been repaired by me if I had been around. She returned to her old haunts, or believed she did, but all her old haunts had gone. At the shore end of one of the docks, where in the old days she used to hear a permanent gabble of street boys, thirty or forty of them, who had fixed up a regular club-room down there, a scrap metal dealer had moved in with his hoists and barges and there was no sign of any boys. She crossed Halsted and turned up Madison in search of the coal-chute down to the bunker under the post office but could find neither post office nor coal-chute. While she had not been looking the buildings had been torn down and the block rebuilt. Funny, she said. All the old buildings have gone.

She told me about it on the telephone when I called her in the evening, exhausted by the demands of the public that had been poking and prying at me all day. I failed to hear what Littlewood was telling me between the lines. She was scouring the nineteenth precinct for those nooks and cran-nies favoured by street children as accommodation. She peered into man-size pipes, even crawled inside them in pursuit of inmates she suspected were in residence there, on her feet all day, poking around in outhouses, in hay barges at the wharves on the river, looking under bridges and even rummaging in trash cans. This was no longer the young woman who had waylaid the evangelists with pies when they came up from their cellar for air. Littlewood was now a grey-haired lady with deep wrinkles of care across her face.

At nightfall she came home empty-handed. Sometimes she continued the search after dark. One night she was taken for a scavenger by a policeman who cautioned her to move on. She turned on him and demanded: where have all the children gone? — getting angry when she received no answer and attacking him with her umbrella. Dishevelled and incoherent, she was taken to the nineteenth precinct police station where she was remanded as a disorderly vagrant and would have been locked up in one of the pens if the police chief hadn't happened to recognise her. They brought her to the Dream Factory. I called in a doctor, who prescribed sedatives for her, and a woman of her acquaintance came in to sit with her during the daytime while I was gone. It was just a temporary arrangement, I said. In a month, when the Fair ended and my contract with it, we would go back to Straight

House. Life would return to normal. How it would do so I did not know, for I had invested everything in Edgar's failed corner and lost it all.

Littlewood spent her days looking at the Fair. From our apartment on the third floor she could walk out directly into the Manufactures Building. It was like living with a department store in her back parlour, she said. Shopping for the last twenty years of her life had meant making up lists for wholesale purchase, medicine, soap, food and clothing in large quantities. I couldn't remember her ever having bought anything for herself. All her life she had been a provider. There had been no time for shopping sprees downtown in the fine stores along State and Madison. Now she went out for the sole purpose of pleasure. She couldn't believe her senses. She bought nothing, she just looked, and still they treated her like a queen. It's all so beautiful, she said. It was not just for display, the wares were on sale, too, although she never saw anything so crude as an exchange of money on the store floor. There were no price tags. She was surrounded by beautiful things so free and easy in their permissive surroundings that no one minded if you touched them. She could pick them up and admire them to her heart's content. Something new was on offer all the time.

Just imagine, she would say, today they were operating a gold mine in the lobby of Marshall Field. Yesterday there had been live crocodiles on display in a case in the cloth department at Leiter's emporium to advertise a clearing sale. The day before that Leiter's had offered a saucer of ice-cream to every visitor and a bicycle suit to the woman who looked prettiest on her wheel. Littlewood was enchanted by these department store displays. They provided her with shelter from a world she found unbearable. So long as she was in the Manufactures Building she seemed able to cope with her grief over the death of John.

This respite was granted her until two men wearing important-looking moustaches, brown check suits and brown derby hats approached me one evening as I was stepping out of the elevator. They said they were plain-clothes detectives and their job was to keep an eye on everything that went on at the Fair. In this function they had frequently had dealings, as they ominously expressed it, with a lady they understood to be my wife. I asked them why, and they escorted me to a room in the basement of the Manufactures Building. From floor to ceiling the room was lined with shelves containing every kind of article stocked by a department store. The men showed me a section of these shelves and said that everything I saw there represented a week's work. They showed me the ticket attached, on which my wife's name was written. Everything I saw in this compartment had been stolen by my wife. She had commenced her activities here a month ago. Just a casual swipe here and there. They had apprehended the culprit, twice she had been warned. But during the last week she had begun stealing in earnest. She had the stealing sickness. My wife was a kleptomaniac. She was unable to help herself. Time had come to settle matters on the side. The men in brown check and derbies took turns in delivering these sentences, short and sharp jabs, like boxers working me over. One incredible accusation piled in on another. I was floored from the start. Every time I came up for air they kept on knocking me back down.

I asked them to call Mark in his office and he came over immediately, accompanied by one of the floor managers. This compulsion, as the floor manager described my wife's stealing habit, had become surprisingly common, nowhere more so than in the best social circles. In nearly all cases the culprits were women. The temptation was so strong, the circumstances so easy, the desire so irresistible. Perhaps women had been deprived too long of *pleasure*. No doubt the department stores themselves were at fault. Afterwards, said the floor manager, his choice of words sliding perceptibly in the direction of Dwight Moody and his tent tabernacles, all the considerations of honour would attack the unhappy spirit and bring forth remorse. But in the moment of accomplishing the act, pleasure — he repeated the word, giving it a whiff of something most unsavoury — *pleasure* was everything.

I liked this insidious charge even less than men in derby hats calling my wife a Greek name for an incurable thief. What had the poor woman in fact stolen? Jewels, furs, gowns, luxurious household goods? No! Her shelves were crammed with soft cuddly things, cushions and counterpanes and animals that squeaked, toys, toys, and more toys, with half a hundredweight of candy thrown in for good measure. This wasn't stealing. This was a woman wanting to propitiate the spirit of her dead son, to lure her boy back from the far side of the grave. With extraordinary clarity an image rose up in my mind, a Pig Indian woman who had lost her child over four hundred year before, standing outside the malocca milking her breasts into the air, weeping and calling on her little one to return to the places where it used to play. The great river in which all creation flowed ran from this woman's unhappiness straight to Littlewood's sorrow in the Manufactures Building.

I opened my old turtle jaws to give voice to my grief, but no more than a squeak came out. I wanted to cry, but the sacks of my eyes were empty. Not a drop of moisture was left in that parchment of a body. Even the expression of the most basic human feelings — it was unbearable. In my despair I struck up the most resolute attitude a Pig Indian warrior could muster, flinging all my strength into my shoulders to prop up my falling sky. Mark was deeply uncomfortable at the sight of his diminutive father groaning and scowling fiercely, arms raised above his head, pressing upwards into empty air. The floor manager danced around me, skittering on the tips of his toes. They persuaded me to sit down and Mark asked the floor manager to leave us alone.

He stood behind me with his hands of my shoulders. Things could not go on like this, he said. Surrounded as we were by a warehouse of stolen articles, I thought for a moment the shoplifting business was still on his mind. But Mark went on unexpectedly: both of you must come and live with – Lavinia – Miss Manning – actually my f-f-fiancée – thinking we might – me and Lavinia – get married – set up house together — f-f-f-family. Mark fell silent, crimson with embarrassment, and when he came up for air again said all in a rush: you shall come with Ma to live with me and Lavinia, and we will take care of you.

Straight House stood vacant, its inmates dispersed, the furniture auctioned off to raise money. When I heard the grain traders were paying rent for abandoned premises in which to store wheat I let them have the house. An immense incoming crop flooded the market at the end of that summer. So much grain poured into Chicago that disused depots, former water towers and coal bunkers were being taken over by the merchants. Grain seemed to pour down on us out of the sky, filling our ears, mouths and lungs with dust. Elevators burst, spewing tens of thousands of bushels out into the streets. Women came out to gather the grain up in their skirts, stuffed sheets and pillowcases and bore them triumphantly back home. In the streets, grain covered the ground like pellets of ice left knee-deep after a hail storm. An army might have been fed just on the spillage during unloading at canals and railroads.

Wheat fell to a quarter a bushel. The bottom dropped out of the market. Wheat was for free. The laughter heard coming out of the pit at the Board of Trade after the ruin of Edgar Stanton echoed all over the city. He owed millions of dollars. He was a bankrupt; worse, a man of dishonour. Edgar had fled his creditors, skipped town, a fugitive from justice as Lee Stanton had been before him. The harvest was in and left behind it a swathe of dry stubble across the Northwest, an empty field where Edgar lost the fortune he had found.

The White City had lost many of its subscribers a fortune, too. Now it was to be dismantled. The buildings had been ravaged by weather. Roofs began to curl at the edges, walls buckled in the summer heat. The Goddess of Liberty still occupied her pedestal, her cap gone and several of her fingers missing. Steel salvaged from the buildings went into the furnaces of the Pittsburgh and Illinois steel company. Other buildings travelled wholesale on rollers to Kansas City. The trusses from the Transportation Building had gone to Milwaukee. Its famed Golden Door was in the hands of a Chicago art dealer. Fish, frogs and lizards, the plaster ornaments of the Fisheries Building, were sawed off and sold as souvenirs. Half a million square feet of glass that had gone into greenhouses was destroyed by storms. The four lions that had stood at the base of the obelisk outside the Electricity Building now lorded it over chickens at a Wisconsin farm.

The rest was soon ashes, gone up in flames at the end of a dry fall. On the tinder-dry prairie, fires ignited by spontaneous combustion. Sparks flew. Rumours were that the fire had been laid deliberately by insurance racketeers, subscribers to the White City who had lost out and wanted their money back. I took a carriage with Mark and Anna to watch the final spectacle that was being offered in Jackson Park. The huge structures caved in like toys, girders buckling and writhing in the terrific heat of the flames. To the accompaniment of fire I had arrived in Chicago, to the accompaniment of fire I would leave it. This beacon was lit on the summit of time, signalling forward to the new century already visible in its gleams, back to the fleet of ships that had discovered the New World, the caravels of Columbus, rebuilt for the anniversary celebrations and moored off-shore where they were weirdly lit up by the fire, ghost ships lying motion-less at anchor on the burning lake.

THE FIFTH NIGHT

The Neon Rainbow

"Through my fifth century," said the old man, "I shrank as a performing freak, even smaller, in the end, than my midget wife. In Hollywood they shrank the film of my life, or the life of someone like me — I couldn't tell things apart, new stories from old, true from false. Do you remember, Father Anselm, our discussion of palimpsests?"

" Palimpsests? "

" How the Pig Indians used to graft one story onto another, overlaying one version of events with another, inventing the history of their tribe? You can dig down through the layers of a palimpsest just as archaeologists dig down through the layers of a site to reveal preceding civilisations."

" I remember."

" Perhaps the batteries are beginning to fade, Father Anselm. I'm not feeling quite myself tonight. I hope I can last out until the end of my story. Might it be better to begin with the benediction, just in case?"

Father Anselm spoke the benediction standing, concluding with the words *absolvo te* as he made the sign of the cross over the box.

" Thank you. Where was I? In Las Vegas, perhaps, where Minnie and I were hired as curiosities at the Last Frontier motel, it was all just a money game anyway. The interest that accumulated on the years, the measure of our lives....."

The voice faltered and petered out.

" In the end.....in the end I found myself on the backward path through time, shrinking to the nothing as which I began. It is unlikely you will ever again have the opportunity of hearing someone describe the circumstances of his own extinction. Apart from the inherent interest of such an experience, it may provide you with insights extremely useful to a man in your line of business....now where was I, Father Anselm.....? "

Landfall

When he moved into the twentieth century Pawfrey discarded the past tense and had not been heard to use it since. His wife lay buried back there on the road, just outside Springfield, Illinois, which the show passed through on its way west. Pawfrey carried her memory over into the present tense, and you were half expecting her to step into the room, or rather the car, as it was in railway cars we spent most of our lives. Through the door that always stood open behind him, almost as a testimony to Pawfrey's principle that nothing in life would ever be closed to him, it was in fact Littlewood whom I sometimes saw pass through the brightness around the entrance before she slipped into the shadowy interior and faded away into the gloom of the car. Spring through fall we worked the big cities in the north, closing with the Christmas show in New York. Then we headed south to winter in California.

At a junction near Santa Monica Pawfrey paid the railroad corporation to lay a private track down by the ocean. Along this couple of miles of railway siding the cars backed up for the winter, surrounded by cactus thickets where we installed the privies, with open rolling country to the north, interrupted only by long wind-breaking rows of eucalyptus trees which for the most part hid Los Angeles from view. If you kept going straight up the dirt track you eventually arrived at Main Street, the Plaza and Sunset Boulevard. Traffic passed down this road on its way to the coast, horses and wagons and soon the first automobiles as well, among them a gasoline-powered Studebaker, containing a man accompanied by a large camera and a small boy. A fringe community of Santa Monica had accumulated around the railway junction even before Pawfrey's road show began to spend the winters down there. After our arrival the population doubled, adding three restaurants, a Chinese laundry, an undertaker and a hotel. The man in the Studebaker checked into the hotel for a few days before he got back into his automobile and drove away again. From our car in the siding the duchess and I watched him taking pictures in the distance, of the sea breaking on the shore and the boy running in and out of the waves all day long, until the light was gone.

Our private car accommodated just Minnie and myself. My professional car, which served as a sitting-room too, we shared with Professor

Bergonie from France. The car, and Professor Bergonie, were sponsored by Edison and Westinghouse. My earnings in sponsorship from these two companies amounted to considerably more than the salary I was paid by Pawfrey. The only drawback was the intrusion of a third person into my private life. Professor Bergonie came with the car, my scientific attendant on a two-year contract to supervise the electrical experiments on myself to which I had agreed in exchange for sponsorship.

I sat for an hour each morning in the electric cage, facing east, one side of the car cranked down to admit the morning sun. Twice a day my legs and arms were strapped into an apparatus and my withered muscles submitted by the professor to mild electric shocks. Though unpleasant at first, I soon became addicted to them, as these were about the only sensations I had left. On tour the shock therapy was part of my programme. The sight of anyone strapped into a machine and wholly dependent on the mercy of its operator never failed to pull in a crowd. Then people read my name on the car, and gasped, and pointed. I was the World's Greatest Living Wonder, first presented at the Exposition in Chicago, and everyone had heard about that. I endorsed the Edison-Westinghouse patent electric rejuvenation cage, retailing in the stores for $290 but available on site at the bargain price of $120. Professor Bergonie showed how it worked. I showed *that* it worked. I was the oldest man in the world.

Testimonials from America's most celebrated physicians were plastered all over the car. I might be rather a small man these days, having shrunk to three feet and seven inches since first displayed in Chicago, but I was a much more appetising sight than I had been then. Certainly I had taken on flesh, whether as a result of Prof. Bergonie's professional attentions or because of Minnie's cooking it was not for me to judge. I wore a wig to cover my discoloured bald head. I had had my teeth fixed at great expense. My complexion benefited from the sea air and Californian sun. Above all I benefited from Minnie.

When Duke Malmesbury died of a heart attack at the age of only twenty-seven I had inherited the baby sister of his duchess as my professional companion. To amuse his patrons His Grace had worn a frock coat and top hat from the age of five, begun to puff cigars at seven and preferred his brandy neat before he was ten. This tiny adult in miniature fascinated the public, and to sustain that fascination he was left with no option but to entertain himself to death. He died heroically in the cause of duty and was buried with the highest honours of a state funeral that could be accorded by Pawfrey's republic of freaks. The Duke's two foot nine inch bier was followed by thousands of his loyal admirers on a freezing day in New York, bringing the traffic along Fifth Avenue to a halt.

Malmesbury's death devastated the duchess. She felt in some way responsible. Had she not been absent on tour for so much of the time she might have kept him from those bad habits, she thought, which had brought about his premature death. Minnie's loss coincided with mine. That same winter my wife was found frozen to death on the sidewalk outside a Madison Street building, formerly a post office with a basement boiler room that had long ago been patronised by a gang of street urchins. I clung on to the duchess and the duchess clung on to me and the grief we accumulated between the two of us in time became less heavy for the sharing of it. Discovering a quality of tenderness in such little people, magnified all the more in his eyes because of their diminutive size, Pawfrey persuaded us to share not only our grief but a midget billing in his show. When Minnie eventually subsided under the weight of her sorrow Pawfrey induced me to build up a new partnership and a new act with her vivacious younger sister. It would feature my vast leathery age set off by Minnie's sparkling youth, her doll-like porcelain features and a soprano coloratura, superior even to that of her sister's, which a critic in Buenos Aires had once memorably compared to the sound of metal-shod mice scampering through glass ears of corn.

I did age. She did youth. Together we did comedy, a father-and-daughter, Beauty-and-the-Beast routine. Age kept on dying, Beauty kept on reviving the Beast with electric shocks administered by the Edison-Westinghouse patent electric rejuvenation machine. The gags and professional banter we developed for our routine of the decrepit old man and the sprightly young woman strayed over into our private life. I was the fall guy, mostly mute, while Minnie kept up a line of ribald wisecracking the audience loved. I was content in my passivity, my role of infancy in old age. It was a relief to me to inch down into the smaller circumstances dictated by Minnie's size. I was beginning to claim the privileges of a childhood that had been stolen from me.

The boy we had seen on the beach came back for a second look and saw what he'd missed first time round. We were all on vacation, lying in the sun. The kid got himself a free show. He walked along the railway siding past the Three Kentucky Mammoths, the Horned Woman of Cyprus, the Wild Australian Children, the Thunder family, bearded females, phosphorous Indians and aquatic Indians living with sea creatures in an aquarium, and his mouth must have hung open for the best part of a mile.

Pawfrey went up to the hotel where the Studebaker was parked to speak to the boy's father. Then he came running down the siding, telling us all to come up to the hotel to witness the most extraordinary thing he had seen in his life. This was a challenge to everyone's professional pride. The hotel dining-room was packed within minutes. So many people had never been seen in the street at one time. A queue formed round the block all the way back to the Chinese laundry.

A sheet hung down from the gallery at one end of the darkened dining-room and the driver of the Studebaker was cranking a machine at the other. Light flickered across the sheet. And there was the sea. We saw it in the distance, undulating with the ripples of the sheet hanging at the end of the dining-room and stirring with little eddies of air that came in through the open door. It was there all right, it was the sea, and nobody knew what business it had being there on that sheet. The aquatic Indians swam round behind the sheet to find out what was back of it. The Wild Australian Children set up a terrific caterwauling as the sea moved in on top of them and a wave began breaking right over them. People in the front row turned and fled. Panic broke out. There was an attempt at a stampede. Then the lights went back on and the sea disappeared from the screen. The machine operator spoke to us. He told us there was no need for alarm. No one would come to any harm. What we had seen was only a moving picture of the sea. Would we please sit down and enjoy the illusion without any fears for our safety. Any spectators who got wet would be given their five cents back.

Sheepishly we returned to our seats. The lights went out again and the machine operator cranked the sea back onto the sheet. We watched speechless with amazement. The little boy appeared like a leprechaun out of the waves, a ghost in shades of black and white, floating towards us on a spar, growing bigger and bigger, until his face filled out the sheet with a silent shout that rang in our ears. Land! A castaway had come to us from across the ocean. Hands reached out to pull him ashore. Cheers rang through the hall as the boy washed up on the beach. I watched the vision approaching from far, far away, from a corner in a kitchen where some-one remarkably like this boy had been removed and taken on board ship four hundred years before, ascending and descending the great tree of rivers by which he had travelled from the Sleeping Sea to the Atlantic Ocean on the first passage across the New World solely by water. This was the vision thrown back at me from a flicker of lights in which my likeness had been recreated after a copy made by Héloise and passed on to Edgar P. Stanton, his son Lee and Lee's half-sister Thelma Louise, and out of that incestuous union the arrival of my great-great-grandson, transferred onto nitro-cellulose stock on an illuminated spool moving jerkily through a projector in the dining-room of the Ocean View Hotel.

Capability Straight

The boy's name was Capability Straight, had been Stanton, Matthew said, but when his mother took off and gave Matthew the stewardship of her child they teamed up as father and son and since then he had called the boy Straight. Matthew had been grinding out a living in Pittsburgh, Pennsylvania, cranking out sixteen shows a day until Thelma Louise got tired of nickelodeon life and had left to seek her fortune more quickly making moving pictures with the American Mutoscope and Biograph Company in New York. The nickels in Pittsburgh had kept piling up and Matthew invested in a film distribution company and sold out and had made fifty thousand dollars while Thelma Louise was still on five bucks a day.

Pawfrey had a proposition to make to Matthew right after that film show, and Matthew accepted it, and the deal was that he would spend the winter making actualities, film records of all the living wonders in Pawfrey's show. They would jointly market these pictures and share the profits, out of which all the artists would be paid a percentage to be invested in an old-age pension fund. This scheme met with unanimous approval at a meeting in the dining-room of the Ocean View Hotel. The assembly unanimously passed Pawfrey's other motion too, which was that they might as well make the owner of the Ocean View an offer for his hotel and have done with it, so that they could use the premises as and when they desired. A momentary upheaval on the part of the Wild Australian Children was understood to be an expression of dissent, but this was rather one of those roaring manifestations of joy to which they were prone when overexcited, and their thumb marks were duly appended to the documents drawn up by the lawyer and signed by all present.

Actualities had been the bill of fare from the early days of the kinetograph. Thousands of them had passed through Matthew's hands, from Jim Joyner's historic yawn on. The cameraman put his subject up against a sunlit flat and cranked till the reel ran out. Madame Histrionia performed her Siamese Butterfly dance under these conditions, Annie Oakley shot clay pigeons, the famous strongman Sandow flexed his deltoids and hefted a two-hundred pound pig with one arm.

What Matthew did was to put his subjects in a story, like the shipwrecked boy coming out of the sea. He began with those whom he knew best, myself and Minnie, accommodated in an apartment next door to the Thunder family. Carpenters built the set in the yard of the hotel, two rooms in cross-section open to the camera, one of them a single room where the giants lived, the other occupying just the same amount of space but floored off as a three-storey apartment with miniature stairs and furniture scaled down to fit the midget family in residence there. Matthew filmed the two apartments wall to wall inside the same shot. A one-reel sequence showed the giant and midget families synchronised as they got up in the morning, washed, dressed, ate breakfast and went out to work. No special gags were necessary. It was brilliant for the simplicity of the contrast. Never had Minnie and I been made to look so minute, or the Thunder family more gigantic.

A film company in Los Angeles printed copies of these actualities as fast as they could be processed through the laboratories. They were distributed for screening all over the country and became enduring favourites. Theatre managers found their customers coming back week for week and still wanting to see more of the same. The public couldn't get enough of the freaks, nor could the freaks themselves. Night for night the former dining-room of the Ocean View hotel, since converted into a moving picture theatre, was packed with entertainers entertaining themselves to tremendous applause. Dignity seemed to have been conferred on their outlandishness as a result of the nitro-cellulose treatment. It made them immortal. They fell in love with their own shadows. They were bewitched. They were proud of these souls they had been given. They streamed care-free out into the night, leaving their shadows behind them to entertain an empty hall. Then there was Capability Straight. Again and again they called for the boy. He came up big on the screen. He opened his mouth, and everyone shouted "La-a-a-nd!"

Where had the boy come from? How had he got there? And where was he headed? They plied Matthew with questions. The boy had to have a story. Matthew scratched his head. Everyone agreed the boy couldn't just be left there on the beach. They plied Matthew with suggestions. Soon they began making demands.

I sat in the electric cage, one side of the car cranked down to admit the morning sun. My legs and arms were strapped into an apparatus and my withered muscles submitted by the professor to mild electric shocks. It was my first script conference and I was very much a captive participant. Minnie brought me a glass of orange juice. Bergonie charted a graph. Matthew was thinking out loud just beside my left ear, quite insistently, rhetorical questions that required answers, and I said, more to be rid of them than anything else, the first thing that came into my head, the first thing that had occurred to me when I saw Capability Straight floating ashore on a spar.

"Boy comes from Lisbon. Fleet of three caravels, two of them gone down in a storm just off the coast of Brazil not long after the discovery of the New World. One ship has survived, the *Santa Cruz*, but the boy does-n't know that. He's about to be picked up by Indians, and that's where he'll be headed for the next few years, into the jungle, to become an Indian himself......"

Caravels? Where would he get hold of three caravels? Matthew was still thinking about this when Colonel Kirkpatrick arrived.

Ghost Indians

The Colonel bought the property with the Chinese laundry next door to the Ocean View Hotel, a vacant lot comprising five acres of cactus thickets and a derelict house that had not been used as a laundry or for any other purpose for as long as anyone could remember. The Polyscope Motion Picture studio was established on these premises. The roofed area at the back of the derelict building serving as a dressing-room, with the stage in a room at the front still missing the ceiling and one wall. The floor was covered with carpets, debris, uncollected laundry, but as Sid Blumenthal, the director of the Polyscope pictures, never cut below the actors' knees the rest didn't show. The Colonel did a brief reconnaissance of the lot, paid cash, moved in and began making pictures the next day.

Kirkpatrick would hand Blumenthal a business envelope on the back of which he sketched in minute handwriting the outline of six scenes supposed to run a hundred and fifty feet to the scene, which was as much as the little Moy camera would hold. Sometimes even the action would only be told verbatim, the actors clustered in a circle to pick up the Colonel's lugubrious whispers, because the Colonel famously had a throat condition and a whisper was all he could manage. Sid then rehearsed the scenes, but if he found they were running behind, or clouds were beginn-ing to pile up, or wind was mussing the girls' hair, he would take a chance on getting it without rehearsal. Obsessive about running costs, Kirkpatrick always stood at the cameraman's elbow throughout the actual filming. When he heard the cameraman murmur "Speed her up, Colonel", Kirkpatrick would begin jigging up and down, whispering anxiously "Hurry up, folks, film's running out. Grab her, Jim. Kiss her, but not too long. Quick! Don't bother with her coat, c'mon, just get her out of the scene.....hurry! Out!"

Polyscope had made a week's worth of these one-reelers when the Colonel looked over his lot fence one morning and belatedly took notice of what was backed up just below his own yard. There were Sioux Indians camped down in those cactus thickets who danced the Ghost Dance and had fought at Wounded Knee. He spent the day scribbling continuities on the backs of used business envelopes, went through some scowling, moustache-tugging calculations of the expenses involved in making an unprecedented six-reel motion picture with a running time of over an hour and finally walked over to have dinner with Pawfrey in his suite at the Ocean View Hotel .

Kirkpatrick said in a whisper to Pawfrey: Have a fire break out, an elephant escape or a train derail just outside your house – put it under contract and worry about the story later. Pawfrey's show parked down on that siding was like all three of those things happening at the same time. Chance in a lifetime, Colonel Kirkpatrick whispered with a touch of pathos, slumping back in his chair, exhausted by so much talking. How much was a chance in a lifetime worth? Pawfrey leaned forward and asked the Colonel to repeat what he'd said as he was a little hard of hearing these days.

A deal was hammered out. If Kirkpatrick intended to put the whole show under contract Pawfrey wanted ten thousand dollars a week. That was too high for the Colonel. Then just the Indians, he said. How much the Indians? Pawfrey said the Colonel could have all the Indians he wanted for twelve hundred and fifty a week.

These were Sioux braves, who did the Ghost Dance, and some of whom had fought at Wounded Knee. The Colonel went down to talk to them. His idea was to make a moving picture of the battle. The idea popped up out of nowhere. One minute it was a shadow in the Colonel's head. The next it was fluttering around in the California sunshine, browsing among the thickets, a new kind of creature which had never been there before. There was a leap from actualities about strongman Sandow to recreating an Indian war on film that we sensed would give us a different order of things. But that was only the beginning. After the Sioux had consulted with Colonel Kirkpatrick and told him the idea was not possible, because the site of the battle, the Pine Ridge Reservation in South Dakota, was now a sacred burial ground, the Colonel said that was no problem. There was a mountain location just down the road near the Santa Monica canyon where he would shoot the battle instead.

After this discussion the Colonel was gone for a week. He returned with a gentleman attired in the uniform of the US cavalry. His name was Lieutenant General Nelson Appleton Miles, and if that wasn't enough for the Sioux the sight of him on a horse picking its way down through the cactus thickets, riding out of the noonday sun towards them with the light behind him most certainly was. Some of the Indians immediately retreated into their cars. Others fled to the beach. Lieutenant General Nelson Appleton Miles had commanded the US cavalry at the massacre of Wounded Knee, and the Colonel had just persuaded him to do so again. On the Colonel's entreaties the Sioux mustered their scattered forces. But they wanted all members of Pawfrey's road show present as witnesses. They wanted an attorney to inscribe any agreement that might be reached on an indestructible tablet of stone. Under these conditions a parley was called.

Negotiations continued for days. Colonel Kirkpatrick sat in the middle of a clearing at the back of the laundry lot, surrounded by several hundred people, whispering at them through a megaphone. He held a stack of business envelopes in one hand. He referred to these, and occasionally gesticulated with them, when matters weren't proceeding to his satisfaction. Lieutenant General Nelson Appleton Miles sat on one side in the shade of a eucalyptus tree, rocking without interruption in a rocking-chair. The Sioux spokesman sitting on the other side demanded a rocking-chair for himself, too, but he settled for an ottoman brought out for him from the Ocean View Hotel.

A breeze spread a smell of oranges through the clearing where I sat in a kind of memory haze associated with the clicking sounds all around me. To the accompaniment of these clicking sounds the Colonel talked on and on about the Ghost Dances. The Colonel said Paiute prophet-dreamers had promised the disappearance of the white man and a return of the buffalo to the plains if certain rites and dances were performed. The Sioux carried these dances out, in fact a veritable craze of Ghost Dances had swept all across the American West, because Indians believed they would induce the dead to come back and build life again on their devastated lands. But this craze for Ghost Dances had made white folks uneasy. Then they got panicky. One thing led to another, the continuity was unclear, but the next thing that happened was that the US cavalry arrived at the Pine Ridge Reservation one winter morning and massacred more than two hundred Sioux men, women and children.

The Indians sat in the shade, clicking their tongues as they listened to this recital of their destruction, and then I recalled where I had heard the sound before, against a backdrop of dried fronds creaking in a palm tree and waves lapping gently on a shore. This was the sound the Indians had made when the Admiral Dom Pedro Felipe read the Requirement to them on the coast of Brazil four centuries ago. The Indians were clicking their tongues and rallying, other Indians in another time and different circumstances, but it was an echo of that sound nonetheless. This time they understood. The Requirement was a document which sentenced them to death, again and again, if necessary, as often as it was read to them. Lieutenant General Nelson Appleton Miles continued rocking after the Colonel had finished speaking, and the Sioux brave sitting with his feet tucked up under him on the ottoman began to weave speech through the rocking-chair runners as if he were laying snares, threading speech softly with his hands through the eyes of invisible needles, but it wouldn't go, he reached an impasse, rewound his speech and put it back in his mouth where it fell silent again.

The Colonel put the megaphone up to his mouth and whispered: so what is Little Bull saying to us? Miles said: Little Bull is saying the Ghost Dances were done wrong. The Colonel wiped his forehead with a handkerchief and snarled into the megaphone: then for Christ's sake they can do the dances again, can't they. Sure, said Miles with an open-handed gesture, then they do them right. What the hell is all this about, the Colonel demanded angrily, and his voice made a leap into cracked sound, like a barking dog jumping out of the megaphone. Then they do the dances right, Miles repeated, and the Sioux win the battle of Wounded Knee, the white men disappear from their lands and the buffalo return to the plains, because the road out of the past is forked and the same path can never be trod twice. That is what Little Bull is saying, said Miles. He continued rocking for a while before he was gradually brought up by the silence spreading out round him and past him until it reached the shore where it calmed the surf and stilled the sway of the sea.

They shot the Ghost Dances on the beach with the cameraman in the sea and the sun behind him in the west, and the dancers with long shadows trailing from them like the streamers of kites. It didn't look like Dakota. It didn't resemble any Ghost Dance that had ever been seen at all. The braves looked as if they were in a desert moving along a narrow tunnel of storm, swept by tangle wood cast up by the ocean, the giant shadows of their movements billowing on a crest of wind. In the wind-still evening they sat in the dunes with outstretched arms, pointing to the sea where they saw the Great Plains, and the rushing waves that were the herds of buffalo returning to their lands. The cameraman did a double exposure using stock footage, so that the animals massed up out of the troughs in the waves and came thundering towards the spectator right out of the surf, and the sea and the plains became one.

The picture was completed in three weeks. A detachment of US cavalry rode into the Santa Monica canyon one morning filmed through filters that turned the dark gold sand pure white. A winter morning in South Dakota, deep snow in the dunes standing in for the Pine Ridge Reservation, a light cross-shadow in the trees. In their visions the prophet-dreamers of the Sioux had already seen the white man riding out of his stockade and prepared their people against his coming. In dapple of shade and sunlight a piebald horse moved with kicking steps in the lee of the dune. Lieutenant General Nelson Appleton Miles, flush in the sunshine, tending his glossy mustaches with a white-gloved hand, led his men onward into a narrowing ravine, urged his horse into the water, knowing the same river could never be crossed twice. The hooves of a hundred horses splashed into Wounded Knee Creek. A hundred arrows splashed. The Sioux sprang their ambush. Close-up butchery followed in the frothing white shoals by the bank, throats slit ear to ear, knives to foreheads, hands ripping scalps, a white glove floating downstream. Light was shut out of the camera, fading back into an image of a woman putting a child to sleep.

It was followed by a very long sequence of settlers' wagons coming down the Oregon Trail, or rather up, because they were inexplicably moving backwards. The projectionist ran the film the other way round and reversed the passage of the white man across the continent after Sioux had annihilated the US army at Wounded Knee Creek. Like toys on little bickering wheels, a swarm of scuttling cockroaches, the settlers' wagons scraped back up the mountains they had descended in their tens of thousands, swam rivers in reverse, crossed plains and deserts for two thousand miles and were sucked back into doom-masted ships that sailed backwards across the ocean.

Indians on horseback watched them go, outlined against the sky on the Pine Ridge Reservation, or a bluff of the Santa Monica canyon, or just a promontory of cloud standing in for solid ground. A draught from a door left open upstairs sent ripples across the sheet hanging from the gallery in the former dining-room of the Ocean View Hotel, tugging at the Indians' faces, ghost Indians, screen Indians, the only ones we had left, because the day after they finished shooting Wounded Knee the Sioux had upped and gone, disappeared from the white man's history forever.

Palimpsest

Creating an illusion of reality wasn't confined to Colonel Kirkpatrick's movie-making career. The entire man was an invention, beginning with the title, ending with the name and covering much of the life in-between. He had not been an officer serving with the Confederate army, as he put out, nor had the limp he cultivated in support of this claim been incurred during action in the Civil War. It was the result of a leap from the third-storey window of a hotel in the course of evading custody.

This had happened in the Yukon a long time ago. According to Sid Blumenthal, who was an old associate, the accident nearly killed him. It had certainly buried what Sid called the Colonel's bad days. Sid got to know him when he was in the decorating and upholstering trade in Buffalo, working part-time in the evenings as a vaudeville magician. His name had been César then and his nationality Canadian. Before that Sid thought he may have been a Greek by the name of Dandalos. It was as César, at any rate, that the decorator-upholsterer invested in the vaudeville business, took a travelling show on the road and hired Blumenthal as manager. On a poster advertising the show in the first town they played the name Kirkpatrick appeared suddenly as presenter. From then on he grew long moustaches, wore tall hats and called himself Colonel. Vaudeville was maybe the only thing to which he remained loyal in his life. It *was* his life. Polyscope films always ran close to twelve minutes, the usual length of a vaudeville number, and that is how they were received by the vaudeville audience Kirkpatrick knew best, as novelty turns between the singers and clowns.

On a rotating stage turned to face the sun stood the first malocca ever seen north of the Panama isthmus. It was the most authentic set on the lot, built to my specifications by the German carpenter Fritz working under a brilliant Hungarian designer by the name of Kadar. Capability Straight plus about a hundred Mexican-Indian labourers hired from the railroads to play Taiassu tribesmen lived in or around this malocca twelve hours a day six days a week. From the lot with the Chinese laundry you could still look down and see the mile-long siding where Pawfrey's wagons regularly used to winter, but it had been a while since the circus last came to the site. Fast-spreading cactus and rampant yellow shrubs had niched themselves in the railroad cracks and were soon going to cover it up altogether. All that was left to remind us of the world's greatest travelling show was the Bearded Infant, Jemima, now grown up into an extraordinarily hirsute girl the same age as Capability Straight. The Colonel bought her out of her contract with Pawfrey, offering her a part in the Polyscope motion picture series *Castaway*. The series featured Capability in the title role and was directed by his father, Matthew Straight.

But what actually happened in the *Castaway* story, what characters it featured and how they were developed, this was staked out as the Colonel's province. He was paying. He overruled Matthew's objections that Capability's Pig Indian playmate couldn't possibly be played by a bearded Circassian girl. Kirkpatrick was a man with clear and simple articles of faith. He didn't give a damn about authenticity. He said all that mattered in the movie making business was to create an illusion of reality.

Castaway was fodder for the five and ten cent parlours with folding wooden chairs, dingy community halls into which millions of working-class Americans crowded night for night to watch greedy corporate tycoons, villainous landlords, corrupt politicians, flamboyant suffragettes and striking workers flicker across the bed-sheets that usually sufficed for screens in these makeshift movie-houses just after the turn of the century. Two or three times a week they also watched Capability Straight playing himself in *Castaway*. Matthew had originally shot three reels and then abandoned the boy to the Indians. The uproar in the Ocean View Hotel exceeded anything we had seen on the night of his first screen appearance like a leprechaun out of the waves, floating towards us on a spar. What country had the boy arrived in? What happened to him after his rescue by the Indians? Had they eaten him? Questions poured in from concerned customers, reinforced by distributors' requests for more of the same.

The Colonel asked me to step into his office where we talked for the better part of a day. He retired to soak in the bath tub in his tower over-looking the set, emerging the next morning with a six-inch stack of used business envelopes on which he had sketched a hundred episodes of what he called a continuous feature entertainment with the title *Castaway*. Unknown to the former decorator and upholsterer, Kirkpatrick alias César alias Dandalos had just brought the world's first moving picture series into being.

It was a love story, the Colonel said, plain and simple. So he put the love element right in at the start by having Lemon Grass rescue the white cast-away on the beach. In three episodes she took him home to her tribe, nursed him through mortal sickness and at a powwow under the rain tree she pleaded his case with tribesmen who were more in favour of eating him. By episode ten Capability had been mauled by a jaguar, survived a hundred-foot plunge down a waterfall, mastered the art of the blow pipe to greater perfection than any Pig Indian before him, and was presented by the tsushaúa Great White Bird with a rat-skin pouch symbolising his elevation into the tobacco-licking tribal council under the rain tree.

A marriage ceremony with Lemon Grass seemed imminent when war broke out with the White Earth Indians beyond the swamp. The audience had to wait another two years for the consummation of the love affair between the castaway and his rescuer. At last, in episode one hundred and ninety-eight, Capability and Lemon Grass were married. As I recalled, the Pig Indian marriage procedure, the bride-groom gave the bride's relatives arrows, an axe and a piece of shingle, hung up his hammock in her father's malocca and that was that. It wasn't good enough for the Colonel. He sub-stituted an opulent wedding to boost the romance his audience craved, with bride and groom passing between lines of drum-beating men and flower-garlanded girls officiating at a ceremony much more reminiscent of Hawaii than Brazil.

Substitution was the by-line of the business, Mexican-Indians for Taiassu tribesmen, pumas for jaguars, a revolving stage with overhead Aristo arc lamps to put shadow into the potted plants and create the impression of an impenetrable jungle. Another life was substituted for mine. I might and often did find that other life incredible or ludicrous. Pig Indian life as represented in *Castaway* had no filth, no ugliness, no overt cannibalism, no sex at all, but it didn't seem to me that the one was more

332

true or false than the other. It was not that a lie replaced a truth. One version merely superseded another. Most astonishing of all was to watch my wife Lemon Grass superseded by Jemima.

Pawfrey had long done a successful line in Circassian beauties, the first of whom had been a genuine original from some obscure territory near the Black Sea. Her successors were mostly barmaids, well-endowed and wearing low-cut blouses, discovered by Pawfrey's tireless scouts in towns en route and taught to rinse their hair in beer for the crinkly Circassian effect. Jemima was the real thing, a granddaughter of the original beauty, but her own beauty had unfortunately gone wrong. Hair grew from the girl's face almost as luxuriantly as it grew from her scalp. Jemima parted her hair in the middle of her face, combed it out sideways over forehead and cheeks and fixed it with a clasp behind her head. She looked like a Chinese dog with a hair curtain over its face. But it was just a matter of becoming accustomed to Jemima. Her hair was silky and fine. She had a small shapely nose and extraordinarily appealing eyes. They seemed to look out from her matted face, appealing to be rescued from her prison of hair. It was these eyes that had summoned the Colonel's finest theatrical instincts to the fore. Jemima was not obviously native to any place on earth. She was a freak. This was her universality. She was no more Circassian than she was Pig Indian. Jemima belonged to the world.

Close-ups so characteristic of Matthew's cinematic style originated with Jemima and the need to show her to the public. The Colonel never forgot his origins in the decorating and upholstery trade. As a salesman you got ahead in the world by paying attention to what your public wanted. Whenever he tried out something new he got into his car with the cans of film and drove around southern California to the towns in the boondocks where they showed movies at the front of the general store. He ran the movie himself, making notes how the public reacted. He could tell from the way the audience was leaning forward and peering at her whenever she appeared on screen that people wanted a better look at this most unusual Indian girl who had rescued Capability. He went back to the lot with instructions to Matthew to come in close on Jemima in at least a couple of scenes every episode. She didn't need to do anything but appeal to the camera with her unquenchable eyes.

In the tenderness her eyes expressed for Capability the public discovered her beauty. The poignancy of seeing that beauty in close-up, thwarted by irredeemable facial hair, reduced millions of moviegoers to tears. Lemon Grass became a name with unfortunate associations beyond anything Pig Indians could have imagined. Hair hysteria swept the country. Fan mail arrived at the Polyscope Motion Picture studio by the sackload, among it thousands of letters with hair-removal recommendations. But there could be no question of removing Jemima's facial hair. Jemima's facial hair was pure gold.

Kirkpatrick exhausted a carton of business envelopes writing the bearded girl into the next two hundred episodes. It was she who would plead with Dom Pedro Felipe to spare Capability's life after the Spaniards torched the White Earth Indian village and put its inhabitants to the sword. It was she, not Grasshopper, who sailed with Capability and the Spanish fleet for Santa Maria de la Antigua, formerly Titumate, the first mainland settlement in the New World. It was she who paid for it, with box-office receipts that were second to none at the height of her fame.

Kirkpatrick went up to Chicago to take a look at the caravels that had been lying moored on Lake Michigan since the World Exposition. I told him how Vasco Nunez de Balboa once built a fleet of wormwood ships on the Gulf of Mexico, had them dismantled by Indians and carried over the mountains of Darien, only to watch them sink like stones in the Sleeping Sea. Russian carpenters in Chicago and the shipping clerks of the Union and Central Pacific railroad, between them substituting for the Indians, dismantled, packaged and transported the caravels all the way down to the disused track where Pawfrey's circus wintered, reassembling them on the beach, and one fine day they were back again, Balboa's ghost ships, riding at anchor in the Pacific Ocean just a couple of hundred yards from the shore.

Where I had sailed north up the coast of Brazil to Titumate, Capability sailed south down the coast of California to the Mexican border town Tijuana. *Castaway* was now a million-dollar business. It went on location with electrically driven cameras on mobile pedestals, miles of cable, a hundred and fifty stock actors and five times as many extras recruited locally in Tijuana, doubling for Santa Maria de la Antigua. Polyscope bought the town, knocked most of it down for the first of the next fifty episodes and built it up again for the last. Kirkpatrick transformed the

Dom Pedro Felipe I had known, the ascetic, God-crazed priest-admiral, into a combination of Long John Silver and Bluebeard who devoured virgins for his breakfast while a captive Lemon Grass looked on in terror.

The intrepid castaway did a deal with the admiral. With a promise to lead the Spaniards to the whereabouts of a fabulous Inca gold hoard known only to him, Capability rescued Lemon Grass from Dom Pedro's clutches. Where the small expeditionary force of the conquistadors had blundered from west to east through the mountains and swamps of the Panama isthmus, an army of thousands marched in disciplined Roman columns from east to west across the peninsula of Baja California four hundred years later, dragging behind them on rollers the refurbished Chicago Exposition caravels with which they would eventually sail the Pacific.

It seemed the Sioux Ghost Dancers had been right. The road out of the past was forked and the same path could never be trod twice. Another life was substituted for mine, another many-branched tree of events for the tree that I had known, and what we call history was neither the one nor the other but an accumulation, a palimpsest of stories laid over stories which had been laid over other stories again and again.

When war broke out in Europe we were filming Dom Pedro's first encounter with an Inca trading vessel in the Sleeping Sea. For Kadar, the designer, I drew a picture of the ocean-going balsa raft with cotton sails, which was built by carpenters on the set. Kirkpatrick was so taken with it that he ordered a dozen more. He wanted a battle between the balsa rafts and Portuguese caravels. Their lombards would begin to demolish the Inca fleet before it was able to manoeuvre and implement the *qu'zoa*, blinding the Portuguese with the rays of the sun reflected in silver mirrors. The sea battle turned out to be difficult to film, so it was moved onto land.

A shallow pit with an area of a square mile was dug in the desert and flooded. Lighting the set posed new problems. Matthew wanted the glitter of the sea. White flats to catch the sunlight and throw it back onto the set were moved into position along the perimeters and overhead wires run across it, enabling muslin diffusers to be drawn over the set and soften the glare at any point the director desired. Kirkpatrick, Matthew and the actors lounged in the shade sipping daiquiris while the technical staff prepared the set.

The subject of the war in Europe came up during the conversation, and the Colonel remarked that unless they put the war on film it was going to remain a phantom. Unless recorded, the war would not have happened. Matthew asked him what he meant, and the Colonel said that it took ten thousand eyes to see a modern battle. There was too much of it for any one person to see. Only batteries of motion picture cameras had ten thousand eyes. You could cross-cut between the images provided by ten thousand cameras and edit a battle into shape. It might be an illusion, but, godammit, at least you saw something. The reality of the battle as a whole was something you didn't see at all. Just for the scrap on this pond, the Colonel said, they were putting in fifty cameras.

All fifty were rolling all the time during over two hundred takes, providing tens of thousands of feet of film. Polyscope had its own processing plant and a projector room to screen the footage on site. The sea glitter Matthew had asked for was there. Light technicians had put it into the pond and given it a mysterious, thrilling quality. The sea shimmered. It seemed to be glowing with the imminent expectation of the appearance of the Inca civilisation for the first time in western history. The balsa rafts with cotton sails hovered like moths with half-closed wings in a sweeping shot of the horizon. Nothing I could remember from my experience of it in life remotely resembled what I was watching on screen.

Kirkpatrick sat in his rocking-chair in the projection room rocking faster than we had ever seen. He was so pleased with the results that the entire crew was given the weekend off before returning to Los Angeles to begin filming the scenes in Tumbez. I sat in the shade with Capability and Kirkpatrick, sipping daiquiris and translating Mexican newspapers. During the last week we had spent shooting the sea battle in the desert a quarter of a million men had died on the Western Front. A phantom, the Colonel said, and a night breeze crept in off the ocean, ruffling the shells hanging over the table with a sound like the splintering of fine porcelain.

The Warping of Capability Straight

In the gospel according to St. Matthew it was the machine heart of the world once more — at bottom just another variation on the same old pump, he declared with something like scorn — expanding and contracting, sucking everything in and spewing it out, whatever could be exposed to the camera's eye, deconstructed by chemical process and put back together, filtering through beams of light to be resurrected as a play of shadows on a screen. It was the same old pendulum stirring in an unquiet universe, the to-and-fro movement, systole and diastole, becoming and unbecoming, the never-ending reconstitution of all things in the perpetual restlessness of their selves. My son-in-law Stanton, about a hundred years before, had invented mass production without knowing it, a system of gears, chains and cog wheels that would co-ordinate the energy coming in at one end of his factory with a product leaving it at the other. In the middle was what Stanton called the energy transformation space, machine heart of the world, at bottom just a pump.

Here now was a difference we had not seen before. Between the motion picture camera and the projector a transformation of time took place, measured in units of five-hundredth parts of a second. This was the exposure time of the moving camera's eye. It blinked sixteen times a second, open to take note of what was happening in front of it for sixteen five-hundredths of a second, or three percent of the time. For ninety-seven percent of the time the camera's eye was not recording what was happening. Yet when a projector presented on screen what the camera saw, it fooled the audience into thinking it was being shown an uninterrupted action. The projector pulled off this trick by reversing what the camera had done. The camera worked in jerky quick-step, a quick wink of the lens during exposure followed by a long period of darkness between exposures. The projector stretched the time flashes the camera had compressed, using rapid movement between frames and a much longer pause with the light passing through the projection lens, allowing plenty of time to let the picture register on the screen. These were the facts behind the magic: a motion picture audience spent three-quarters of a second seeing something that had taken place for only a thirty-second part of a second, or an hour and a quarter watching a five-reel film, recorded in exposures totalling just two minutes and twenty-four seconds.

Matthew knew the details because before he worked with motion picture cameras he had spent years projecting motion picture films in nickelodeons, up to sixteen shows a day. He could explain why the projector had to make up the time the camera had lost. The chemical recording process of a film was much quicker than the picture-processing functions of the human eye and brain. That was why. It wasn't difficult to understand. What Matthew could less accurately gauge was the effect on Capability of a sixteen-shows-a-day diet from the age of six or seven on. He had seen his first movie at four, a passion play filmed on the roof of the Grand Central Building in New York, and had lived in the shadows and flickering nickelodeon lights ever since.

What alternative did Matthew have, with the mother of the son who wasn't his just up and gone one day? He took the kid with him to work. On screen was one place where Capability could see his mother regularly. After she left to join the Mutoscope company in New York it became the only place. Matthew found it hard to gauge say how the boy saw his mother or how he felt about the waif-like types she played on screen. How much of her did he remember from real life? On screen he saw Thelma Louise Stanton weeping, wilting, enduring, always sacrificing herself or being sacrificed by others. The boy may have asked himself: where's the sacrifice for me? He may have had an idea how different she was in real life, cut and dried, hard and clear as the diamond she wore as her talisman. It was difficult to figure out what was going on in Capability's mind after he had seen the same feature ten or a hundred or maybe a thousand times. He had seen them so many times that maybe there was nothing but motion picture junk all twisted up in his head. With a granite solemnity disturbing in a child he sat through the Keystone slapsticks among audiences disabled by laughter. With the same rock-like seriousness he watched his mother's self-effacing shadow flit back and forth across the screen, and maybe he was already thinking to himself: bitch is a fake.

Very early on the duchess remarked there was something about Capability that made her feel he wasn't quite there. She didn't mean he was weak in the head, nor was she referring to the fact that he drank too much, because it was the other way round, not being there was why Capability had a serious drinking problem by the time he was twenty.

Ironically, the daiquiri deluge set in the year the studio moved from the laundry lot to Hollywood, another bone-dry cactus thicket waiting for the desert to take over; so dry that it was forced to appeal to the city of Los Angeles, eight miles away over dusty country roads, to be incorporated in the municipality and qualify for help with its water supply. Rumours wouldn't go away that Scott Chester, the mayor of Hollywood, had been helping the natural shortage along, diverting water onto private properties and making huge profits on real estate deals the moment the community was absorbed by Los Angeles. Scott lost the next election. Indicted on charges of malpractice in office, he was convicted and sent to jail. None of this affected Scott's popularity. People still preferred him to his successor, as a man if not as a mayor, and ever since the purchase of some prime real estate off Sunset Boulevard, when the Polyscope Motion Picture Company had been advised by Mayor Chester to their mutual advantage, he had no more staunch supporter than Colonel Kirkpatrick.

Both men went through life in a tremendous hurry, as if everything they did were subject to a stop-motion camera effect that dramatically condensed the time in which it happened. The weed that took a week to struggle up out of a pavement crack achieved the same result in fifteen seconds of camera time. Scott sentenced to jail for a couple of years? Only yesterday, it seemed. Already we saw him back in town, raising his hat to the ladies on the street and funds in back rooms to finance his re-election campaign. Going into or coming out of jail, there were always short-cuts on the way.

It was the same with the Polyscope studio that became known as Kirkpatrick Town. First there was just one stage in the lot off Sunset Boulevard, then three, then five. Two hundred dressing-rooms surrounded them, with scene docks at either end, housing five hundred sets, an arsenal for thousands of firearms, saddlers, stables, a corral, a power house, a reservoir, a fire brigade and half a dozen standing sets, permanent locations. Among them was Boa Vista, a seventeenth-century town in Pernambuco, complete with colonnades and tiled walks, a house of Misericordia, a Jesuit seminary and an Episcopal palace designed according to my instructions. The set remained unused and was partly demolished before serving as the location of a battle-scarred city on the Western Front. After the war there was a change of mood. The popularity of *Castaway* declined, but even in decline the series remained a money engine and the studio still ran its star like a machine.

Minnie saw through the illusion of Capability being there all the time. Between exposures Capability had been leaking away. Bits and pieces of him had been crumbling away. He was the first Stanton to look prematurely old, reversing a family characteristic which had continued for four generations. Little grains of time, measured in five-hundredths of seconds, fell here and there and everywhere out of the picture of Capability Straight. They added up to big gaps, but the audience didn't see them. Projection mechanisms stretched the picture back to cover the missing bits, dwelling so long on the bits which were there that you didn't notice those that weren't. The screen star was like a tanned hide, stretched and stretched to the point he must tear, and even with ninety-seven percent of him missing we still saw him in what seemed to be one whole piece.

Childhood had disappeared through one of the gaps, but it didn't show. Capability played on camera instead and seemed to be enjoying himself. Sex was another of the bits that had gone missing. About the time he got married, when he was already deep into the daiquiris, he was spending more time in his den in our house than he was in his own. Jemima lay in bed alone at night, waiting for Capability to come home and for her marriage to be consummated. She knew her husband hadn't gone out on the town. It might have been better if he had. He was just over at our place, happily roaming around on all fours, only sometimes drunk, switching points and shunting trains on an electric railroad presented to him by Westinghouse.

Was that natural, Jemima asked Minnie, a grown man playing with trains in the middle of the night and not with his wife? Uninterested in making love to a woman, moved by no intentions more lustful than to comb her hair? Minnie was sure it wasn't. The duchess remained a virgin all her life, but instinctively she knew about these things and was quite sure it wasn't.

When the last instalment of *Castaway* had been filmed the set was closed down. Matthew was released from the contract that had tied him to Polyscope. The Colonel had agreed to produce a film called *Defamation*, starring his old friend Scott Chester, former mayor of Hollywood jailed for malpractice in office. Matthew was invited to direct the film but he declined. Scott's idea, triggered by the reversal of victory and defeat he had seen in a movie of the battle of Wounded Knee, was to play himself in his own version of the events that had cost him his job as mayor. *Defamation* told the story of a man unjustly condemned, fighting against the odds to clear his name. In the movie it turned out that Scott had been framed by an unscrupulous opponent, conveniently now dead, who proved to be guilty of the manipulations he had laid at Scott's door in order to oust him from the office he aspired to himself. Grass had long since grown over the affair. The record was blurred. Always a likeable man, Scott played the innocent version of himself very well, and to most people who saw the movie he was more persuasive innocent than guilty. *Defamation* rehabilitated the former mayor.

In the transformation space between camera and projector the truth, at least as Matthew remembered it, had been turned into a lie. There once was a time, as a young man in Chicago, when the motion picture seemed to Matthew to supply the link between one image and the next, the reassurance that between frames one didn't fall into nothingness but continued within the same film, woke up the next morning inside the same life. Naively he had seen it as a recording device, a phonograph of images. But between the recording of an image and its projection on a screen was the transformation space where the nature of the image changed.

Matthew imagined this space as a factory, at bottom just a pump, sucking images in from the world and pumping them out, but not to the place from which they had come. They constituted a secondary reality, a parallel universe. He imagined Capability on a passage from one place to the other. Capability would be sucked into the camera and travel on a strip of perforated cellulose through periods of brightness interrupted by darkness. This was how Matthew remembered riding on the El through the sweaters' district in Chicago a long time ago on his way home from the Fair. He remembered illuminated windows of sweaters' apartments seen in flashes interrupted by the darkness of the tenement wall. Capability would play Matthew, a director making a film of his own life, searching for the continuity in the flashes, and the darkness, telling the story of the director's own life.

Naturally, for Matthew, the continuity didn't exist. That was what the film was about. But the Colonel shook his head. Had to be a continuity. *That* was what movies were about. Polyscope's business was depressed, however, and the Colonel offered Matthew a cheap lease on the unused lot down by the Ocean View Hotel, if he wanted, so that he could make the film himself. He came over to see Minnie and me, to ask if we were good for a fifty-thousand dollar stake in the film. Minnie wanted to know how the film would end. Matthew said it would end with the director getting lost in the labyrinth between the camera and the projector. He would disappear inside his own film.

Minnie didn't like that and neither did I, though for different reasons. Movies had to have happy ends, Minnie said. That was why people wanted to see them. Matthew told her a happy end was one of the variants the director would be considering when he edited the film of his life, but he would reject it, because among the infinite number of ways images got warped in the transformation space between camera and projector the happy end was the worst warp of all. The more he talked about his project the less Minnie and I liked it, but we advanced him the money nonetheless.

It was the grey world of Prohibition, but the parties that went on at Scott Chester's place were being pioneered in Technicolor, the booze piped up from the beach in a reassuring flow when Scottie turned on the tap, the multi-coloured junk pills and the snow-white heroin handed out free by Beau Peep, an unemployed but always smiling actor in Scottie's entourage, to anyone with a hangover. Hangover was the password. Everyone who took drugs in the industry got started by this charming man. He put the set designer Kadar on the junk. He went up to him and told him he had a hangover and the guy said "I'll fix it for you," and a few years later Kadar was dead.

Eighty percent of the world's movies were being made in Southern California. About as many of the guests at Scottie's parties were movie actors in search of work. Scottie's parties must have rated as the most hilarious get-togethers of the unemployed ever held on earth. They were on camera all the time, flappers single or in pairs who smiled unflinchingly as they paraded up and down the terrace twirling parasols advertising their talents. *We're not just pretty Buddy We can Act Sing & Dance.* One regular at the parties was a Theda Bara type, a sneering, hip-wriggling, cigar-smoking vamp who pioneered T-shirt logos with *Kill any man at fifty yards* in spidery letters across her back. This was not the Colonel's type. The ageing sybarite preferred farm-raised, big-breasted, clean-cut girls whose willing faces spelt out the message *Instantly Available* with no strings attached other than hopes of employment that would disappear the next morning when a servant showed them the door. Scottie's parties belonged in the orbit of that giant body which had formed suddenly out of nothing, with a force of attraction that sucked everything in and spewed it out, whatever could be exposed to the camera's eye, deconstructed by chemical process and put back together, filtering through beams of light to be resurrected as a play of shadows on a screen.

Capability's passage through this party landscape could be plotted by the detritus he left in his wake. He knew the hangover password without ever having to be taught it. He often applied for relief to Beau Peep, the smiling man who fixed hangovers. Capbility led the field in the contest of least appropriate names. This game was popular among the casting agencies. Here, just a few years after the immense success of *Castaway*, was the actor in town least capable of walking in a straight line for more than a few yards whatever the time of day. He was a drunk. He took dope. He was thirty. He was finished. Capability Straight, once a child star. These days when people heard his name mentioned they shook their heads with the kind of funereal satisfaction that in Hollywood passed for sympathy.

The Cellulose House

Matthew kept him locked up in the tower on the Chinese laundry set if he wanted to work with him the next day. Capability begged and threatened and finally wrestled with him until he was so tired he fell asleep in his father's arms. Stone-cold sober on the set in the morning, white-faced, trapped inside a set from which all the inside door handles had been removed, Capability brought to the role of the traveller lost between realities a desperation he could never have played. On the lot they referred to the set as cellulose house. The name stuck and became the title of the film.

The walls, floors, corridors and stairs were all a continuous strip of film, winding like a roller-coaster through a windowless interior representing the inside of a motion picture projector. All these elements were quotations I recognised from Matthew's life. The roller-coaster dated back to the amusements parks of the streetcar companies he had worked for in Chicago.The dark windowless interior was the Madison Street post office coal cellar. The endless loop of film represented Matthew's Pittsburgh years as a projection operator in a nickel-odeon, the endless footage he had cranked to make a living.

Somewhere at the back of the director-cameraman's mind remained a traumatic continuity gap between his lost origins as a Lithuanian immigrant child and the beginnings of his remembered life as a street child living in a coal cellar. It supplied the emotional charge to a merely technical curiosity that never ceased to fascinate him, the discrepancy between the time it took to register an image and the time required to project it. In the story told by Matthew's film, a wanderer between two worlds, like the mermaid in the fairy tale who fell in love with the prince, would pay a high price in an attempt to close that gap. When she left the sea for a life on land, shedding her tail and growing human legs, the mermaid felt each step she took as if she were walking on dagger points. She smiled at the prince she loved while she walked on dagger points, smiling and in agony at the same time.

In Matthew's version of the fairy tale Capability played an Edison-Frankenstein hybrid inventor who fell in love with the movie princess he had created. The princess was played by Thelma Louise Stanton. She never actually appeared on the set in person. The footage was pre-shot and delivered in a can.That was the condition on which Capability agreed to work with his mother. It seemed a freakish idea to have the inventor fall in love with a woman played by his mother. In the event, it gave the film an extraordinary poignancy. Capability was made up to appear a lot older, but even without make-up the son already looked older than the mother. He had a haggard, nightmarish look. She was long since famous as the woman who seemed eternally young.When the inventor took his leave of the world and moved into the cellulose house to live with the princess he found himself separated from her by the different time she inhabited there. The princess was printed into the film strip that unrolled through the roller-coaster house. Her life ran at a different speed from his. While the inventor in his time grew older the princess in hers never changed. He knew she was an illusion, created from exposures lasting only tiny fractions of time that had been stretched inside the cellulose house to make her seem wholly there. So long as she continued to be projected at such a slow speed she was indeed wholly there. Her image splashed languidly like liquid moonlight up and down the walls and stairs and ceilings of the cellulose house, and the mad inventor was happy just to have her around him all the time. Her face shone down on him in his bed like the moon staring in through a window. Her face lit up the floors and walls in all the rooms of the house. She smiled under his feet when he walked up and down the stairs. She went flowing around and over him, his shining talisman, the sun and the moon, watching over him through all his days and nights.

But after a while the inventor could no longer be content with just a celluloid image of the princess. He began to experiment on ways to deconstruct the image and restore her to her original life. Half way through the movie the first title card appeared on screen. "Don't! If you do that, you know that I shall disintegrate!" The inventor ignored the warning. He pulled a lever and brought the moving film to a standstill. For the first time since he arrived in the cellulose house the image of the princess remained fixed, a still picture. In Matthew's film the moving image seemed to have stopped. He shot a photograph of the princess, five times sixteen frames a second or eighty successive images over a period of five seconds. The whole fantastic machinery of cellulose house came to a halt. It was as if the motion picture itself had broken down. The face of the mad inventor froze momentarily in horror. Then he began running up and down the stairs, along the corridors, in and out of the rooms, a slight silhouette seen against a dimly illuminated giant film strip, kneeling and cutting with shears, kneeling and cutting, an excavator of images, a mad miner with a lamp scurrying across a dark coal face. Here and there in the coal face bits of light showed through. As the mad inventor cut the film and piled the frames on the floor, demolishing the cellulose house, light perforated the darkness wherever a frame was removed. Studio backdrop, a white cyclorama representing the sky, began to show through the holes in the house. The cellulose house was dismantled. In his laboratory the mad inventor placed stacks of cellulose frames in the chambers of a transformation machine and pressed a plunger.

Smoke filled the room. The door of the transformation machine opened and out stepped the restored princess, a three-dimensional, lovelier than ever Thelma Louise Stanton. She walked across the room, turning to look back at the inventor before she disappeared from his life. In double exposures she began to disintegrate. Wall became visible through her as she gradually turned transparent. Then she was just a blur, a faint wash outlining the figure of a woman as she walked out of the door and vanished into the light.

Pa Jones

Seven hours through the desert on Highway 91 and only a few miles short of Las Vegas Scott Chester's Studebaker blew up. Minnie had a gig at La Vega Royal and Scott said he'd drop her off on his way to Salt Lake City. Hardly a minute passed before the first car pulled in at the side of the road to ask if he needed help. Scott said all he needed was a tow truck to get the Studebaker into town to a garage where they could fix it. So there we were, right in the middle of the desert for all we could see, with sudden pumps of winds rocking the car and spray-gunning sand at the windshield. Minnie had the two eldest children sitting on her lap, Horatio and Winifred. These were her travelling dolls, allowed along for the ride, while their younger brothers and sisters, all nine of them, had to stay at home. Horatio and Winifred were good. They didn't mind sitting in the desert in a hundred degree heat, waiting for the tow truck to arrive. Minnie told them a story and they were good as gold.

A rasping noise in the front seat accompanied the story. This was Scott rubbing his chin reflectively, goddamned if that wasn't the third car he had seen passing in as many minutes. I sat in the back next to Minnie, wrapped up in coat and scarf and thinking I was now beginning to feel warm enough to take them off. Scrub brush with hundreds of miles of emptiness to blow around in came hurtling at the car as if it had all collected in this car-wide bowling lane out of spite. The wind blew and blew the scrub brush at us and Minnie added another loop to her story because the tow truck still hadn't arrived and I was thinking, strange, in a broken-down car in the middle of nowhere it was the first time I had really felt comfortable that winter. Scott rasped and goddamned away to himself, so absorbed counting the cars with out-of-state license plates passing on the highway he forgot about us in the back. When the tow truck pulled up alongside he wound down the window to tell his rescuer that no less than thirty-two cars had passed in the hour since the car had broken down, how about that, he said jubilantly, winding the window up again, as if the tow truck man had made the trip out from town especially to get that piece of information and now he had got it he could head back.

But for the Studebaker blowing up just south of town Scott would most likely have driven on to Salt Lake City the same day. He changed his mind, said he'd stop over with us at the Adobe Inn on Fremont Street for a couple of days, take in Minnie's show and see himself the town, and that was the last we saw of Scott. We clean forgot about him. A sensational discovery in the lounge of the Adobe Inn put everything else in the shade. This was a cowboy asleep, dead to the world in a rocking-chair to one side of the reception desk, staring with blank eyes into space as if had been shot.

Edgar P. Stanton was the only man in the world who slept with his eyes open, the only person to have been exposed to the biological slow-motion effect of Tahuantin-suyu when rolled up in a quipu as a child. He must have been well into his eighties but looked sixty, on the gaunt side, a little desiccated these days, not a trace of mould, all river damp dried out of him by the desert climate. With no more than a change of focus in his eyes he still came at you unnervingly straight out of sleep, and with an unfamiliar rolling accent said welcome to the Adobe Inn folks Pa Jones at your service 'blige any way.

P was about the only item from Edgar's previous life to have survived into his new incarnation. He registered as P. Jones in the succession of doss houses, roadside inns, jails, hotels or wherever his luck had landed him for ten years after running away from the million-dollar debt he owed syndicates in New York and Chicago. He always travelled in the opposite direction, south-west, south-west, in a straight line that took him all the way through Kansas and Colorado until his pursuers were getting so warm he dipped down to cool off in Mexico for a while. These were very persistent people, he said. They knew they weren't going to get their money back. That made them all the more determined to kill him out of sheer spite. It was south of the border that somebody mistook for an *a* the flourish in the tail of the P he signed in a rooming-house ledger, making Pa Jones of him at a stroke. He adapted a persona to go with the name, grew a beard, cultivated a battered prospector-style look, wore western clothes and learned to speak with a twang. He turned himself into a cranky old guy, watching shrewdly all the while from under the brim of his hat until he reckoned he must have outlived all his enemies and the coast was clear. Pa Jones surfaced in Arizona the year the Titanic went down.

About ten years after the founding of Las Vegas he arrived at the meadows in the middle of the desert. Not much of a place then, arrive wasn't the word, and that suited him fine. The dry climate was great for his rheumatism. The meadows were just a watering hole, a road station for people passing through. He could live there and continue to pass through, doing a little prospecting, without much success, now that he had acquired the Pa Jones role, a little gambling, with even less, and a little marrying, which had worked out best of all. Pa Jones, as I was asked to call him now and for the rest of his new life, drove me a couple of blocks to show me home, an improbable mock-Tudor bungalow housing his wife, a half-Norwegian half-Paiute woman with strong arms, a bright smile and three brawling children, swinging carousel-like on the hem of her skirt as she stood out in the yard pegging washing to what looked like a movie backdrop of snow-capped mountains against a hard blue sky.

This heat suits me, I said, I shall come and live in Las Vegas. Nobody lives here, Pa Jones said as we drove back up Fremont Street. He waved an arm at two-storey shacks with false fronts lining a covered sidewalk. To me it didn't look in any way different from the western set in Kirkpatrick Town. Men with grizzled beards, perpetual sunburns, sweaty underarms and silver stirrups, rather like Pa Jones in fact, walked, lounged and talked in the shade. He said they were all just resting up here on their way through. All the people here were on their way to some place else, which was why it was only natural the highway from Los Angeles to Salt Lake City had been routed through this town, a town pretending to be a town for the sake of the people who were passing through. Las Vegas stuck around only so long as people continued to break their journey here. It would go with them when they left.

I wondered how comfortable a three-storey brick structure like the

Adobe Inn would feel about that, and Pa Jones laughed. Welcome to collapsible America. Few years back the Adobe Inn had been just that, he said, an adobe dwelling that had a false front and a couple of storeys tacked onto it so that it qualified as a hotel to comply with the liquor laws. It was a saloon disguised as a hotel. You could dismantle it and pack it up in a few days and if need be take it with you. The highway was just an asphalt version of its forerunners, the wagon trail and railroad lines that had moved people west. Tollhouses, livery stables, train stations, taverns, hotels and gas stations lining the road sprung up to piggy-back travellers on their way to someplace else. Pa Jones knew those travellers. They were fugitives like himself. The towns out here were no more than parking bays on the road, cars the tents of the new nomads. The road was where they were headed, just pushing the white line, as Pa Jones said.

La Vega Royal

Tony Galiotti and Baby Shoes Beretta remembered the duchess from way back in Naples. She had been in her early twenties then, an extraordinary midget presence with an extraordinary vocal organ, scattering Puccini arias from a balcony overlooking the market place. No greater honour for these admirers of the lady they deferred to as Puccini's minimalist donna than to have her sing for them at the gala opening of La Vega Royal. Only — twice the age she had been then, when she sang in Naples, the donna's voice was now no longer what it was. Dark spots lurked in the silvery moonlight where the sublime voice could no longer reach, cracks opened up in its once perfect melodious smoothness. Age, said Minnie with a sigh. These days she stood on a table and sang duets with a six-foot mezzo soprano beside her who hailed from Hannibal, Missouri, a visual *frisson* which helped to distract from the purely musical aspect of the performance. In the tricky passages, where the duchess was apt to go under, the mezzo provided the soprano with a sonorous background in which she could safely disappear. The thin light patter of her voice still reminded me of tiptoed footsteps in the moonlight. Accompanied by the booming organ of a more than full-grown woman from Hannibal, Missouri, her staccato sprinkling of notes sounded like a toy piano in concert with a grand.

The men who owned La Vega Royal were all of East Coast Jewish or Italian origin. The combination of Gus and Moe Greenspun, Solly Rosenberg, Tony Galiotti and Baby Shoes Beretta, with the way they looked and the clothes they wore — dark men, glossy men, vibrant and smiling, muscled dandies in pin-striped suits who came from the streets and operated in a town that still had hardly any — left an unmistakable, a quite overwhelming impression. They always moved in a pack, their star-sapphire pinkie rings flashing at the chandeliers, driving half a block in a convoy of black Cadillacs with swamp-coolers to take a soda at the State Cafe on Fremont Street. There they parked their cars next to the horses at the down-town hitching posts and had the waiter bring the sodas out to them, hissing at the horses to discourage them from dropping manure on their immaculately shined fenders. I liked to imagine their pack life by day continuing into the night, sleeping side by side in a giant five-bed fixture, ten hands resting on the coverlet, unsleeping star-sapphire pinkie rings their sentries, watchful eyes reflecting beams of neon light from the sign outside the window and glittering with just a suggestion of menace in the slumberous dawn light. This was the time of day when someone might invite you to step outside and take a cab.

La Vega Royal was the first sign to print a name on the sky a couple of miles outside the city limits on Route 91. The name cocked a snook at the club's maligners and sneerers who were watching from downtown. In flowing neon across an empty desert night the sign must have seemed to be a fata morgana to car drivers riding in to Las Vegas from the south, some meteorological freak, tangled lightning lashed to a hundred-foot pole breathing dragon letters of fire sideways into the night. A night, a club, nothing else: a night-club called La Vega Royal, maybe catering for a clientele of coyotes and kangaroo rats within a radius of two hundred miles. Downtown at the re-opened Arizona Club, the Northern Club, the Golden Camel, where men in sweat-lined hats still spat on the sawdust floors, there was no end of jokes about these eastern dudes who paid a couple of hundred dollars for a few acres of sand and a thousand times that amount to put up some dude fantasy in marble and mahogany which any fool knew would be bankrupt in a month.

Within a month of the purchase of the night-club site the US government coincidentally approved the building of the Hoover Dam. Even prospectors used to sweltering in hundred and twenty degree heat could work out that it wouldn't be long before the largest building site in the western hemisphere started pumping out plenty of cheap electricity, enough to keep cool a city ten or twenty times as big as it was now and at whatever heat the desert furnace chose to fry it. The Dam would put thousands of single men down in the desert within drinking, whoring and gambling distance of the road station on the old Mormon trail. Planners, engineers and constructors would be spending their weekends in town and flying their families down for vacations. This was a whole new thing, a whole new kind of customer. All of a sudden the dude night-club in the desert was looking like a working proposition. Somebody had friends somewhere. It looked like pretty good timing.

Downtown wasn't invited to the party. Downtown was unwashed, didn't have the right attitude, didn't have the right clothes. The swells rolling in at dusk from the Los Angeles highway and heading back again at dawn wore tuxedos and low-cut gowns with diamond tiaras. Guests flew in from Chicago and New York to a brand-new airport north of town. They drove right through town without stopping, staying in the hotel on top of the night-club where they house-warmed sixty brand-new rooms with carpets on the floors, and flew back again the following day. They entered the night-club in the middle of the desert through a foyer with a white marble floor. Arched entrances opened out on one side into the ball room where the duchess sang, on the other into the casino, a well-ventilated, high-ceilinged room festooned with Lady Luck frescoes reminiscent of fleshy Neapolitan cinquecento madonnas. Door handles, light fixtures, all the metallic decorative panel work set into the walls, was executed in gold and silver leaf. It was crass. It was gorgeous. It was a miracle merely for being where it was.

On a roof-terrace patio with swamp-coolers concealed behind the palm trees, Minnie and I sat looking out over a vista of the Bay of Naples with Etna smouldering in the background. It had been done by the set designer who painted the backdrop of the Andes for the Tumbez scenes in *Castaway*. Many old acquaintances were there, including Kirkpatrick, Scott Chester and his eternally smiling sidekick, Beau Peep, the man with the candies who fixed people's hangovers. Solly Rosenberg had soon button-holed him. Together they disappeared into the thickets surrounding the back entrance to the club office. Tony Galiotti registered this with a frown and went in pursuit. Solly's habit of shooting up in the counting room was becoming a liability. Every half hour or so Baby Shoes came dancing by to bandy with Minnie. He stood behind her and she seized his hand when Etna unexpectedly exploded with a bang. Fireworks puffed and shimmered over the painted backdrop of the Bay of Naples. It was a marvellous illusion. The guests whooped and stood up to applaud. The top of the mountain had been blasted away, and there was suddenly a hole in the wall with nothing between us and the desert outside where a transparent nail-clipping of a moon swam somewhat unrealistically in the sky as the sun burned up over the mountains.

Queen of Hearts

I belonged in the desert, along with the stones and the birds that hung still with spread wings in the high skies and the cold-blooded creatures that gaped on the ground. Sinews jutted out like ridges along my back and up my neck, taut strands of muscle under my chin, forming deep fleshy caverns in the hollows of my throat. The furrows across my brow had become indelibly corrugated. I was a corrugated, sinewy old lizard with a hardening skin condition more or less all over my body, notably on my spine, my feet and hands. These days I saw the world rather dimly through milky irises indistinguishable from the whites of my eyes. Like all cold-blooded creatures I needed to lie motionless in the sun every day and absorb the heat I required for life. I had my lounge chair by the pool on the roof terrace of the Adobe Inn where I would lie gaping and unblinking like a lizard during the middle of the day when no one was around. Towel, sun glasses, sun lotion, an ice-box and a glass with a straw, all the sun-worshipper's equipment lay on the table at my side, but I had no use for any of them. I was there to warm the corpse of my life. Just don't understand how you can take that heat, Mr Straight, the young ladies would say who occasionally came up for a dip in the afternoon. Even with my bathrobe on I took care not to expose myself to their sight for too long. The arrival of the first guest on the roof each afternoon was the signal for me to withdraw.

In all the years I lived together with the duchess I was never given proof that she took off her clothes. I saw her in various cocoons of night wear, all of them as inescapable from as the hide-bound and buttoned-up restrainers which passed for the clothes she wore by day. The duchess was born and bred a late Victorian and would follow that fashion, I was quite sure, until the day she died. Like many of her colleagues I had got to know in Pawfrey's travelling exhibition, the duchess either harboured in herself more contradictions than I had noticed among ordinary people or those contradictions were more violently juxtaposed within such a small person. She was a prudish exhibitionist, a bawdy moralist, a coquettish spinster, a parsimonious spendthrift. At the bottom of all the ambivalences of her insecure life the duchess was a child woman.

In the wake of Horatio and Winifred came nine more dolls, with their dolls' house and garden, their wardrobe and their diet, carefully packed and crated for the seven-hour drive in the truck that arrived with the things she considered essential for our longer stay in Las Vegas. Not a single article of mine or hers were among them. All the essential things were the children's. I had a notion Minnie and I were in retirement these days. That and the heat were the reasons why it had seemed not a bad idea to settle in Vegas, free of all the buzz that had begun to jar on me in Hollywood, movies that flopped and wiped out half of our savings, a great-great-grandson who played trains round the house all night and was now into his fifth year of intensive psychiatric care. But now we were back in the family business, running a home out of the Adobe Inn for eleven children.

I went down to talk things over with Pa Jones. Since we were planning to be long term residents we got special rates. We took a second room for the children. Pa Jones entered into the spirit of things. He arranged for a caterer a block down on Fremont Street to deliver eleven miniature lunch portions each day at a reasonable price. His eldest daughter was happy to come and play with the dolls, as she understood it, or baby-sit, as the duchess did, whenever we planned a night out. A new mayor in town, irritated by the custom attracted to the new resorts outside the city limits, tax revenues lost to Vegas, was beefing up its western image in order to attract tourists. Recently I had heard gunfire down in Fremont Street. Looking out of the window, I saw a man lying on the ground, another standing with revolvers still drawn. Bystanders testified to the sheriff that the survivor had been challenged by the dead gun-fighter and shot back in self-defence. In the competition for tourist revenues such stunts were becoming common. Minnie's fantasies were nothing unusual in this town.

Las Vegas was perfect for the duchess, the duchess was perfect for Las Vegas. The residents appreciated her midget status, her mock-noble title, her fashions half a century out of date. They deferred to her illusions, her secret imagination, because almost everyone, like Pa Jones, secretly inhabited their own. No one questioned that Minnie's dolls were her children, no more than that she was two foot five and three-quarter inches tall. The miniature duchess represented a world in which make-believe became true.

With the children's move to their own room at the Adobe Inn I ceased to be merely a spectator of their proxy life in Minnie's imagination. They became a presence in which I was physically involved. This began one night when Minnie woke me and asked me to go next door because the children were making such a noise. You could go and tell them a story, she suggested, until they go back to sleep. What was there to say to that? Dutifully I got up and pushed open the door to the adjoining room. A night light was already on. Six girls lay in one bed, five boys in the other, hands resting symmetrically on the coverlet, rather as I imagined Gus, Moe, Solly, Tony and Baby Shoes, frozen in their nocturnal chorus-line routine inside their gangland tap-dance bed. Well, queried the duchess next door. Things had instantly quietened down, I said. A show of force had been enough. This was not a happy choice of words. I heard Minnie sniff. There was a pause. You could tell them a story all the same, she said.

She was a woman who had neither sex nor marriage nor children, a child woman who played at all these roles by make-believe, still a woman, scaled down to tiny dimensions, not at all reduced in the stature of her desires. She had acquired her last doll in her mid-thirties, accepted she was past the doll-acquiring age when the twins died of tuberculosis ten years later. She knew there could be no replacements for dolls that got broken. She mourned their passing with a finality that to me was not perceptibly different from the way Littlewood had mourned John in Chicago or Mijou the daughters she lost to yellow fever in New Orleans. The great serpent-river in which all creation flowed watered the meadows in the Nevada desert no less than the Pig Indian igaripé in the rain forest, the same mourners stood on the same banks with the same feelings in their hearts.

Only weeks after the twins had been put away in the old Mormon burial ground on Clark Street a third and a fourth child died of asphyxiation in their sleep, seizures that had literally shaken them to tatters. I began to spend more than usually sleepless nights, watching over Minnie's unpredictable imagination, the wayward, violent passage my little woman was now in, haunted by lurking frenzies which might drive her to get up in the night and kill what was dearer to her than her own life. She mourned herself in these children of whom she bereft herself, her own passage in theirs, punished herself in their deaths and through them groped after a miracle of resurrection, the will to believe she could triumph over death.

What agonies I watched over my little woman's ageing, mundane process all the world went through! How is my figure these days, she would ask, taking a few turns up and down the desk. Trim as it had been in her twenties. It was true, and she needed to hear it. She wanted to hear it several times a day. She bounced back, announced a new concert series, finding her pitch, she said, for a couple of weeks at La Vega Royal before departing for the East Coast. She practised her arpeggios in the bathroom and light overlaid light. Back in the bedroom, however, I noticed less fluidity in her voice than when she sang at the club opening less than a year back. Dryness had crept into her music. If Baby Shoes heard it, he concealed it behind his smile. She was engaged for three weeks, and then her agent planned engagements in Pittsburgh and Philadelphia before taking Boston and New York by storm. But before she was through even the first week of the night-club gig her voice fell out of the sky. Her vocal chords could no longer sustain its flight. The flawlessness cracked. All that was left of her most famous tribute were mice with bloodstained paws crawling through a field of broken glass.

During the night after this disaster, at some unguarded moment when I was asleep, mass murder was carried out in the children's room. In the morning I went in to find six dismembered corpses of dolls, stabbed with scissors, seams ripped open and stuffing scattered, arms and legs all over the floor. By an oversight Horatio survived in a cupboard, where he had been locked up overnight as a punishment for being insolent.

Minnie lay curled up under the bed-side table for a week, didn't move or speak, just lay in my arms as light as cushions when I carried her around the room, tight-lipped and dry-eyed until she found Horatio in the cupboard and at last released herself in a torrent of tears. They weren't really children, after all, she said, although I used to pretend they were. They were. They were just, you see. They were just dolls.

In the aftermath of the murdered dolls, the make-believe children disowned, Minnie buried the child woman and reinvented herself, changed her clothes, her style, her century. I shall cut off my hair, too, she announced, and have it bobbed, but before I do so I shall have my portrait painted, something for you to remember me by, the woman that I once was. She wanted it to be a nude portrait. Whether she succumbed to this long-standing request of her admirer Baby Shoes for money or vanity or as an expression of her new-found freedom it was impossible to say. A professional woman from the day she was midget-born, a trooper who had always pulled her weight, the duchess was well aware of the precarious state of our finances after losing half our savings in support of Matthew's *Cellulose House*. The twenty-five thousand dollars Baby Shoes was offering for her portrait to hang in the club entrance seemed an enormous sum to us at the time. But the duchess also knew, and only she knew, just how much there was to the little she had to show off. Smallness, childlessness, the lessness altogether of her physical presence on earth, had preserved the duchess at forty-five with a perfect miniature of a body barely different from what it had been at twenty.

Lorenzo, an Italian movie set painter who had succeeded Kadar after he had killed himself with drugs, flew in from Los Angeles to paint the portrait. Sittings took place in a penthouse apartment of La Vega Royal. The skylight brought in a white brilliance of desert light that supercharged the whiteness of the duchess's bare body with the whiteness of seashore bleached shell, an altogether deathlike pallor, breathtakingly set off by the tender pinkness of her nipples, the rich redness of her lips, the storm-brewing blackness of soon to be bobbed hair that reached down to her hips. Nakedness released it like a trapped bird, the miraculous flight of a beauty that had remained grounded until now.

The painter portrayed his subject reclining on a sofa viewed from overhead. With one hand on her stomach, the other resting nearby on her thigh, the duchess looked as if she would have preferred to cover her sex had the painter not persuaded her otherwise. This woman in two minds, to show and not to show, was perfectly caught by Lorenzo. The pièce de résistance, in an engagingly literal sense, was an amazingly luxuriant triangle of dark pubic hair. This was a bush beyond belief, almost surreal, prompting associations in the painter's mind, as he admitted to me, of the head of a Negro closeted between the duchess's thighs. Here was a declaration of sex so subversive it took us all aback. Everything surrounding it was restrained, suggesting modesty, even primness. But this centre-portrait pussy where all lines seemed to gravitate leapt out of the picture right at the viewer, arched its back and rubbed itself up against his legs.

Minnie and I chose not to attend the official unveiling of the picture that in future would always hang at the entrance to La Vega Royal. Later she did agree to officiate as the club muse, however, when, as a homage to the painting which was attracting so many visitors, La Vega Royal was renamed the Queen of Hearts. The naked lady became famous far beyond Las Vegas, due to a deck of cards on which she was featured as the Queen of Hearts; not bad for a duchess, she liked to boast. She must have guessed the sort of milieu in which her life as a playing card celebrity would be spent, in sweaty palms, pawed, pinched, liquor-stained, leered at, slammed down on tables or left crumpled on saw-dust floors and swept out with the night's trash. She guessed it and whatever she thought about it she kept to herself. After a lifetime of being stared at the duchess could will onto her face an unfathomable expressionlessness. But possibly she saw her playing card incarnation as the apotheosis of her career as a midget, a miniature accommodated in miniature, a woman for exhibit, what more natural than to expose herself, a naked queen, surrendering her last stitch to the public, to whom alone she felt she had always truly belonged, before finally bowing out.

The Last Frontier

Scott Chester, sitting smoking in his blown-up Studebaker counting out-of-state cars passing on Route 91 while waiting for the tow truck to arrive, was a man having a vision. This was still before the projected Hoover Dam, or Boulder Dam as it was then called, had been built. Some boot-leggers to the carriage trade whose paths he had crossed back in LA bought into a chunk of desert at the intersection of Fremont and Charleston to put up a night-club called La Vega Royal — something of an annoyance to Scott Chester, who found the price of desert outside the city limits had risen by $50 an acre six months later. It seemed the boot-leggers had hired people to count cars too. Scottie moved just a bit further away from the city limits, bought fifty acres for $150 an acre and hired the LA firm that had built similar properties for him in Fresno and Sacramento to design a motor hotel which featured a settlement of the Old West combined with a ranch-like Spanish mission motif. By the time The Last Frontier, as Scottie wanted his vision to be called, lit up its hun-dred and fifty foot cow-horn neon sign in the desert night the Boulder Dam had finally been built and the number of cars coming in on Highway 91 during any twenty-four hours already averaged over a thousand.

This was the vision: you didn't count people, you counted cars. It was cars that counted. They had their feedings habits that needed to be catered for, so where the stable used to be you now put the gas station, and you gave them a large forecourt with acres of space where they could be dumped for the night. The vision of the world was the view through the windshield of a car. Maybe as far as fifty miles away, depending on the weather, the windshield framed a small atmospheric disturbance on the horizon. Twenty to ten miles in it became apparent as a man-made source of light. At this distance people with good eye-sight thought they could make out a pair of illuminated horns, and someone sitting in the back who was a reader of life-style magazines and a diviner of signs would say Yep, Last Frontier coming up. And the cars pulled in, hauled in as if on mag-netic rails.

Everything at The Last Frontier was a quotation, a nod of the head acknowledging once famous, since forgotten western icons. The bar was the original from the Arizona Club, the first gambling establishment worthy of the name in Las Vegas around the turn of the century. Swing-doors to the bar area were done in bevelled glass with inlay silver fittings. In its time the bar's owner Jim McIntosh claimed it was the longest in the world. Yard for yard it must also have been the most expensive, costing $20,000 even back then. The casino boasted log beam trusses, palisander panelling, fringed leather drapes and Navajo artwork. Spindle legs on the craps tables and redwood trusses inlaid with Paiute designs brought a dignity of tradition, as Scottie saw it, to the ephemeral business of gambling. Above the main pit hung a circular structure made of coiled sticks and switches and leather thongs, concentric circles that moved out like ripples, resembling a spider's web, a Paiute dream-catcher streamlined by interior designers but still close enough to the original for the movie star Thelma Louise Stanton, in town for her fifth divorce, to look up and give an inexplicable scream of terror when she recognised what it was.

That must have been around ten o'clock in the evening. The duchess and I did our last walkabout at midnight, so I missed Capability's mother by only a couple of hours. We heard she had left town immediately. Scott Chester, the permanently sun-tanned, ever-youthful owner-manager of the Last Frontier, came over from his office at once to find out what the hell had happened to give offence to the celebrity, but she was already gone, and with her the answer to his question. She just didn't like it, said Katz, the casino manager. What didn't she like, demanded his employer. The Indian art stuff, said Katz with an upward jerk of his chin. It spooked her. So why the hell didn't you take it down, snarled Scott. Katz gave a shrug and his boss stormed out. The next morning the dream-catcher was gone.

Mr Chester was also the sheriff of Last Frontier Town, and in the occasional gunfights that were part of the show it was always the other guy who went down. These days you called him Scott. It was no longer Scottie, not even to his old Hollywood acquaintances. What he said when he hired us was: Paul, why don't you and the duchess come and settle in the Last Frontier Town at my expense? He would provide us with a downscaled, midget-sized residence in rolling green golf country with whatever amenities we cared to name plus a salary of fifteen hundred dollars a week. In exchange we agreed to wear the Old West costumes that went with the Last Frontier theme and show ourselves around the location from time to time. He was in effect paying us, as Minnie said, to live.

All his entourage was small. The casino manager Katz, Little Beau Peep, the unemployed actor who was Scott's boyfriend — people with whom Scott had intimate dealings were smaller than he was or they weren't hired. The logical extension of this preference was the particularly soft spot he had for midgets. There was no call for Old West midgets in the Last Frontier Town, not on historical grounds. Scott put us in because he liked having little people around.

We lived in a western town as all western towns had looked in the decades between the Civil War and the turn of the century, with a traditional Main Street, sidewalks and storefronts and nothing else at either end for the next hundred miles. In fact it looked pretty much as downtown Las Vegas might have looked half a century ago, even incorporated parts of it, like the remains of the Mormon fort, an original whorehouse on Block 16, the Union Station at the head of Fremont Street which Scott had dismantled board by board and reassembled on the site of Last Frontier Town ten miles south on Route 91. Original cars on the Topeka-Santa Fe run, including such attractions as the armoured car containing a crank-operated multi-barrel machine gun of Civil War vintage with which Lucky Chinee Lee had killed five bandits in six seconds, departed twice daily from Union Station on a tour of the Last Frontier landscape. There were visits to a mine, an Indian village, a Joss house for the Chinese labourers who had worked on the railroad, ending with guaranteed bloodshed during a hold-up at Dead Man's Creek.

As for the extras on the set of Last Frontier Town — no one counted them, they kept coming and going and there were always so many of them. They lived in shanty towns on the perimeters of the site, Hoovervilles, they were called, because when the Hoover Dam was being built they came in search of work. Hoover Dam had been completed long ago, but there were still people in shanty towns in search of work, fringe people collected all along the rim of a geological fault known as the Great Depression.

They were going to give the people in the shanty towns a new deal, but to my knowledge they never did. There was a whiff of magnesium in the air which kept the population fluctuating throughout those years, some giving up on old hopes and others coming in on new ones, and suddenly there were boom times, because of the magnesium ore being mined in the desert, top priority, top pay, because magnesium mining was a war related industry and in war you didn't count the cost. You could tell there was a war on by all the money that was being brought into the whorehouses and poker dives on Block 16, fully licensed working ventures back in business in Last Frontier Town just like they had been in Las Vegas a few miles down the road and half a century before.

There was no way Sheriff Chester would beat the shanty towns on the other side of the fence around Last Frontier Town, so he joined them, putting them on the payroll and including them as attractions on the railway tour. By the time tourists started asking questions about the shanty towns, like why people were living in these miserable places and what had brought them out to the desert in the first place, Hoovervilles were sufficiently far away to qualify in the same historical department as mining families in Conestoga wagons and Chinese railroad labourers in Joss houses. Tour guides no longer waited for folks to ask what theme these carefully preserved hovels represented. And here we have Hoovervilles, they announced, whose theme was the immigrant labourer pushing into new territories in search of work as he had done throughout American history.

Scratched and erased, makeshift communities suspended from time cropped up on the shore, came and went with the flotsam disgorged and retracted by the sea, the bareback Indian riders on ponies with soft hooves, castaways of life from the far side of the continent, the rims of their hats thick with brine, their garments sun-bleached, dazed from the seemingly endless journey, the wagon-stopping, brain-jolting halt when they came up smack against the ocean. It all came to an end here. This was the border finalising emptiness. It stopped travellers in their tracks. Nothing happened. No more place. Lean-to houses creaked on shifting foundations. Wind blew through shadows. Sand drifted across the porch and buried the rocking-chair runners, slowing down the old man's rocking sleep until he reached a complete standstill and woke up with a start. At the pool side in rolling green golf country I gaped and dreamed I had been here before. Here was the watershed. Here the roll-back began, on this desert shore I found the flood brought things back I had already seen before. There had been an ocean in this desert, long, long ago, and on the rise and fall of its invisible tides the flotsam of previous civilisations came and went with a never-ending ebb and flow.

A Cab for Mr Straight

Nobody died in Las Vegas. They made a point of not doing so. They took a cab, like Solly Rosenberg, when he was out of town on a visit to LA. For staff members at the Last Frontier and Last Frontier Town, not dying in Las Vegas was specified by contract and you were in breach if you did. There were fake deaths, two or three a week, the result of encounters between gunfighters claiming to be the faster draw, but that was to be expected in a western town. They were our colleagues in Last Frontier Town, unemployed actors, former stunt men with working schedules of mowing lawns and painting woodwork between interludes of gunplay. They waved to us when Minnie pushed me round town in a home-crafted wheelchair, an antique contraption we had built according to the design I came across in a home self-help book that pre-dated the Civil War. Great idea, great idea, beamed Scott Chester with approval when he saw us trundling out with me in this Heath Robinson run-around pushed by the duchess. Our antique wheelchair lent a distinctive, wholly authentic note to the ambiente of Last Frontier Town. That was our job, to be the town's original old folks. Scott believed the wheelchair was a new feature in the act. We didn't tell him morphium was part of the act, too, and arthritis that had stopped me dead in my tracks. I wasn't even able to stand without crutches. But I was paid to impersonate old age, not to live it, and these were unappetising, visitor-unfriendly attributes of the old folks' role which Scott wouldn't have liked. He'd have stopped paying us to live in Last Frontier Town.

We had lived so long with it, inside it, surrounded by it not just here in Las Vegas but in Hollywood and at the Santa Monica railway siding, in fact all the way back to Pawfrey's Dream Factory at the Chicago Exposition, that we had become used to it, Stanton's secondary reality with its Over and Over Again effects of reproduced life, we had aided and abetted it and forgotten we were accomplices, forgotten it was there, the false bottom in the suitcase out of which we had been living for the last half century. My irreversible shrinking process, dehydration, arthritis, pain — they belonged to a primary reality with which I had gradually lost touch. The duchess and I talked about this late at night when the floodlighting was out and the last tourists gone. She was so used to the midget view of the world that she had difficulty with what I called ordinary life.

So where is it, Paul, she would say, this ordinary life of yours — who are you to tell me about ordinary life? I told her I no longer felt comfortable here. I felt like an impostor. Was that a right state of affairs, that someone genuinely handicapped felt he was committing a fraud whenever he was out in a wheelchair? Minnie came and put her head in my lap. For better or for worse it *is* the suitcase we have lived out of for the last fifty years, she said, as I stroked her hair in silence. Did I really want to move again? And where? And what made me think it would be so easy to make the passage, even, with a record like mine, to make it at all?

It wasn't that I was telling Minnie I felt ready to die. I wanted to let go, to be disembodied, but that didn't mean I wanted to die. I wanted to be shot of all the stuff, the clutter that accompanied life. I wanted to hold Minnie's hand, my sole cable to life, and watch it undulating behind me as I drifted around in space, pumped by the same blood that flowed in her veins, echo of her heartbeat, in orbit round her planet. Down to two foot eleven inches now, living in a room hung with wet towels, providing the air I breathed with the moisture I needed no less than air to keep me alive, all I wanted was to continue to the vanishing point at the end of my passage, becoming smaller and smaller until I dwindled to nothingness. I could see this parabola like a neon rainbow in the Las Vegas night sky, an arc suspended in emptiness, emerging out of nothing, re-entering nothing, a passage of light in-between.

In Stanton's secondary reality that had come into being at the Last Frontier I no longer felt sure of my footing. I kept on falling through the apparently firm surface of the here and now inhabited by Minnie. In the dark room hung with wet towels in the midget house, surrounded by a golf course in a desert, I was having trouble finding my bearings. I lived in a cellulose house where the wallpaper was changing all the time. I couldn't say with certainty if I was in a corner of the kitchen in Zarate's house, the admiral's cabin on board the *Sao Cristobal*, my hammock in the malocca, the car in the railway siding at Santa Monica, or where. The sea sucked at my feet and they sunk into the sand as the tide flowed back into the desert, flooding the present with inexplicable marine deposits, coral and sea shells in which I heard the past.

363

These days I was wary of Hooverville. We went on the tour, twice daily, at Sheriff Chester's particular request, in order to lend colour to the outing. But in a landscape whose appearance was quite as likely to change as the wallpaper in cellulose house the inhabitants of Hooverville were also no longer to be reckoned with. Where, for instance, had all the trees gone that had once grown in this desert?

Other days I would see them, the trees in the park around the big house, spreading their shade over the courtyard and the mill house, the refinery, the distillery, with a view of plantations beyond where Negroes slashed cane from dawn to dark. Sometimes this sight was accompanied by a long noise of masses of people on the move, like cattle, and I knew the theme must be back of the yards in Chicago, a long drawn out conveyor belt of motion shuddering between places of work and places of sleep, clattering down a corridor between one dark room and another, human energies, sweat, muscle, always straining hope that were bundled like bright filaments, passed through spools and transformed into products, until the worker had been worn out and was thrown away. These were travellers, as Pa Jones said, just pushing the white line and passing through, lives that went cheaply, anonymously, extras on the lot making up the history that counted, the grand projects so quickly forgotten, the mass charges of renewable humanity, wave after wave that went down, followed by replacements that surged back up, these days with an actors' union card, as Minnie reminded me, lunch breaks in mid-battle, welfare benefits to puff them through the doldrums when struck off the studio payroll.

Come the end of the war and the US government annected the land adjacent to Last Frontier Town for troop demobilisation, put up their own Hoovervilles, khaki tents inhabited by khaki warriors who had seen real action all across the Sleeping Sea from Midway to Okinawa. Some of these soldiers took the railroad ride around Last Frontier Town and grinned when they saw our gunfighters. Throughout the hold-up at Dead Man Creek they sniggered and said "Bo!" to the bandits. When the tour guide showed them a crank-operated multi-barrel machine gun and told them how Lucky Chinee Lee had killed six bandits in five seconds with this weapon they told the tour guide about the weapon that had erased a whole town in just a few seconds more. Fire one time, boom! Fire two time, boom boom! End of war. We should stick around and see for ourselves, because boys from the Nellis Air Force Base would be dropping more of these big firework sticks on test sites in the Nevada desert. And they would be in ringside seats themselves, official observers, battened down in trenches right by the blast, courtesy of the US Air Force. Scott Chester was the first man to promote the idea of holding a fireworks party for viewing one of these atomic events from the roof terraces of the Last Frontier motel. The whole town was invited.

The fireworks party coincided with Halloween. This was still Capability's favourite time of year, masking, merriment, homicidal pranks that could slip through as seasonally legitimised lunacy. In his early fifties, with a ravaged face turned inside out, lobotomised to let out the night-mares that had rampaged through his head, Capability looked like a mix-through of all the characters ever imagined by Edgar Allen Poe. Matthew accompanied him, setting up a projector and a screen behind the buffet in the ball room on which a reel of film with greetings from the stars ran end-lessly all night long. Thelma Louise Stanton, a shimmering mirage of age-less beauty I had yet to meet in real life, wished us all a great party and regretted she couldn't be with us for the occasion. The Colonel was there, in a chrome wheel-chair pushed by a starlet, dressed up as a nurse in a see-through white uniform with a jaunty cap. When he spotted me in my Old West contraption he rolled over for a whisper. Age had taken him all fifteen rounds in the vanity ring before sending him slam-jawed into retirement, lopsided after a stroke, still groping with lecherous hands, a mottled, trembling, toothless, gaping old lizard like myself. The old magi-cian confided obscenities in a barely audible whisper, complimenting the duchess, cranking out a tirade against his old friend Scott Chester before he ran out of breath and wheezed shut.

To the duchess Baby Shoes said afterwards: sheriff of Last Frontier Town, first real estate developer to get out there and really mine the Strip when it was just a piece of asphalt with a night-club and two gas stations, a man like that makes enemies as fast as he makes money. Envy, you see, greed. Greed aroused, unsatisfied: dangerous. Somebody's got what you haven't, but want. There are plenty of people who might want to kill a man like that. Which was where Hiram K. Myers entered the picture, as the *Las Vegas Sun* leader writer speculated in an editorial headlined *Who shot the sheriff of Last Frontier Town?*

This was something of an overstatement. Mr Myers didn't enter anything, pictures least of all. Rumours nonetheless persisted that an avatar of Hiram K. Myers had been spirited into town and was holed up right there under the parabola I had seen in the sky, the Neon Rainbow. This man was a friend of presidents and secretaries of state and was alleged to have made out of the war only slightly less than the government had spent on it. He had loose cash to acquire a town. He wanted to plough that Old West trash back into the ground and build a last frontier in concrete towers right out into the desert, a Hiram K. Myers Wall, an Iron Curtain all the way across the state of Nevada, to keep germs and barbarians from contaminating civilisation. He wanted to build himself a monument on the planet. But old Scott Chester refused to sell.

The invitation was for a masked Halloween ball, which for employees of The Last Frontier meant business as usual in workaday Old West outfits. The same went for representatives of a whole new clutch of theme hotels that had emerged in The Last Frontier's wake — managers in blackface from The Minstrel Show, nautical types from Riverboat in caps and blazers, whores in high rouge from Place Pigale, deep-sea divers up from Ocean Floor, robots down from Outer Space. A big band was flown in from New Orleans, dancers from Brazil, waiters from New York, food from Brussels and Paris. An Atomic Cocktail had been created for the occasion, a smash concoction of sugar soaked in angostura bitters, rolled in cayenne and sunk like a depth charge in champagne. The motel lobby was transformed into Moment of Impact. Chairs flew up and stuck to the ceiling, melted clocks hung like drapes on the walls, projections of postblast Hiroshima city centre drifted across the floor to a big band accompaniment that sounded like engine roar.

It might have been anyone. When the sun rose over the desert guests were already beginning to troop up to the flight deck to be in position for the test blast scheduled at dawn. It might have been anyone, any one of a dozen people at the party who came costumed as gunfighters. There was a call, a fair call loud and clear, even if Minnie and I didn't hear it, for the sheriff to turn and face his man. A challenge was issued, conforming to standard gunfighter code. There was no argument about that. Scott Chester swung round, already firing as he turned, turning he already fell, pitched onto the long banqueting table, his hands in pies and cream cakes, his heels slipping, skedaddling five, ten, fifteen yards of table length and ripping cloth all the way, pulling what was left of the dessert down on top of him. It was a fantastic performance. Bravo, Scott! You could tell that man had once been an actor. Everyone applauded. Upstairs came a sound like a long moan in crescendo until it burst into a shout. Bombs away, baby! In thirty seconds the lobby was empty. All the guests were up on the roof.

The duchess and I remained frozen in the window niche on the far side of the banqueting table where she had parked my wheelchair away from the party swirl. No one could have spotted us over the table unless they had been on the look-out for midgets. But we could see under the table. We could see Scott's tanned face crushing a pineapple meringue pie. Scott didn't look like a man who was going to get up in a hurry. Footsteps approached. We saw black boots, a hand reaching down under Scott's chin and peeling off a skin-tight mask. Scott's tan came off with it. His face somehow seemed to have come off with it, too, leaving behind it a white rot, a soggy mass. It looked like something the damp had got into and the maggots had been working at since. The boots disappeared and we heard footsteps fading away outside.

When the coast was clear the duchess wheeled me out from behind the table and made for the entrance at top speed. Up on the wall ahead we saw Thelma Louise Stanton smile as she said she wished she could be with us for this great occasion. Bye Scottie, bye everyone. We reached the entrance and the dawn light sprang out of the sky. I could see what seemed to be an approaching hurricane, a spirally twisting mushroom-shaped cloud. It was heading straight for the The Last Frontier, beating its millions of angry wings, a storm front of white moths sucked down through a funnel to the motel entrance. As we looked back across the street, watching the swarm descend, filling out the lobby with a fluttering white cloud, a large black limo pulled up with a scrunch of tires beside us at the kerb. A door opened and a voice inside asked: Cab, Mr Straight?

The Neon Rainbow

There was a hum throughout the building I could never place. When the level rose I felt it vibrate and heard a faint shimmering of glass. Whatever direction I went in I seemed to be approaching it. Sometimes it faded away and left a tingling silence, nerve ends sawn off from any actual noise but still shrieking, registering a phantom sound. I woke up in the night with it ringing in my ears, glass rod music, like spears in my brain. The duchess diagnosed tinnitus. One of the Mormon bodyguards said it was radiation. Right at the bottom of the building, beneath twenty-six floors of administration, underneath the gold vaults in the basement and still some more below that, Myers Global Incorporated stored its uranium reserves. Hiram said it was the sound of high-tone corporate muscle flexed, the hum of beehive power, the music of the spheres. I never saw the word in print but the logo was everywhere: a neon rainbow. By an ingenious arrangement of mirrors you could stand right under it on the top floor and still see it, a parabola of coloured lights that seemed to beam down out of nowhere. It descended on a ladder of gradually intensifying wattage until it hit the roof of the building, Hiram's chief marketing director said, and the hum you heard inside was the fallout of exploded rainbow light.

For a while the duchess was unsure in her mind whether we were Hiram K.'s guests or his acquisitions. We dropped in and stayed for years. We never asked to leave. But if we had? So far as I was concerned, it was Hiram doing us a favour and not the other way round. Hiram was an old man himself and he knew what we wanted. We vacated our previous life all in one go, let it fall like a bathrobe, stepping into the Neon Rainbow naked of a single possession, a single encumbrance, to tie us down to the past. The top two floors of the building, reserved exclusively for the CEO of Myers Global Incorporated and his entourage, were like no place on earth. It was a space station lounge with the back-up of a surgical clinic, the ambiente of a private hotel, the restfulness of a sanatorium. All the way round the top floor led a walk with viewing bays where one could sit looking out over the desert through tinted glass. All the windows were tinted, toning down a roaring sun by day and the neon roar at night, putting the world outside in permanent twilight. The duchess used to push me round once or twice a day, then once or twice a week, before she limped into retirement.

Maybe it was the hum of the ventilation system, or the air-conditioning, or the humidifier installed to preserve me from terminal dehydration. A mobile humidifier was made to my design, a bit like the palanquins that had been popular in Boa Vista. It was electrically powered and I could drive it myself. I was lifted in and out of it by Jim, complete with the ergomatic driving seat. Jim was one of the five or six physiotherapists in Hiram's entourage. A label on me read: handle with care! Extremely fragile! Sockets for the driving seat were installed at strategic points in the apartment. I would say: desk, Jim, or dining-table, and Jim slotted me in as required. Mornings and evenings he lifted me in and out of bed. These days I was smaller than the duchess. I weighed the same as a two year-old child. The duchess could no longer bear the humidity in which I lived, a humidified glass-partitioned habitat referred to by Minnie as the reptile house. There I had my bed, WC, paddling rock pool and marble-floored sun terrace equipped with infrared solar system; my terrarium, as Minnie called it. At night Jim cleansed me of my daily excretions, anointed my parchment body with salves to prevent the skin from cracking even more, sweet essences of cinnamon, rosemary and thyme against the stench of putrefaction, and hooked me up to a saline drip feed to compensate my daily fluid loss.

Jesus Christ, said Jim the first time he opened me up, I mean, if you don't mind me saying so, this is really quite something quite, er, un*u*sual, Sir. It became a conversation piece between Jim and me. And since all people, old people no less, retain a coquettishness so long as they retain an interest in life, the revolutingess which was my showpiece became something I took a sort of pride in.

Maybe, in the end, it was the hum of money, radiating out of the pot-of-gold building at the end of the rainbow, at the hub of the Myers Global Incorporated empire. It became stronger the closer one came to the operations centre where Hiram lived, worked, ate and slept in antiseptic isolation, and when you saw him, the lean, mean old man sitting naked on a plastic sheet, it became almost tangible, the hum emitter, a semi-solid sonic ring hovering over his enormous skull. His body had long shed its bulk, he had lost all his hair or shaved it off, but the head, so huge and fleshy, seemed even more prominent for the spareness of the rest of Hiram's physique. *Make money make money make money...*the money-making pulse, a visible throb at Hiram's temples, was the energizer and the ionizer, emitting sonic rings to spread wavelike through the corporate universe and carry the hum of the CEO's mantra to the far corners of Myers Global Inc. His visitors looked down at him from a glass gallery surrounding the semi-circular amphitheatre that constituted Hiram's living space, and Hiram in turn looked down through a curved perspex window reminiscent of a cockpit at the bank of TV screens with information from the world stock market in the control room below.

In his glass menagerie the celebrated recluse had as much privacy as a medieval monarch, sharing with an always present audience his toilet, his sex life, his sleep. Sometimes he turned on us and bayed: see the beast! Here is the beast! He would stand in his amphitheatre, urinating into a plastic bottle, plucking at his genitals, wagging his long slack penis at the visitors in the gallery, and mockingly he would challenge them: behold the beast and see yourself!

A white moth struggled futilely to get in, beating its wings against the glass.

The Land under the Belly of the Earth

My eyes were weak, but the powers of recognition in my fingers still undimmed. A roll of cloth was brought to me and I was asked if I knew what it was. I fingered the strands of wool. It was a quipu I had in my hands. Hiram's agents had bought it from an antique dealer in Spain. The antique dealer had acquired it from a monastery. A monk had brought it to the monastery from Peru a long time ago. Nothing more was known. Hiram asked me to investigate it during my residence at the Neon Rainbow.

I fingered my way into a quipu code quite different from the one I had learned from the *quipu camayoc* Xiahunaco in Tumbez. I had to decipher, sometimes conjecture its meaning. The roll was a record of one hundred journeys, made at intervals of a hundred years, from the tip of Tahuantin-suyu to an island that began at latitude 70 degrees south and extended under the belly of the Earth. I recalled that I had once seen what was probably the outline of this island burned onto a lama hide and wrapped up into a ball in the quipu archives in Ki'zak. At the time I had no idea what it was. Now I knew. It was a globe. The quipu the monk had brought back to the Old World appeared to be a history of the cartography of the southern reaches of the Sleeping Sea over a period of ten thousand years. The land it described as lapping under the belly of the earth was the continent of Antarctica.

The first ten journeys recorded the exploration and colonisation of the island. The northern coastline was mapped, then the rivers, lakes and mountains of the interior of this vast land mass with a sub-tropical climate. Settlers from Tahuantin-suyu cultivated the land, built irrigation systems and roads, cities where a growing number of people came and lived. Trade between Tumbez and the land wrapped under the belly of the earth flourished for what seemed to have been thousands of years. But from about the fiftieth journey onwards the quipu recorded a gradual process of cooling, then an extremely rapid one, leading to a change in conditions of life on the island. In the course of the next few thousand years, as the land reverted to steppe, then tundra, then ice, the island became uninhabitable. Ice formed in the surrounding sea, transforming the coast line. Life died out. When the voyages to the freezing island became too risky, the cartographers of Tahuantin-suyu who had been continuously mapping it and describing its topography for a hundred times a hundred years abandoned it to its fate. The quipu provided no absolute chronology. But from research into ice formation in Antarctica, conducted by modern geographical institutes, I came to the conclusion that the first voyages to the ice-free continent described in the quipu must have been undertaken fifteen to twenty thousand years ago.

Most mornings at sunrise, when the bank of TV screens switched off and the CEO of Myers Global Incorporated prepared to go to bed, I related to him these findings and we discussed their implications. The cartographers who carried out the survey documented in the quipu must be assumed to have had technology we believed had not existed before the second millennium of our time. They had knowledge of longitude and spherical trigonometry, devised precision instruments and drawn navigation charts with which they explored the globe. They had known the Earth

371

was round and how to calculate the orbits of the planets. They were the protagonists of a pre-history wholly missing from our record of the world.

If our record of the world was just a matter of chance, said Hiram, because the evidence for it was just what you happened to have dug out of the ground or found lying around in an old library, history could never be anything more than conjecture. Showing what might have happened, I said, quoting Pawfrey, would be about as close as one ever got to showing what actually had. When you changed the beginning, mused Hiram, you changed everything that came after. You could make out of history pretty much whatever you wanted it to be — germ-free, for example.

Myersworld / Take 1

Snug in the lee of the land under the belly of the earth, where he took shelter from the head winds of too much fact, Hiram set out to dream the history of the New World all over again. Money was the index of everything, he said, emerging from the Ten-thousand Year Quipu at about the time of the birth of Christ. He would invest a penny at 5% and see what had become of his speculation by the time we got to the twentieth century. Hiram wanted input from me, and I obliged with reminiscences, beginning with a Portuguese voyage of discovery to Brazil, which it had been my task to record as ship's writer on board the *Sao Cristobal* some five hundred years previously.

Hiram queried 'voyage of discovery'. It had been more like a commercial venture, he said. At his prompting I could still recall the inventory of goods we had on board to barter with the inhabitants of the new lands — the mirrors, coloured glass, ivory combs, Venice glasses and shoes of Spanish leather which the Portuguese carried with them in exchange for gold and precious stones. God for gold, interjected Hiram, in that inventory of the goods we had brought along for barter I had forgotten to mention God. It was mainly gold we had got from the Indians and mainly God they had got from us. A commercial venture was the exchange of one article for another. "God worth his weight in gold — and the Indians shall pay dear." Hiram proposed this as the working formula of the Conquest and I raised no objection. He reckoned the Portuguese had got the better half of the deal.

Thanks to the injection of precious metals into the commercial blood-stream of the Old World, the 5% interest on his penny investment had accumulated a mass in the intervening fifteen hundred years worth many times more than the Punchao, a solid gold effigy of dawn reputed to weigh several tons, still hidden somewhere in the mountain forests of Peru. Here was the difference between Indians and conquistadors that counted. If the Indians had invested the Punchao at 5% at the time of the discovery of the New World instead of stowing it away in the woods.....the CEO of Myers Global Inc. was so overwhelmed by this thought that he got up from his plastic sheet and went to the window, where he stood silently staring out at the desert.

In the aftermath of my account of the Conquest, the mass extermination of indigenous people as if they had been irritant lice, Hiram began to develop his notion of historical hygiene. At the window of the Neon Rainbow he saw his vision of Myersworld taking shape in the desert, and that it was jeopardised by irredeemable faults in its ancestry. Hygiene would have to be introduced to history in order to clean it up. At bottom, Hiram's theme park landscape was the place he had lived as a child, a small town in Louisiana. He was putting it together in his mind, at first remembering it and then reconstructing it, adding bits here and taking away bits there, notably the bits about the town's former slave population. He wanted a blueprint and I obliged with reminiscences from the very deep South at a time some three hundred and fifty years ago, when Pedro Joao Pilar had stood on the wharf in Boa Vista, watching the first consignment of Negro women to arrive in the colony as if they had been breeding-mares for improving the local stock. He pledged the value of a year's sugar crop to the merchants in exchange for their entire cargo of slaves, riding back to his plantation the same day with two dozen men, women and children in tow like a mule train behind him.

Hiram asked me if I had witnessed such scenes myself, but because of some fault in the wiring of my box I didn't catch the question. The oxygen-enriched air with a high moisture content and backed up by a saline drip-feed, all part of the life-support system I needed to survive, could no longer be conveniently supplied inside the same environment that other people lived in. I had been fitted with an airtight glass case, rather like an old-fashioned carriage clock, sixteen inches high and equipped with a handle on top so that it could easily be picked up and plugged into the nearest socket. For my conversations with Hiram Jim placed the case on a shelf directly beside the auditorium, allowing him to come over and see me at close quarters if he wished. Speaking through walls to each other, as we now did, we had to use an intercom. Sometimes it broke down. In this event, Minnie, who liked to come along with me for a change of scenery, installing herself in an easy chair on the shelf over-looking Hiram's menagerie, would get up and fix it by delivering a couple of raps to the front of the case.

In reply to Hiram's question as to whether I had been on the wharf in Boa Vista myself and seen the Negroes coming in chains off the ships, I said no. He began to speculate if we maybe had here another case of incomplete evidence, like the land under the belly of the earth with a civil-isation gone missing from the official history of the world simply for lack of evidence. He wondered if the black immigrants from Africa might in fact have come to the New World of their own free will, just as the white immigrants had, but I said there could be no question of that. On arrival in Boa Vista black immigrants were sold at auctions at the slave market in Vallongo, white immigrants bought them. Hiram asked me if I'd attended such auctions myself, and I said no, but I had seen slaves sold at the mock market in Vista, an echo town of Boa Vista, founded by a troupe of travel-ling entertainers at about the time of the Great Earthquake in Lisbon.

Hiram wondered ruminatively if the echo town had been a forerunner of the kind of theme park landscape he had in mind for Myersworld. I said that in a way it had. In fact, it had run forward so hard that it threatened to overtake the town of which it was an echo, putting future before pres-ent, a subversion of the God-given order of things, which had persuaded the authorities the echo would be better suppressed and the ring leaders with it. Minnie got up at this point and rapped the front of my case. I had lost Hiram way back in the conversation during the Great Earthquake in Lisbon. The intercom had broken down again and I had been rattling away to myself. Meanwhile Hiram had been doing calculations in his head, coming up with results which so overwhelmed him that he got up from his plastic sheet and went to the window, where for a long time he remained looking silently out at the desert. At last he came over and peered at me in my box.

Paul, he said. If you use a flow of time to chart the passage of history it's the same as a two-dimensional map, giving you no idea of the contours, the elevations of the landscape through which you have passed. From the discovery of the land under the belly of the earth to the Great Earthquake in Lisbon the events of the world seem to recede on the constant horizon of the same plane. There is a sameness to events, whether they occurred yesterday or ten thousand years ago. But if you use money as your index, a quite different story is told.

The index is a penny invested at 5% at whatever zero date you determine, for convenience sake let us say at the birth of Christ. This introduces an idea of arithmetical progression into the two-dimensional historical plane. Contours push the map into a third dimension and a sharp rise in elevation becomes visible in your view of history, or acceleration, if you like, as you grow aware of your increasing speed on your passage through time. The progression of 5% interest accumulating on your investment in zero year takes place by the most astonishing leaps and bounds, still negligible at the Sack of Rome, trudging uphill through the Middle Ages to the discovery of the New World when it is disclosed to be a kind of Punchao, a solid gold mass with the density of a small satellite body, already weighing hundreds of thousands or perhaps million of tons. But what happens in the two and half centuries between the arrival of Dom Pedro's fleet on the coast of Brazil and Porphyry's tableau of Lisbon in Ruins in the market place of Boa Vista? Progression is such that 5% interest on your original penny has generated a value equivalent to the weight of the planet Earth in gold — a mass of 5882×10^{18} tons, far beyond anything your poor old head can imagine, Paul, let alone count.

In the lee of the land under the belly of the earth, in fact a penny, which by means of a mere 5% had been converted into a gigantic blob of gold, I talked to Hiram for forty days and nights illuminated by freak snow falls that turned the desert white. My daughter Héloise was about to re-enter the story, and with her the subject of compound interest that had always been close to her heart. I told Hiram about the man with the tin nose, the smugglers of Chief Liar Island, Garrault's trading house and 10% commission for Zarrate et Cie., which my daughter's endeavours raised to twelve and a half, subject to an exemption regarding trading in slaves. In practice there had been no exemption of slaves, however. There was no way round that peculiar institution of the South, whereas the peculiar institution tended to find a way round anything, notably an embargo, let alone a twinge of conscience, with the greatest of ease.

I told Hiram about my enlightenment in the marshlands of Grande Terre and the Temple, how I had tried to think of a commodity untainted directly or indirectly with blood or the labour of slaves and was unable to come up with a single one. The world and all the trade of the world resembled that ghost-ridden, skull-strewn Indian temple in the swamps after which the maroon smugglers had named their island. Never-ending sacrifices had to be brought to sustain the flow of commerce. All wars between nations were fought on its behalf. Wars were commercial ventures, as Hiram said. All the written instruments, contracts, promissory notes and letters of credit on which trade was based were nothing other than blood pacts, recognising the primacy of commerce above everything else on earth.

After I had finished speaking we sat and listened to the hum of money radiating out of the pot-of-gold-building at the end of the rainbow. The CEO of Myers Global Incorporated was back on his plastic sheet, plucking his penis, and he nodded approvingly, I thought, and after a while I heard him mumble out of the corner of his mouth: nothing wrong with that. That was business. That was just the way things were. I said that the drawback with Hiram's money index of history was that in the end it only showed how much you'd got, not how you got it. Hiram said that was its great merit. It provided a dynamic model of history that was free of all sentiment. It demonstrated a simple design capable of endless repetition. What else had my daughter Héloise done when she started tracking the growth of compound interest in her own lifetime and the shift in the distribution of wealth, resulting in more and more wealth owned by fewer and fewer people the further you went? What had been the ratio of dollars to dollar owners when she began to keep her records? Before the Civil War, twenty percent of the families had owned fifty-four percent of the wealth, I said, and by the time of the Exposition in Chicago it was more like seventy percent of the wealth in the hands of nine percent of the nation's families. Hiram thought it was only a question of time until one percent of the population owned ninety-nine percent of the wealth.

Surely it was just another variation of the same design when my son-in-law Stanton, of whom I had so often spoken to Hiram, made his prediction about mass manufacture: that more and more would be produced of less and less? Or that producers would manufacture commodities in quantities that increased in inverse proportion to the decreasing number of producers? Or that cities would come to be defined as specific gravities of higher and higher density, with increasingly more people in increasingly less space? Synchronised, standardised people amounting to not much more than consuming agents between a commodity on one side and a desire on the other, more and more people with converging desires and consuming a narrowing range of commodities – in the end the same virtual commodity infinitely reproduced.

In Hiram's view of history from the twenty-sixth floor of the Neon Rainbow, accretion of matter accompanied by concentration of power were consequences of the same law of progression that transformed a penny invested at 5% into a gold nugget the size of the Earth. Ultimately they were consequences of the second law of thermodynamics, which stated that as the universe expanded entropy increased, until everything contracted back into a state of infinite density at the end of time. Ownership of beasts of burden, whether oxen, mules or slaves, was incidental to this process, however undesirable it had been. On our approach to a ratio of 99%: 1% as an expression of how much wealth was in the hands of how many owners at the end of our millennium, surely a more extreme disproportion than at any time in history, Hiram wished to point out that a condition of restricted freedom, though not yet comparable with slavery, was now more widespread than it had ever been before. Hence the need for Myersworld.

Myersworld wasn't business, said Hiram, spreading his hands as he turned and appealed to me inside my glass case, sensing my suspicion. Myersworld was a refuge where folks in bondage to reality could escape for a nice weekend. It was going to be a good, clean, wholesome place with echoes of way back home. At bottom, Myersworld was where Hiram had lived as a child, a small town in Louisiana. As he talked me through his scheme it was clear that he was still very much in the lee of the land under the belly of the earth that had gone missing for lack of evidence, leaving history wide open for reinterpretation. On the principle that the main things wrong with the world in the present had already been wrong with it in the past, Hiram was putting it back together in his mind, adding bits here and taking away bits there, notably the bits about his home town's former slave population, because he reckoned the only way to deal with what had been wrong in the past was to go back there and fix it.

Here Hiram got pretty excited and walked around wagging his penis. History had potential as a fantasy toy place, a gigantic playground for the recreation of mankind in its modern bondage. But first you had to edit out of the picture what was wrong with it, bury the corpses, turn the thugs out of the playground and lock them up before you could move on to a wholesome present not mortgaged up to the hilt in the past. What obligation did we have to keep on and on paying that debt?

I asked Hiram if he was thinking of digging up the corpses that had already been buried under the foundations of the Big House and burying them some place else. Now to be perfectly frank with you, said Hiram slyly. Way back home in Louisiana, the place where he'd been born and grown up — frankly, not the great place he'd been making it out to be. Plenty of niggers in the wood-pile down there. His mother a whore, his father a drunk. He was brought up in a depressed area. Mostly his father didn't have a job and he would whip the daylights out of Hiram if he found out he had wet his bed. The black population scratched a living out of the soil and were housed in sties not too different from the cabins their great-grandparents had lived in as slaves. Did anyone want to go back home to a place like that? People wanted to go back to a place where the things wrong with it in the past had been fixed. That was the principle of Myersworld.

Pushed to its logical conclusion, the Myersworld at the back of Hiram's mind called for a remake of the New World. Wherever cultures had clashed, Hiram admitted, problems had arisen, but you could eliminate those clashes by eliminating the indigenous people. You retouched the photograph, snipped a few frames out of the film, shrunk the tape. *Blip!* And they vanished. Settlers arrived in a New World cleansed of indigenous populations. Effectively that *was* where they had arrived, in the end, but it had taken them centuries of bloodshed and would take them centuries more of recrimination. Our values had since changed.

Was Myersworld going to have a wharf like the one I described in Boa Vista, where black men and women in chains were unloaded by the slave traders who had stolen them from Africa? You bet not. It may not have troubled people then but nowadays it would discourage the tourists. Africa was this goddamn big black continent that wouldn't go away. The further you went back, the deeper you got into it. The niggers in the woodpile down there were a couple of million years old. Difficult to go *blip!* on a place they were now making out to be the cradle of mankind. It couldn't easily go missing like the land under the belly of the earth. But you could come up with other scenarios. You could *postpone* the discovery of Africa until the colonisation of the New World had been accomplished. You could retroactively *upgrade* African labour, put it in steerage with the later immigrants, rough, tough, ill-paid, but acceptable to our moral standards. You had to go back and fix this thing in the past, fix it all the way through, otherwise you would never get shot of the problems. They showed up every night in his Las Vegas hotels, in the shape of great entertainers, big names, audience loved the show, didn't love black people, which was why when they came off stage they knew without being told that they had to exit by the back door and go stay in a boarding-house on the West side of Vegas, because no way could black performers live in the same hotel as the white audiences they entertained on the Strip.

Early Myersworld hotels with thoroughly sanitised Old South themes such as MinstrelShow, RiverBoat and NewOrleans rose one by one along the Strip while Hiram was holed up with me in the lee of the land under the belly of the earth, talking his way back through history and turning it on his head. He had a pile of blueprints, History As It Really Might Have Been, transferred onto slides which he projected onto enormous screens, discussing their merits with his Mormon advisers, Minnie and me.

On sentimental days he would favour something folksy like the rural town he seemed to remember having grown up in, themed as the Back Home Motel. Reception would be in the courthouse, guests in farmhouse units with views of picturesquely uniformed staff employed profitably at cottage industries. No one but Hiram wanted to stay in the Back Home motel, however, his marketing directors least of all. In a more grandiose vein he tried to rouse their enthusiasm for a thousand-acre golf-plantation hotel with the main casino in the Big House and slot machines in the slave quarters, but his marketing directors didn't see that one, either.

Myersworld / Take 2

Hiram was so busy weeding out things wrong with history that he overlooked the things wrong with himself, incontinence being the most conspicuous of these. The spillage on Hiram's plastic sheet was not merely there for everyone to see. It was thrust into their face. It took the resources of Minnie's imagination, latterly fading though it was, to forge links between Hiram's self-indulgent infantile-billionaire behaviour now and the whippings he'd been given for bed-wetting then. Under the bedcovers of Hiram's obsession with going back to fix the past the duchess detected a whiff of urine, and she came to the conclusion he had liked it. She thought that Hiram's reeking nostalgia for home, which was the moving force behind Myersworld, was not so much a longing for a place as for a feeling of security associated with the reeking of urine when he wet his bed and his mother had managed to cover up for him, conspiratorially changing the sheets in the morning while Hiram's Dad was still sleeping off last night's drunkenness. In Hiram's memory he could go *blip!* on his father, leaving the son unchastised in a warm brew of bed with an indulgent mother on call in the background, a smile on her lips and a supply of fresh bed linen in her cupboard. Here was the original blueprint for Myersworld.

Myersworld / Take 3

In Hiram's Mormon entourage the key to understanding Myersworld was considered to be his fascination with casinos. Myersworld only took off as a commercial concept rather than as a mere rich man's plaything after the dollar floated free of the gold standard and heavy speculation entered the currency market. By later standards this was still pretty modest stuff — a daily investment volume of maybe ten billion dollars. The Mormon fascination with high finance was itself a fascination with power, hence the ready association it found in their minds with attributes of deity. This attitude had rubbed off on Hiram after years of seclusion among exclusively Mormon attendants. Money was Hiram's religion — not in the sense of a trite saying but as an avowal of his belief in things transcendental.

For Hiram, floating currencies symbolised a world already far gone in the process of detaching itself from its foundations. Liberated from the gold standard, money was no longer bound by a covenant, offered no quid pro quo on which you could depend. It repealed the law of Moses and built a highway all the way to Mammon Plaza in downtown Babylon. Money was worth whatever the market liked. In the lee of the land under the belly of the Earth, gone missing for lack of evidence, history could now be openly united with its demiurge, Money, and formed howsoever the personification of the market, Hiram K. Myers, desired.

According to Hiram's dynamic law of history, accretion of matter accompanied by concentration of power saw to it that within months of the dollar coming off the gold standard Myers Global Incorporated had virtually become a bank, with all its capital deployed in currency markets. Twenty years later, this would be true of investment the world over. The funds speculated on the currency markets in a single day were a hundred times more than the global turnover of raw materials, finished goods and services. Billions worth of hot money flowed electronically in or out of national currency markets in a matter of seconds. Money was a terminal greed with no appetite left for anything but self-ruinous speculation. The bank reserves of the world were swept away by this torrent. Hiram cleaned up. Before he died he had the pleasure of proving to me that the penny invested at the birth of Christ, which by the time of the Declaration of Independence had generated wealth approximately equivalent to the weight of the Earth in gold, was worth the equivalent of a hundred billion planets Earth a mere two hundred years later.

These figures suggested a view of the planet as a spinning ball on some kind of galactic roulette wheel, a pop-up target in a cosmic shooting-gallery, as rudderless in itself as it was subject to the arbitrariness of extra-terrestrial influences — collisions with wandering stars at trivial intervals of millions of years, gigantic bursts of speed from outgassing comets, acceleration, accretion, deceleration, implosion under an insupportable density of matter, extinction. Hiram's choice of metaphor for these astro-nomic developments was the Casino of the Universe, enjoining as always a down-to-earth, hands-on Mormon application of any Hiram K. Myers' figure of speech, which was to own and operate as many casinos on the Strip as possible. Thus the way was paved for the chief to ease himself into his final incarnation as the Pharaoh of the Neon Rainbow.

It took Caesar's Palace to open Hiram's eyes to the grand synthesis of all his ideas and how this melange was to be realised within the terms of Myersworld. Snarling and pacing up and down his menagerie as he watched the gala opening of the Strip's latest theme hotel on TV, Hiram followed the changing of the Pretorian Guard, Cleopatra on a walkabout, first through an ancient Egyptian setting, then in Rome, then in a shopping mall in a Renaissance Italian town. The house lights were slowly dimmed to reveal stars on the ceiling as evening stole gently across the sky before she left the shopping mall and boarded her perfumed cedarwood barque to snuggle down for a cabaret night featuring a folk-singing Caesar, Octavian commanding a sea battle in drag and a tap-dancing Marc Antony who was eventually downed by a chorus line of girl gladiators in bikinis. This ketchup of entertainment, a hotchpotch of all periods and styles, was a revelation to Hiram. He had been honing authenticity all the while, striving to perfect a genuine fake atmosphere of the Old South where folks could feel at home with a good conscience, but what they really wanted was to get the hell out of anything that reminded them of home. People wanted to get out of their cars — nowadays it was their planes, Scott Chester never got round to installing this update of his vision — and step into a fantasy land where they shed responsibility for themselves, the families, wives, lives that were to be put on hold until such time as reality recalled them when the bank roll ran out.

Hiram realised it had been a mistake to go back and fix the things wrong with the past. You junked history, grabbed the swag and made a run for it. You shook it all up and took it just as it came out. The Mississippi riverboat restaurant could float as an airship above the roof of the Inca Palace Hotel, accessed via an elevator inside the Eiffel Tower, and who the hell cared? Couples made up to look like Marilyn Monroe and Napoleon, Helen of Troy and Elvis Presley could get married in a dungeon of the Bastille that metamorphosed into the Cheops Pyramid or a Honolulu hotel the moment they stepped outside. Auschwitz could become an adventure theme park featuring famous survival-of-the-fittest games such as Tarzan in the jungle, Robinson Crusoe on a desert island, passengers in lifeboats escaping from the Titanic and much, much more besides, with a free weekend in Myersworld as prizes for the lucky winners.

A warm smell of urine led Hiram with infallible instinct into everyman's toyworld of infantile wish fulfilment, offering cleanly commercialised libido, emasculated evil, perversions yanked out of the shadows of leering privacy and given outlets in pleasure domes as intimate as supermarkets. He was the first to introduce adult fun brothels where housewives could play safely at being whores, adult fun nurseries where middle-aged men could have their diapers changed, their bums wiped and their tiddlies tickled by extra-tall strong-arm playmate persons. This was what the Myersworld public wanted. They didn't want a brush with reality even inside a space suit. Reality was the killer germ from planet Earth. Who wanted to go back and live any time any place in the history of the Earth? Just look at its rat-seething garbage-dumped poison-packed surface. *Earth?* Unfit for human habitation. So how about joining us for a vacation in the present, folks? How about a touch of something *real?*

Yuck!

Reality was the killer radioactive agent, you had to build a Hiram K. Myers enclosure in the middle of the desert to keep contamination at bay. Come to Myersworld! Just unreal! The ads ran on TV all day and night. Hiram in his pharaonic twilight used to watch them as if they were a full-length feature, uninterrupted, as he never tired of joking, by a single commercial break.

Come to Myersworld! Just unreal! Family-friendly! Join the happy crowd! Guaranteed germ-free! It drove even the Mormons crazy.

The Pharaoh of the Neon Rainbow

Within hours of Hiram's death a small Lebanese gentleman with a completely hairless head arrived from Los Angeles. He had been contacted long in advance and paid half of a very substantial fee in order to ensure his co-operation at short notice. The Lebanese had a mortician's practice in Bel Air. Before he arrived in America from the old country he had been initiated in the rites of ancient Egyptian embalmers and could prepare a corpse in accordance with an art that had been practised in the Valley of the Kings four thousand years ago and came back into fashion in twentieth-century Hollywood. The mortician was blindfold when he was fetched by a Mormon escort from his home and again when he was returned to it. All he saw between leaving and returning to his house on two visits to the Neon Rainbow was his dead client on a table in a curtained room. The embalming was recorded on video projected onto a large screen and attended by Hiram's entire entourage, in accordance with arrangements laid down in precise detail in his last will and testament. Hiram died just short of the new century it had been his ambition to reach, no one knew at what age, his ambition unfulfilled. I never heard he caught a cold or was ill for a day. Shut off from all risk of contamination, out of harm's reach, Hiram had been out of love's reach too, the duchess said, and in her opinion the illness he died of was a dearth of contact with humankind.

The wasted corpse with the hypertrophic head lay on a pathologist's anatomising table in the centre of the amphitheatre where the deceased had spent the latter years of his life naked on a plastic sheet. I felt a curious sympathy between the mortician and his client when the rotund little Lebanese bent down to remove the sheet from Hiram's body, and for a moment the two huge bald heads side by side seemed to be engaged in conversation. A slight air turbulence that arose when the sheet was pulled back caused a fine down that Hiram must have forgotten to shave or allowed to grow to stir along his temples like something suddenly come back alive. The mortician ran his hand over the crown of his head as he stood mustering the dead man. Then he looked up at the audience watching from the amphitheatre like students at an anatomy class and without any preliminaries announced that he would first be removing the brain of the deceased. He would take out the brain without opening the skull, for to damage the skull would be to damage the soul. To make this delicate operation easier he had poured an acidic fluid into the nostrils. He had done this as soon as he arrived, he explained, in order to soften the tissue and facilitate its extraction, although with a corpse still in such a relaxed condition this was not strictly necessary. And so saying he went over to a table where various instruments were laid out, picked up a bent piece of wire with a hook at the end and held it up for our inspection.

Despite our failing sight the duchess and I were able to follow this operation in detail on the large video screen. Underestimating the effect of a lifetime spent among gross distortions to the human body that until recently had been publicly exhibited as freaks, I had expected she might be squeamish, but the duchess watched the disembowelling of Hiram with the same level curiosity she brought to bear on whatever she looked at in life. How much truer this was of myself, who already as a child had witnessed the truncation of the Pig Indian dead so that their limbs could be compressed as human parcels and buried under the floor of the malocca, not to mention the dismemberment, roasting and eating of my tribal brother Woodcock by the White Earth Indians. We now learned what an apparently simple matter it was to draw a man's brain through the holes in his nose. The Lebanese twisted and gouged with his hooked wire as deftly as if he were prying out oysters, bringing out a debris of blood, spatter and discoloured membrane onto a large plastic bib arranged like a surplice around the dead man's neck. Then he inserted tubes into each nostril, pumped in a fluid and drew it off into a bucket under the table — a dark viscous slime, all that was left of Hiram's brain to be flushed out of his skull.

In the time of the Pharaohs, the Lebanese said tonelessly, bodies had been cut open using a particularly hard stone from Ethiopia, but as this stone was no longer available and modern surgical steel far superior to any tools possessed by the ancients in any case he employed a pathologist's knife. With two swift, almost negligent incisions he cut the skin across the chest and down to the groin. He put one hand into this T-shaped cavity and drew out the inner organs, snipping here and there with a pair of scissors to release them from their anchorage inside the body. The whole came out like an engine block, heaving from the elasticity of its own mass as it stood on a side-table while the operator prepared a solution in which the inner organs were subsequently placed. Now he stood at another table, like a chef mixing the ingredients of a dish as he explained to us that he was grinding pure myrrh, to be mixed with cassia and other incenses, making up a substance that would preserve the interior of the body from putrefaction and give it an agreeable smell. With a painter's brush he applied the substance to the walls of the stomach, filled the cavity with chunks of unground incense and sewed it up in the most brisk, workmanlike manner imaginable. Then he turned the body onto one side, filled a syringe with essence of cedar oil, injected this clyster into the rectum and slowly drew it off, removing any remaining impurities. It seemed to me that nothing could have conveyed deadness better than this spring-cleaning of Hiram's tumble-down bone-house within hours of his life having vacated it.

The body was now ready to be placed in a lye to halt the further decomposition of the flesh, a sodium hydrate solution in which it would left to soak for a period of seventy days. This method of conserving human bodies, the Lebanese mortician remarked in passing as he cranked up the anatomising table, seemed to have originated in the observation that flesh buried in shallow desert graves was preserved better due to the quartzose composition of sand. It was gradually understood to possess natural conservatory properties and put to use in ancient Egyptian embalming techniques. At an angle of about forty-five degrees the corpse began to slide feet first off the anatomising table into the sodium hydrate solution, eased in with the help of the mortician, who was unable to prevent a slight splash when Hiram's head plopped into the tub. It came to rest not fully submerged. The Lebanese was obliged to insert a gloved hand to push it under before he placed a lid on the tub and Hiram finally disappeared from view. That, said this coolly methodical workman, as he allowed his hand to rest momentarily on the lid in the first gesture we had seen indicating anything approaching piety, was that. We would meet here again in seventy days to conclude the embalming procedure.

While Hiram lay in his sodium hydrate bath having his body fluids leached in preparation for being mummified — bed-wetting for eternity, Minnie said corrosively, anticipating an infinity of blissful diaper wrapping by a transcendental mother beyond the sky — his Mormon entourage began to dismantle the other remains of his life. The no-contamination rule continued to apply in death as rigorously as it had in death. Nothing the Pharaoh of the Neon Rainbow might have touched could ever be used again. Banks of TV screens were scrapped, light fixtures, door handles, even the Ten-Thousand-Year quipu, were crated up and driven out to the desert to be dynamited.

All that remained was money, but of hard, spendable money, dollars, quarters, nickels and dimes, there was not the slightest trace. In the last months of his life the wily old man had manoeuvred a planet-sized fortune past his Mormon guards and sunk it in forms of liquidity fathoms deep where they were never going to be able to find it. Somewhere in the system Hiram's money was anonymously circulating, gathering pressure, a time bomb which had begun to tick even as the Pharaoh of the Neon Rainbow lay being leached in his sodium hydrate bath, fulfilling a posthumous mission of accretion of mass and concentration of energy until one day it would implode under its own density in accordance with Hiram's Law and destroy the system with it.

Oh, the family was taken care of, naturally. Hiram's will made provision for his retainers to be housed and fed on the same terms during his death that had applied during his life. Our posthumous loyalty was taken for granted just as it had been in life. The Pharaoh's entourage would move to the Hiram K. Myers Building in New York, possessionless, naked as new-born babes, to be incarcerated in his tomb with him. Overnight we would be spirited out of the Neon Rainbow and leave an empty building behind us.

Seventy days later the Lebanese returned, accompanied by a suitcase containing a collapsible winch and a human-shaped coffin, with a wide-eyed Egyptian painted in royal blue and white on the lid. Hiram emerged from the sodium hydrate bath as lean as a board, all the adipose tissue skimmed off him or sucked out of him, leaving just a hide stretched over bones. He was lowered in and out of freshwater baths, dabbed with linen and laid down on the floor with one end of a long bale of bandage under him. The Lebanese rolled him into the bandage just as I had once rolled Edgar P. Stanton up in the quipu that had been his undoing, like a sausage into pastry, layer after layer, until he looked like a spindle, tapering somewhat towards each end, daubed all over with a gelatinous substance that looked like glue. The Lebanese at last opened the coffin, like a magician coming to the grand finale of his act, revealing the interior of the lid spangled with stars on a dark blue background. The duchess thought that a fanfare might have been appropriate at this moment, some solemn Water Musicke to float the coffin-bound prince of night downstream into the measureless beyond, the eyes on his coffin lid fixed emotionlessly on a prospect of eternity that was hidden from us. But all we heard was the familiar theme tune of the Neon Rainbow, the hum of air conditioning at full blast, working up a desert chill, seizing up and slowing down, freezing to a halt as crystals of frost formed on floors throughout the building and gradually turned the carpets white.

End Game

In the hundred odd years since Pawfrey used to play Coney Island as an annual Christmas fixture I found New York had changed a lot. So did the duchess, but how was she to know, Minnie hadn't even been born at the time. Minnie was getting a lot of things wrong these days. She claimed she had been Duke Malmesbury's midget sidekick way back in Pawfrey's original show, but that was another Minnie, my Minnie had simply taken on the name when she moved in as her elder sister's successor. Minnie thought she had a panorama view of the city from our apartment at the top of the Hiram K. Myers Building. She didn't understand that there were no views these days, because there were no windows, and that what she saw was an image projected onto a wall screen. Where Minnie admired New York by night she watched soap operas by day, all on the same wall-size screen she kept on confusing with a window. I asked how she could be watching soap operas through a window and she said because that was where the soap operas were, out in the streets of the city, the stuff of life you looked down and saw from the window of your apartment.

The window of our apartment had been replaced by a wall screen on which images were projected, but Minnie didn't understand the difference. Intuitively astute though she was, certain things could not longer be got into her head. The shift from what the duchess called the stuff of life to a virtual reality rendition of the same had taken place so gradually she remained unaware of the difference, while her increasing infirmity left the duchess with an ever dwindling source of real-life experiences that might have provided her with means of comparison.

Minnie had always been fascinated by TV, whatever was on, for the reason that a 22-inch screen brought her into a feel-good world of folks her own size, but after our arrival in New York and the sealing of the tomb which we had more or less voluntarily entered with Hiram she became a full-time TV junkie. On a wall-size screen where the characters were larger than life she no longer had the excuse of mixing with other little people. The soap operas on the wall gobbled her up and she disappeared inside. What else was there for her to do? When we first moved in she still tried to keep house after a fashion. She dusted her knick-knacks, watered her orchids, played xylophones and occasionally even sang, accompanying herself on the toy piano. What could I do for Minnie, now that I lived permanently behind glass? I hung bat-like inside my carriage clock case, apparently tethered by my ears, in fact supported by a wire brace fitted to my spine and anchored to the back wall of the case. My head, though shrunken, must still have appeared gross on a body now withered to nine inches, its natural functions long since suspended, gutted and equipped instead with an artificial circulation system sewn up inside me. I was no more than a ghoulish thing in a cabinet, still alive by clinical definition, but able to move only the fingers of my right hand to push buttons on my life-support system, unable to speak except by voice synthesiser, unable to hear except by a device that digitised speech and fed electrical stimuli to my brain, unable to see except what I saw by means of laser guided vision on the wall-size screen of the apartment.

Since the days I did Coney Island at Christmas New York had changed beyond recognition. Sometimes I had my doubts if it really was New York I was looking at out there. This may have been due to the medium through which I saw it, processed images, deconstructed and digitised and fed to me as visual perceptions only at the end of a long chain of conversions. What was the Chrysler Building doing in Battery Park, for instance? How come the Statue of Liberty had moved to Greenwich Village? And from there again to Central Park? Wired up in my box, facing the wall screen all day and night, I came to the conclusion that what I saw there must be some kind of quotation New York, excerpts quoted from the original work. The New York I got was a promotion package, with the more famous bits of the city duplicated and constantly shuffled around. Times Square showed up one evening no less than six times in as many different locations. The whole of Lower Manhattan was dominated by a Wall Street stretched beyond all proportion. Icons of New York were rehashed so often in this virtual reality product of Myersworld advertising which we saw on our screen every night that the actual city of New York, made up of streets crowded with people and garbage and smells and stray dogs just passing through, had disappeared behind the icons. Jim, my former phys-iotherapist and still the only real friend I had made in the Mormon entourage, looked in once a day to see how I was, but it was no good asking Jim what was going on out there, because none of the Mormons ever left the building.

Minnie used to be able to climb up on a stool and tap the front of my glass case. She could no longer see too well. Minnie was fading. Are you still there, Paul? Are you warm enough? She would tap my case in just the same way she tapped the barometer and the clock she had inherited from Duke Malmesbury. Weather was changing. Twenty past six. Are you there Paul? She tapped three times, checking the weather, the time, and me. I told her I was still there all right but that I was losing track of New York, and that way back in his warehouse on the Tschopitoulas Road Stanton had been right all along when he foresaw that more and more would be produced of less and less. Aren't you cold inside that case, Paul? Thank you, Minnie, I'm just fine. These were the exchanges I had with Minnie day after day until she could no longer climb up on the stool to tap the front of my case and spent all her time in bed. My synthesised voice sounded like something sucked out of a drain. New York had died of its fame, I said, only icons were left and even they were beginning to wear out. Minnie asked if I was warm enough. We were all beginning to run down and wear out wear out wear out wear out, I said, entering an infinite loop I would never find my way out of again.

The Ocean Sea

If I was the microcosm of the universe then the universe would end with me, and how it ended was just this process of retrograde creation, the backward path through time, shrinking to the nothing as which I began. The passage between the splicing of atoms from which I emerged and their dissolution towards my final decay was no more than a flash in the dark. Travelling through space at the speed of light, I could observe in one flash the fusion of events which on Earth were as distinct as birth and death and the apparent passage of life in-between. Still, for the duration of that flash the growth of mass existing in the form of me had been incomparably greater than the appreciation of Hiram's penny. Hiram's penny investment, yielding an interest equivalent to a hundred billion Earths of gold after two thousand years, was still negligible when compared with the growth of me from my molecular beginnings to the labyrinthine mind-matter system I became. Hiram's journey into space seemed to have been planned in accordance with an ancient Egyptian belief that after death the souls of pharaohs ascended into the sky in order to be united with the stars. His mummy, standing in a casket with eyes painted on one end, looking up through a cone-shaped skylight, became the tip of a projectile on a journey to the stars. Whether that journey was undertaken actually or as a figure of speech it was difficult to say. Jim and I were the only persons still left aboard the Hiram K. Myers Building, and we disagreed about quite what had happened. Jim claimed that the tower took off, proving the supporting structure below to be a rocket-launching gantry in disguise. On leaving the Earth's atmosphere the tower had discarded its first fuel stage, or sixty-seventh storey, but not until we were increasing accelera-tion to exit the solar system did it shed its second stage, or the sixty-eighth and top storey (by Jim's account) of what until then had reliably been reported to be the Hiram K. Myers Building on the Avenue of the Americas. But Jim was a space buff, a great reader of science fiction comics. If he could only learn to shed his Mormon materialism and allow his spirituality rather than his imagination to run away with him he would understand that space, space travel, the ascent of the soul and its passage through the stars by rocket or otherwise were all paradigms of becoming and unbecoming as we experienced them in life and death on our way to becoming something still else again thereafter. For me this took place in a region of space that reminded me of the Jesuit Seminary in Boa Vista. After lift-off from the Avenue of the Americas the Seminary was where I eventually arrived after passing through an Oort cloud of white dwarf stars. The stars regressed to a familiar swarm of white moths surrounding a padre I knew, deep in contemplation in his interstellar bower, and I understood now what I had not understood before. The moths were man-ifestations of corruption, tainted spirituality, my own decomposing flesh, buoys or marker dyes in the Ocean Sea of heaven to help me trace my way back to my beginnings. Welcome to the infinite loop, the padre said. I had arrived at what he called a turn-around area in space, where spent matter was reconstituted and put into reverse time — the narrative of my own journey along with everything else, played back and forth, back and forth on an infinite loop. The padre represented all journeys as being paradigms of existence in which there was no stasis. All were travellers moving in and out of matter on an infinite circular path, carrying out infinite revolutions.

I wondered if this was a figure of speech, something merely in the mind, a spiritual encounter with a padre who was explaining these things to me, or if we were part of an event taking place, as Jim claimed, on the edge of a black hole in the region of the Oort Cloud. No more was left of me than a brain wired up in a flask, a biological chip with fungus growing spontaneously around the rim, while Jim had turned into a little old man with wisps of hair, the last attendant worthy of the name in Hiram's tomb, still jogging each morning for eternity, running if necessary upside down round the projectile walls in order to reach eternity. I watched him plucked down off the wall and sucked violently into his retro-passage through time, shrinking back through the configurations of his prime, his proudly swelling runner's legs regressing in, oh, no time at all to spindle-shanked childhood and the virtual leglessness of infancy. Then he split into two, a fish-tailed sperm docking with an ovum inside a woman on a bed in a motel on Highway 91. I tried to catch a glimpse of the neon sign identifying the motel as it flashed past, but it was gone too fast, the entire desert contracted to a dune, and on the far side of the dune was the sea. The cameraman stood in the sea with the sun behind him in the west, and the dancers with long shadows trailing from them like the streamers of kites looked as if they were in a desert moving along a narrow tunnel of storm, swept by tanglewood cast up by the ocean, the giant shadows of their movements billowing on a crest of wind. In the wind-still evening they sat in the dunes with outstretched arms, pointing to the sea where they saw the great plains, and the rushing waves that were the herds of buffalo returning to their lands. The animals massed up out of the troughs in the waves and came thundering right out of the surf. Light was shut out of the camera, fading back into an image of a woman putting a child to sleep, and I saw settlers' wagons coming down a trail, or rather up, because they were moving backwards. Like toys on little bickering wheels, a swarm of scuttling cockroaches, the wagons scraped back up the mountains, swam rivers in reverse, crossed plains and deserts and were sucked back into doom-masted ships that sailed backwards across the ocean. This was the unique, solitary nature of everything that lived, being a record of a journey special to itself. A journey that *was* itself. Here was I, the sentient, reflective traveller riding like a bright buoy on the surface of my narrative, dipping and rising, marker of submerged movements, tide pull and swell and whatever rhythms ran through the sea. I sat on deck with the little girl, watching the rhythms of the Ocean Sea, the plunging porpoise schools and the silver arcs of flying fish tensed in mid-air, shimmering fishes all around us as far as the eye could see. The voyage proceeded by varying shades of blue, from transparent green seas with turquoise tints, laid out like a flowing mosaic floor through a deep royal blue streaked white to a blue-black swell as dark as night. I looked up to see dense swarms of stars glittering in the inky heavens. The waves came charged with phosphorescent light. As they broke against the side of the ship they opened into chasms of fire, so that she seemed to move in a surface of flame, leaving a long train in the burning wake behind her. At night the sea was like a river, the breezes sweet and soft. I could feel the respiration of the sea, of the tides rising and falling on its shores, of rivers flowing down from mountains into estuaries, and all the earth's breathing through the great watery diaphragm of the ocean and the streaming firmament above. I listened to the inhalations and exhalations of a universe in perpetual motion, and I knew that I flowed in this sea-river just as it flowed in me. The ship sailed alone without a visible sea or roof of sky, imprisoned in the fog that swallowed up its wake and shut off whatever lay ahead. Wave by wave the vessel rode each stretch of sea as it was unravelled, moment for moment, as if it came from nowhere and had no destination. The ocean seemed less to be carrying the vessel forward than moving along with it, so that I wondered if I had put any distance behind me at all. The sea passage narrowed to a river between banks of fog. All around me stood walls of darkness and fog. I began to feel the cold and wondered where Minnie was. I heard the splash of dipping oars beyond, a voice saying we had been taken in tow. Although there was no wind the ship slid mysteriously into the estuary with furled sails, casting anchor in the river. I felt the cold right through into my bones, and as I grew numb I let go, why should I resist, knowing as I did that when the ship's writer died during the night they would send factors ashore to obtain a replacement for the dead man, someone to take my place, and finding Pablito asleep in a corner of the kitchen they would make do with the boy and carry him off with them to the New World.